Praise for Tiffany Clare's

THE SURRENDER OF A LADY

"Tiffany Clare writes a swoon-worthy romance filled with rich details and vivid characters. Any readers wishing for a bold and sweeping historical romance need look no further—Tiffany Clare is a treasure of an author!"

—Lisa Kleypas, *New York Times* bestselling author

"A unique, unforgettable, sensual love story sweeping from the harems of the east to staid Victorian ballrooms. Watch out for this sizzling new talent to rise to the top."

—*RT Book Reviews*

"Exotic, bold and captivating. Tiffany Clare's rich, sensual prose is a delightful indulgence!"

—Alexandra Hawkins, author of *All Night with a Rogue*

"Dazzling, daring and different! Exotic and erotic! *The Surrender of a Lady* will have you turning the pages until you finish, no matter how late it gets. Tiffany Clare is a brilliant new talent in historical romance."

—Anna Campbell, author of *Midnight's Wild Passion*

"Tiffany Clare has written an exceptionally exciting and heart-wrenching story of the devotion and survival of a young mother, sold into the most despicable of circumstances...Fast-paced, full of suspense, and totally exciting with each turn of the p‌ ‌s been woven for the rea‌ ‌

"Emotion-packed...a l‌ ‌-
cal romance that will t‌ ‌

Romance Junkies

St. Martin's Paperbacks Titles
by Tiffany Clare

The Surrender of a Lady

The Seduction of His Wife

The Secret
Desires
of a Governess

TIFFANY CLARE

St. Martin's Paperbacks

This is a work of fiction. All of the characters, organizations, and events portrayed in this novel are either products of the author's imagination or are used fictitiously.

THE SECRET DESIRES OF A GOVERNESS

Copyright © 2011 by Tiffany Clare.

All rights reserved.

For information address St. Martin's Press, 175 Fifth Avenue, New York, NY 10010.

ISBN: 978-0-312-38184-4

Printed in the United States of America

St. Martin's Paperbacks edition / June 2011

St. Martin's Paperbacks are published by St. Martin's Press, 175 Fifth Avenue, New York, NY 10010.

10 9 8 7 6 5 4 3 2 1

For Loolie. Because you're always available, girlfriend!

Acknowledgments

I don't think there ever comes a time when a book is not the product of a village. Ely, what would I do without you? I'd like to thank the Vixens, Courtney Milan and Janga, Monique and Holly.

A very special thank-you to the art department at St. Martin's. You're bloody brilliant. Beyond, in fact!

Helen, how could I not mention you! You're always there when I need you most, especially during the crazy author-chick cliff-walking times. You rock!

Chapter 1

In the Kingdom of Brahmors, there was a young prince who lived under the shadow of his father's rule. He wished to stand up to the king, but the prince was young and did not have the strength needed to do so. The land around the kingdom was sad and oppressed and the heavens no longer rained down atop the grains that sustained the land.

—The Dragon of Brahmors

1848, Northumbria

Elliott Taylor Wright, the Earl of Brendall, stilled when he heard footsteps. A squelching wet sound drew nearer to his study. Definitely not a usual occurrence. He flicked his watch open: ten after nine. No one came up to the castle if they could help it.

Martha, his housekeeper, would be gone from the main house for the evening. She always made sure to put his son down at eight. That didn't mean it couldn't be Jacob wandering around, finding some sort of trouble when the hour was still early. If that were the case, the boy would find his bed before long.

Not worried about unwelcome guests, Elliott stood from his wide desk, papers scattered over the surface. He stretched his back, then rubbed his eyes. He'd been looking over a stack of meaningless letters for too long and a break was in order, maybe even for the remainder of the night.

Striding toward the hearth, he picked up the poker and turned over the burning logs. The room was chilly and a bit damp. A lick of frost teased the air.

Elliott looked toward the door when another faint sound reached his ears. That was not his son; the tread was too heavy for a boy of eight years.

With the unlikelihood that the noise was his son . . . who could be wandering the castle? There were a handful of servants, but they rarely spent time in the main house this late in the evening. They had everything they needed at the keep—another building on the castle grounds. They left him well enough alone once the day closed. As he preferred.

It *was* possible someone was looking for him. And if that were the case, they'd know where to find him.

Except . . . the noise continued right on past his study.

He walked over to the door, slid it open soundlessly, and peered down the dimly lit hall.

A figure in white turned left at the end of the long corridor. The mud-caked hem of her skirts snapped with the twirl of her heel before she disappeared from sight.

Elliott stepped out of his study, shut the heavy door as silently as he had opened it, and followed the evening prowler. He was careful not to make too much noise. Padding quietly down the hall, he wondered when he should make his presence known. He was intrigued by the notion of having a trespasser.

Everyone who lived in the area was superstitious and thought his home to be haunted. Cursed since his mother's death. Not a surprising assessment since his mother's demise had come when she'd walked out into the sea; he was only a boy of seven at the time.

Elliott was curious as to why the woman was wandering his home. She would have passed the village long before finding her way here.

She was a tiny thing, probably a good seven or eight inches shorter than he was. Elliott studied her slender figure. Her hair was straggly and soaked right through; the pins had released a long braid to fall down to the middle of her back, and dripped a trail of rainwater down her skirts. He couldn't make out the color, but he guessed a light brown.

Wetness clung to her like a second skin, making the line of her underthings beneath the worsted muslin visible to the naked eye. Not an ideal material for the unreliable climate in Northumbria. Her shoulders were narrow. Her waist couldn't be more than what his two hands could wrap around.

Her skirt painted a muddy path along the hardwood floor with every step. The sloshing sound he'd heard earlier was still audible. It must have been coming from her waterlogged shoes. She carried a dripping shawl over one arm, a valise in her other hand.

She turned down another corridor. Did she not realize she was headed back to the entrance she'd come through? She mumbled something under her breath, but either he was too far off to make out the words or she wasn't muttering anything intelligible.

With no desire to wander the halls of the great house all evening, and curious to know who she was, he called out to her.

"I see few visitors here, madam."

He set his shoulder against the darkly paneled wall and waited for her to face him.

She froze at his comment and turned with more grace than he thought possible in her sodden, bedraggled state. Raising a dainty chin, she narrowed her eyes, making tiny wrinkles form between her brows. Her features were clearer now that she stood next to a lit lamp on the wall.

She resembled a drowned rat. Better yet, a mutt left out in the rain that had done nothing more than roll in the mud and filth for the better part of a storm.

"You!" She pointed a castigating finger at him.

He raised a questioning brow. Who did the little witch think she was?

She seemed to think herself mighty important and marched right up to him, her chest rising furiously with every breath. He said not one word more as she seemed to size him up, her nose scrunching as though she would bare her teeth in a snarl.

How dare she treat him like a lesser in his own home? In the house she trespassed in.

"How is it you've found your way here?"

On closer inspection, she was unusually nice to look upon. Her complexion was clear, freckles dotted across her nose and the upper portion of her cheeks. Her lips, he imagined, were full. Right now, though, she pinched them tightly together, either in anger or to keep her teeth from chattering since the edge of her lips held a tinge of blue. How long had she been standing out in the rain to come to this state? It occurred to him then that he should offer her the warmth of a fire before he sent her on her way.

"I walked," she spat like a feral cat.

He pinched his lips tightly together and swallowed his offer. It was then he noticed her eyes were as rich and clear a green as peridot, with the slightest hint of gold, and as fiery as her nature proved to be.

"I had to walk fifteen miles because no one arranged

for a carriage. I couldn't even hire a coach to bring me this far."

Who was this woman to act so familiar with him? He didn't know her. Didn't recognize her. Did she require a warm meal and a place to sleep until the storm passed through? If that were the case, she went about it strangely. Snapping and snarling at the master of the house was no way to win a free meal and lodgings.

He looked her over once more. Even though it was damaged from the rain, her dress was well made and of a fine, expensive material. A lady would have traveled with a maid. A ladybird on the other hand . . .

Elliott crossed his arms over his wide chest at that thought. He watched her gaze flick to the open throat of his shirt, trailing lower to the exposed skin of his forearms where his shirtsleeves were rolled up. Then she met his gaze head-on, weariness making her lids heavy. She had traveled far by the looks of it.

"Madam, do you always address your betters in such a fashion?"

"How—how dare you speak to me thus. I'm here on your invitation!"

That gave him pause, and he stood away from the wall. He hadn't invited a woman up to the castle for more years than he cared to count. When he wanted the company of a woman he rode over to Alnwick, one of the larger townships. But he'd been too busy over the past few months to indulge in a good tumble.

His earlier thought that she might be a lady of the night would not quit his mind. She might do if she wanted to warm his bed. After a bath, this woman would clean up nicely.

Admittedly, she wasn't his usual type. He didn't like them to talk back.

But once the thought of this woman in his bed was in his mind, it stirred his blood. Before he even realized, he'd dropped his arms to his sides and took a step closer to her. Her eyes widened, smoothing all the creases from her pretty face.

He was half stiff when her hand came between them, pressing the tips of her chilled fingers against the exposed skin of his chest briefly before pulling away. The skin-on-skin contact did more than set fire to his arousal. Her cheeks and neck flamed a cherry red in the golden light around them. He wasn't sure when he had last made a lady blush. It made his body taut with need.

He wanted.

Until she stuttered, "I—I'm the governess."

The governess?

Elliott forced himself to take a step away from her. What was he thinking? Better yet, what was he doing? Obviously he wasn't thinking at all about the consequences of his actions.

It was his turn to narrow his eyes. The housekeeper had been corresponding with someone, but for some reason he'd pictured the new hire to be an old crone. Much like all the other *older* women who had taken on the impossible task of teaching his son. This young woman, who couldn't be a day over her eighteenth year, didn't fit his image of a governess. How could one so young take on the task seasoned women had failed at?

"You're the governess?" The disbelief and disappointment were evident in his voice.

"Yes . . . I put an advertisement in the *Northern Times* last month. I was asked to start immediately."

And she looked ready to hit someone—whether from his briefly untoward behavior or from her uncomfortable, bedraggled state was hard to determine.

Damn it. What was wrong with him?

* * *

Furious didn't even come close to describing Abby Halla-way's current state of mind. *Livid, manic, enraged*, and *in-furiated* weren't strong enough words, either. *Violent* was an apt description. For the first time in her life, she wanted to hit something. Or someone. To say that her first day of employment had not gone as planned was an understatement.

Never mind that Lord Brendall's staff had not arranged for a carriage after she'd given Mrs. Harrow the precise time of her arrival into the Alnmouth railway station in a letter set for fast post more than a week ago.

Lord Brendall's reaction to her had only made her night worse. The infernal man. If she wasn't mistaken, he'd thought her no better than a common harlot before she'd blurted out the truth of her circumstance. She had barely kept herself from stamping her foot over his. At least he had the decency to take a step back with her admission.

Perhaps a gentleman hid beneath his wholly improper form. She'd never seen a man look and act so uncultivated in all her years. And to direct that incivility toward her was too shocking for words. The stark intent on seduction she'd read in his clear eyes was outrageous. Deplorable behavior on his part.

He stared at her in confusion. His eyes were rather striking: the lightest, eeriest blue she'd ever gazed into, like a cloudless summer day.

She had assumed he would be older—in his fourth or fifth decade. He wasn't supposed to be near her own age. Or handsome for that matter.

Lord Brendall was a rather large man, bigger than her sister's affianced, considerably greater in bulk than most she'd ever met in London society. It was quite an attractive feature, which she well knew she shouldn't admit. He was tall, too. A couple of inches over six feet was her guess. His formidable height was topped with dark hair—black in the current lighting—that had the slightest wave to it. His face was shadowed with evening stubble, lines slashing down the middle to indicate that he probably had dimples if he smiled.

For some reason, she doubted he ever did anything so common as smile. The cleft in his chin was slight. His lips were thin, the lower marginally larger than the upper, and she imagined she could fit the curve of her thumb into the enticing dip at the center of the top one.

Then . . . there was the rest of him. There couldn't be a more fitting description than: *a bear of a man*. She doubted she'd be able to wrap her hands around the thickness of his forearm. That thought had more gooseflesh dancing up her cold arms. His shoulders were wide, and they weren't soft and squishy to the touch, either; she knew because she'd pressed up against him. The man was like granite, only much warmer.

She'd peg him for a common laborer if not for the finely cut shirt, trousers, and suspenders he sported and the air of command sucking all the warmth from the air around her. Her teeth chose that moment to chatter.

"I wrote to say I'd take the position immediately. As was requested of me. I sent a note for Mrs. Harrow to arrange for a carriage to meet me at the train station since I couldn't make the arrangements myself on such short notice."

He looked puzzled, the side of his mouth rising in a snarl-like fashion.

Abby had to close her eyes and take a deep breath as she counted to ten. She would not cry after the trials she'd endured on her trip north. She refused to show any emotion that made her seem weak. Yes, she was overset in her emotions—and rightfully so. It had been a very long, very cold day. The only thing that would make it better was a hot bath followed by equally hot soup.

"You didn't receive my last letter, did you?"

He shook his head once. "I didn't expect you. Nor do I think Martha knew of your imminent arrival."

That was stating the obvious, since her feet and legs now ached something fierce from trudging fifteen miles through mud and rain. Her toes were icicles; she couldn't even feel them. She'd never walked so far in one stretch before. Not in all her life. There were carriages to take a lady so far, or horses to ride. But no one had been willing to lend her a cart once they had learned she was in Lord Brendall's employ. And who was Martha? Was that Mrs. Harrow's given name?

"What is your name? I can't recall."

"Abigail. La—" She pinched her mouth together and bit the inside of her cheeks. She definitely was overtired to have almost let it slip that she was a lady. She inclined her head as a way of introduction. "Miss Abigail Hallaway."

Finally, a gentlemanly reaction from him; he dipped his head in greeting. "Miss Hallaway. I'm sure you've concluded that I am Lord Brendall."

"I have. I've been incredibly rude. Apologies, my lord."

He said nothing in response. Just stared back at her. What a strange man he was. Did he not have the decency to ring for a servant or at least show her to her room? There was a curious glare to his eyes that left her speechless for some moments.

"I'd like to retire to my quarters, if you don't mind. It's been a hellish day."

His head jerked up, and he seemed taken aback by her harsh wording. Wording a polite governess should never in a million years use. Curse her luck right now. Curse this whole day!

She gave an exasperated sigh, and added, "It's been a

difficult day, my lord. I am chilled right to the bone and liable to catch my death if we stand here and chat the remainder of the evening."

She should guard her tongue better and be less snappish with his lordship, even if his manners left something to be desired.

"Yes, of course. You need to be shown to your room. If you require hot water, Martha keeps a pot on the stove in the kitchen. There is a hip bath tucked in there somewhere as well."

Did the castle have no modern amenities? Was she really expected to bathe in the kitchen? Or as a servant, was she expected to use a common facility? She'd save that question for later. It was trivial when she was chilled to the bone.

"Thank you. Will you ring a servant for me?"

She'd consider having a bath just as soon as she got out of her wet clothes.

"There is no one in the main house. The staff lives over in the keep. I don't make them work past the supping hour."

No servants in the main house? And six people living close by did not count. In this monstrous place, how could that be? How did the master of the house function on a skeleton staff?

She was too tired to question why he didn't keep serving staff on hand. If he could not pay them—or her—she'd know soon enough. The worst that could happen was her going back home to her sisters and having to advertise for another position.

"Will you please show me to the keep so I might settle in? I assume that is where I will take my room?"

Before answering her, his gaze traveled the length of her, from knotted hair to mud-covered skirt and feet, with a scowl. Then his sharp blue eyes met hers. Yes, she was an awful sight to behold, but it couldn't be helped. She glared at him for his rude survey of her person.

He said not a word as he turned around, grabbed a candleholder from a long side table in the hall, and lit it against another candle's flame.

"You'll be staying in the main house."

He had said all the servants lived at the keep. Was the keep fully occupied? Or was she expected to stay close to her charge? Did that mean the child's nurse wasn't at hand?

She was too tired to barrage him with so many questions. Too tired to utter another word. She cared not where she slept tonight, so long as it was warm and dry.

Without another word, he headed down the hall she'd just come from. He did not offer to take her lone bag, as most gentlemen would do. But she kept forgetting, she was the hired help now, not a lady. She'd left that honorary title behind two days ago.

Chapter 2

When the prince was of age, he wished to marry the local wise woman's daughter. The young prince loved her and wanted her always at his side, but the king refused the union.

—The Dragon of Brahmors

As Lord Brendall took her up a wide set of stairs, Abby couldn't help but scowl at his back. His white shirt stretched taut over the defined muscles of his shoulders. She also couldn't help that her gaze slipped to his buttocks, which appeared quite firm under his trousers.

Her head tilted to the side as she watched the material tighten, then slacken with each step he took. The man should have the decency to wear a jacket; he probably turned many a lady's eyes with his form alone.

The light-veined marble of the railing was cool under her bare hand. She'd taken her gloves off on entering the house and stuck them in the side of her valise since they were soaked right through. Her foot snagged on the lip of the step while staring at his enticing backside and she tripped forward on the stairs. At least she had the good sense to grasp the rail tighter to keep herself upright.

He turned to her with a sharp, disapproving frown. She swallowed against the nervous giggle that almost escaped her throat and forced her gaze to her surroundings as she took the next stair, then the next.

She shouldn't admire her employer's buttocks. But she'd always appreciated brawny men. They were so different from the simpering society gentlemen she was used to. Powerfully built men seemed so raw and untamed. Dark and dangerous. And so very much a man compared with the effeminate peacocks who tried courting her on every trip she'd made to Town with her sisters.

Abby shook her head and focused on the large picture frames lining the wall with what had to be images of long-ago relatives. The eldest portraits were near the bottom. Seventeenth and eighteenth century by the style depicted in the oil paintings. One was of a man wearing a white wig, green hunting coat, and tan breeches. He held a gun over his lap, and he sat astride a great white warhorse. The man had a carriage of command about him. Two Brittany spaniels stood next to the horse, tails erect, their heads high like their master. A grandfather or great-grandfather, she guessed.

Halfway up, there was a beautiful woman wearing a clean Grecian style, the white sprigged muslin gathered and cinched enticingly under her breasts, her dainty feet peeking out from beneath the hem of the frilly dress. Her dark tresses were coiled in the fashion of a few decades past. Quite possibly it was an image of Lord Brendall's mother.

On the first landing hung a great large tapestry. The lady was dressed in a medieval burgundy-colored gown. Thin braids bound her hair back from the face, but the rest of her golden tresses fell well past the flare of her hips. There was a spark of mischief in her eyes, as if the mysterious lady held a secret from the observer. It was a newer piece, not actually of the time period it depicted since the woven threads seemed to be in pristine condition.

She turned to ask Lord Brendall who the woman was, but he'd already taken the second flight of stairs, forcing her to cease her curious study of the paintings to keep up with him.

The higher they climbed, the more tired she felt; it didn't matter that it wasn't more than a dozen steps to each landing. It had been such a long day. She doubted she'd be able to drag herself back downstairs to the kitchen for a hot bath. She just wanted to strip out of her wet, sticky clothes and climb under a multitude of warm, dry blankets.

A small pang of longing for the comforting arms of her sisters stabbed at her heart. She did her best to ignore it, but it wasn't easy. She was on her own in the world now. It was always meant to happen this way. Her sisters were enjoying marital bliss with babies probably not a year off.

That was never the life she'd envisioned for herself. It seemed so meaningless, so dull to fall into the trap of marriage and then the heaps of children that were sure to follow. And she certainly didn't want to be the spinster aunt caring for her sisters' children. That was not her idea of a fulfilling life. She wanted more than that for herself. Needed more than that. She wanted to be an independent woman. It started here, at Brendall Castle. And by God, she'd do whatever was in her power to make it work.

To her surprise, they stopped on the second floor. "Is the nursery on the second floor?"

He'd shown her down a hall with half a dozen doors. All insignificant, all the same.

Lord Brendall turned up the latch on the old-fashioned darkly stained oak door. Pushing it open, he motioned with his hand that she should enter. "This will be your room. It's where all the governesses have slept," he said.

"The nursery is not used. It's in another wing of the castle that has not withstood time."

There definitely couldn't be a nursemaid if she was to be on hand for the child at all times.

It didn't surprise her that part of the castle lay in disrepair, either. Not so uncommon in the larger, older estates scattered throughout England. She'd have to explore the grounds tomorrow with her charge. The overall condition of the house might tell her a lot about the family and about his lordship.

She approached Lord Brendall warily before peering inside. It was a good-sized room—not as big as the one she had occupied at her sister's house, but decent enough. The damask bed hangings were dated. A heavy brocade curtain covered the lone window in the room. The candlelight held forth by his lordship illuminated the gold-and-blue motif inlaid on the heavily woven material. The walls were papered in gold and light blue.

She stepped inside to further inspect her new surroundings. The door shut behind her and Lord Brendall was gone a moment later. She heard the click of his booted feet as he walked away from her room. His steps faded before she could figure out which direction he went in.

Did he head to his own room for the evening—which she wasn't sure was even in this wing of the house—or did he make his way back down to the main floor? It didn't matter. There was a wide comfortable-looking bed calling to her with its layers of blankets and pillows of varying shapes and sizes.

Setting her valise on the writing desk, she opened it and pulled out her night rail and dressing robe, the only articles of clothing she'd been able to carry with her. What a shame that the sole dress she had was the one currently sticking uncomfortably to her. Hopefully it would be dry by morning and she could brush out the caked-on dirt before making her way back to the train station to pick up the rest of her luggage.

Stripping down to her unmentionables, Abby opened the wardrobe in the hope of finding a few pegs inside. To her surprise, there were more than a handful of dresses hanging neatly along a wooden pole. How strange to find clothes in here when this was a room designated for the hired help.

Stranger yet, the dresses were not a governess's. Rubbing her fingers over the soft material, she knew they were of fine silk and twilled muslin. She'd ponder why they were in her wardrobe later. Riffling through the clothes, she found some empty hangers.

Now that she wore next to nothing, she realized how cold the room was. Making her way to the fireplace, she set the logs inside, opened the flue, and struck the flint that was stored in a box on the high mantel. It took her a couple of tries to get the wood lit, but she managed. Her first task as an independent woman accomplished, she warmed her hands by the flames that licked up the logs. Pulling off the rest of her damp clothes, she set them on a chair close to the fire so they would dry quickly.

Donning her night rail was the last thing she remembered before waking to a frigid room. Her cheeks were frozen where they were exposed to the night air. She stared around the dark chamber, making out bits of white molding against the papered wall. Had it not been so chilly, she'd have opened the curtains to let in the moonlight. If it happened to be this cold at the beginning of the fall season, what would the winter months bring?

That familiar ache of homesickness sent an unpleasant shiver through her body that had nothing to do with the winter-like air and everything to do with being away from her sisters. She didn't want to believe that her hasty action in removing herself from under her sisters' noses might have been the wrong decision.

She had to believe this life would be better than living under the pressure of watching her sisters—with their beloved husbands—building families that no longer included her.

She wanted the old days back. The time when it had been the three of them and no one else. Selfish of her to think that way, but it was that way of thinking that made her realize she had to move on. Permanently, temporarily, she didn't know for how long, just long enough to carve her own way in life. Enough time to decide what she wanted to do for the rest of her days since her fortune wouldn't come to her until her twenty-fifth birthday.

Unless she married before then.

What an utterly depressing thought. She had rejected the very idea of marrying any of the boring gentlemen of London society long ago. Actually, she'd decided against marriage at her very first ball.

Sighing, Abby sat up to lean against the stack of warm pillows at her back. She should add more logs to the fire. Unfortunately, that required getting out of bed.

Pulling the uppermost blanket around her shoulders, she made her way to the fireplace. There were no more logs in the iron rack. Even if she didn't want to leave the room, she had no choice since the fire had to be built up again.

With a heavy sigh, she rummaged through her valise in the dark, found a pair of dry slippers, and put them on. Hardly warm enough, but they'd do for wandering around the house. She squeezed the material of her clothes hanging over the back of the chair. They were still damp and too cold to wear yet. Hopefully this wasn't a sign of how her day to come would play out. She did not want a repeat of yesterday.

Opening up the chest of drawers, Abby found a che-mise. She shook it out and held it up in front of her. It looked about her size. Maybe a bit short and a bit wide for her, but it would have to do. Taking out a bar of soap and other personal items, she found some linens in the ward-robe and then left the bedchamber in search of the hip bath his lordship had mentioned on her arrival last night.

Elliott's night had been sleepless, so he'd decided to get up despite the fact that the sun had yet to crest the hori-zon. There wasn't much sense lying abed thinking about the governess all wet and shivering. Wanting to warm her in more ways than one.

He scratched at his unshaven jaw and wished he could focus on something else. He'd busy himself in his study till it was light enough to go and fix a few more of the fallen stones on the west wall with Thomas.

Intent on scrounging up some food in the kitchen, he was brought up short by a soft but colorful curse. Miss Hallaway was a curious creature. For a proper governess, she seemed rather accomplished in using a number of expletives even he didn't know the meanings for.

Heat spilled from around the open crack in the kitchen door, and he peered into the dimly lit room. A candela-brum was set on the cutting table; the lit wickers of the candles gave the room an ambient glow. The old hip bath was set near the woodstove, steam rising from the surface. There were a number of items set on the floor: a folded stack of clothes, soap wrapped in paper, a counterpane from the bedroom fallen in a heap on the floor.

Once he realized that Miss Hallaway wore nothing more than a night rail and dressing robe, exposing the clear outline of her willowy figure, he was helpless to move away from the door. Elliott swallowed tightly at the sight of her slender beauty.

There was a slight roundness to her breasts shadowed beneath the white material. Her waist was tiny without the cinching of a corset so many women relied upon.

A long, silent huff of air escaped him and he grasped the door frame to stop himself from moving forward.

She pulled her braid forward and loosened the strands by brushing her fingers through the long tresses. He still couldn't tell the color of her hair in the dimness of the room, but he could see that it was a light shade. Brown, he decided, since he preferred brunettes. It was incredibly long. Fanning around her like a curtain of wavy silk right past her elbows, and just past the slight flare of her hips.

She leaned forward, her hair stirring the surface of the water as she tested the temperature with her fingers. He could imagine the feel of her fingers on his body caressing him in the same way she gently swirled them over the surface of the water.

With a sigh, she stood and shed her robe, and then his thoughts narrowed down to only her. Her arms were as milk white as the rest of her. Smooth and perfect-looking. Elliott itched to touch and caress her with his rough hands.

He should leave her to her privacy, as a gentleman would. He was no better than a blackguard. No better than his conniving father, because for the life of him, he couldn't walk away. This desire he had for her was new and unsettling for him, and something he didn't want to deny himself just yet.

Perhaps the attraction was that she wasn't a normal governess. Not compared with the last. This one swore—crudely. She was younger than the batty crones and other women who'd tromped through his and his son's life over the last few years. And, he could admit, she wasn't hard on the eyes. Not in the least.

Releasing the buttons at her throat and down the center of her chest, she pulled the garment over her head and dropped it to the floor. Elliot closed his eyes and tried to inhale the breath that had been punched right out of his lungs. The next time he saw any garment flutter over her head and to the floor, he vowed to be the one removing it.

Shit.

He had to stop thinking that way. Had to stop thinking about *her* that way. Had to walk away before he did something stupid.

His eyes snapped open again when she sank deep into the water with a heavy sigh. Her shoulder blades and the upper half of her arms were exposed to his gaze when she gathered her hair to one side.

He had to walk away.

When women became involved with Wright men, it seemed to end in madness and death. The last woman he'd cared for was dead, the circumstances surrounding her death just as strange as his mother's final walk into the North Sea.

Still, he couldn't move away from the door. Head tilted to the side, she wet her hair and lathered soap into it from a small container. The smell of crushed flowers made its way to his nostrils. It seemed familiar, but he couldn't place the fragrance. Her fingers were slow and methodical as she combed them through the wet strands. He'd been so entranced by her every move that he hadn't expected her to dunk her whole body beneath the water to wash out the soap.

When she came back up, she reached over the lip of the tub to grab one of the folded linens on the floor. All the breath left his lungs when the deep rose tip of her breast pearled on being exposed to the air. His mouth watered to taste her. To suck that firm peak into his mouth and lave it. His hand gripped so tight around the frame of the door that it groaned in protest.

He couldn't continue to torment himself like this.

He'd definitely been too long without the company of a woman. So why in hell couldn't he leave her in peace?

She hummed something while she rebraided her hair. Nothing identifiable, but something low and melodic. He must have been standing there for some time without re- alizing it, like an asp charmed by her music. He shook his head like a bloody mongrel—which he was, considering his inability to leave her be—and forced his grip to loosen from the door frame.

Elliott found a shred of decency niggling at his mind and grasped the thin threads before they escaped him. Finally, he managed to turn away from the kitchen. He headed toward his study and away from temptation.

Hard labor was the only thing bound to clear his mind of Miss Hallaway and rid him of the stiffness beneath his trousers. He'd have to take better care not to find her un- aware again. It wasn't fair to her. And she most certainly wouldn't appreciate the kind of thoughts running through his head right now.

Abby paused with one foot on the edge of the bath, her ear tilted toward the door. Was that noise a creak in the floor? Was someone up and about in the house?

Stepping completely from the water, she grabbed up the folded linen and wrapped it around herself as she dripped her way over to the kitchen entrance. The door was cracked open the tiniest amount. She furrowed her brow. She'd definitely closed the door behind her. Hadn't she? She stuck her head out from the warmth of the kitchen and peered down the dark hall. No one to be seen any- where. No moving shadows. Just stillness.

It was an old house. It was bound to make strange noises.

Shutting the door firmly, she dressed with quick effi- ciency. She was reluctant to leave the warm sanctuary the kitchen had blazed into now that the woodstove was going strong.

It had to be coming up to five in the morning, so the cook should be here any moment. Were governesses required to help with the preparation of breakfast? She hadn't a clue. She had limited experiences with governesses. Her own father had taken it upon himself to educate her once her mother had died.

There was a bucket under the table. Filling it with the water from the hip bath, she took it to the door that led outside. It was a heavy door to pull inward, but once it was open, she made quick work of tossing all the water into the gardens.

Abby warmed herself by the fire once more before gathering up her belongings and finding her way back to her room.

If she recalled correctly, the child she was to instruct was eight. She'd ask Mrs. Harrow, the woman who had corresponded with her, what learning tools would be available to her. Her first priority of the day—after a warm breakfast—was to retrieve her luggage from the train station. She'd have to wear one of the dresses she'd discovered in the wardrobe.

She found her room with better ease than she'd found the kitchen. Shutting the door behind her, she looked at the logs aflame in the fireplace. Her breath froze in her lungs as she peered around her shadowed room looking for any imposing figures, any moving silhouettes. She exhaled once she concluded she was alone.

Who had lit her fire? Was there a maid already in the house? Surely it hadn't been the lord of the manor? If it had been Lord Brendall, she'd have to make sure he understood he couldn't enter her private bedchamber whenever he pleased.

Chapter 3

The prince was set to marry a princess of his father's choosing. He refused to abandon his lady love and left the castle to find his own way in the rough.   —*The Dragon of Brahmors*

The first members of the household Abby had come across were the housekeeper and her daughter, Lydia, who appeared to be about Abby's age. Abby had been given immediate instruction to call the older woman Martha, because calling her Mrs. Harrow made her think of her husband's mother. Abby could only surmise that Martha did not like her mother-in-law. Not with the way her lips curled in distaste when she'd mentioned the long-deceased woman.

Martha had also apologized for unknowingly abandoning her at the railway station. But she didn't seem to care that Abby had had to walk fifteen miles in the most horrendous torrential downpour she'd ever been caught in. Abby wasn't generally one to cast judgment on people until she fully knew them, but it was very hard not to judge Martha for her lack of caring.

Presently, Martha kneaded into some dough on the long table in the kitchen while her daughter cut up potatoes, onions, and carrots and tossed them into a pot on the chopping block set between two deep bronze butler sinks.

Abby sat on a stool close to the table and Martha. This was the first time she'd ever watched someone make bread. The way Martha pounded into it looked like a good way to release anger, if one were so inclined. How useful it would have been to do something like that last night.

"You came with exceptional letters of recommendation and you're well written so you've had a respectable education, but you seem too young for this post. How many years have you got, child?"

The woman didn't seem convinced that Abby was quite capable of filling the position. Was that why she spoke so gruffly to her? Was that why she pounded into the dough with more vigor than she probably needed? Martha had seemed so much more cordial in their correspondence than she did now in person. For some reason, Abby had been expecting a more motherly figure.

Lydia didn't look up once during the whole conversation. Had Abby done something wrong in coming to the castle on her own? Was it the fact that she wore their old mistress's clothes? It wasn't as though she'd had any choice in the matter.

"Three and twenty, madam." Abby knew she looked younger than most thought. It was her lack of bosom and hips that made her seem youthful. "My father groomed me well for this position. I was his last hope to play the role of the son he never had."

"You have sisters, then?"

"Two older sisters, yes. Both married well." They'd done so much better than marry well. She'd not reveal that her sisters were both countesses.

Stirring a lump of sugar in her tea, Abby watched the older woman's weatherworn hands flexing around the dough. Not wanting the conversation to focus on her life, Abby said, "I've been unable to find my charge all morning."

Actually there'd been no sign of the child. She had checked all the rooms she'd come upon, explored every parlor, bedchamber, dressing room, study, nook, and cranny she'd found in the giant house. There were no misplaced toys, no child-like clutter. It was as though the house were childless.

Martha took a small handful of flour and tossed it into the open oven. It turned a golden brown. She gave a harrumph—satisfied with the outcome, Abby assumed—and set the dough in the rising pan for a fourth time, then put it in the oven to bake.

"Have you checked the stables?"

"She's fond of horses, is she?" Abby loved horses, but she was not an accomplished rider. Papa had had to sell their horses to keep their family in coin and cloth. They'd lived on necessities until her first sister had married.

"The young master's father had *him* on a horse before *he* could walk," Lydia interjected. The first words the young woman had uttered since her good-day wishes first thing this morning.

Abby looked directly at the young woman, sure that her face clearly revealed the shock she was in. In her confusion, she pushed her teacup away and stood from the table. The hot liquid sloshed over the side and scalded her hand. She yanked it away and wiped it on her skirts. The pain was nothing compared with her thoughts.

He?

A boy?

What was she to do with a boy? She had no experience with boys. None. Why in the all the world had they hired a governess instead of a tutor? Didn't little boys, and heirs to earldoms, receive an education from the finest tutors and later attend the finest schools throughout England?

"I did not realize I'd be teaching Lord Brendall's son." She busied her hands by smoothing her braids against her head. She'd been duped into coming here. She felt foolish. Naive.

Was there a possibility that the boy was from the wrong side of the sheets? Did bastards go to the finest schools? She wasn't sure since she'd never been to a school before. Since she'd never met a bastard before.

"We discussed it in our correspondence." Martha looked at her with her innocent round face, with her dark brown eyes and a heavy fist to another batch of dough.

Abby was positive she'd never been told so. She would have remembered, and probably would have refused the job had she been given that knowledge to begin with. As soon as she retrieved her luggage, she could prove that fact.

Yet proving she'd never been made aware she was to educate a boy would not change her mind on taking this post. She could not leave. She didn't want to go home. She needed to make this work. If it turned out terribly, she'd advertise in the paper for another position. If she ran home to her sisters at the first hint of a problem, she'd never make the kind of life she wanted for herself.

Not that she knew exactly what she wanted for herself. Maybe she was merely amusing herself till her dowry could be released to her. Maybe she wanted only to escape the love and joy that her sisters indulged so openly in. Was she jealous of her sisters?

Oh, what an awful thought to have. She adored her sisters, and was happy that they had found loving, adoring, disgustingly smitten husbands for themselves. Oh, dear, she *was* jealous.

She focused on Martha, wanting to concentrate her thoughts elsewhere, like on the fact that she'd never been told about educating a boy.

One skill that Abby had honed well, since she liked to wager on a great many things, was that she was an accomplished liar. She'd pretend she was not caught off guard by this small quandary, despite her earlier reaction belying that fact. She was determined to have her independence, and Martha would not have her tucking her tail between her legs and running home. And she'd not be thrown off course after coming this far.

"I hadn't thought to check the stables for the *boy.*" Abby tapped her mouth in thought. "Speaking of stables, is there someone who can take me to the train station? I need to retrieve the rest of my belongings today. I did not mean to help myself to the clothes in the wardrobe, but the dress I wore on my trudge up to the castle is still quite damp."

Abby didn't mind repeating that she'd been all but forgotten at the train station. For some reason, Martha didn't seem to like her. Maybe given her youthful appearance, the older woman thought she'd been duped into hiring her. She'd have to prove Martha wrong.

"Thomas will be out helping the master. They'll be working on the west wall. Been out there most of the summer to fix what tumbled down some decades ago."

Interesting that Lord Brendall was the one maintaining the castle and not the local tradesmen. Unless he was overseeing the workers? Come to think of it, she doubted that to be the case with his brawny physique. The man was built like a laborer who worked in the fields at her sister's home.

She shook her head as though it would clear the unwanted thoughts. She must stop admiring her employer's most exceptional physique.

Martha placed the last bit of dough in a pan, clapped her hands to remove most of the flour from them, and gave them a final wipe on her apron. Taking one of the warm loaves that had cooled by the window ledge, she cut fat wedges off the loaf of fresh bread.

"I'll prepare you some sandwiches to take. They'll have worked up a fierce hunger by now."

Martha said nothing more, just went about her task of setting up a luncheon, while Abby finished her tea. Lydia came over to the long table and cut up some cold meat to put between the thick slabs of bread.

Basket in hand, Abby stared up at the clear blue sky with its faint smatterings of clouds stretching across the horizon like bolls of cotton yet to be picked.

The weather was decidedly better than it had been on her whole trip north. It had rained for most of the train ride and poured buckets when she'd been forced to walk to the castle. A shame it hadn't warmed a great deal with the appearance of the sun.

Her gait quickened with every cool slap of wind to her face. It was a relief to know her first day of employment didn't seem nearly as dreary as it had only a day ago. Aside from the fact that she knew next to nothing about little boys, she would do her best to make this situation work for her. She hoped she wasn't biting off more than she could chew in this instance.

In the distance, the sea slapped noisily against the shore. She couldn't get a glimpse of it from where she stood as there was a great sandy-white wall surrounding the bailey, but she tasted the salt on the air, heard the call of gulls in the distance, and fought to stand against the cool wind that swept over the wall and through the castle grounds.

The grass around her was a cropped field of emerald

green. Taller rushes of brown grass lined the inside wall. There were few flowers aside from the vines of morning glories near a large square building a good hundred paces from the main house. She guessed the building to be the keep that the Harrow family lived in.

There was a drive that went around that second structure and led into a section of the castle that seemed mostly in disrepair. Bits of stone lay crumbled, and littered the interior walls of the castle. Where stones had once filled the cobbled path, only pockets of sand and dirt remained. Half the stable was missing its roof, and what looked to be an old church lay in ruins, just a few walls still standing. The bell, long fallen and rusted to a lime color, lay dejectedly on the ground.

The grass had not been cropped in the old churchyard; it grew like a wild field, swallowing its secrets beneath the tall rushes of dancing greens and weeds. Beyond that, at the farthest end of the castle grounds, she could see the men bending over and lifting a great square block waist-high and placing it onto the white ledge of the new wall.

They did not immediately see her approach, so she slowed her pace to see how they went about mending the wall. There was a whole section of crumbled stones that had fallen and tumbled down to the sand dunes surrounding the castle on the north side of the property.

Where the wall should have been was an open view of the water. It was her first view of the North Sea. It was as dark as a night sky without stars to light the way. The water churned and rolled not far off in the distance. It made her dizzy staring at it. Made her feel as though she'd fall if she didn't close her eyes and turn away from the rhythmic slap of waves against the shore.

She focused on the men. Busy at their task, they still hadn't noticed her.

The weather might not be particularly warm—she did require a thick wool shawl—but it was obvious the men had been doing heavy labor for some time. Especially with the way Lord Brendall's sweat-dampened shirt stuck to him at the shoulder blades and lower back. Outlining all the strength and sinew beneath.

What would a fine layer of perspiration look like against his bare flesh? What would it feel like under her fingers as she explored the hard planes of his body?

Abby snapped her eyes closed, wanting to dispel her thoughts along with the images hampering her mind. It didn't help; her imagination conjured up the image she'd hoped to banish. Lord Brendall was like some long-forgotten warrior. She pictured him brandishing a sword, cutting a swath through enemy lines. She made a strangled sound, and had to focus on the ground in front of her.

It wasn't her fault she was imagining him in half dress. The man was never decently clothed whenever she'd happened upon him.

Taking a deep breath, she forced a smile on her face, hoping the desire she'd felt moments ago wasn't obvious. Hopefully they'd think the red of her cheeks an effect of the chilly wind and not something she seemed to experience whenever she looked upon her employer.

Ignoring her unruly thoughts, she studied what the men worked on. Strange that there were no local tradesmen helping them reassemble the wall. Did his lordship not have the money to pay them to do the task? Was that why they'd hired a governess for a mere pittance, instead of hiring a tutor for his son?

The man working next to Lord Brendall must be Thomas. He had a full white beard beneath his straw hat. His eyes crinkled at the sides as he squinted against the sun. A red kerchief was tied about his neck, and his sleeves were rolled up to the middle of his forearms. He wore a kind, welcoming smile, one that encouraged her a few steps closer. She did not wish to interrupt them overly much. She could wait for them to finish their work before she asked for a hand in retrieving her belongings.

Lord Brendall stood and drank water from a skin: his head tipped back, his damp shirt revealing a clean, strong outline of the muscles on his back: the indent at his spine, the outline of his shoulder blades, and the solid bulk of his shoulders and arms. She watched his throat work as he swallowed the liquid.

Perhaps the journey to Northumbria had tired her more than she thought? Perhaps this attraction she felt would subside after a decent night's sleep? He was very different from what she was used to in a man; that must be where her fascination stemmed from.

He hadn't looked up at her yet. But she didn't doubt that he knew she stood silently by. Thomas nodded in her direction and said something too low for her to hear over the wind whistling around them.

It wouldn't do to be distracted by the lord of the manor. As quick as the thought came, her eyes trailed back to his strong form. She had to force her gaze to Martha's husband. Goodness, what had gotten into her? She'd never spared a glance for any man. This was thrice now that he had captivated her attention wholly and completely.

Someone ought to hit her over the head to clear the nonsense from it. Where were her sisters when she needed them most?

She curtsied when Lord Brendall turned to her fully.

"Good morning, my lord. I've come bearing gifts from the kitchen." She held out the basket.

Lord Brendall didn't glance her way. He'd gone back to mortaring the stones with a gray slop mixed in a large wooden pail.

It was Thomas who spoke. "That wife of mine is spoiling

us too soon in the day." He raised his hand in her direction. Beckoning her closer. "Come sit closer to us. Who be you, lass?".

"The governess and new hire, Miss Hallaway."

"Well, Miss Hallaway. Let's see what you've got in that basket there. I've worked up an appetite this morning."

She opened the basket and set out the small linen spread enclosed with the sandwiches. She supposed it was her duty to lay the food out for them since they were mighty filthy with dirt and sweat. She busied herself with the task, trying to ignore the fact that Lord Brendall was ignoring her.

It shouldn't bother her. She shouldn't want him to pay her any mind. Yet it stirred anger in her gut to be disregarded so thoroughly.

She handed Thomas a sandwich filled with ham and cheese. "I've come to ask a favor of you, Mr. Harrow. I had to leave my luggage at the rail station. I'd like very much to borrow a cart, or get a ride into town so that I might reclaim my things."

When she offered up Lord Brendall's sandwich, he looked at her briefly before going back to his work.

"I'll take you after we've eaten. We had an early start this morning, and my back's not going to take much more lifting today. There's not much good to be said about getting older if you were to ask me."

Abby couldn't help but smile. Thomas was very friendly, and so different from his wife. She needed friends right now. She missed her sisters, and had felt so alone since leaving them. To be welcomed in any small way in this farthest reach of England seemed a bit of a blessing.

She ducked her head again, feeling unusually shy. She was never shy. Perhaps she was just sentimental when thoughts of her sisters clouded her mind. Or perhaps it

was the blatant disregard she received from Lord Brendall
that was making her feel uncomfortable in her own skin.
He had a way about him. He looked right through her as
though she weren't standing five feet away.

Did the man dislike everyone, or was there something
she'd done to offend him? She was sure it was the first and
not the latter. Because, for the life of her, she couldn't think
what she'd done wrong since last night.

"Where shall I meet you, then?" she asked Thomas.

"Come sit here with an old man for a bit. I find I like the
company of a beautiful young woman."

Beautiful? Hardly. Emma, her oldest sister, had always
been the beauty in the family. Abby had always thought
herself rather plain. No sense in dissuading him. Every
girl liked to be charmed with pretty words. Just because
she had no desire to marry didn't mean she couldn't enjoy
a little flattery once in a while. And it wasn't as though
Mr. Harrow was a contender for her hand.

"I've yet to meet my charge." Abby hesitated before
drawing nearer. "I really should look for him before we set
out."

"Jacob will be in the stables," Thomas said. "I wish
you luck. He's a wily one. He'll slip out of your fingers the
second you blink."

"I'm sure I'll manage." Perhaps the child was a little
wild. She'd been like that: daring, adventurous, clever . . .
slippery as an eel, her father had always been wont to say.

Thomas chuckled and bit into his sandwich. Lord
Brendall finished up with the mortar and sat on a tree
stump nearby with his sandwich in hand. He seemed content in remaining silent and continued to ignore her existence.

As though her thoughts were carried on the wind, he
suddenly turned his head and stared directly at her, the

silvery blue of his eyes trapping her like manacles about her wrists. His sudden regard robbed her of breath. His eyes were even more beautiful in the full light of day. The blue so light, so clear and unusual that she couldn't stop staring into them. She was making an imbecile of herself, but for the life of her, she couldn't drop her gaze.

"If Jacob's not in the stables, he likes to wander the ruined parts of the attic and upper floors of the main house." His voice was gravelly and deep.

"This is a usual occurrence, then?" At least she had found her voice. "This wandering around and hiding?" She couldn't blame the child when the father seemed so cold. Distant. There was something dark about him that warned her to guard herself carefully around this man. "Does he ever leave the castle grounds?"

"He's got no need to. There's nothing outside the walls that would interest him."

"Why is it, my lord, that you've accepted an advertisement for a governess and not a tutor to prepare your son for school?"

She bit the inside of her cheek and clenched her fists in her skirts. A bold tongue was a sure way for Lord Brendall to send her away.

"You ask too many questions, Miss Hallaway. It's my business what I do with the boy."

Taken aback, she stood from the rock she'd perched herself on and gave a curtsy. She ducked her head more to cover her glower than as a sign of respect when departing from his company. Lord Brendall might not know it, but he was not her better. She'd not let him treat her with any condescension. The man was incredibly rude, and she'd not endure his company any longer than she needed to. The castle was big enough that they should be able to go a whole year before setting eyes on each other.

"On that note," she muttered to herself, then clearer for

the company present: "I'll take my leave, my lord. Mr. Harrow, I will meet you at the stables in . . . shall we say, fifteen minutes?"

Mr. Harrow nodded as he lifted his hat and tipped it forward to her in farewell. "Till then, madam."

She gave him a smile before turning on her heel to head back to the stable. As much as she wanted to run, she kept her pace steady. She swore she could feel Lord Brendall's eyes glaring at her retreating form.

No wonder Martha had seemed bitter to her. It must be near impossible to work for such an awful man. She clenched her fists at her chest as she held the shawl closed over her. Was this what she should expect as a governess? Cruel treatment from employers who thought themselves better than her? Lord Brendall would have to learn to refrain from treating her as though she were no better than a commoner.

It was deplorable behavior on his part. It wasn't a wonder she'd never met him at any of the balls she'd been to in London. The man was uncouth, boorish. It shouldn't matter that she was under his employ. She'd never treated a servant so poorly.

On reaching the stables, she stepped inside without hesitation, happy to have a reprieve from the cold wind. There were six full stalls and a tack section on the far wall. No names adorned the doors.

The first horse she passed stuck its head out and nudged at her shoulder as she passed. She scratched her hand between its eyes, right along the white stripe decorating its chestnut-brown coat.

"Have you seen a little boy? I happen to be looking for one. Can't say as yet what he looks like, since I haven't had the pleasure of meeting him. I'm told his name is Jacob, and he's rather fond of you and your brethren."

The horse bobbed its big head. The shushing of little

feet sounded. Though she was having trouble locating the direction from which it came, she did not move from her position. She'd let the boy come to her.

"Strange that no one has come forward. I would really like to know your name, horse. Don't suppose you could tell me?"

The horse blew out a snort of air. Still, there was no sight of the boy.

"I suppose I'll just have to name you myself. How do you like the name Maybelle?"

"That's a girl name," came a soft voice.

Not wanting to scare the boy off now that she'd made progress, she continued talking to the horse. "Well, if that name is too much like a girl's, how about Zeus? Why have a masculine name if you can't be a great Greek god?"

The shuffling of feet grew louder, then a dark mop-headed boy came and stood close to her. She turned her head to the side and looked at him. He looked rather like his father with all that dark wavy hair.

There were several things she noticed that seemed at odds with being an heir to the Brendall earldom. Young Jacob needed his hair trimmed. It was a ragged mess. With all the knots, she had to wonder if he had lice. He wore short trousers and a white linen shirt already smeared with dirt. Suspenders held up the trousers, which looked a slight bit big on him. His eyes were as blue as his father's. And he did not smile. He looked at her as any curious child might. Only there was something else in his gaze. Was he afraid of her? Quite possible, being that she was a stranger.

"His name is Ivan."

"Well, Ivan," she said to the horse, "I think that is the perfect name for such a handsome equine." Scratching him once more along his muzzle, she turned back to the boy.

He was making a study of her. She could tell by the way

he looked over her dress and scratched at his head. He'd need a bath first chance she got.

"Why are you wearing that?" he asked of her.

She frowned and looked down to her borrowed dress. "The majority of my belongings are still at the rail station. I had nothing else to wear. So I borrowed something from the wardrobe in my room."

"You shouldn't wear that. Father won't like it. Who are you?"

She smiled, hopefully giving the boy a friendly face, one he could trust and maybe even make him chance another step closer. "I'm to be your teacher."

"You don't look like the last one."

"No?" She looked down at her dress and fanned out the material. "Is that because of the way I'm dressed?"

"You're not old. Their faces looked like a wrinkled old apple and their hair like muddy straw. Last one was as big as Ivan."

She nearly chuckled at the comparison, but managed to refrain. Barely. "How many governesses have you had?"

"Lots."

"Why did they all leave?"

He shrugged. Abby wondered if it had anything to do with the treatment received from Lord Brendall. Perhaps he wasn't liable to pay her wages? She'd have to broach the topic of her annual pay with Martha, not that the money was of any significance to her—it was a pittance compared with her money sitting in trust. She just didn't want anyone taking advantage of her.

"Thomas is taking me to town shortly. Would you like to come?"

Jacob shook his head vehemently.

"No? I don't suppose it sounds like any grand adventure for a boy your age. We will start our lessons very soon,

though. Hopefully this evening. Is there any particular
room designated for your studies?"

Again he shook his head. Weren't children generally
more talkative than this? She took a couple of steps closer
to him. Quicker than the blink of an eye, he took off at a
run.

That didn't go nearly as badly or as well as she had
thought it might. Would she have to search him out again
this afternoon? She'd have to ask Thomas, by far the friend-
liest inhabitant of the castle, how best to handle Jacob, or
better yet how best to find him when it seemed he didn't
want to be found. She was interrupted from her thoughts
by the sudden presence of Lord Brendall. A shadow blot-
ted out the light from the door, and it was as though his
presence sucked all the fresh air from the stable.

She scrunched up her brow, wondering if *he* planned
to take her to town. That wouldn't be proper. Besides, she
needed some information about the past governesses that
she could not ask of Lord Brendall. He was much more
the silent brooding type, whereas Thomas was a kind and
ready talker—at least that was the impression she got.

Smoothing her skirts, she gave him a long look. He
appeared intent on ignoring her as he went about setting a
saddle on the horse she'd been petting a few moments
ago. She wasn't sure if she should address him, or ignore
him as he did her.

Knowing he was apt to remain silent, and wholly uncomfortable with that silence, she finally asked, "Are you
going for an afternoon ride?"

He stopped in the middle of checking the belt that
wrapped around the barrel of the horse. A gruff, "In a
sense," was all he replied before he stepped quickly toward her. She hated that she took a couple of steps away
from him, allowing him to back her into a supporting
beam in the middle of the stable.

"You talk too much," he said and pulled on one of the braids at the side of her head till it was free of its pins. Tugging it forward, he studied it, rolling it between his fingers before meeting her gaze. "It's like fire. Perhaps you're a witch."

She reached up and loosened his fingers from where they grasped the braid. His fingers were rough, not those of the privileged class but of the working class. They were warm, too. Before she could pry his fingers away, he released the strand of hair. However, he did not move away from her.

"Never thought you'd be pretty."

That comment brought her up short.

Why had everyone assumed she'd be some aged and gray spinster? And why was he making any such assessment? What was wrong with the man? Did he have no social skills to speak of?

She put all her focus on wrapping the thin braid back around the bun at the back of her head.

His gaze followed her hand, watching her tuck her hair away, then made a slow study of the dress she'd borrowed. So the boy had been right: She was not invited to wear the clothes found in her wardrobe. Why hadn't the dresses been removed before now?

"All my belongings are at the rail." She shouldn't have to justify her reason for wearing something not her own.

He made no response. And he did not make eye contact with her again. With a strained ruffle of his hand through his hair, he frowned and turned away. Wherever did he learn his manners? Ha! It was quite clear he'd never learned any.

Thomas chose that opportune and most awkward moment to enter the stable. She turned and greeted him, happy to not be in the sole company of Lord Brendall. "I hope I didn't make you rush your luncheon."

"Not at all, Miss Hallaway. Besides, a break'll do me good this afternoon. Even if it's only a few hours."

He opened the stall door that housed a horse farther down than his lordship's. An old hag of a horse, half asleep where she stood, blinked one large brown eye at her. The beast blew out a breath of air as though she didn't want to do any human's biddings today. Abby stepped forward, offering her hand to scratch the horse. Thomas stepped in front of her.

"You don't want your fingers too close to old Betsy here. A bit temperamental she is. She'll nip them right off. When she wants some attention, she'll give you a nudge."

She pulled her hand away and shoved it into the pocket of her dress.

"You can go outside, miss, I'll be there in a minute with the cart once I get Betsy here set up."

She left the stable without further word. How odd for the master of the house to ignore her as he'd done. Then suddenly approach her and impulsively touch her. What a strange man. Did he dislike her, or dislike his servants in general? Maybe he was trying to figure her out as she was him.

Thomas came out with the horse and cart a few minutes later. The cart was as old and decrepit as the horse. All rotting grayish wood, with a wooden bench full of knotholes in the seat. No cushions adorned the bench for comfort. Well, beggars—though she was far from that point—could not be choosers.

Grasping the handle of the chair, Abby tried hoisting herself up. It was a rather high perch. Before she could reach out to grasp Thomas's proffered hand, another set of strong hands—Lord Brendall's—grasped her around the waist and lifted her to the seat.

She felt the heat of him through every layer of material she wore. His touch lingered even after he released her and she was set up in the cart. She turned to glare at Lord Brendall, but he'd already turned away from her.

She muttered a thank-you, then turned her attention to Thomas. She would not allow her thoughts to be consumed by her employer. To think of his strong grip wrapped about her and the ease in which he lifted her to her seat was unsettling and thrilling. She disliked him for making her feel at odds with herself.

She pinched the bridge of her nose. Lord Brendall was a bit of a mystery, so that explained her curiosity toward him. It did not explain why her heart felt as though it would skip right out of her chest whenever he looked at her, or why her face grew flush under his regard, or why she kept stealing glances in his direction.

Lord Brendall mounted his horse next to Thomas. The muscle in his legs flexed beneath the tight trousers as they gripped the barrel of the horse. She swallowed the sound of appreciation that threatened to spill from her throat and focused on Thomas.

"How long till we reach the rail by cart?" she asked.

"Maybe an hour and a half. Betsy's hardier than she looks."

With that last comment, the horse bobbed her head and pulled forward.

The ride was mostly silent. It was very hard to concentrate on the surroundings with the brooding presence of Lord Brendall. Whenever she glanced his way, she was sure he'd been staring after her, but she never did catch him in the act.

On leaving the castle grounds, Abby turned around in her seat to better look upon the castle in all its grandeur. It had been too dark last night to see the formidable, imposing sight.

A rocky outcrop surrounded the walls; the trees looked as though they climbed the great white stone. The castle could only be described as a medieval monstrosity. The outer walls stretched past what her eye could see.

The fields around her were filled with tall grasses and rushes of yellow flowers. On any other day she might appreciate the natural beauty of the place. But she was all too aware of Lord Brendall following close behind them on his horse.

He kept to the side of the cart she sat on. She had the urge to scratch the back of her neck where the hairs prickled up. She knew he was watching her. She also knew that if she turned to face him, he'd look away and pretend as though he had never been making a study of her.

What did it suggest about her character that she wanted him to meet her gaze? Wanted to see some of his thoughts flitting across his mind by reading his body language? She should not care about him in the least. But he was a hard man to ignore outright. He was so silent and brooding, like a character right out of a gothic novel. She wanted to crack through his rough exterior just for a moment and see what he was hiding of himself.

Who was to say he hid anything, though? She didn't know this Lord Brendall, had never had prior association with him, and hadn't ever heard his name whispered once in her circle of acquaintances.

When they arrived at the rail, Lord Brendall dismounted from his horse and lifted her from the cart before she could climb down on her own. She pretended that this strange, out-of-place, and very unnecessary chivalry didn't make her hands shake in nervousness—even though she had to grip her palms together in front of her once she was set on her feet. Why did he affect her so?

Some men liked and even preferred to treat the fairer sex as though they were helpless, inferior.

The only rebellious thing she could do in her position, and out in the open with passersby, was put her nose in the air and refuse to thank him. Though she did pry his fingers away from the underside of her breast where they'd grasped and this time lingered. And damn her for liking these stolen liberties of his. He suddenly released her, and she was left to find her footing so she didn't teeter over.

Cool as ice, he turned to Thomas as though she were no longer there. The two exchanged no words as they walked into the rail station.

"Well, Miss Hallaway"—Thomas turned at the entrance—"let us retrieve your luggage."

Abby pushed between the two men and made her way to the clerk. The same man who had checked her baggage. The same man who had declined to help her find a coach or cart to take her to her destination the previous day. Of course, she'd learned soon enough he hadn't lied about people refusing to take her up to the castle. She'd walked through two villages on her way to her new posting; everyone she'd met had refused to offer her a horse for the remainder of the journey.

The attendant was in his fifties, if not older. His wizened face and white hair gave him a fatherly air. He looked up from the ledger of names he was copying from a loose sheaf of paper to a bound book.

"Madam," he addressed her. Setting his pencil down, he folded his hands over his work. "Did you make the trek well yesterday?"

"There was a spot of rain and thunder rumbling across the skies quite frightfully last night. The walk was not comfortable." Cool as ever she had set him down, though he didn't look away from her.

"I'm sorry to hear that." There was no sympathy in his voice for her ordeal. "How may I be of assistance?"

"I'd like to retrieve my belongings, if you please."

The attendant's kind expression turned dark. The laugh lines scrunching the corner of his mouth moments ago turned to scowl lines. His gaze shifted to her left and narrowed. All the kindness in his expression was void. Absent. Not so fatherly now.

She didn't need to turn to know Lord Brendall stood close to her like the very devil on her shoulder. She imagined—it had to be her imagination because she was wearing so many layers of cloth and linen, it couldn't be the truth—that she felt the warmth of his body engulf her. Nearly suffocating her with its heated proximity.

His penchant for invading what she liked to call her personal space needed to stop. It overwhelmed her. Made her feel less in control.

The old man finally tore his gaze away from Lord Brendall and pulled open a drawer on his desk. Picking something up from the top—a key, most likely—he stood, straightened his jacket, and squared his shoulders as he led them to the storage room.

Opening the door wide, he pulled out his fob, checked the time, and announced, "Your cases are all there on the right. If you could please take them quickly, I have a train arriving in three minutes."

Abby didn't need to be told twice. On entering the room, she made her way to her portmanteaus. She was intercepted by the men who had followed in on her heels as though she were some great dame. She nearly snorted at the image that presented in her mind. Too bad she couldn't be more lighthearted about this. Not with Lord Brendall dogging her every step.

He took the larger of her trunks back out to the cart, giving her a much-needed moment to pull herself together so she could face him again with cool regard. She dragged one of the smaller cases too heavy to carry.

She'd only made it outside the door of the station before the very man she was trying not to think about took the case directly from her hands. She then squealed in surprise when he once again picked her up by the waist and set her in the seat of the cart.

"I'm far from helpless, my lord," she said as she settled her skirts around her.

Hard to say if the anger she felt was directed toward him or herself. What was wrong with her? She didn't want to think about the infernal man another moment. Ignoring him would be best.

"I understand perfectly."

What did he understand? Did he realize it made her uncomfortable when he was in close proximity? She gave an annoyed huff and stared at the twitching ears of the old nag set to pull them home.

Home?

How interesting that she'd already labeled the castle as her home. Was she so desperate to be out of her sister's manor that any house would do in its place? She'd never considered anyplace a home aside from the one she'd grown up in with her sisters and parents. That house had gone to some cousin of hers last in line to take her father's title.

Thomas did not immediately join her. She guessed the men were parting ways since they spoke for some minutes away from her range of hearing.

"Miss," a woman said to her from the side of the cart.

She was older, in her sixth or seventh decade. Her black-and-gray hair was braided and fell like a thick rope down her back. Her clothes were tattered and moth-eaten; tears and holes the size of a shilling speckled her burgundy plaid shawl and old sackcloth dress of the same ratty material.

Was this a beggar? She loosened the string on her reticule to find a farthing.

"Miss," she said again, shaking her head at the coin Abby held out. "All's fair in warnin' thou. Yer young, miss. Don't be taking up with the likes o' that man."

Not only did the woman's words make the hairs on her forearms prickle, but Abby also felt insulted and rose to defend herself, as any Hallaway woman would. "I'm the governess for the boy. I shall never allow myself to be 'taking up' with a gentleman."

"Smart lass. A brain in thy head. Be thee warned, nothing good comes out o' that castle." The woman pointed a knobby cane in the direction of her new home. "Bad things be happening to those who stay. Be warned." Her cane pounded against the wooden floorboard of the cart as though it added to her decree.

"Bethesda," Thomas scolded with a firmness that seemed contradictory to the man she'd been charmed by since midmorning. Abby turned her head up to look at him. It was as though everything in time and space had slowed as she eyed the man she'd chatted kindly with over the past few hours. He was not that man anymore. In his place stood a man who was as much a brute as his master. The look in his eyes seemed vicious. Pitiless and angry toward the old woman.

"Be off, witch," Lord Brendall growled in his deep, rumbling voice. This was a man who had many shades of black. She saw that now as she hadn't before. There was something indefinable in his expression. Something she couldn't quite comprehend passing between the old woman and the men. What that secret was she was not privy to.

Abby sat frozen in her seat, shocked and outraged at the abuse they showed toward a woman who clearly did not have her wits about her. But she was wary to interrupt, for fear of missing something important. Something that defined her employer's character, which she was all too interested in uncovering.

The old witch pointed her cane in Lord Brendall's direction. Even coming from a feeble old woman, the move seemed threatening. "Yer no better than your father."

As repulsed as Abby was by the whole situation, she felt the old lady was unjustly attacked by the two men.

"She means me no harm."

To show her goodwill, and her support toward the woman, she pressed her hand upon the woman's bony shoulder and gave it the lightest of squeezes.

The woman looked back to her with a wicked smile full of holes where her teeth should have been. Abby swallowed back her disgust and attempted a smile. She feared she failed miserably. There was an unease snaking through her veins, skittering up her body in a nervous, uncomfortable shiver.

"Miss," the woman crowed. This time when she spoke, she grasped Abby's hand and pulled her down with unexpected strength so she could say something of import next to her ear with her fetid, humid breath.

She felt a prick at her wrist. A buzzing in her head seemed to drown out all the others—except the hypnotizing voice that spoke to her.

How odd that Abby then noted her surroundings. A crowd had formed since the woman had approached the cart. Half a dozen citizens of the town stalled their daily activities in the street to see what transpired; a lady and a gentleman who came out of the rail station stared at the scene with barely concealed disgust. Thomas attempted to pry the old woman's bony hands away from Abby's hand and wrist.

Lord Brendall trotted over on his great horse. The bay, feeling the agitation in the air and in his handler's hold, stomped his foot in annoyance and neighed. The sound was like the screaming of a soul in the hands of the devil. It was no benign sound, and it crept through Abby's mind like a serpent over her bare flesh.

Through all this, the woman maintained her hold.

The long nail of Bethesda's thumb pressed into the soft

tissue of Abby's wrist. The pressure, even through her gloves, seemed to relax Abby and make her light-headed.

She swore she swayed in the witch's hold. For how could she be anything else but a witch, when the old woman had bewitched everyone around them?

Nothing could have stopped the hissed warning from reaching Abby's ears. There was desperation in the old woman's slurred speech. Stark belief resonating in each consonant uttered, and firm conviction was laced in the tone of the message conveyed.

Abby was not wont to believe in local fables, legends, curses, and whatnot. She'd never been one for stories of this nature.

But the way in which she was warned made her want to caution herself. Made her wonder. It was as if a spell was being put on her. Suspending her thoughts and allowing impossible slander to root into her head and worm its way so deep, it could never be plucked away. So deep, she'd have to explore every facet until she knew the truth of the matter. A sliver of apprehension embedded itself right into her bones.

"Too late, Tommy boy." The woman gave a bitter laugh. "Too late. Truths have a way of coming out. Just helped her along in figuring it out sooner."

When the woman released her arm, Abby swayed where she sat. She felt as though she'd been sitting in a room full of cigar smoke from her father and his acquaintances for too long. It lent to the light-headedness—the feeling of disembodiment.

The woman set her knobby cane to the cobbled road and wobbled away on rheumy legs. She limped with every step down the center of the town's road, cutting a swath through everyone. Another cart went around her, pedestrians moved away, even the village children who were more focused on one another veered far out of the woman's path.

Lord Brendall's fingers were light under her chin as he tipped her up to face him. His lips were pinched in an angry frown, his eyes softer than they'd been since she'd met him. What he searched for she didn't know.

"Thomas," he called over his shoulder as he released her and turned his horse away from the cart.

Abby said nothing on the ride home with Thomas. He did not ask her any questions, did not ask what the old woman had whispered for her ears alone. She felt dazed with all the questions going through her head. There was a mystery to be solved. Secrets to uncover. And she hadn't even been here two days. She would find the truth in the old woman's words. If there was any truth in them.

Lord Brendall did not follow them back. When they arrived at the castle and her luggage was unloaded and taken to her room, she had no more energy after climbing the stairs.

She did not search out the child she was there to teach. She could not. She could hardly think. There was one thing aside from finding the boy she must do on the morrow.

She had to find the grave that had been whispered about in her ear.

Chapter 4

In leaving, the prince allowed his father's rule to stand, despite his promises made to the woman he loved true. —The Dragon of Brahmors

Abby did not find the grave. She'd had plenty of free time to herself in the last few days since she could not find her charge. Her search had been to no avail, so she doubted the grave's existence. The woman who'd spoken to her in town had lacked a sound mind. In fact, Abby had given up the silly notion that there was a mystery to solve in regard to Lord Brendall.

The less she thought of him, the better.

The simple fact of the matter was that she shouldn't care to know more about him. Giving in to the urge to find the grave showed she wanted to better understand him. Good thing she'd come to her senses after a couple of futile and rather frustrating searches.

Another mystery she had yet to solve was where her pupil whiled away his days. She'd seen neither hide nor hair of him. It was understandable why the governesses hired in the past didn't stay on long. Without a child to teach, their days were spent idle. She didn't like idle.

It seemed strange that the staff went about their day without looking after the boy. It shouldn't surprise her that the boy was intentionally avoiding her. She thought maybe Martha had something to do with that. The woman didn't believe in her ability as a teacher. Had made a point in saying she was too young on the first day they'd met. Had further questioned her abilities whenever they'd chanced to meet. The dislike most likely stemmed from not successfully having even one day of studies with Jacob. It wasn't precisely her fault she couldn't find the child.

How did a child of eight go about his day alone? How was it that the staff allowed such a thing? Or that Lord Brendall permitted his son to be left to his own devices morning, noon, and night? It wasn't right. It stirred up empathy in her breast, and a desire to help the child in any way she could. She just didn't know what she should do.

Lord Brendall was no help. She'd not seen him since she and Thomas had taken the cart back from town. He kept to himself as far as she could tell. She was a bit thankful for that.

Finishing a bowl of warm oats and tea for an early breakfast, she left the women to their meal preparations to search for Jacob. She was determined to find him today and would leave no stone unturned in doing so. Wrapping her shawl around her shoulders, she headed for the stables hoping to have a smidgen of luck on her side.

All six stalls for the horses were occupied including Ivan's—which meant Lord Brendall was in residence. Not that she cared. She was simply taking notice that he often didn't leave the castle.

She turned where she stood, studying the inside of the stable area. There were two doors. One was painted a deep red and led back outside, the other a ruddily worn wood door that probably housed the stable hand.

She walked over to the adjacent room and opened the

door. Empty, aside from a cot and small table. It was dusty enough to attest to the fact that no one had slept here for some time. She shut the door and pressed her back to the hard surface. This old castle had too many hiding spots to name.

If she were eight, where would she hide?

There was a ladder that led up to a hayloft. She'd have to check there before she searched the abandoned half of the stable. Setting her shawl over the door of Ivan's stall, she rubbed at his muzzle before making her way to the ladder and climbing the steep steps. It was quite high up. There was plenty of hay stacked up here, but no dark-haired child.

"Jacob?" she called.

Not that she expected an answer. All she hoped was that her search wouldn't take her the majority of the day. Would the little rascal hide in among the stacks of hay? She climbed up off the ladder and hunched over so she didn't hit her head on the low-hanging beams of the ceiling.

"Jacob," she called again.

There was a small square window set into the east wall. The wood planks beneath it were cleared of hay, and a few marbles littered the inside of one of the larger knotholes. Evidence that the boy did spend time hidden away up here. With that knowledge, Abby reluctantly made her way back down the ladder.

If she didn't find him today, she might sit up there for the full day tomorrow. It was better than sitting in the library, where she'd set up her teaching things, or in silence with the kitchen staff.

She looked over her shoulder to assess how much farther she needed to climb down and met the stoic gaze of Lord Brendall.

She lost her footing. Foolish of her to be distracted by the man. He habitually showed up without warning.

To say he caught her before she could land on the ground both was and wasn't quite the truth. It was much more than simply stopping her fall. Her chin hit one of the ladder rungs, leaving a sharp sting and a light ringing in her ears; her knee smacked against another step lower down, and her skirts rode up high enough to reveal her drawers. She knew this last fact because she felt Lord Brendall's warmth seep right through the frivolous, impractical silk.

"I'm sorry." It was the best she could come up with by way of apology. Her arms still hugged the ladder. Lord Brendall still held her tight to him with her back to his front. Not a predicament she wanted or ever planned to be in.

And good Lord, why wasn't he letting her go? And why was she starting to feel flushed in his hold?

"I'm fine now," she pointed out.

Since her feet finally reached the ground and she no longer needed the support of the ladder, she released it. Lord Brendall, however, did not let her go. She stilled, her body as rigid as a board, as she felt the heat of his body through her clothes.

Abby knew she should at the very least push him away, but the adrenaline pumping through her body from the fall did something funny to her. Her legs felt unsteady, and her hands shook a little as she waited for him to say or do something.

With a deep breath, Abby found the calm she displayed to everyone in her acquaintance. "Do you wish to intimidate me, my lord?"

One of his hands moved to her chin and tilted her head to the side. "Only to make certain you've not caused yourself any lasting damage."

He was surprisingly gentle, his hands a little shaky as

he skimmed over her jaw with the blunt tips of his fingers and inspected the spot that had smacked against the ladder rung.

She remembered how those fingers had felt against her own hand. What would they feel like on other parts of her exposed skin? Her stomach flipped at the thought. She should pull away; she should slide out from under his arms. It wouldn't be that difficult. It was the right thing to do.

She pinched her eyes shut and focused on herself. Only herself. Why didn't she want to do the proper thing? She had no answer to that question. Admittedly, she had pictured herself in this type of scenario with Lord Brendall over the past few days. Idle time was dangerous to one's thoughts and imagination. Especially hers.

It was true that she'd always walked a thin line between right and wrong, but always on the side of propriety. Doing what she ought to do suddenly seemed dull and mind-numbing.

She hissed in a breath when his finger prodded under her chin. He stopped his inspection immediately upon hearing her pained sound.

"The skin is only reddened. You've bruised yourself, nothing more."

"I'll be fine," she assured him, but her voice wavered, which was probably due to the fact that he was still touching her.

Lord Brendall turned her around to face him, moving his warm body away from her. She didn't like the loss of his warmth one bit. And that wasn't good . . . wasn't right.

"What else did you hurt?"

"My knee, but it's no worse than my chin."

She was beside herself when he slid his big hands down to gather up her skirts and went on bended knee to inspect the damage. She tried not to think about what he'd reveal in lifting the heavy twill. She should put a stop to his actions. Should but would not, because she liked the excitement that coursed through her with his surprisingly gentle inspection.

Her knee throbbed in time to her heartbeat. She couldn't meet his gaze when his hand skimmed over her calf and then around her lower thigh as he lifted and studied her knee.

Was it her imagination or did he toy with the ties that held her stockings in place? Her breath caught in her lungs.

"Only a scratch, but you've torn your stockings right through." His finger traced the edge of that hole, making her heart skip and speed up to double its normal tempo.

"Yes," was her pathetic reply.

As Lord Brendall stood, her skirts fell back around her legs. Casually, he grasped the ladder behind her with one hand and gave her a thoughtful look.

The shiver of anticipation she'd felt earlier now did a jig throughout her body. What was he about?

"Why is it that you don't find me intimidating, Miss Hallaway?"

She didn't miss the note of wonder in his voice. But it was an odd question to ask of her. Was she supposed to run shamefaced and embarrassed from the stable? She supposed should have protested his improper inspection of her injured knee.

"You are a bit of a brute at times." She was proud of herself for keeping her voice level, uninterested. Even a bit superior.

"So I've been told," he replied.

The remark was made in a light bantering tone, and it made her grin to hear a teasing side of his lordship.

His free hand traced the line of her jaw, stopping well before he reached the tender part of her chin. His action had all the air leaving her lungs in a rush, and she closed her eyes. Was it her imagination or was there a tremble to his hand as he held her almost reverently?

She forgot how to breathe in that moment. Felt her heart skitter and stop, skitter and stop. She swallowed against her dry throat and gasped for a breath of air. It didn't fill her lungs easily, and the second and third breaths were just as hard to take.

He made no move to touch her further. Why was she disappointed by that fact? When she opened her eyes, she said, "I doubt that."

What was wrong with her? Why wasn't she stepping away from him? Whatever her reason was, it must have had something to do with the kick of excitement coursing through her, like the instant jolt you got upon tipping back a whole shot of liquor. What game was Lord Brendall playing at?

The bigger question that needed to be answered was: What would she gain in continuing this game whose rules she didn't fully understand?

This was exactly how her sister Grace had ended up married. Doing things like this with a gentleman. Not a predicament Abby wanted to be in. The thought of marriage somehow cleared her mind and allowed her to breathe easier.

She met his gaze with indifference. At least that was what she hoped he read, before his pale blue eyes hypnotized her. Silenced her. She could drown there, she decided. Lose herself so easily. So completely.

The only question left on her mind was, what would happen if she just let go? Just this once?

Elliott had come to the stable with no other purpose than to ask his governess why lessons had not commenced in the last few days. He'd talked to Jacob briefly this morning, asking his boy what he thought of Miss Hallaway. Jacob had done nothing more than shrug and say he hadn't seen her since that first day in the stable, then had relayed a story about a young red squirrel that had fallen out of a hole in one of the trees on the property.

After he'd assured Jacob that the mother squirrel would look after the baby with great diligence, the boy had scampered off to make sure the animal was well looked after. He'd taken that as his cue to find Miss Hallaway immediately to remedy the fact that she hadn't yet started any sort of schedule with Jacob.

Elliott certainly hadn't meant to cause Miss Hallaway to fall from the ladder. Hadn't meant for her to hurt herself. Definitely hadn't meant to touch her inappropriately.

Well, that last bit was a lie. He'd wanted to touch so much more of her but had refrained. She was a temptress. A veritable siren luring him into the water and farther from the shores of decency and sanity.

His long-dead wife, Madeline, would be laughing in her grave right now knowing he couldn't keep his desires in check. Wright men had no business where women were concerned. He had his heir; he did not need a companion.

But it was hard to resist Miss Hallaway when she'd given no indication that she objected to the liberties he'd carefully taken. His attraction toward her had not dimmed one whit since he first met her. He'd gone out of his way to avoid her for the past three days, but couldn't continue to do so when his son had yet to sit for a lesson.

He should leave her be; it was obvious she was searching for Jacob. And he'd been about to turn away and let her find the boy on her own when he'd had a peek at her pretty underthings, embroidered in a delicate pattern of fine pink and green fleur-de-lis. The French silk undergarments were enough to make his feet move forward instead of retreat to the house.

Then when he'd made her fall from the ladder and had put his arms around her . . . he couldn't keep himself from touching her, if only to reassure himself that he'd caused no lasting damage.

For more years than he cared to remember, he'd awoken early in the morning, broken his fast alone in his study, headed out to some part of the castle that needed to be repaired, and had spent his days out of doors, rain or shine. The evening didn't fare much better. He dined alone in his study as he went over grain counts and the investments he'd made in the early days of his marriage. Without that money, the castle would still lie in ruins around him. His father had squandered the Wright fortune on bad investments.

But with Miss Hallaway . . . his whole routine had changed. She was a welcome distraction from the monotony of his daily life. He watched for her first thing in the morning. She liked to walk the grounds before taking a quick breakfast in the kitchen. By lunch, he had done at least one round of the castle in search of her, hoping to catch a glimpse. At night, dining alone in his study held little appeal. He craved more.

The idea that she might feel the same desire he did was far-fetched. Once she better knew him, and understood that his son was not by any means a normal child where his learning was concerned, she'd grow to despise him as all others eventually had—even his dead wife.

The smartest thing he could do, for her, would be to cut her loose. Let her find a more fitting path. She was young and had a long road ahead of her in life. Yet that voice of indecency whispered temptingly: A small hiccup in her path now would not hurt her future employment.

And he did not want to let her go. If she left, his life would follow the same boring path it had for years. Foolishness was what this was. Utter foolishness. Four days with her living here and he couldn't fathom letting her go.

With a sigh filled with too much longing for his liking, he ran his knuckle down her neck and stopped at the froth of silk tucked into her bosom. *Tempted* wasn't a strong enough word for the emotion roaring through him right now. *Beguiled* or *bewitched* seemed about right.

Fair would be showing her only the side everyone else saw and assumed about him. Fair was not taking advantage of a woman who had to be at least a decade his junior and under his employ. Fair was scaring her off, because the things he was feeling for her would do neither of them any good in the long run. No, not when the last two women he'd loved had killed themselves for being shackled to a Wright.

He had no desire to drive one woman mad after another as his father had done. Madeline had been a decent woman when he'd married her. Then she'd grown paranoid, claiming ill will toward her right up to the time she'd had Jacob. That was when the madness had completely consumed her mind. She'd not been a fit wife. Nor a fit mother when she'd tried to claim Jacob's life with her own. His son would never be put in a life-threatening position again.

"Are you playing games with me, Miss Hallaway?"

"What do you mean?"

"I don't know what arrangement you had with your previous employer, but I can well imagine how you spent your time."

Because there wasn't a man sane enough to not notice the finer wares of Miss Hallaway. Elliott could envision exactly how he wanted to spend time with her.

Her mouth dropped open in shock and he groaned to himself. He hadn't meant to accuse her of any such indecency.

"How dare you! I have done nothing except come into the stable to find your son."

An idea struck him then. If he angered her, made such a bold accusation against her character . . . she'd go out of her way to avoid him, stop his advances, and disallow him to touch her. Prove to him that he harbored hopeless fantasies. Though he doubted he'd stop thinking about her.

"You haven't managed a single day of lessons with my son since your arrival. Now that I've caught the songbird, one might wonder why she hasn't tried to fly the coop."

She blew at a strand of hair that had fallen over her cheek. She was unsuccessful. He longed to brush it away, but held himself still.

"It's hard to teach a pupil who is nowhere to be found. Your assumptions are misaligned, Lord Brendall. I am no nightingale for you to cage."

A challenge if ever he had heard one.

He didn't want to cage her. He wanted to shed the constraints that bound her to being a governess, layer by silky layer. And because of that, he must play the beast.

"How much do you really want this post?"

She made no response. Though there was a flash in her eyes of some unspoken emotion he couldn't quite place his finger on. Dislike? Anger? Surprise?

"You can't mean to send me off, Lord Brendall."

He wrapped his hand around the soft creamy white skin of her neck. *So much for not touching her.* He could cover the whole expanse of her neck with his giant hand. His thumb massaged the pulse beating frantically there; he couldn't stop touching her. Couldn't pull away.

She swallowed hard beneath his callused palm. When she didn't object, he tilted her head to the side to expose the line of her neck, wishing he could taste her there instead of simply studying the smooth perfect arch.

With more difficulty than it should have taken, he dropped his hand from her temptingly soft skin and took a step back. It was not far enough to douse the need thrumming through the whole of his body like the tension in a rope ready to snap.

"No, I won't send you off, yet." He might have no choice if he couldn't keep his hands off her.

He didn't miss the spark of relief that flashed across her green eyes with his announcement. Maybe she had nowhere else to go? He couldn't send her away if that were the case. Damn. She'd do better to find a post elsewhere.

"What exactly is it you wish of me, my lord?"

"Only what I've hired you for."

Only that wasn't all he wanted.

"You come with excellent recommendations as a governess, so I wouldn't dare interfere with your teaching my son."

His earlier actions belied those words. What was done was done. He must learn constraint while in her presence.

Abby almost snorted at his observation of her skills as a teacher. It would remain her secret that the letters of recommendation were forged by her own hand. Not that she doubted her ability to teach a child—she had every confidence in herself.

The fact that Lord Brendall thought she could play some sort of mistress to his whims *and* teach Jacob put her in an interesting predicament. Why else would he touch her as he just had, if he didn't want something more intimate between them? And why did a liaison with Lord Brendall hold such great appeal?

She'd always been a bit of a daredevil in the family, so long as she didn't skirt too much over the lines of respectability. As tempting as it was to succumb to the seduction, she would not lower herself to appease her desires.

She stepped away from the ladder. He needed to know she'd not be swayed in her decided course of becoming an independent woman, reliant on no one but herself. She'd not be ruled by a man. Especially him. It was not her fault she couldn't find Jacob. Not once had anyone offered to help her find the child. No one had offered her any word of encouragement, either.

"I've seen you but a handful of times since my arrival, we've barely spoken a word, yet you advance like the hound on the fox."

Let it be known he was not chasing the proverbial rabbit. No, she was no creature so simple and easy to catch as a rabbit; he no better than a hound bent on the chase and nothing else from what she'd witnessed of his actions so far. Perhaps he'd tire of her once she accomplished what she'd been hired on for? Provided she could find her charge.

He did not respond. He did not smile. He did nothing but steady his gaze on the pulse at her neck. He wasn't much of a talker. No sweet words would come from his lordship's mouth. Not that she wanted any such thing.

"My first priority is to educate your son," she reminded him. "As I was hired on to do. I am more than qualified for this position."

He nodded his agreement.

"I believe you will be pleased with the results as soon as you locate him and bring him to me." If his lordship wanted to put himself in her path, she might as well make good use of him. "He must attend his lessons daily and without issue."

His eyes locked with hers. A man shouldn't have such eerily beautiful eyes. When he stared at her with such intensity, thoughts fled her mind.

He reached toward the lower portion of her throat and ran his hand over the sheer linen scarf tucked into the top of her bodice. She did not stop him. Testament to the fact that she was welcoming his advances. This was a mistake, of course, but she was a slave to sensation right now.

The slide of the scarf over her flesh was erotic and arousing. Her nipples peaked to firm tips beneath her corset, and her stomach fluttered in anticipation of more. Did he know the effect it had on her?

She could not bring herself to push him away when she wanted to feel such carnal, sensual delights.

That was a mistake.

She didn't want to stop him but knew she had to.

Placing both her hands to his chest, she pushed him away. Far enough that she could no longer feel his heat warming her already overheated flesh and fogging her brain. Far enough that she was not tempted to rub up against him like a cat in heat.

There was a long moment where they stood and studied each other. Neither of them said a word for some moments.

Neither moved.

Lord Brendall's expression was devoid of emotion and intention. Well, not of intention. She knew perfectly well what it was he wanted, and it just so happened she wanted a piece of that temptation, too.

In her limited experience, men treated women one of two ways: like bone china, liable to break if handled without extreme care, or like a ladybird ready to sing whenever commanded by its owner. Though she was not liable to break, she was not inclined to follow any demands set out by a man.

He gave another glance over her person, one that nearly ate her up and licked a wicked heat over her body. She turned and left him standing there.

"You can find me in the library once you have found your son."

She grabbed up her shawl and walked back to the main

house, her steps brisk. She did not turn around to look at him. She couldn't. She was angry about her reaction and her own lack of restraint, never mind his. She was out of her depth whenever he was around.

Chapter 5

Heartbroken, the wise woman's daughter shed tears for weeks on end. She did not eat, nor could she sleep. Over time she withered away to a husk of the woman she was until finally she slept, never to awake again.   —*The Dragon of Brahmors*

What in hell was wrong with him? Elliott smacked his hand against the ladder she'd leaned against moments ago. He wavered between a strong desire to possess her and an equal need to send her away. He didn't only want her in the basest of ways, either. He wanted to just be in her company. Watching her pretty green eyes assess him and measure his worth.

Why? He'd talked to her thrice since her arrival. But every time, she'd tested her will against his. Had stood up to him. Had told him without hesitation or reservation that he was nothing but a brute. Which there was no arguing against.

She was playing havoc with his emotions, his feelings. He didn't like losing control. But the more she tested him, pushed him, the more helpless he felt to resist her. He had no right liking her. She was such a free-spirited woman, and crushing that exuberance would tear him asunder.

He'd have to settle for watching her from afar, because he refused to ruin another perfectly good woman. It would do him well to remember that he *was* a brute. His wife had hated his constant attention and coddling. Had spat hated and cruel words at him on a daily basis.

Miss Hallaway might prove no different if she understood just how simpleminded a man he was. *Dumb as the day he was born.*

He shook his head, turned away from the stable, and went to retrieve Jacob. He found the boy standing under a tree in the west courtyard, staring at the ground. Could it be the source of Jacob's morning excitement and agitation?

"Jacob," he called when his son didn't raise his eyes from the ground at his approach. "Miss Hallaway is waiting for you up at the house."

His son turned to him with sad eyes. "I don't want lessons. What if a bird comes?"

His son had his heart in the right place.

Elliott stared down at the squirrel that held his son's attention rapt. The animal hadn't fallen far. There was a hole in the trunk about eight feet up. He knelt down next to Jacob.

"Shall I put it back?"

Jacob's eyes widened. "Would you?"

Instead of answering, he picked up the little ball of red fur and reached high in the tree to put the critter back in its place. It nipped his finger in the process, but its teeth were new and its bite weak.

Task complete, he wiped his hands on his trousers and turned back to Jacob.

"Now up to the house with you. Miss Hallaway is not to be kept waiting again."

Jacob wiped his nose on the cuff of his shirt before saying, "Do I have to?"

"Yes." Elliott turned to walk back to the main house, knowing his son wouldn't be far behind.

Her need to be behind closed doors and in the relative safety of the main house where Lord Brendall was less likely to catch her off guard and put her in another compromising position was a spur to her flanks.

She was not so lucky to completely escape Lord Brendall. After taking her spot behind the desk, he was minutes behind her and led Jacob into the room. Of course he would know where to find his son where she had failed, though it was through no fault of her own.

Well, she supposed, it seemed she was well set with the boy attending lessons—at least for today.

Lord Brendall had shown no interest in staying to test her knowledge or the basis of her curriculum, both of which were without fault.

He left shortly after asking his son to sit in a chair and stay put till lessons were over and he was dismissed for the day. Jacob nodded in agreement, then focused on her. Abby did her best to ignore Lord Brendall's retreating form. She wasn't very successful until he was completely gone from her sight.

"Good day to you, young master."

The hostility with which the boy gazed upon her could probably set flame to rock. How like his father he was. They both seemed so angry at the world. She would uncover the reason for that as time wore on.

For now, her sole focus was Jacob. There was no room for Lord Brendall in her mind. She'd worry about *him* when she faced him later; they would have to discuss Jacob's lessons, and the sooner the better.

"Since I'm not sure where your last governess left off, we'll start with some light arithmetic."

Jacob crossed his arms over his chest. "Math's dull."

"Would you prefer we read something aloud, then?" She raised one brow in question. It mattered not to her what they worked on first.

With a huff of annoyance, Jacob slid his chair closer to the desk. Paper and pencil were already spread out for him. She'd set this room up on her second day here. It was nice to finally have a student to fill the quietness.

"Can you chart out a multiplication table up to fifteen?"

He nodded and set his pencil to the paper. Abby leaned over him, interested in how fast he worked the numbers into the chart. He didn't pause to count, or think about what the numbers were, as he went higher.

"How high can you go on the table, Jacob?"

He shrugged and continued writing out the numbers. He was done in less than two minutes.

She frowned down at the completed chart, wondering how much more advanced a boy child might be with numbers than the girl she'd thought she was to teach. No use fretting over such a thing. She hadn't been prepared for his strong show in math on his first day, and with the absence of a steady teacher, so she would have to present him with something more advanced on the morrow.

"Tomorrow we'll move on to something more challenging for your young mind. I'll prepare the lessons tonight. Perhaps some geometry would interest you?"

He gave a noncommittal shrug.

Abby slid a chair closer to Jacob and sat next to him. His hair was mussed up and tangled; she wasn't sure if it had been brushed today, let alone all week. She wanted to brush her fingers through it to smooth it out, rid it of some of the knots.

Some strange maternal notion had her wanting to wipe

the smudge of dirt from his cheek, too. She refrained from doing so. She'd ask the kitchen staff to make sure the boy came to her bathed and dressed as befitting his station tomorrow.

Jacob stared down at his paper, looking over his numbers. She couldn't be sure, but she thought he was avoiding her scrutiny.

"I found a wonderful book of fairy tales in the library." Reaching across the wide desk, her fingers grasped the edge of the leather-bound book to pull it closer. "I read it yesterday. I've never read it before, so I guess it's based on a local legend."

Jacob kept his head downcast. His fingers fidgeted and tangled together in his lap. Abby screwed her lips tightly together and wondered how best she'd garner his interest. She opened the first page of the book. There was a picture of a young man—a prince—sitting next to his father's throne. She'd been positive that all little boys would be intrigued by a story featuring a dragon hero.

"It's about a prince who's turned into a fire-breathing dragon. I thought perhaps we could read it together."

Jacob's eyes wandered away from his lap to the room around them. His feet kicked backward and forward between the legs of the chair.

"If you'll take the time to read part of the story with me, I'll let you go till after lunch. How does that sound?"

He turned and faced her. His forehead scrunched up as he frowned. Even his little lips pursed together in anger. Or was it distrust? Did he not believe her?

"I promise." For some reason, Abby felt the need to add that last comment.

What else could she do to assure him that she wasn't some evil crone? She'd thoroughly enjoyed learning everything her father had taught her. Had sat on his lap as a child and absorbed every story, every bit of knowledge he had wanted to share with her impressionable young mind.

Maybe Jacob hated fairy tales. Maybe he hated this story in particular. But the boy had to start somewhere with her. She didn't know what kind of education he'd had before her arrival at the castle. Though it was obvious his math skills hadn't lacked.

Pushing the book closer to him, she pointed to the first word. Jacob took a deep breath and pushed it out, and then slumped in his chair. Was he shy?

"I can read along with you, if you like. Repeat after me: *In the Kingdom of Brahmors, there was a young prince . . .*"

Abby looked at her charge. He had crossed his arms over his chest, and his feet kicked between the legs of the chair with more vigor than he'd previously shown. How had she angered him? And in less than half an hour.

"Why don't you read the next line?" she offered.

"No."

"Let me ask you something, Jacob." Abby leaned back in her chair and waited for a response from him.

"What?"

"Is it simply the story you dislike?"

His feet stopped kicking, and he finally turned his head toward her, his blue eyes narrowed.

"Or do you just dislike all your governesses?"

"Don't like learning. Martha says it won't do me no good."

Abby had to bite her tongue on that. She'd discuss that inappropriate comment with Lord Brendall later on in the evening.

"Learning, when done with a competent teacher, can be a great deal of fun and very rewarding. Will you at least trust me in that matter? Trust that I can fill our days with fun?"

He looked back to the book, his eyes narrowed as he gave her a reluctant nod. So she hadn't won him over yet. She'd work on that as the weeks unfolded. He would come to trust her and maybe even like her.

"I simply wish to assess what level we need to start at in your curriculum. Is there another book you wish to read?"

"No."

It took a great deal of will not to snap the book closed in frustration and toss the bloody thing across the room. Abby was beginning to wonder about her sanity in deciding on teaching as her path in life.

"I'm trying to work with you, Jacob. If you dislike the story, we'll find another."

He shrugged as if it didn't matter. "It's not that."

"Then, pray tell, what is it?"

"I can't read the words."

Abby barely managed to suppress her gasp of surprise. He couldn't read? How was such a thing possible? The poor child. And those bastard tutors and awful governesses before her! How dare they not teach him the most important thing there was to learn. He must have been sorely neglected in his studies. For heaven's sake, she'd been reading by the time she was five. Both her sisters, too.

"Then I will teach you." There was no questioning that.

He let out a long-suffering sigh. A boy of eight shouldn't be driven to make such a sound.

"Can I go now?"

Had she been sure he wasn't embarrassed about the situation, she'd have made him stay. But the child had trusted her with something he obviously didn't share with everyone. Or perhaps he did, and they'd been too frustrated with Lord Brendall and the boy's illiteracy to stay on.

Closing the book gently now that all her frustration had dissipated, she replied, "I want you back here after luncheon. That should give me plenty of time to prepare some lessons for you this afternoon. If you don't come back, I'll have to get your father to retrieve you again and I don't think he'll be happy to know you disobeyed him."

Jacob looked at her, waiting for her dismissal.

She sighed. "You can leave. But I want to see you back here in one hour."

He was on his feet and out the door before she could even finish her sentence. Had she been that impetuous as a child? She shook her head with a smile. Yes, she had been.

While Jacob ate, she'd have to look for some lettered cards. If there weren't any, she supposed she could make them. She wasn't an artist like her sister, but she'd be able to paint something decent, and even a little fun for Jacob.

It was that exact moment she realized that there was no question of her not staying.

Now that she'd had the opportunity to sit with Jacob, she wanted to help him, especially since it seemed no one else cared for the boy's welfare. Aside from his father, who had gone to the trouble to hire her and all the governesses in the past.

She wanted to make a small difference to someone in the world.

Added to that, she did not want to leave when she saw more to Lord Brendall than the casual observer might. There was something in his character that she craved to explore.

Chapter 6

Distraught at the fate of the woman who filled his heart, the prince vowed never to return to the monarchy. —The Dragon of Brahmors

"I'd like a moment to speak with you about your son, Lord Brendall."

The demand was clear and firm. Her tone brooked no argument.

He turned his head toward her. Strands of hair covered one side of his brow, shading a clean view of her. He'd been doing nothing more than stare at the dying embers of the fire for the past half hour. Trying desperately to forget their morning run-in. He couldn't get her out of his head and thoughts.

His tumbler was balanced on the arm of the leather chair he relaxed in. He made no move to stand. He couldn't get closer to her; if he did, he'd want to touch her.

He looked over the prim, proper woman glowering before him. Her lush lips were pursed. Her eyes narrowed in question. Her stance stiff, immovable. Rather as if she were frozen to the spot. Her gaze focused solely on him with pique.

That look was answer enough for him. She knew. And she most likely blamed him for Jacob's shortcomings. He supposed he was to blame.

Elliott turned back to the fire, wishing he could dismiss her. But she would not be denied answers; her presence here said that. The soft shush of her leather-covered feet over the carpet inched closer. He spun the crystal glass around on the arm of the chair. It caught flecks of light from the fire and reflected rainbow hues in the dark liquid that swirled in the bottom.

With a motion of his head, he indicated the chair across from him.

"I'll stand, my lord."

He did raise his eyes to hers then, glaring for a moment before pushing himself to his feet. She didn't back down when he towered over her smaller frame. Her breast rose on a stubborn air and she tilted her head in a way that reminded him of his dead wife. A young Madeline—not the *personality* she had evolved into. But a woman full of fire. A woman who refused to back down from what she wanted. It was a useless venture trying to frighten this governess into submission. Into doing his bidding without question. Had his mood not been so black, he'd have smiled at her boldness.

"I'll not stand here all night, Miss Hallaway. Say your piece and be off." The words cut through the silence like alcohol tossed on a fire. He hadn't meant to sound that harsh, but he didn't know how else to act when she was around. It was seduce her, or try to frighten her off. And the former was definitely a bad idea.

"Though you may be master and commander in this castle, I'll not be spoken to as if I were an annoying bug."

"Interesting metaphor coming from someone who is buzzing around my study, doing nothing more than stir the air."

He walked over to the sideboard, topped up his glass of whiskey, and tossed another fiery shot down his throat. Tonight he wanted sweet oblivion. To forget the nuisance that was Miss Hallaway and the damnable desire he had for her.

He did not want to want her. He simply couldn't help himself.

"I see you hold the same regard for your son as most men in your position."

Her observation was incorrect, but he understood how she might come to that conclusion. He cared a great deal about his boy. Why else would she be standing here berating him? Why would he allow it if he didn't care?

It hadn't been by design that his son was often wary of him, but it seemed to be the normal course for these things among the men in their family.

Afraid his son would hate him as he had hated his father, Elliott only dealt with the child on a minimal basis. It was probably wrong to let the household staff raise the boy. But he couldn't help that he feared his son's hatred as much as he feared his son would turn out just like him: *dumb as the day he was born*. That term had haunted him daily since the arrival of Miss Hallaway.

At least he was never cruel to Jacob. Not like his father had acted toward him.

"You're too young to have a great deal of experience with men in my position."

She folded her arms over her chest. She was small, but still, he wanted to peel off her gown and . . .

He rubbed his palms over his face, wishing to banish every image he had of her naked form. He should have walked away on seeing her at her bath. It might have saved him some sleepless nights; every time he closed his eyes he recalled that image with perfect clarity.

"It is obvious, my lord, that your son has lacked a decent education. I can only guess what the reasons are."

"What is it you expect of me, madam?"

"I wonder how many governesses before me were made aware that your son is illiterate? I thought at first it was neglect on their part, but I worked with him on some letterings this afternoon and he could not make heads nor tails of anything I read."

He raised one brow and took a drink from his tumbler. Liquid courage, he told himself. She'd think less of him and his son now that she knew the truth. All the governesses before her had thought his son a simpleton beyond any help and learning they could impart. That alone had been enough of a reason for them to leave.

"You are here to teach him whatever it is he needs to know, Miss Hallaway."

"Is this why you've hired an unassuming governess when tutors are more befitting the child's station? Perhaps you wish the world to remain unknowing of his inability? You do him more a disservice than good by remaining silent on the topic. I assume this is some dreadful family secret I've unwittingly come into?"

It did not escape his notice that she hadn't said she was leaving. Nor had she blamed him.

"Not dreadful. Merely blown out of proportion by one vexing governess."

He ground his teeth together. His tongue was liable to get him in trouble tonight. And he could admit that he needed her. His son needed her.

Elliott set his glass down on the sideboard with a heavy clank.

He should have indulged with his lusty widow when he rode into town. Might have staved off his interest in the pixie woman who was currently glowering at him as if he were the devil incarnate. But he hadn't been able to bring himself to see his widow in town when he'd been thinking of an entirely different woman.

He scratched at the back of his head. Why in hell did he want her so badly? She was far from his type with her strawberry-blonde hair, her delicate small features, and her brazen disposition.

"As much as it pains me to admit when you've been nothing but a brute . . ." She drummed her fingers along her folded arms impatiently. "I do wish to help Master Jacob. And while you don't deserve any kindness from me, I wish to make an ally of you."

"Is that so?"

She nodded. "You must care for your son enough to have hired me, and the long string of governesses in the past. I believe you wish to correct your son's inability in reading and writing. Whether you admit his underlying incapability or not."

He *did* want his son to be normal. And though not one person he'd hired in the past five years had been worth their salt—nor had they been able to help Jacob with his letters—he still held out hope that his son would not turn out like him.

Could there be a chance that this governess would succeed where all the others had failed, simply by sheer determination? She hadn't castigated the boy and claimed him too stupid to learn as some of the others had. That had been reason enough to send her predecessors packing.

But would she be worn down and still leave once she realized that Jacob's grasp on words wasn't what it should be for a boy his age?

"I also believe that you're running out of options and will not let me go despite my strong dislike toward you."

Taken off guard by her unabashed comment, he almost gave her a smile, which surprised him. No one had dared to say such a thing directly to him before. So why did he like that she spoke so fiercely and gave him the truth of her thoughts? How did this pixie woman have such a strong effect on him?

"I believe you to be the right woman for this task. Jacob is my heir, Miss Hallaway. He cannot do this position justice if he's unable to do such a simple task as read and write."

How it pained him to admit that truth.

He'd never enjoyed talking about his son's illiteracy, his failure to learn something that was so easy for any other child. It served as a reminder of his own failure. Maybe if he had been a better father, a more learned father, his son wouldn't be in his current predicament. It reminded him of times when his own father would soundly cuff him whenever a tutor had berated his stupidity.

Desperate to steer this conversation elsewhere before he revealed too much about his own character, he turned away and asked, "Are you here solely to lecture me on my son's education, or lack thereof? Or did you need something else, Miss Hallaway?"

"Nothing for the moment."

She did not retreat from the room.

Aside from reprimanding his failure in being a good father figure for his child, maybe she desired to see him again after their run-in this afternoon at the stable.

She kept her hands busy by wrapping the tail end of a bow on her dress around her finger. She was nervous. After telling him she disliked him with so much conviction, how was it that she was nervous now?

"Do you often fidget?" he asked.

Her hands immediately dropped to her side.

"I can't quite figure you out, Lord Brendall. You are always snappish with me. Or silent and domineering. If I'm to stay on for any great length of time, which I have every intention of doing, we need to come to some sort of agreement that will make our living arrangements more comfortable."

"Why is that? This will be for the better."

Though he could admit that she was right: He was a boar's ass whenever she was around. It was this damnable need he had to loosen the pins in her hair and run his fingers through the silky strands. The want he had in running the back of his hands over the delicate arch in her soft neck and the slight swell of her breast. The ache to press his mouth to hers and see if she would drive him more insane with lust.

A most inconvenient desire.

"It's no way to live. I'll not fight with you merely for the sake of fighting."

"Then you are a better woman than any I've ever met."

Elliott advanced on her, unable to help himself. He liked that she held firm, her chin tilted at that stubborn angle as he approached her.

"If it's your intention to frighten me off, you'll have to try harder."

Backing her up against his desk, he placed his fists on the dark-stained top and leaned in toward her. She smelled like spring after a light rainfall. Fresh, clean, and new.

"This complicates things," she said so quietly it was like a whisper against his skin.

"It certainly does."

He did not step away from her as he bloody well knew he should. This was not the way to scare her off, keep her from his company. She must harbor some kernel of yearning for more, too.

Her eyelids lowered, and her throat bobbed on a swallow. Despite her bravado, it was possible she was slightly uncomfortable in his presence. Good. That made two of them.

"Is this why governesses don't stay on? Your abuse toward them? Your inappropriate advances?"

"No."

"So why start now?"

"The matter is simple, Miss Hallaway." He moved his arms closer to her, his biceps pressed against her linen-covered ribs. "I want you."

That want was turning to need at a rather drastic rate. If she said no, he'd not force the issue. But he'd do his damnedest to get her out of her pretty silk underthings. The mere thought of running his hands over the soft silk beneath her skirts had his cock swelling in the confines of his trousers.

She shook her head and looked at him through narrowed eyes. "Should I simply submit because you want me?"

No. But that was not something he'd admit. He stared back at her instead, forcing her to arch her back over the desk when he leaned in closer. She did not push him away.

"Your actions tell me there is something to be explored between us."

Instead of denying his words, she nibbled on her lower lip. What would she do if he nibbled at that lip? Sucked it into his mouth to lave it with his tongue?

Reaching up, he brushed a wisp of hair from the corner of her mouth. Like silk, the soft strands slid smoothly between his fingers. "You are the only complication, Miss Hallaway."

But his son needed her.

"I'll not risk my position here, my lord."

"Then let us think of this as a position with . . . certain benefits."

Because she still hadn't demanded he stop, he pulled the scarf from her bosom as he had in the stable. Again, no objection passed her lips. She wanted this. She'd not convince him otherwise if she didn't stop him. What a fool he was for continuing this game.

"I am at a disadvantage."

"Not in the least, Miss Hallaway. I am nothing if not discreet. There is no one else in the house to catch us out or gainsay our actions."

"How many women in your employ have you whispered those words to?"

"None." And he knew he was a bastard for the advances he'd already made. But damn it, he couldn't help himself. "I've tried avoiding you." And had managed to do just that since her first morning here. "Tried focusing on other things. But then I see you again and I want you more."

Slowly, he pulled the other side of the scarf from her bodice. The sheer white material was of fine silk.

Her breast rose rapidly beneath the light grazing of his knuckles along the edge of her dress. To hell with staying away from her.

Push him away. Push him away. That sound suggestion kept running through her mind. She really ought to say no and be done with it. Be done with him. She'd come here for one reason—to lecture him on his son.

Oh, God, why had she stayed after he'd admitted wanting her so badly? Instead of leaving, as she should, she stood before him, indulging his sense of want and her sense of curiosity.

This seduction was not a respectable path in which to become an independent woman. Not the way to prove her worth in the working world. This was not the way to start her future.

But with Lord Brendall, it was as though no other man existed. Maybe, deep down in the recesses of her mind, she didn't wish to be independent? Or didn't want to play the meek role of governess? If her sisters knew what thoughts she harbored, they'd lock her away until they could safely marry her off to a respectable man.

For shame, the only thing she liked the idea of right

now was threading her fingers through all the thick dark hair of his and pulling him down to her mouth. Or asking him to slip his hand beneath the material of her bodice and massage her flesh instead of teasing his fingers and knuckles so lightly over what he'd exposed.

She barely knew this man. Could it be that his rough exterior intrigued her? Perhaps his barking, demanding, gruff ways would continue to vex her but his strong, masculine manner would tempt her by night? Maybe she wasn't meant for a life alone, but for wedded bliss. Though it was doubtful Lord Brendall held any thoughts of wedding her. Bedding her, on the other hand . . .

And despite her earlier words, she didn't dislike him.

What a ninny she was.

Abby pressed her hand atop his, stalling his progress. So warm and tempting. As much as she would prefer tangling her fingers with his, she had to stop whatever it was he had planned.

Focused on his hand flattened against the top swell of her bosom, she swallowed the lump of regret in her throat and lowered her eyes to steady her gaze on the wrinkled folds of his shirt where they were rolled up his forearms. He had very nice, strong arms. What would it feel like if he wrapped them tight around her? The outline of muscle was well defined like that of a racehorse. She could reach out and trace the sinew . . .

She closed her eyes and let out an unsteady breath. She could not throw caution to the wind. Would not jeopardize her position here. And certainly would not lower herself to playing the role of mistress of the night.

She was worth so much more than that. Her unruly desires would have to be trampled and beaten into the ground.

Before she could push him away, though, he took a step back, sliding his hands from beneath hers. Was he fighting his desires, too?

She had never been so horrible at reading a person. To her, his eyes, his intent could not be made out in his sharp gaze. She saw no anger. No upset. Not even a reflection of the arousal she certainly felt right now. Was the man devoid of all emotion?

"You don't want to stop," he said. His voice was like brandy in coffee. Smooth, practiced, and warming . . . just intoxicating enough to loosen inhibitions.

"You do your son a disservice in your attempt to seduce me."

She hated to admit the truth now. Not when living in a fantasy world filled with erotic promise held so much appeal.

"Drivel."

Abby pinched her lips together. He was right. What would she have done had he not moved away from her? Submit? She hoped she had more control over her body and mind than to do something so foolish.

Walking to the middle of the room, she turned her back to him and tucked her scarf back into the bodice. Had she had her wits about her, she'd have pushed him away before he had started undressing her. But she hadn't.

She said nothing. Really, what was there to say? She felt gauche. Awkward. Confused by her conflicting feelings to flee when really she wanted nothing more than to allow him any and all the liberties he wished. Any and all liberties *she* wished but couldn't voice aloud.

There had been a thread of need in his voice when he'd told her that he had tried to avoid her—and that admittance had been a sharp hook luring her in.

With a deep inhalation and a determined firmness to her stance, she headed toward the door before she could change her mind.

She made it close, but didn't quite escape before Lord Brendall gently grasped her by the hand and spun her around to face him. She didn't need coaxing. She allowed her body to be pulled flush up against his. He was like a blazing fire down the front of her. So hot, she melted against that warmth and swayed more firmly into his grasp.

Gone was the frigidness she'd hoped to display and in its place a wantonness she had never felt toward any other man. Definitely not for any of the men who had attempted to court her in London, nor any of the men who had sequestered her on a darkened balcony to steal a kiss.

Lord Brendall was none of those men.

He was brash and unkind.

Ill-mannered and cross.

She should despise him for those traits alone, yet she couldn't. She also sensed him to be a caring father, a man who could take advantage of her in his position but held back. Why did he hold back? If he wanted what she wanted, why stop himself in his own domain? Because he was a decent man under all that gruffness, that was why.

And what did it say about her character that she so badly wanted him to take? And take. And take.

When Lord Brendall lowered his mouth to hers, there was a spark, like a jolt of lightning, hitting her dead center and setting her heart to a frantic pace. She moaned as the impact of his mouth to hers forced her lips open.

He did not coax, did not tease. He took. And before now, this was not a liberty she'd given to any man. Everything in the past had always been done on her terms. But she hadn't pulled away, she'd invited his actions. She wanted him to do so much more.

Curse her stupidity to hell and back, she didn't want to protest or deny him anything at the moment.

Her fingers curled over the bulging muscles in his upper arms. He was tightly strung beneath her fingers, whereas she was clay in his hands.

His tongue slid into her mouth, playing and wrapping

around hers. Unsure how she should respond, she wrestled her tongue against his, indulging when she ought to think twice about what she did with her employer.

Now that she'd done the unthinkable, she couldn't stop herself from taking a little bit more of what Lord Brendall offered. She wanted a taste of the forbidden. A taste of him and everything he offered her in the moment.

Her arms rose of their own accord, curling around his neck, forcing her to stand on her toes so he could better assault her mouth and she his.

Lord Brendall did not remain idle, either. One hand tangled beneath the chignon at the back of her head, while the other spanned over her back, rubbing in small hard circles, drawing her closer despite the fact that she was already plastered as tightly as she could be against him.

The friction of their bodies rubbing together made her all too aware of the state of arousal he was in. The state of arousal she was in. A heavy dampness flooded her core. Her body ached. The material of her drawers pressing intimately to her wasn't near enough to the pressure she desperately craved. She wanted to wrap her legs around him, rub against him. Feel his body sliding over hers as he eased both their needs.

Obviously her senses had left her the moment Lord Brendall laid his hands upon her. How far she was willing to take this was anyone's guess. Thankfully, that question would remain unanswered, for a knock sounded at the door.

Quick as a bucket of cold water thrown on them, she tore away from Lord Brendall. His expression was dark, his carriage tenser than it had been moments ago. She pressed her hand to her mouth; the sting of his lips and beard lingered. She didn't want to lose that feeling. She wanted more.

He stared at her and silently mouthed, *Fix your dress*

and hair, then waited for her to put herself to rights. She smoothed back her hair and tucked the loose strands into the pins.

"Come," he called just as she gave a hard yank at the creases in the front of her skirts, smoothing them out.

She put her shoulders back and held her head high as though nothing was out of place when Martha entered the study. The older woman looked her over from head to toe very quickly—had Abby not been so sensitive to her surroundings right now, she might not have noticed the strange regard, one of pure malice, as though she shouldn't be sequestered in his lordship's study alone—then Martha focused on Lord Brendall.

Martha's entry gave her the perfect opportunity to escape.

Abby cleared her throat and dipped her head. "As we have concluded our discussion on your son's curriculum, my lord, I'll not bother you a second more."

Abby did not wait for him to respond. She did not look up to Martha, either. Could Martha guess what they had really been occupied doing in the study? Certainly not. That was impossible.

She left quickly without looking back, thinking that she must do better to avoid Lord Brendall in the future. She could not trust herself around him. What if they hadn't been interrupted? What would have happened? How far would she have allowed their intimacies to advance?

Once in her room, she locked the door behind her and pocketed the key. Lord Brendall would not be making any nightly visits to her room. Not that he'd be so bold as to do so. Not that she'd admit to herself she hoped he would take that kind of liberty.

She groaned on realizing her feelings were in conflict with her hunger for something of a more carnal nature.

She had to keep away from him. She wanted to run to

him too desperately. She wanted to experience more of what she'd only had a small taste of tonight. That small piece of pleasure he'd shared with her had unfurled a beast inside her . . . one hungry for more than the meager sampling she'd gotten.

Throwing herself down on her bed, Abby pressed her hand to her erratically beating heart and closed her eyes on a deep inhalation. She pressed her fingers to her kiss-swollen lips.

Why did she want his kiss? Why did she want another? For that matter, why couldn't she think about anything but seeing him again?

She couldn't focus her every thought on her employer like this. She had to forget about Lord Brendall's mouth on hers. Forget about his body pressed against hers, making her feel so many things a lady shouldn't want. Making her question her refusal to ever marry.

Letting out a noise of frustration, she pounded her closed fists on the bed.

The only important thing she should be focused on was young Jacob. He needed all the help she could give him. And she'd not let her longing for Lord Brendall deter and distract her from that goal.

Chapter 7

The prince set out to regions far and fought in the harshest of wars to appease his heart.
—*The Dragon of Brahmors*

Abby looked for the children's fairy-tale book she had left on the table yesterday after working with Jacob. At least she thought she'd left it on the desk. Perhaps someone else had borrowed it? She checked all the shelves in the library with no luck in locating the old book of fables. Rifling through the drawers on the desk, she still came up empty-handed.

She stood up on seeing Lord Brendall and his son walking through the open library door. He walked ahead of his father today. Maybe yesterday had made Jacob realize that his lessons were worthwhile, even a bit fun.

Abby nodded to his lordship, then did her best to ignore him because her thoughts seemed to belong wholly to him since waking this morning.

Last night, sleep had not come as she had tossed and turned in her lone bed, wanting. Wanting something she understood the basic fundamentals for but did not understand why she was so desperate to explore with this particular, more-than-aggravating man.

Their eyes met for a fleeting moment, then the connection snapped the second he turned to leave the room. It wasn't surprising that he didn't greet her. It was probably better that way. To feel any hurt by his disregard was silly beyond reason. Did he regret their actions yesterday?

She said nothing to his retreating form, not even giving him a good morning. After her sleepless night, she'd resolved to check her yearnings for an inappropriately intimate relationship with Lord Brendall and focus on the task at hand.

Jacob needed a strong teacher to help him with his studies. She'd not abandon him now that she knew how much he needed her guidance.

Smiling down at the boy, she said, "Good morning, young master."

Jacob screwed up his nose and scowled down at the floor, kicking at a bump in the carpet. "Good morning, Miss Hallaway."

She beckoned him over with a motion of her hand. With one final kick to the offending carpet, Jacob came around to the desk.

So Jacob still didn't want to come for his lessons. She let out a long exhalation. Perhaps the classroom was not an ideal place to start enjoying his studies?

"Have you seen the fairy-tale book I read from yesterday?"

"No."

"Such a shame to have misplaced it." She sighed. "I had hoped to bring it with us. We'll have to look for it later. I propose a simple lesson today."

"I don't want any lessons."

"You haven't a choice in the matter. You will be the

Earl of Brendall someday, and therefore you must learn all you can to fulfill that role. Besides, I believe you'll enjoy our day together."

Jacob turned his head and looked up at her with disbelief in his eyes. She grinned and walked around the desk so she could kneel in front of him.

"As you are a native to the grounds, I suggest we take a historical expedition."

His eyes sparked with interest and his expression quickly changed from a scowl to one filled with boyish curiosity. That was much better, Abby thought.

"What do you mean?" he asked.

"Well, I'm sure there are a great many things about this old castle that you know and I don't. How about you play the teacher this morning, and I will help you with your letters in the afternoon?"

It was an excellent compromise, and Abby hoped it would soften the child's feelings toward learning and maybe toward her. For a moment, she thought he was going to refuse the offer. However, before he could protest, she grabbed up her bonnet and started out of the room. Thankfully, he followed.

"Where are we going?"

Abby turned and looked down at her charge. "Wherever you wish to lead. It is your morning to teach me something. You have much to teach me since I know nothing about the castle."

He scratched at his head.

"Is this some sort of trick?" he asked earnestly.

She grasped his hand, saying, "You'll never know if you don't come away from the library."

He pulled his hand from hers once they were outside. Feeling a bite in the air, Abby realized she should have taken a warmer shawl with her, but she'd not turn back now. Tying her bonnet under her chin, she waited for Jacob to pick a direction. He was still scratching his head, looking about them as if deciding which path was best to take.

It was then she noticed that his hair was washed, his face clean, and his clothes not smudged with dirt. She had relayed to Lydia the previous day that she wanted the young master better tended to. It seemed her request had not fallen on deaf ears. It pleased her immensely to know she had an ally in at least one other member of the household.

She waited patiently and was rewarded when Jacob finally walked toward the keep. She strode by his side, keen to hear what he would say about her new home. He didn't disappoint, either. He took her up to the parapet wall. The walkway looked to go on for at least a mile. Some stones had fallen over the years and littered the path, but the walkway was mostly intact.

"The castle has been here forever. Hundreds and hundreds of years. Thomas told me there were lots of wars here. But no one could ever take the castle. It's got a lookout over on the sea, so no one can invade by water. And the rocks below make climbing the wall impossible."

Abby looked over the parapet wall. It was a long drop. "Very true and intuitive of you to make such a clever observation."

That earned her a smile.

The village was about half a mile off to the south. There were only three or four dozen houses in the village. Wind rolled over the tall grasses stretched between the castle and the village below, making it look like a sea of brown wheat beneath them. Jacob stood on a fallen stone next to her so he could better see above the wall.

Over the years, tall deciduous trees had grown along the base of the rocky wall, adding to the formidable appearance. A dirt road curved around the castle and into the inner grounds. She followed it with her gaze as far as her eyes could see, then focused back down the wall of the parapet.

"It looks very hard to climb. I can't imagine it being an easy feat for anyone to take the castle."

"But it did fall to one of our relatives," Jacob piped in, his excitement evident in telling her the rich history of his home. "Father said it was two hundred years ago that the Wrights came here."

"I daresay the Wrights were a formidable family and not easily defeated." She turned and looked to the inner bailey. The sea frothed in a black-and-white mass in the north, seabirds rode the invisible current of the wind, and shags dove from the sky and into the water to catch fish. "The view is spectacular. I don't think I've seen a more magnificent sight."

Jacob turned to see what she watched on the seaside.

"We'll have to walk the dunes someday soon. Before winter has a chance to set in," she suggested.

"Father doesn't like me going down to the water."

"Well, you'll be with me. And there is a great deal to be learned about the animals that call this place home."

"I've been down by the water. Father said not without someone to go with me. He just prefers me not to walk there."

Which made perfect sense to her. Lord Brendall was more doting and protective of those he loved than she had given him credit for.

"Now you've someone to go with. I'm afraid you're stuck with my company for an indeterminate amount of time."

He looked at her strangely after her teasing comment. Did he not believe her?

As they walked the remainder of the parapet, Jacob talked animatedly about the wars that had happened against the castle before his family had taken their seat here. There was a section of the wall tumbled down on the south side. Abby pulled Jacob away from it, forgetting that he probably knew where not to walk better than anyone.

After they stepped carefully over the crumbled rocks, small bits of stone tumbled and bounced to a ledge about ten feet below.

The damaged parapet wall was far more dangerous than the fallen wall on the west end of the property that Lord Brendall and Thomas were busy repairing. Why hadn't the parapet wall been fixed? Especially since the boy made a habit of walking up here. Though it wasn't her place to suggest anything, she would point out the danger of the walk to Lord Brendall and ask if it could be restored.

They exited at the opposite end, taking a set of stairs that spilled out into the stable yard.

"Where are we going next, my young historian?"

That comment got her a lopsided grin. The innocence in his gaze had her stumbling a step. Jacob was akin to a little man, never child-like in his outward disposition. But in that moment, she saw the child beneath: a child who yearned for the companionship of an adult, one who wanted nothing more in the moment than to be a child.

With his hands in his pockets, Jacob brought his shoulders up in a shrug. "What else did you want to see?" he asked.

She took his arm in hers, and led him around the yard and toward the old churchyard. Surely there was a great deal of history to be learned there. They had another hour till lunch and she'd not hide away indoors when the day was finally warming.

When her feet edged toward the tall, uncut grasses, Jacob yanked his arm away from hers. "We can't go in there."

Taken aback by his sudden refusal to explore the grounds, she went down on her haunches so she was level with Jacob. "I'm rather curious to know more about this place."

"Father said to stay clear of this place. It's where the ghosts are the worst."

"You think the castle has ghosts?" It was hard for Abby not to chuckle.

Jacob nodded his head vehemently. "Plenty of ghosts in the catacombs. Sometimes you can hear them on a day like this, but mostly you hear them when the tide is high."

"I had no idea there were catacombs here! As fascinating as it sounds, we'll have to save that story for another day." She stood and held her hand out. "This is an old church, is it not?" At his nod, she continued, "There won't be any ghosts on consecrated ground."

He shook his head this time, and his eyes were as round as tea saucers.

"I, for one, want to see what the inscription on the bell reads. Do you know why the bell is lying in the grass? Why it's never been righted? Do you think it fell in a long-ago battle?"

She hiked up her skirts to aid her in walking through the tall grasses. She hadn't thought to explore the old church grounds before now for some reason. It had seemed like a sacred, untouched place and she hadn't wanted to disturb it, afraid to ruin the wildness it had sprouted into over the years.

"Father will have my head if we go in there. You can't go, Miss Hallaway. Please . . ."

He tried to grasp onto her hand, but she was already steadily moving forward. Jacob remained in the clearing, just on the other side of the tall grasses.

"Nothing bad is going to happen." The only way to prove that for fact was to show him, she figured. "I promise."

She stepped toward the lime-crusted bell, her fingers outstretched. The old bronze was cold and rough beneath her hand, and she stroked over the long-faded inscription, barely making out the words CORAM DEO and nothing more. How many battles had this very bell gonged through, warning the inhabitants of an imminent battle, warning townsfolk of an incoming enemy from the seaside?

"Have you ever touched this church bell?" Abby walked around the bell, skimming her bare fingers over the alloy as she went. "It's almost as if I can hear it ringing as it once used to."

She closed her eyes and trailed her fingers over the cool rough surface as she inhaled the sea air deep into her lungs. She loved the sound of church bells.

When he didn't respond, she looked to where she'd left him standing on the cropped grass. All the color had drained from his face, making him look a phantom next to the brown-and-green weedy field she'd stepped into. Yanking her hand away from the rusted bronze, she headed back toward her charge.

"There's nothing to be afraid of. It's just a bell long fallen. It probably fell in one of the battles you told me about."

Holding out her hand, she waited to see if he would take it. So odd to see a child deathly afraid of anything, especially something that was a part of his home. When he placed his small sweaty palm against hers, she grasped it gently, and beckoned him with a nod of her head to step into the tall grasses with her. He came reluctantly.

"Father says to stay away from here. Says it's haunted and the ghosts want revenge."

She gave him a skeptical look. Why would Lord Brendall want to instill fear in his own child? Make the boy afraid in his own home? That didn't make any sense to her. A home was meant to be a safe place. A refuge. That empathy she'd felt yesterday swelled in her breast. While she was here, Lord Brendall would have to stop making up tales to scare his son.

"Are you telling me you've never been curious to explore this section of the castle grounds?"

She didn't walk toward the bell again, but toward the remains of the stone walls where the church had once stood. There was no feeling of malevolence here. No fear. Just a solemn peace in the beautiful surroundings.

"Why are you to avoid this part of the castle and not the fallen wall on the parapet, or the ruins of the attic in the main house?"

"I want to go back up to the house," he replied instead of answering.

"It's not so frightening now that you're in here, is it?"

When he didn't answer, Abby led them away from the sacred grounds of the church. She would not add to his fear by forcing him to stay.

"Go on up to the castle," she encouraged him. "I'll meet you in the library after you've had something to eat."

He seemed reluctant to leave her side, despite wanting to steer clear of the old church. He looked from the main house, back to their surroundings, and then to her.

How endearing that the child was worried a ghost might cause her any harm. Perhaps she'd already won the boy over.

"I won't be far behind you," she promised and gave him a little chuck under his chin.

Now that her curiosity was irrevocably snagged, she'd not leave the old church grounds without looking around a little while longer. There was still the matter of the missing grave. Luck, she had a feeling, was on her side in solving some of the mysteries the old woman had whispered about.

Jacob finally left her there, looking back every ten

paces, as though he was afraid she'd disappear altogether. She waved back at him until finally, he was out of view.

She turned her back to the main house and looked at the fallen walls around her. What secrets did this place hold?

Jacob had mentioned ghosts. Why would Lord Brendall insist on such rubbish? It made little sense that the boy had been frightened from searching this particular area of the castle, considering he explored more dangerous and ill-repaired portions of the house and grounds. It was evident that his lordship was hiding something.

Walking beneath what must have been the old vestibule doors, she entered a clearing filled with more tall grasses and wilted wildflowers. It was so desolate and dreary that the scene before her seemed at odds with the bountiful beauty found in the flora growing everywhere the sun's faint rays touched.

She'd never seen ruins before. Had the church been long abandoned before it had tumbled to the ground? Had it fallen in a siege as the bells rang out their warning above?

She trailed her hand over the weatherworn pillars that remained standing in the old garden enclave. For what reason had this whole structure not been taken down? Surely there was a story here. One she was most interested to uncover.

Would she find the grave? She'd not checked here previously. And there were obviously a great many places in the castle she wasn't aware of, like the catacombs. There were so many places for her to discover that it made her heart skip a beat in eagerness.

Abby's foot caught on a rock slab hidden beneath the tall grasses, bringing her to her knees. Her hands smacked down in front of her on the ground, holding her steady. A large white piece of broken stone lay dismally beneath her.

"Damn it. I haven't an ounce of luck with me in this bloody place."

Dusting off her hands against her skirts, she got her feet back under her and threaded more carefully through the grounds, taking slower steps so she didn't trip again. The old churchyard looked about a quarter mile square. It was tucked against the south wall on one side, the back of the stable on the other. It was hidden away, and she supposed easily forgotten in this less traversed part of the castle.

On the west, there were markers indicating an old graveyard. Interesting that it wasn't better looked after out of respect for the dead.

She gingerly made her way closer, wondering if she'd be able to read any dates on the stones. Most were so faded and pale that her fingers couldn't even trace the names etched into the stone slabs. The sea air had eaten away at them, fading and erasing the history of this mysterious place with time.

The farther into the small plot she walked, the newer the stones were. Newer in the sense that one was dated 1620. Another, 1710. How old was this castle? Quite possibly it dated back to Norman times.

What an interesting history such a place must hold. She was determined to find some books in the library on this castle when she went back up to the main house. It was fascinating to discover new secrets and hidden places on a daily basis. She certainly wouldn't be bored in a place where every day brought her something new.

Toward the back of the graveyard there was a taller and newer grave marker, standing out from the rest. It was shaded by the hedgerow growing wildly on the right and a solid chunk of what remained of the church wall on the left. Abby stood in front of it, making out the inscription clearly on this one.

The breath left her lungs at the realization that the old woman's words had come to fruition. Here lay the grave she'd whispered about.

The inscription read MADELINE HARRIETT GRAHAM, born 1820, died 1841. Seven years ago. One year after Jacob had been born. Had she died trying to birth another babe? Had she died for other reasons? Why was her grave hidden away from everyone? Including her son?

Abby traced her fingers over the letterings of her name. There was no epitaph marked on the cold stone. No loving words for the woman who had given birth to the next heir to Brendall Castle. Only her name and date. What a gloomy and lonely death for this woman. Abby wiped away a stray tear, feeling overwhelmingly sad at the thought of Jacob's mother buried and all but forgotten where people daren't tread. Where Jacob would never visit with a bunch of picked wildflowers.

Abby screwed her lips together in thought. There had to be a reason to bury her in the back of the unkempt grave-yard. Now she wondered about everything else the woman from town had accused Lord Brendall of. Could those words hold the same amount of truth as they had for find-ing the grave? Could he have been the cause of his wife's death?

She was making fanciful leaps with her imagination and let out a frustrated exhalation. Lord Brendall was no murderer. He might seem coldhearted, but he was not cruel.

She had tarried long enough here; it was time to get back to the main house for a quick luncheon before the afternoon lessons began.

The sun shone high in the sky ahead of her. She had to shade her eyes as she picked her way back to the front of the church. Just as she reached the edge of the wall of the origi-nal building, she stepped into the path of Lord Brendall.

He had a penchant for finding her in the most unusual and private of places. Had he been following her? Certainly not, or he'd have stopped her from exploring the grounds sooner. Wouldn't he? How had he seen her tucked so deeply inside the shaded churchyard? Prying eyes on the outside world should not have seen her. This place was its own forgotten sanctuary.

A thousand questions came to mind on seeing him. Thank God none came flying out of her mouth. She wasn't sure what to say, when he had a peculiar look on his face. Not precisely anger, though it was clear he wasn't thrilled to find her. Should she rise to defend her whereabouts? No spot on the castle grounds had been forbidden to her entry.

It wasn't as though he had forbidden her to come here. No, there was no reason for her to apologize for being caught exploring her new home. She lived here in this monstrous castle, too. She had a right to know her surroundings and whatever secrets they guarded.

He looked behind her—to where his wife's grave lay forgotten—then back to her.

"Find what you were looking for?" he asked.

Chapter 8

The prince prayed the day would come when he could forget the woman who haunted his dreams.
—The Dragon of Brahmors

Sweat beaded at his temples. His shirt stuck to his chest in the front, and the sleeves were loose and rolled up to his elbows; dirt smeared his forearms and his shirt. His hands were loose at his sides, his chin high and haughty, lips pursed together in disapproval. It was as though he were saying, *how dare you.*

"I was on my way back to the main house."

She attempted to step out from his path, but he followed, stalling her escape. His eyes were narrowed as he studied her, and he'd shoved his hands in his pockets.

"Where you should be, but aren't."

"I decided to explore the castle grounds a little while longer before heading back," she felt the need to explain.

"This is not a safe place to explore."

She narrowed her eyes. More likely he wanted to hide his wife's grave where no one would see it. And for what reason? So many questions burned at the back of her mind, eager for explanations to appease her curiosity. She'd not utter a single one of them. She was a stranger here. It wouldn't do for her to stick her nose in things that had nothing whatsoever to do with her. She would have to employ other means of weaseling out the information she wanted.

"Stay clear of these grounds. There are loose stones that could tumble down at any time."

He had a point that was hard to argue. The grounds didn't look the least bit safe. But if this place was so dangerous, why not just level the whole structure to the ground? Set up the grave markers more clearly so the dead could be properly respected? Why bury his wife here in the *unsafe* rubble, where no one could lay down flowers next to her marker?

Lord Brendall took a step closer to her. She held her ground, cocked her head to the side, and let him approach. She should have probably avoided him, run back to the house and just stayed out of his path. But she was too busy trying to read his expression, trying to interpret the reason for the tic that had started under his eye. There was no anger in his carriage. It was some other indefinable emotion.

She had this inexplicable need to understand this man. She said, "I found your wife's grave."

He remained calm. His look, his stance, none of it changed.

"It was inevitable that you eventually would."

She'd thought he would deny it. Now she had a host of more questions.

"How did she die?"

It was a bold inquiry, but one she couldn't help but ask.

"You can't guess?"

"There is the logical part of me that would assume she died bearing another babe. My mother died birthing a fourth child. A son. He came too early and neither survived."

"The situation with my wife was far from logical."

"I keep coming back to that woman's words. The woman at the rail. Bethesda, Thomas called her?"

"You shouldn't trust the words of a woman scorned."

"Scorned by whom?"

Instead of answering, he said, "Bethesda has long hated the Wrights. My family's history with the village goes back to the time we took over the castle. They were dark times."

He scratched at the back of his head in thought. She'd not stop him from revealing tidbits of information about himself. She wanted to know more. Everything.

"Though she despises the ground I walk upon, Bethesda probably wasn't too far off from the truth. There's a lot of speculation surrounding my wife's death." Why was he so forthcoming all of a sudden? She hadn't expected him to reveal any of his secrets.

Certainly the witch's words were a lie. This man might be frightening in his grand size, but he was as gentle as a . . . a puppy.

"She said you were the cause of your wife's death." She'd not worded it quite so gently as that, but that was essentially her meaning.

"Not too far off at all."

"I don't believe you. Tell me what happened instead of dancing around the subject."

"You are new to the castle, Miss Hallaway, what right have you to know its secrets?"

"Because I doubt anyone has ever bothered to ask for your side of the story before."

Lord Brendall slowly wheeled them both around and put her back to the last standing portion of the interior wall of the building.

"She killed herself, Miss Hallaway. There's your truth. Nothing so romantic as having another child. Or death found in sickness. Unable to bear life anymore with me . . . or Jacob, she killed herself."

Abby looked away from the hurt blazing in his eyes. Her fingers plucked at a blade of grass shooting out from a crack in the stone wall behind her. What could she say to that declaration? She was ashamed to have asked, but surprised he gave her the truth. A lesser man would not have admitted that fact.

"I'm sorry," was all she could think to mutter.

"I haven't asked for your pity."

Is that what he thought she offered? Not pity, but condolences for his loss, and for the pain her death must have caused. His expression was difficult to read, but she thought maybe he was waiting for her to reject him after his admission. Storm away from him and run back to the main house.

"Now that you know my secrets, why don't you tell me what you are running from, Miss Hallaway?"

"Why would you assume that?"

"Because anyone with your youth and brains would have thought better than to stay on here. Would have found a more biddable life."

"You shouldn't misjudge me."

"*Misjudge* isn't the right word. You're a distraction I could do without."

"I will endeavor to stay out of your path, then."

"No. Don't do that."

He stepped closer to her, so close there wasn't any space between them and her breasts heaved against his chest, and then *her* body was moving closer, forming and shaping more firmly to him. Her nipples went taut, and her breathing grew erratic.

The press of his body was solid and masculine against

hers. They both held perfectly still and tight against each other—neither, it seemed, willing to move away. What did it say about her that she wanted to rub up against him? To feel the firmness of his body beneath hers as their limbs tangled together and his lips explored hers?

Excitement for something more flowed through her veins. Her body warred with her mind on the matter of Lord Brendall. She needed to avoid him because this man would make her hunger after something she shouldn't want . . .

"I want to know your secrets, Miss Hallaway."

"I have none." None worth sharing.

His hand came up, and the back of his forefinger trailed a path down her cheek.

"Your son will be looking for me."

"But he's not so foolish as to come here in search of you."

"We should leave." Not that she wanted to.

"Soon." He leaned in close, till his lips were a fraction above hers.

"Soon," she repeated and swallowed any rebuff she thought to utter.

"When you came to me last night, I had hoped—" He shook his head slightly and pressed his lips together for a moment. "There is something to be explored between us."

"Are you so sure?"

"Yes. And not wholly in a bed, though the idea holds great appeal."

If he knew how badly she wanted to be in his bed, what lengths would he go to to ensure such a thing happened in truth?

What was wrong with her? In the company of Lord Brendall, her brain ceased to function.

With more effort than it should have taken, she mentally shook the thought away, burying it deep in the back of her mind. She needed to think with her head right now, not with her unruly yearning for another touch from this man.

She'd not become a senseless simpering female, throwing herself at every eligible, handsome bachelor in the hope of shackling herself to one. Doing so would mean she was no better than any of those silly chits she'd been unfortunate enough to meet in London, and that her worth rested purely in becoming some man's wife, or in the case of Lord Brendall . . . his mistress of sorts.

Without kissing her, his lips brushed over her cheek and around the shell of her ear. His breath was hot against her skin.

Her eyes slid shut as he whispered in that gruff tone of his, "What do you want, Miss Hallaway?"

Nothing.

Everything.

Oh, God, she was so close to falling into a trap that she daren't speak of in fear of making this whole situation worse. There wasn't a sound to be heard, except those that occurred in nature. A lone warbler chirped a soft song in the nearby shrubbery; gulls cried in the distance, their wails carried in on the wind whistling through the castle grounds. The constant chirp of crickets hummed around them as they stood quiet and still against the wall.

Then there were the even, deep breaths of Lord Brendall, awaiting the answer she could not give. Refused to give him. She clenched her hands into fists so she wasn't tempted to flatten them against his chest and feel the muscle so taut and brawny and just within her reach.

"Why should you want me at all?"

"I've been asking myself that question since you arrived."

What could she say to that?

His hand glided firmly over her arm, then around to the

small of her back. His long fingers spread wide, his arm strong as he held her away from the cool stone wall.

Move away, she told herself. Slip beneath his arms and tell him he should stay away from her. Tell him that she wanted nothing to do with him, even though it was a lie.

No objection made it past her lips. Her fluttering, frantic heart did not beat in protest, either. Her mind, on the other hand, insisted she do what was proper before she acted on rash impulses. But right was relative, wasn't it?

"I have to go back to the house." What a feeble excuse.

The words were the right thing to say, her actions the opposite of what she should do to follow through on that suggestion.

"Not yet," he said, brushing his thumb over her right cheek and then cupping it with his palm. At least she held herself back from nuzzling into the rough feel of his hand.

She looked up into his eyes; the blue was eaten up by the black centers. They were so intense and full of lustful hunger. Need. Want. It all mingled there. So many emotions, she couldn't pinpoint just one.

She shouldn't have looked so closely at him. Because now she didn't know why she should deny herself something she wanted. Deny herself something that felt so right to indulge in.

Fists unfurled, she pressed them against his shirt and went up on her toes. She'd do the kissing this time. Because there was definitely going to be kissing. Lots of kissing if she could help it, since she liked the way his tongue rolled around in her mouth. The way he tasted faintly of coffee and brandy.

"Oh, damn," she whispered.

Before she could think better of her hasty actions, deny herself what she wanted most right now, her mouth pressed against his.

She didn't start slow and gentle. She didn't want any

such thing. She took and took. Delving her tongue into his mouth, thrusting her tongue against his, with his, around his. This was a very bad idea. But no one would know what had transpired between them, except them.

Mayhap it would be their little secret. She nearly snorted with that thought. It was as though she were reaching for a glittering shilling in a deep, deep well. Instead of clasping it, she was tumbling over the precipice. Eventually she knew she'd crash to the bottom, broken and dejected. Yet she still reached for that shiny, tempting coin.

He should have marched her back up to the main house and told her to get on with her lessons and not to wander the castle in idle musings.

Elliott had planned to chastise her for entering the old church, not engage in intimacies that never found a satisfying completion.

Instead all he cared to do was see how far she'd be willing to take this kiss. Would she let him touch her? Feel her? This obsession he had for her made no sense. What was the attraction? Certainly not her snide, quick remarks. Maybe it was her sudden interest in and desire to help his son? Or maybe . . . maybe it was Elliott's need for a companion?

He'd gone a long time without the company of a woman. It wasn't just the physical intimacy he wanted, but the presence of another in his everyday life.

It had been so long since he'd had someone at his side. Miss Hallaway's nearness made him want those things. Things he hadn't realized he had missed all these years. How could you miss something when you didn't know you were in fact missing it in the first place?

So here he was, with her in his arms, instead of demanding she hie it up to the house.

The second she'd stepped up onto her toes and kissed

him as passionately as she had, he couldn't stop from wanting more. Now that she'd initiated the kiss—showing him just how much she desired him, and not vice versa—he wanted more.

She arched her body away from the wall and threaded her fingers through his hair, effectively fusing their bodies from pelvis to pelvis, breast to chest.

The crush of her small breasts made him want to feel them naked against his body. He wanted to cup those small mounds in his hands, pluck at the tips till they stood firm from her body, and suck them into his mouth as he thrust his cockstand inside the velvety warmth of her sheath.

He dropped his hands and tilted her more firmly and comfortably against his burgeoning prick. What would she do if he took her right here, right now? Would she welcome him with open arms? Would it be as passionate as the kiss they shared?

Pulling her skirts up, he encouraged her to hook her leg over his hip with his hand so they were more intimately in contact. So that he could grind against that sweet feminine part of her and rub his hand along the smooth skin of her thigh—though there wasn't much to feel with her unmentionables covering everything he wanted to touch most.

Had she not been wearing so many damn layers, he'd be inside her right now.

Pulling his shirt from his trousers, she ran her hand along the corded muscles of his stomach that flexed under her tickling touch. Her fingers danced over the taut flesh with a mixture of hesitation and anticipation. He groaned into her mouth when she pressed the flat of her hand against his pectoral and grazed her nail unintentionally around his nipple as she slid her hands over him.

He wanted to tear her clothes away and feel her flesh beneath his as she arched up to meet his body. He wanted to turn her around, bend her over, and take her from behind.

Goddamn it. What was wrong with him? He could not do this.

Elliott forced his hands away from her body. Forced himself to unfuse their mouths. Arms now at his side, he took a step away from her and looked over his thoroughly disheveled governess.

Lips red and swollen, bonnet askew, and dress wrinkled and nowhere near set to rights, Abigail looked like a woman entrapped by lust. Her breasts rose and fell rapidly as she attempted to gain control of her breathing.

Maybe she had expected—had wanted—him to take her against the wall. His cock jerked in the confines of his trousers with that thought. Those cat-like green eyes of hers stared warily back at him, then at the ground. She pressed the tips of her fingers to her parted mouth. Was it possible he'd rendered her speechless? Had she shocked herself by that kiss?

"Go back to the house, Miss Hallaway." Her eyes went wide at his gruff demand. When she made no move to fix her dress and leave, he added, "Go. Before I take you here in the middle of a churchyard." This was no place for a dalliance.

Her nose pinched up and her eyes narrowed. She glared at him as she shook her skirts out and smoothed her hair back into place, hiding it away under her ugly straw bonnet with steady hands.

Brave woman that she was, she didn't take her eyes from him as she righted herself. When she stormed past him, her shoulder knocked into his arm.

He'd put a fire under her bonnet now. And he couldn't regret doing so.

Maybe now she would focus on the fact that she had

found Madeline's grave, buried where no one would find her. She should hate him for doing that.

After the misery Madeline had put him through, she deserved to be forgotten. Sometimes he wished he'd never dug her body out from the rubble of the burned-down church. Couldn't be changed now, though. Couldn't be changed.

Chapter 9

The king did not worry of his son's journey into the world, for he set guards on the prince to ensure that he would live and return to the Kingdom of Brahmors.
                              —The Dragon of Brahmors

Abby was such a bloody, bloody fool. Following the *incidents* in the library and in the churchyard, as she liked to refer to them, she'd managed to avoid spending any more time alone with Lord Brendall.

She couldn't trust herself when in his company—she had a tendency to throw caution out the window.

Jacob had left her for the evening—some hours ago now. His recognition of the alphabet was sorely lacking, so she'd busied herself painting out some cue cards to use as a teaching aid. She wanting nothing more than for him to succeed.

A light tapping at the door had her raising her eyes, hand clenched around the small detail brush she was using to paint a rhinoceros to depict the letter *r*. She wondered if it would be Lord Brendall and almost gave an un-ladylike curse when her heart began to pound.

Instead it was Martha who poked her head around the

door. Even though the housekeeper had not warmed to her, Martha was both a welcome and a disappointing sight.

"You're still in here. Thought you'd be in your room for the night."

The cherub ormolu clock chimed the half nine hour. Abby wiped her wet brush on a rag and set it on the desk. "I wanted to finish painting these cards before I retired. It's rather late for you, too."

"Aye, we stay late in the main house on Thursdays to get all the laundry done and away." Martha stepped into the room, a stack of linens piled up in a wicker basket perched on her hip. "What's that you're working on, child?" Another reminder that she thought Abby too young for the posting.

Cleaning her hands off on the apron she'd put on to protect her dress, Abby picked up the edge of the card and turned it to show Martha the simple painting. Martha didn't usually make an effort to talk to her, so she was thankful for the opportunity to befriend the older woman. Maybe the painted cards would show her dedication to help Jacob. Show Martha that she had no intention of leaving anytime soon and that she was more than capable in doing the job she'd been hired on for.

"They're alphabet cards to help the young master remember his letters."

Martha placed the basket on the leather chair near the fireplace and took the card from her to inspect it closer.

"You've a fine hand at painting."

"Not nearly as good as my sister, I assure you. I thought I'd choose exotic animals, incorporate some lessons on the geographic wonders of the world."

Martha nodded her head in what Abby assumed was agreement as she placed the card back on the desk and turned to retrieve her basket.

Should she say something about the manner in which

Martha treated the boy? How she'd told the boy he wouldn't be able to learn. But the words stuck in her throat. She'd not let the woman know that the boy spoke candidly with her. She wouldn't betray his secrets at the risk of him being treated poorer. She'd have to bring her concerns to Lord Brendall. Which meant she couldn't avoid him for much longer.

"See you bright and early tomorrow morning, then."

Without further ado, Martha left.

Abby frowned at her retreating form. Was the housekeeper only checking on Abby's whereabouts this evening? Martha had never bothered to search her out in the evening before. Had Martha been suspicious that something had happened between Abby and Lord Brendall when she'd interrupted them in the study?

No, that couldn't be it. The housekeeper was probably trying to befriend her. It must not come easy to the staff to befriend the hired governesses when they didn't stay on very long. Well, Abby planned to outlast all the previous teachers. She liked it here. Liked her charge, liked the place, liked being on her own and not dependent upon her sisters for once in her adult life.

Besides, Abby's behavior had been above reproach since the *incidents*.

However, one night away from him had not put distance in her desires. If it were possible, she wanted to spend time with him even more now that she'd gone out of her way to avoid him.

Painting accoutrements set aside, Abby stood from the desk and decided that it was time for bed. It was safer if her fantasies remained in the realm of her dreams and not acted out in the presence of Lord Brendall.

His son was up well past his bedtime. Elliott was loath to send him to bed when they were thoroughly enjoying a game of chess. But it was going on half nine and even Elliott was growing tired after his long day working outside again with Thomas. Winter was coming quick, and the work needed to be completed before first snow because it would hinder their progress. He and Thomas had worked longer, done more today than they had in the last two days.

Jacob had regaled him with stories of Miss Hallaway's most unusual teaching styles between plays. Jacob said that he taught her about the castle half the time they were in lessons, and the rest of the time she tested his skill mostly in math since she didn't have letter cards to teach him to read yet.

He wasn't sure what letter cards were. He'd neither heard the term nor seen them before. Not that he remembered anyway.

Elliott had never seen his son so happy and animated with any governess before.

He leaned back in the leather chair with a yawn. "You need to head up to bed, Jacob."

Jacob got up from his chair with a heavy sigh and a slight slump in his shoulders. The boy would never learn that pouting didn't work on him. Elliott hid a smile behind his hand and gave another yawn to cover his amusement.

Jacob turned back to him before exiting through the study door. "Father?"

Elliott looked at him expectantly, waiting for his question.

"She won't leave, too, will she?"

"You like her, and you've only been in her company for a few days."

"She's not like the other teachers. She's nice to me. She doesn't say mean things when I don't know how to do something."

No, she'd been steadfast and dependable even with the revelation of his son's illiteracy.

It had been Elliott's own fault that the teachers previous to her had treated his son with a firm hand. He remembered with perfect clarity when he'd become actively involved in his child's life—Jacob had been six and had already been through two tutors and four governesses.

It had been after Miss Paisley and her penchant for caning. She'd packed her things immediately after their confrontation, which included him snapping her damn cane right in front of her in a fit of rage. One never raised a hand to a child. Especially his child. It was uncalled for and unacceptable in his household. His son would never suffer as he had. Never.

"I promise to do my best to keep her on as your governess. I do believe she wants to stay." She seemed to like Brendall Castle, a surprise to him because the land and weather this far north were unforgiving to those not acclimated to life here.

Jacob chewed on his bottom lip and seemed to think on his words a moment. "You have to be nice to her. I don't want her to leave."

So his son hadn't been oblivious to his dislike toward previous governesses and tutors. Miss Hallaway was different, though. He'd do his damnedest to keep her on. So long as he could control his lust when she was around, they'd get on amicably. He was sure of it. But damn if he didn't want her back in his arms, feeling her slight form flush to his larger body.

"I don't want her to go, either. I, too, like Miss Hallaway." And not in purely inappropriate ways: She'd not stand idly around and be told what to do; she would push back when he pushed too far, put him in his place if the need arose. He liked and respected all those character traits in her. "Miss Hallaway is going nowhere for the time being. Now go on up to bed, the hour is late."

"Good night, Father."

"Sleep well."

He sat there in his chair, happy for the first time in a long while that his son had taken a liking to someone who was here to teach him and make him a better person than Elliott would ever amount to.

His thoughts ceased with the soft tread of feet outside his study door. He sat forward in his chair, head cocked to the side to better hear. The steps stopped and a soft curse sounded, amusing him to no end. Where had she learned to curse like that?

Should he call out to her or let her come in on her own? He had the distinct feeling that she'd been avoiding him all day. He assumed because of their foray in the church-yard yesterday.

He'd gone too far. But he couldn't regret his actions. Had thanked the heavens she'd felt the same need he did. Had wished he'd been in another time and another place to fulfill both their desires. But the truth of the matter was she was under his employ, and she was here for a different purpose entirely than to appease this need he suddenly had for companionship. *Her* companionship.

If she came to see him, he'd have to do his best to keep from pulling her into his arms and continuing where they'd left off yesterday. From showing her again how much he wanted his hands all over her tiny form. If she walked on by his study, then it was never meant to be be-tween them.

As though his thoughts had summoned her, her pixie form filled the open doorway. Her nose was scrunched up, strands of hair falling from her chignon, and paint was stained along the side of her left hand.

He stood from the chair he'd been reposing in and walked to the edge of his desk where he perched himself so he could be closer to her.

Elliott stared at her a long moment. It took everything

in him to keep himself balanced on the edge of the desk—
away from her, but not too distant. She walked into the
room and stood not two feet from him. Restraint was not
his forte when in her presence.

He could reach out and pull her into his arms. Run the
back of his knuckles down her soft neck, place his lips
there and taste her skin. He crossed his arms over his chest
instead.

He took a deep inhalation of the floral scent she used in
her hair. Gardenias. That was the smell. No wonder it had
been familiar. It was a scent his mother had used; he'd
smelled it often enough as a boy that it was firmly im-
printed on his mind.

"How may I be of service, Miss Hallaway?"

"I wanted to talk to you about something that has come
to my attention."

What could it be now? She knew Jacob's every flaw—
hopefully there was never a day when she learned of his
own inabilities; then she'd definitely think less of him.

"Miss Hallaway," he prompted.

"I've been privy to information I cannot remain quiet
on. Your son, who proves to be rather tenacious now that
he knows I'll not judge him for the wrongs of his past
teachers, has been unnecessarily spoken down to by some
of the staff. I only bring this matter to your attention because he is but a child and children are easily disheartened
when those they are supposed to trust offer nothing but
discouragement."

"What exactly are you asking of me? Everyone living
here has been involved with my son's upbringing." It was
a wild accusation. Who in the house would dare do such a
thing?

"The information is now yours to do with as you
please, my lord." She only stared at him below the long
fringes of flaxen lashes that fanned her round eyes. Those

cat-green eyes of hers beckoned him closer. He barely managed to stay put. "I thought you should know," she whispered.

"Who?" he asked, needing to know. Needing someone to focus his rage on. Rage he hadn't felt since the days his father had been alive and last raised his hand against Elliott.

"I cannot betray your son's trust in revealing the source. But I would recommend speaking to him on the topic."

Elliott never discussed lessons with his son. It was too sore a spot for him. But this was something that could not be left alone. He had trusted every member of the household with his life—his son's life. This felt like the worst kind of betrayal. Would Miss Hallaway have any reason to lie to him? He didn't think so.

He clenched his jaw and gave her a nod. "Thank you" was all he could say as his fists clenched and his body filled with tension.

She stepped closer to him. "I would not have brought this to your attention if I thought it unimportant."

Her closeness made his body tense for an entirely different reason than previously. He looked to the open door behind them, then back to her. It was late, but that didn't mean his son couldn't wander back downstairs.

"Miss Hallaway?"

Dare he hope she had the same thing on her mind as he? Where was his will to avoid temptation? Her mouth parted, her tongue flicked out and moistened the bottom lip.

That was his undoing.

He could resist her no longer. Standing from the desk, he cupped her face between his hands and leaned in close to press his lips to hers, licking at the seam, then nipping as he sucked the soft, plump flesh of her lower lip into his mouth.

He backed them up so far as the door so he could close

and lock it behind her. She did not protest. In fact, she took his mouth with as much enthusiasm as she had in the churchyard.

Breaking their kiss, he pressed his forehead to hers, his hand caressing her hip as he fought for some degree of control.

He had to take this slower even if it killed him with desire to be inside her with an immediacy that bordered on madness. They were both panting hard from a mere kiss.

"I can't help myself," he said.

"Neither can I."

Well, damn. How could he stop himself?

If she had no intention of stopping his advances, then he'd take what he could. When was the last time he'd hungered for the companionship of a woman? There was something about Miss Hallaway that made him forget common decency.

But that wasn't what this was about. He knew there could be something more between them. What the more was couldn't be defined if he didn't take a chance on her. And she on him.

Chapter 10

While his son was gone, the old witch who had lost
her daughter hobbled her way up to the grand doors
of the king's entry. Cold and sick, she sought refuge
from a winter storm that turned the lands out-
side dangerous to those who dared to venture into
the cold.   *—The Dragon of Brahmors*

Lord Brendall's finger trailed a hot path along the exposed line of her neck.

Why hadn't she denied him this pleasure? Why didn't
she protest? The answer was simple, really: She wanted
this.

Abby closed her eyes, savoring the soft touch and the
warmth of his body surrounding her, trying to forget the
fact that what she was doing might be the wrong thing
to do.

His tickling touch was a delicate branding to her
senses.

"What is it you wish of me?" she asked, breathless
from his light caress.

She wasn't sure what had decided her on entering Lord
Brendall's study and subsequently staying in his company.

She couldn't claim curiosity at this stage . . . She didn't want to be curious, she wanted to know.

Instead of answering her, he leaned in and ran the tip of his nose along the shell of her ear, rasping out in a low tone, "I can't help myself when I'm around you."

That made two of them.

She should run off like any demure and sane lady would. Instead she curled her fingers around his biceps. To stop him from taking further advantage or to keep him from moving away from her, she couldn't say.

His hand moved around to her back and caressed her rump in slow circles, tilting her pelvis closer to his.

She wanted this. Wanted him to touch her. Ached to feel his body cover hers in such a primal position that it had all her senses reeling. To feel something other than the cold that had seeped into her bones since setting foot inside this morbid, dreary castle would be more than a blessing, especially given that Lord Brendall would be warming her.

She began to wonder about her wisdom in putting herself in this situation. This position. He'd probably think her no better than a tavern wench.

She hadn't realized how lusty a nature she had. Had she been stifling it all these years? Well, she'd certainly never acted upon her desires—not that she'd ever wanted anyone until she'd met the galling yet intriguing Lord Brendall. Not that she'd ever wanted to act upon her desires—aside from a few kisses that curiosity had prompted her in to stealing years ago.

The back of his finger caressed her cheek. "How far will you let this go?" he asked. "Or I, for that matter?"

Was he as unsure as she? The thought endeared him to her more.

Her eyes slid closed. Her back bowed as she sought to get closer to him, her shoulders striking the door. He followed her. Her hands spanned over his chest. An errant lock of hair fell over her brow, tickling at her nose and lips with every inhalation. She tried to blow it away, but it fluttered back down to tease her cheek.

His hands stopped moving. She didn't like that in the least. It meant her mind had free rein to think. Thinking wasn't good. Thinking made her realize how misguided her actions were. For what reason was she so willing to ruin herself? The answer was obvious: She'd completely lost her wits.

He might think they could be lovers in the evening while she taught his son during the day. But reality wasn't so kind as that. She had to put an end to this.

She had to stop him. Tell him no. She just didn't want to do that tonight. She wanted to feel a man's body against hers just once. And not any man. *This* man.

What was it about him that made her toss years of good behavior out the window?

When his hand curved over the roundness of her breast, stopping him was the farthest thing from her mind. His other hand was lifting the mass of her skirts, so high she felt the brush of cool air on her stockinged legs. His hands skimming daringly up her thigh and around to her rear.

Oh, God, what would it feel like if he touched her bare skin, stroked it as he did her clothed form? She had an inexplicable desire to touch his bare skin. To feel the heat of him along the length of her body as they writhed in mutual ecstasy.

"We shouldn't." The words came out on a moan and not as a sound suggestion.

"We *are* doing this."

"Lord Brendall . . ."

"Elliott. My name is Elliott."

"My lord, there are too many dangers in doing this."

Her mind might suggest that, but her heart suggested otherwise.

"Will you deny yourself this?" His fingers found the slit in her drawers and slid along the damp flesh between her thighs. "Your dew proves what you want. You are wet for me. Because of me."

His lips brushed against hers.

She should be embarrassed by such blunt words. Embarrassed that he touched her so intimately and that she didn't even have the decency to blush like the maiden she was. She should be pushing him away to preserve her innocence. Not encouraging whatever this was they were about to indulge in.

"It doesn't make it right."

"Who's to say what is right, Miss Hallaway?" There was a pause, and then another gentle brush of his lips against hers. "Tell me to stop, then."

She couldn't do that. Refused to deny herself this. Whatever *this* was.

When his finger slid beyond the slit of her drawers and inside her core, her resolve to cease what they were doing completely vanished. They wouldn't have to complete the act, would they? She'd once seen naughty picture cards of eighteenth-century etchings. They'd depicted men licking at the core of a woman, women sucking the rod of a man.

They could find mutual bliss in such an act, couldn't they? Though she'd been thoroughly scandalized years ago when she'd found the bawdy drawings among her father's things, time and curiosity had made the scenes less shocking and more interesting.

For him to pull his hand away from her when she felt like she was coming undone was foolish. She might as well take what he gave her so freely. Enjoy the moment.

Sliding her hand lower, she stroked the length of his erection straining so hard against the front of his trousers.

He stilled in his ministrations, a groan coming from deep inside. Then his fingers were moving again, slicking over her, finding that little pearl she'd discovered only last year. She knew what kind of excitement that would bring her. She wasn't ashamed to have learned such a thing about her body, either. How could she be when it brought so much pleasure?

She couldn't stop the thrust of her pelvis, the grind of her clitoris over his deft fingers. He inserted his middle finger into her sheath, his thumb still rubbing against her nub.

That was something she'd never contemplated doing—sticking her fingers inside herself. She'd only ever rubbed *that* part of herself. The feel of him inside her sent a tingling thrill to her belly. She wanted more. So much more.

She'd not voice that request to Lord Brendall. Could not find the words to voice her desires.

Elliott. His name was Elliott. At least in her mind she'd call him by his Christian name.

He thrust his groin against her hand harder as he pulled his finger from her sheath and slid back inside so slowly she wanted to scream her need for more. His fingers never stopped working their magic against her nub.

When a gush of liquid released from her center, Elliott gave a harsh curse and kissed her again, nipping at her lips, thrusting his tongue to the same tempo his fingers plunged within her—for there were two fingers within her sheath now.

Her strokes were firmer against his hardened member. She wanted to put that piece of flesh in her mouth. Suck at him till he found the same kind of release she'd find any moment.

The titillation of his fingers never stopped. Neither did the thrust of his rod in her palm.

"You're so damn tight, the very thought of fucking you

nearly has me ready to let off with just the stroke of your palm."

She mewled at his harshly spoken words, reaching for the final outcome of what his hands would soon accomplish. She made no response, not with words, at any rate. She was past the simple capabilities of speech. Past thought altogether. She could only feel. She was so close to that final explosion of bliss that she stilled, solely focused on his hand.

There. Right there. His fingers circled over the flesh between her thighs. Rotating tightly around that hidden part of her with practiced ease. Elliott must have felt the tension strumming through her body, for his strokes grew firmer and longer as he swept through the folds of her sex to spread the fluids from her core. His fingers pressed inside her as he rotated his thumb in a steady rhythm.

Her breath caught, her muscles clenched as she hit her peak. He pulled away from her, a deep growl of animalistic approval in his chest just before his mouth found hers again in a deep tongue-dueling kiss.

How she managed to think at all was a bit of a miracle.

Still unable to voice her thoughts, say what she so badly wanted to do, she pushed him away. He stepped back from their ferocious kiss, disappointment clear in his hard gaze. She saw his thoughts reflected in the stormy, arousal-ridden blue, like angry waves crashing on the shore, sucking away the earth into its watery grave. Did he really think she'd reject him after finding such pleasure in his arms?

Not a chance of that happening. She wanted this more than anything. So much so, she admitted, she needed more.

Had someone chosen that moment to intrude—thank goodness no one had—she doubted she could have stopped herself from what she was about to do.

Hiking up her skirts, which had fallen back around her ankles, she placed one hand on his lean hip and dropped to her knees in front of him. She didn't give herself time to think about what she was doing. Because truth to tell, she didn't know the first thing about doing such a thing, she only knew it was possible.

Her fingers were sure and steady as she released the fastenings on his trousers. Her breath held as she pushed the material down from his hips only to reveal the linen impediment of his underclothes.

The sound that came from her throat was one of distress and eagerness all mingled together. When Elliott gave a slight chuckle, she stalled, her hands on the upper edge of his drawers. He'd never laughed before, not in her presence anyway. She did that.

Was it possible her fumbling had made the ice-cold man smile? She glanced up at him. No smile tilted his lips. They were pressed in a firm line. He stared down at her, eyes half-lidded. She was locked in that sharp gaze of his. Unable to continue.

All the saliva dried from her throat, and her heart beat such an erratic tattoo against her chest, she could actually hear it. She parted her lips and waited for him to say something. Anything.

When he pushed his drawers down, releasing the length of his rod, she swallowed again and couldn't quite tamp down the high-pitched sound of astonishment she released.

He grasped the base of his cock with one hand and threaded his fingers in her hair with the other.

His instrument was a great deal bigger than any of the ones she'd made careful study of in the etchings found in the erotic collection still hidden in a pouch at the back of her journal.

Elliott's large hands couldn't even cover his length. Her hand certainly wouldn't wrap around the full girth.

Her instincts had always done her well; she'd rely heavily upon them to do what she'd craved doing the moment he'd pushed her up against the wall for his wicked ministrations. She leaned in and kissed the rounded head that was a darker pink, while the shaft was more flesh-colored with a thick vein running down the underside.

She licked at the bead of liquid that moistened the crown. The flesh was smoother and softer than she could ever have imagined. Men's bodies were so much harder than a woman's that it was pleasantly surprising to find this vulnerability, this unexpected difference. She couldn't help but imagine what that steely smooth piece of flesh would feel like sliding into her body.

Her mouth opened, and her tongue slid around the head as she capped her lips around the whole end of him. She wasn't sure what she should do. The flat of her tongue caressed the bottom edge, feeling the smooth texture, the softness as she sucked him gently into her mouth.

His hand was firmly tangled in her hair, like he was afraid she'd stop or pull away.

He slowly pushed into her mouth and then pulled out, sliding his rigid length along her tongue, showing her what he liked and wanted. His hand fisted at the base of his cock, stroking it with each forward push down her throat.

She wanted to be the one holding the base. Make him wild with the same ecstasy he'd shown her moments ago. She placed her hand over his. He shook her off and led her hand to cup the tight sac beneath his rod.

"Roll them," he gritted out before taking hold of the base of his cock again. Was that to keep from pushing too far into her mouth?

Looking up at him, she was surprised to find him staring down at her. His expression was dark, clouded with lust. She kept her eyes on his. Not wanting to break the intimate contact they shared. It seemed more intimate to stare back at each other while involved in such an act than it did to actually be sucking his thick, heavy rod into her mouth.

"I am going to taste you." There was a firm edge of promise in his voice that made her shiver and groan around him.

She could guess what he meant. Very well. Her imagination was running wild with the possibilities. She sucked at him harder with a half groan, half moan still in her throat. When she continued to make that sound in her throat, he hissed in a breath and clenched his jaw.

She never broke eye contact with him from that point forward.

Hunger. That's what the look was in his eyes. A hunger for more. For her. The thought sent a jolt of pleasure through her veins, and more fluid rushed to her center. Her mouth moved faster, tongue slicking the way and aiding her.

With a growl, he pulled away from her. Too soon. She wanted more. She wasn't done exploring him.

"Why have you stopped?"

Before she could finish her questions, he yanked at her hand, forcing her to her feet, and brought them both to the sofa.

He didn't cover himself. Didn't try to hide the current state *she'd* put him in. That put a grin on her face.

Goddamn. She'd be the death of him. Elliott sat heavily on the sofa. He'd have that taste of her now. Suck at her juices. Fill her slit and rub at her cleft with his tongue to bring her to a second climax.

At first, he'd been surprised by her actions. This was not something she was skilled in. But it had felt so good and so delightful in some primal way that he hadn't the sense to tell her they shouldn't be doing any of this. Where was his will to keep her at a distance? Gone the second she'd stepped through the door.

He was putting her in a bad position—taking her as a

lover when she worked for him. Worse, he knew she had not done this before. She'd been so shy and unsure on her knees that the likelihood she'd never been with a man shouldn't surprise him; it shouldn't give him a secret thrill that he'd be her first.

Her last.

Good Lord, he needed to put an end to what was about to happen. But how could he? His pants and smalls were pushed down, his cockstand a result of her very presence, and he needed to touch her, to taste her, swirl his tongue around the tips of her breasts and the swell of her clitoris. Squeeze the rounded globes of her buttocks as he rode them to sweet oblivion over and over again until neither had the strength to move.

She stood before him, no shyness in her outward demeanor. In fact, she stared at the jut of his cock, which throbbed and jerked at her naked regard. He'd have that perfect mouth of hers around his prick another time. Grabbing her hand, he pulled her closer, going to work on her skirts. The twilled material would only impede what he planned to do.

Maybe after he'd made her come and found his release, he'd stop fantasizing about his governess. Get her out of his system once and for all. The ties now loose on her skirts, he pulled down the heavy layers before she could think to utter a protest.

Not that he'd thought to hear a protest from her lips after everything they'd done tonight. All they would do. It was an inevitable fact that he needed to have her in his bed.

She stood before him, her bodice still in place, her underthings bared to him. He feasted upon the sight. Still too many clothes on her, but he'd be able to do what he wanted. Taste the sweet treasure between her thighs.

Her small hands rested upon each of his shoulders as he grasped her hips between his hands. He'd known she was small, but once in his clutch she seemed delicate. More fragile than a porcelain doll. He'd do his damnedest to be gentle.

His hands slid around to her rear, forming to the rounded globes like a wet towel on flesh. She swayed forward. Her hands running through his hair, massaging at his scalp. She pulled him closer, till his forehead pressed against her sternum and her small, softly rounded breasts.

When he took a deep inhalation, the gardenia scent seeped into his nostrils and his body. It was a smell that reminded him of a home filled with love. Filled with everything that was taken away from him the day his mother died and then the day he'd finally lost his wife to madness.

He would not be ruled by his past. Shoving the memories away—hopefully to never be thought on again, though he knew better—he lifted his head and pressed a kiss against her corseted form.

When he looked up to Miss Hallaway, her expression was filled with desire and lust, and something more. More of *what* he couldn't even guess at.

Maybe she felt the same loneliness he did. Had the same longing to belong somewhere he could call home. This heap of rock was his legacy, one his father had practically beaten him over the head with. Those were thoughts for another time. Another place. Too much misery had filled this house over the years, and he needed just one good thing. One. And here Miss Hallaway stood.

The slight flare of her hips between his big rough hands had his cock throbbing. Her innocent scent wrapped around him like the arms of a lover.

Right now all he cared about was having a taste of his sweet governess. Let her make him senseless for the next few hours. Make him forget anything but her lips wrapped around his cock, fucking him with her hot little mouth.

Not wanting to explain himself, knowing she was

inexperienced, he moved quickly. Laying her out on the couch, he pressed her legs open so that he could clearly see the slit in her drawers and the thatch of strawberry-colored hair beneath. She squealed out her shock, but made no objections.

He actually groaned at the sight in front of him. It made him want to pull at the hair there, slap at the lips of her sex and heighten her passions to a fever pitch. No, he couldn't be so rough with her. Slow and gentle, he reminded himself, not the brute he often turned into during sexual congress.

He couldn't help himself from kissing the linen-covered thatch. Pulling the material aside, he swept his tongue over her wet slit, licking at the juices he knew would be the perfect mix of musk and aroused woman. He thrust his tongue as deep as he could into her core. The muscles of her sheath flexed around the welcome intrusion of his tongue.

It wasn't enough.

He tore at the slit in her drawers, widening the gash, revealing much more of the womanly flesh he would taste. There was nothing of her body hidden to him now. Her flesh was flushed with desire, her cream slicked her entrance, beckoning him closer.

Rolling his thumb around the juices, he wet the whole of her entrance, spreading the fluid so he could lap it up. Sliding his thumb into her core slowly, he felt the flex of muscles inside her inner walls.

She only stilled for a short while. Maybe he had shocked her. The ministrations of his tongue on her nub had her riding her clitoris against his mouth with more vigor.

To his delight, she came again with a downpour of her feminine juices.

He pulled his hands away from her, placed a chaste kiss

against her wet slit, and stuck his tongue into her core one last time with a groan. Looking up, he watched her watching him.

The only thing he read in her expression was satiation.

But he was far from done with her. She scooted up on the sofa, away from him. Wonderment and shock making her actions hasty.

He wanted to ask her up to his room. To continue where they'd left off. But her expression stopped the words from leaving his mouth.

"This was a mistake," she said, scrambling to her feet, gathering up her skirts from the floor.

Disappointment didn't come close to describing what he felt.

Why in hell was she running from him now? "I'd have to disagree."

"That doesn't make it right." She stepped into the material of her skirts and tied it back in place. "I like my position here, Lord Brendall. I don't want to leave, but if we can't stop ourselves from doing . . ." She waved her hands angrily, searching for the right words for what they'd just done. He'd made love to her with his mouth, for God's sake. "Doing things we ought never indulge in, then you'll be as good as forcing me from the castle."

"Miss Hallaway." Elliott sat up and pulled his drawers and trousers back up to his hips. He'd not sit here exposed to her while she rejected him. Not after the pleasures *they* had shared. How dare she!

Goddamn her. Goddamn him. Goddamn every fucking thing in his life that just didn't seem to work out for the better in the end.

She didn't meet his gaze again. She pulled out her remaining hairpins, shook out her long fiery hair, gave him one final long look he didn't know how to interpret, and left him in the study without another word. He sat heavily on the sofa and rubbed the heel of his palms roughly over his eyes.

Shit.

He'd embarrassed her. Gone too far. Done too much. What a bleeding idiot he was. He stood and tucked in his shirt, righting the evidence of all he'd done. Though he couldn't erase the taste of her from his tongue, the lingering softness of her skin beneath his hands.

"My lord," came Martha's voice from the door not five minutes later. Elliott looked over to the older woman. She'd been with his family as far back as he could remember, had cared for him when his mother had died, tended his bruises and cuts after his father's angry outbursts, helped him through the tough times when his wife would rant and rage nonsensically.

Had she been the one to whisper such hated words to Jacob? Martha had disliked Madeline from her first arrival at the castle. She now had an obvious dislike toward Miss Hallaway. She'd even gone so far as to ask him to have the new governess leave. Martha had insisted she was too young for the position.

"You look troubled. Can I prepare you a drink?"

She'd always been rather perceptive of his moods.

Then he had to wonder if she knew . . . could she know that Elliott had spent the last hour in Miss Hallaway's company? If she did, would she hate his governess more? She should have quit from the main house already. Why was she here?

"I'm for bed."

"Of course, my lord. I'll see you in the morning." Head high and shoulders back, she left the room.

Chapter 11

The king was not a charitable man and refused the old woman entrance into his domain. Before the king could lock the door, she whispered words so hateful upon his household that the king banished her from his kingdom forevermore.
—The Dragon of Brahmors

Abby had hardly slept a wink over the past week. Thoughts of Elliott weighed heavily on her mind. Refusing to lie in bed tired, and yet wide awake, she'd dressed and made her way out of doors.

She doubted anyone was up at this early hour. The sun barely speared across the horizon, shading it a warm orange topaz. Not quite day, not quite night. She leaned against the parapet wall, elbows resting against the back ledge, and let the cool morning air infuse her bones.

She was so sapped of energy, she wanted to let the wind carry her away. Carry her so far off the beaten path that she would be back in the warm comfort of her sisters' arms. They would tell her what she should do. Give her the guidance she desperately needed. Because for the life of her, she didn't know what would come next. How she should act. What she should say or do.

What had she allowed to happen with Lord Brendall? That had been on her mind for too many days now. What had she been thinking? Clearly, she hadn't been thinking at all. She'd been incredibly embarrassed when she had finally come to her senses and fled to the privacy of her own bedchamber.

What did Elliott think of her? She hadn't even been able to face him after everything that they'd done and shared. Had barely been able to look him in the eye.

He'd avoided her since that night, too.

She couldn't afford the distraction his lordship presented. Couldn't play this game whose rules she didn't understand. In fact there were no rules, and she didn't like that. It meant not having control over what happened. Turning toward the North Sea, she perched her elbows on the stone ledge in front of her and set her chin on her folded hands.

The sea was rough this morning, the waves high and the water churning angrily. Could the first storm of the season be on its way? Once winter set in, it would be impossible to leave. The roadways were sure to close to travelers.

Did she plan to leave? Walk away from the opportunity of helping a child she'd come to adore in such a short time? Walk away from a man who made it impossible for her to think clearly? The only man who had ever made her feel so much emotion, desire, and passion with a mere look in her direction.

If she stayed at Brendall Castle for the next few months, what would happen between her and Elliott? Resisting the allure of what he offered would be impossible. This was the crux of her conundrum. Stay and become a mistress of sorts to her employer, or leave and reevaluate what it was she wanted in her life. She definitely didn't want to leave, but maybe it was the right thing to do.

If she left, she'd never know what it was to desire a man so much that she lost her wits whenever he was around. That was not a state she'd ever found herself in before. Men had always failed to truly interest her, to the point that she had begun to think there was something wrong with her. That was one reason she'd decided never to marry; the other was that she didn't want to lose herself once she married. She felt as though she'd sacrifice a small part of herself if she gave a man any control over her life.

She pushed out a heavy sigh. As much as she'd like to stay out here and contemplate her path in life, she couldn't brood for much longer. Jacob would be in the library in a few hours for his lessons. And while she remained at the castle, she was determined to teach him the basis for reading and writing. She would succeed with him.

She stood and decided on a walk before returning back to the main house. Fresh air would do her good, despite the light drizzle that misted the air. She missed her daily walks with her sisters and she hadn't been able to cull the habit even though the air was sometimes quite bitterly cold in the early morning. Walking always helped her to think more clearly.

If she did decide to leave, would Lord Brendall continue to go through a string of governesses? If Jacob were her son, she'd do everything in her power to correct the issue as it stood.

When she came to the crumbled wall of the parapet, she held the opposite side and stepped over the fallen stones carefully. It probably wasn't smart to walk this way. Her only design had been to watch the rhythmic slap of the sea against the shore. It was comforting and mesmerizing. Lulling. Though, she supposed, she could have stuck to the sand dunes on the beach below. Or walked the fields of never-ending grass on the opposite side of the sea.

Her foot slipped on the loose rocks. She caught herself before she could fall. That was until a great gust of wind and the force of someone pushing her made her stumble toward the unsteady wall. She grappled for a hold, but the wall had met great damage over the years and it collapsed beneath her fingers.

She screamed as she tumbled toward the wide-open space and a far drop in front of her. There was no purchase to be found as she slid from the walk and into the open air.

There was a ledge some ten or fifteen feet down. She landed hard on her ankle, twisting it painfully as she hit the stone with enough force to send all the air out of her lungs. She bit her lip to keep herself from throwing up from the sharp pain shooting through her leg. The sun still hadn't lit the sky enough for her to see her surroundings— not that she could see anything with her eyes filled to the brim with tears.

The pounding of feet grew louder. The shout of a man sounded, but the words could not be made out with the wind picking up around her.

She was whimpering, tears falling down her face as she felt around the ledge she'd fallen to. She wasn't sure how to get back to the castle, or how to get down from the high perch. As soon as the sun was up, she'd probably find a door that led to some secret passageway in this old castle.

She looked around her carefully, trying to see if someone lurked above.

Why would someone push her? Was it her imagination that someone had done something so cruel? Could it have been the wind pushing her over the ledge? She doubted that. There had definitely been someone there to precipitate the fall.

"Abigail!" someone yelled in the distance.

She swiped the tears away from her cheek with the back of her hand and looked up to the wall.

"Here . . . I'm here," she called back, voice shaky.

Small pebbles and dust rained down on her as someone settled above on the parapet. She raised her arms above her head to shield her eyes from falling debris.

"I ran up here the moment I saw you go over the edge." Lord Brendall. The very man she hadn't been able to rid her mind of.

"Did you see what happened?" She needed to know if someone had pushed her.

"I saw. Don't know who was up here with you, but you didn't fall on your own."

Not her imagination, then, that someone had pushed her.

"Can you move?"

"I think so." She prodded the flesh around her ankle, feeling for broken bones. She hissed in a sharp breath when she hit a sensitive spot and pulled her hand away from the tenderness. "Perhaps not," she cried. Fresh tears fell from her eyes.

"I'm coming down." Elliott's voice was laced with anger.

"Is there a door on this level?" she asked.

"Yes, but it's too dark for you to find."

More sand and pebbles rained down around her. She shielded her eyes again. She bloody well would find the door. She didn't like being helpless. Not in the least. But she couldn't even get her feet under her and push herself to a standing position.

"I doubt I'm going anywhere," she mumbled and bit back a sob.

She peeked up at that ledge she'd fallen off only to spy Lord Brendall swinging over the edge. "What in God's name are you doing, my lord?"

"Coming down to help you."

"You can't do that. I'll wait till you come around to this level. You're going to hurt yourself. I will not be the cause of your death!"

"Someone could be making their way down to your level to finish what they started. I'll not leave you alone."

Abby gasped at the realization that he was right. Someone had wanted to harm her a great deal. Why, though? She'd been here less than a month. No one knew who she really was, not that that would matter to anyone if they were adamant about taking her away from the land of the living. But had they known who she really was, they might think twice about trying to rid the world of her. She had powerful relations.

Still, none of this made sense.

Elliott swung his legs over the edge and jumped down next to her, landing in a crouch. He dusted his hands off on his trousers, and then cupped her cheek, his thumb brushing away some of the tears she was helpless to fight in her pain.

She nuzzled into his palm and felt more tears fall. God, she'd missed his touch. Had craved it while she had been avoiding him this past week. What if Elliott hadn't seen her fall? Would anyone have come to look for her here? Would her attacker have come back to finish the job?

"We'll get you back to the house in a minute. I'm just going to check you for any injuries."

His hands were so warm and sturdy as he checked her arms and her back with a firm, steady touch. She concentrated on the feel of him pressing into every part of her body. Having something else to focus on dulled the pain in her ankle to an incessant throb.

On reaching her palms, he hissed in a breath. She pulled her hands away, curled them up, and hid them in her lap. "They sting, nothing more. They'll heal well enough."

"We need to get you washed up and clean these cuts out." He pulled out a handkerchief and wiped at her tears again. Embarrassed by the fact that she couldn't stop crying, she took the cloth from him, wiped under her eyes and nose, and tucked the material in the sleeve of her bodice.

"Tell me where else you're hurt." The note of worry in his voice made her heart flutter in nervousness.

"Just my ankle pains me. I've been able to move it, so I don't think it's broken."

He tossed up the lower portion of her skirts and loosened the laces on her short boots. Her lip trembled as she bit back a cry when he removed it. At the very least, it was sprained.

"We'll put ice on this when we get back to the house. I'll send for a doctor, but it'll be a couple of hours before he arrives."

She knew who the doctor was. Had seen him when she'd attended church with Lydia last Sunday. Lydia had been quite smitten with him.

"Why do the townspeople dislike you so much?"

She wished the words back as soon as she'd said them. Now was not the time to question Lord Brendall. Elliott. He was Elliott to her now.

"That is a question for another day." At least he didn't seem offended by it. "Come, put your arms around my shoulders; I'll carry you back to the house."

She didn't argue. She wanted to hold him close. She'd missed him. Funny how she'd done everything in her power to ignore him; and he, her. Yet she'd missed him with a fierceness that had her arms tightening around his broad shoulders.

"Did you see who was on the parapet with me?"

"No. But I will find out."

He lifted her, one arm under her knees to support the

other behind her back. The movement made her nauseous and the throbbing of her ankle more noticeable. Her arms tightened further around Elliott's shoulders, and she had to place her forehead against his collarbone to take in steady, even breaths. She did not want to throw up, but the reality was that she might.

"My head is spinning."

"I'll retrieve some laudanum for you. It will dull the pain."

She shook her head. She didn't want to take anything that would dull her senses. She needed her wits about her if someone had set out to hurt her intentionally. She also needed her wits about her if she was to be alone for any length of time in Elliott's company.

To take her mind from the pain, she asked, "Why is this ledge here? Seems counterproductive in defending the castle from intruders."

Elliott hefted her higher in his arms as he reached toward the wall, looking for something, the access point, she was sure. Seemed even he had difficulty finding it in the dim light. A piece of the rock moved and opened up to a long stone tunnel that was as black as a starless, cloudy night and musky with dampness from the sea.

"It was put in when my family took the castle. Wars have long since ceased in this part of the country. I think this perch was put here when my ancestors were fixing the exterior wall. The castle was in great disrepair when we took it over. Not from neglect but from its final battle."

The tunnel around them was cool, the air thick with water. She realized then that she'd lost her shawl and snuggled closer to Elliott, wanting to steal as much warmth from him as possible. Was it wrong for her to want to bask in his arms? It felt right to be held like this. And so wrong. So very wrong that it brought fresh tears to her eyes. This time, she managed to stop them from spilling over the rim of her eyes.

She was overly emotional because she was hurt. She knew that. She laid her cheek in the spot between Elliott's shoulder and neck and inhaled his masculine scent. He smelled clean, like bay leaf soap. That made her think of baths. And being naked with his lordship. She took a deep breath and tried to mentally shake the thought away. She was becoming delirious as her body adjusted to the pain.

"I feel ill," she whispered.

"You'll be fine once I set you down. Then we'll get your ankle looked after. I will send Thomas for the saw-bones."

"No. I won't need a doctor. I just need to rest." She yawned. Too many days of little sleep were catching up with her. "Really tired."

"Sleep, then. I'll watch after you. The doctor is a friend, so you'll be in good hands."

She closed her eyes because she couldn't keep them open a second longer. The thud of his heart in her ear was soothing. Hypnotizing.

She'd fallen asleep as he neared his chambers. He headed there instead of her room because it would be a great deal easier to wash her up there with running water in his bathing room.

Who in hell had been up on the parapet with her? It was too dark to make out any details beyond the dark monk's robe billowing in the wind, obscuring all their features and true size. When he found out who dared to harm someone in his household—and he would find out—he'd have to keep his temper in check, so he wasn't tempted to throw them from the highest tower to meet their own death.

Miss Hallaway's fall brought back long-forgotten words uttered from Madeline. His wife had been too frightened to leave the house once she was pregnant. Had ranted about someone wishing her demise. He hadn't believed her at the time. Now he wondered if his wife ever met with any accidents. Had she been trying to protect herself by staying inside the house? She wouldn't even walk the grounds with him. As her condition had worsened and the pregnancy had taken its toll on her body, he'd called the doctor in. It had been too late. Paranoia had taken firm root in her mind, and the wife he remembered had forever changed.

Miss Hallaway was of a stronger constitution. Her mind and will were strong, whereas his wife's had not been. He need not worry about Miss Hallaway. She would grow angry from this incident, not melancholy.

Laying her as gently as possible on the chaise longue in his room, he went to retrieve towels, wetting them and bringing them back to her to wash the cuts on her hands where she'd stopped her fall.

Superficial scrapes marred her palms. He was happy to see that there were no lacerations that would require stitches.

What would have happened had he not been watching for her this morning? Something he'd done since she'd taken to walking the castle grounds. He was never far behind, but never close enough for her to notice him.

Who would dare do this to someone in his care? It had to be someone who knew the castle well. Knew its faults and dangers. Knew the path Miss Hallaway walked regularly.

Setting a washing bowl in his lap, he submerged her hands in the cool water and picked out a few pebbles embedded into her delicate skin. There was minimal bleeding, but the water turned pink with the small amount of blood she had lost. When her hands were clean, he wiped them on a towel and set a pillow under her leg to elevate her ankle. He needed to get the swelling down so it could be better looked at.

He checked her limbs again, feeling for any broken bones or other swellings that he might have missed in his quick perusal of her earlier. Her knee was bruised an ugly shade of red and purple. That would make walking even more difficult for her. Still, aside from that—and the swelling of her ankle—she would only sport a few bruises from her ordeal.

She'd been very lucky.

Glancing at the tall clock in the corner of the room, he thought about how he should handle this sudden problem with Miss Hallaway. It was too early for anyone to be up and about in the house, so it wasn't an easy task to summon a doctor unless he went over to the servants' quarters to wake someone, or took it upon himself to ride to town.

If he did leave her for a while, no one would dare enter his chambers and cause her any harm. No one would even think to find her in here. But he didn't want to chance leaving her alone.

He'd send Thomas to collect the doctor. In the meantime, he could fetch some ice for her ankle. The swelling needed to be brought down. Hopefully it was no more than a sprain.

When he arrived back in his chambers, Miss Hallaway's eyes were open, her foot still elevated, and her dainty calf exposed on the pillow. It wasn't his imagination that the bruise was growing darker, and larger. It now covered half her foot. Hopefully the ice would stifle further bruising.

"You shouldn't trouble yourself," she said.

As she propped herself up on her elbows so she was reclined against the end of the chaise instead of lying on it, her ankle slid from the support of the pillow. She hissed in a sharp breath when it bounced on the seat.

"I most certainly shall. You nearly fell to your death, Miss Hallaway, and all you have to say to me is that I shouldn't fret over your injuries?"

He moved the pillow back in place for her, and wrapped one of the dry towels around the ice before setting it over her ankle. Hopefully this would do the trick, because there was very little ice left in the well beneath the main house.

"The servants can help me."

"A shame, then, that I am the only person up in the house who can help you right now."

Miss Hallaway looked down at her foot, a scowl firmly on her face.

"For the life of me, I can't understand why someone would wish me any harm."

The look on her face was one of distress crossed with pain.

"It's not the first strange accident to have happened here over the years. Just the first for me to witness."

Accidents had happened often when his wife was alive. Though he was sure Madeline had been the cause of most of those incidents. Including the one that had finally claimed her life and nearly his son's, too.

"Oh," was all she said.

"You've been through quite an ordeal. If you'd like to sleep here, at least till the doctor has looked you over, by all means do so."

"I shouldn't be in here, my lord. What should the rest of the staff think?"

"That you are injured and under my care. Don't read too much into it. You made it clear to me that you abhor my company."

Why else would she have gone to such great lengths to avoid him if that weren't the truth?

"I—"

He didn't want to hear her excuses. He stood from where he knelt next to her and went into the bathing chamber to wash out the linens he'd bloodied in cleaning her cuts.

"The household won't be up for another hour. I'm going to walk the grounds, see if any of the outside entrances have been left open to intruders."

Her face was downcast, the fringe of her lashes covering her eyes from him. She said nothing. She couldn't even look him in the eye after the accusation. That struck deeper than it should have. He shouldn't care what she thought at the end of the day. Shouldn't care that he wanted her to like him even a small bit. If not for the pleasure they had found in each other's arms, then for his rescuing her.

What a fool that made him. He locked his chamber door behind him, not wanting anything untoward to happen to Miss Hallaway as he checked the grounds.

His first stop was his son's chamber. Opening the door, he saw Jacob stretched out on his stomach, blankets kicked down to the end of the bed, hair mussed and sticking up. His mouth was open, a light snore emanating from between his lips.

He stepped into the room and brushed his fingers through his son's hair. It was the first time he'd noticed that his son didn't sport dirt of any kind on his face or on his curled-up hands. Even his nails appeared to be buffed and free of grime. His hair looked to be washed, too. This was new.

Did Miss Hallaway have something to do with this change? He didn't doubt it for one moment. She had come far with his son's appearance, it seemed. With one final brush of his fingers through the boy's hair, he pulled up the counterpane and tucked it around Jacob's shoulders.

He locked the door behind him and made his way

outdoors. First stop would be to see Thomas, who would have to fetch the doctor. Second, he would make sure that none of the old passageways through the castle had been used, and lock the doors that remained open to the outside world.

Chapter 12

Those words, you ask: May a blight fall upon your family and your kingdom fall around you, for your family will not seed another generation to fill the lands around you.   —*The Dragon of Brahmors*

Abby lay back on the high end of the chaise once the click of the lock had tumbled over. Was he concerned she would attempt going to her room, or genuinely worried for her safety?

She wished she didn't feel quite so useless. Helpless. The throbbing pressure she felt in her ankle and partway up her leg made it near impossible not to cry out in pain. But she bit back the sobs. It would only make her head pound as much as her ankle should she succumb to *that* need.

Besides, her head still reeled from the fact that someone had tried to push her to an early death. But who? And why, for heaven's sake? She'd have to be more vigilant from now on. The reasoning behind her fall made no sense.

She'd gone to church this past weekend, had met a lot of the townsfolk, if not all of them. But would they hold some sort of grudge against her for living at Brendall Castle? For being in the employ of Lord Brendall?

Everyone in the village had been cold at first, but had eventually warmed toward her. Even the reluctant vicar's wife had gone from pinch-faced bitterness to lovely kindness in the course of a couple of hours. There wasn't anyone who wasn't cordial with her by the time she'd left for home with Lydia.

Abby was not the type to make enemies. At least none that she was aware of.

Opening her eyes, she stared up at the ceiling. A fresco of angels danced in blue skies. They all wore flowing white gowns in a Grecian style, their long blonde hair hanging loose around their shoulders and wings. One held a hunting horn, two bitches at her heels; another strung an arrow in her bow, pointing it to the clouds painted in the scene. Not angels, then. Warrior maidens? Goddesses from literature?

Strikingly similar to the maiden depicted in the painting on the landing up to the bedchambers. A distant relative perhaps? Had she been a lady of the castle? Or even the master's dead wife? The thought sent a shiver through her. It would be unsettling to know the paintings were of his dead wife. Maybe he grieved deeply for the woman.

She'd have to ask Jacob who the woman was, if only to ease her mind that Lord Brendall no longer pined after his wife. To think that he did seemed ludicrous since he'd had her buried where no one could easily find her grave.

The room she was in boasted a wall of windows. The opulence made her feel as though she were back at her sister's. Rich burgundy fabric covered the large four-poster bed. The rugs on the floor looked Persian, threaded with dark hues of red, browns, and oranges. The walls were papered in gold, the motif too far off to make out the finer details. Sheepskins were placed on the floor beside the bed and in front of the fireplace—a nice place to curl your toes on a cold morning or evening.

The room was easily four times the size of hers. A huge marble fireplace was situated in the middle of one wall, the veining a light gray. Lion heads were carved into either side, their mouths opened to reveal their deadly teeth. The chaise she rested upon was of yellow velvet, the pillows the exact same gold coloring as was on the walls.

The room provided no insight into Lord Brendall's character. She could no more figure him out today than she could upon her arrival. That fact grated since she had become intimate with the man.

His actions today, however, had illuminated a great deal about him. Had he been watching for her in the mornings? She was nothing if not a creature of habit, her routine predictable. It shouldn't surprise her that he'd been there to help her in an instant. Every time they'd run into each other, he'd seemingly come out of nowhere. Maybe he watched for her often. Had she known where to find him, she probably would have watched for him, too, if only to uncover more of his character.

Hiking up the lower portion of her skirts, she looked at her ankle. She had to move the cloth filled with ice to get a good look at it. The swelling had decreased, but not significantly enough that she would chance putting weight on it anytime soon.

How long would she be stuck in *his* room? Regardless of her injuries, she did not want the staff to find her in his lordship's private chambers. What would they think of such folly?

She lay helpless in his room for at least an hour before he finally returned.

"You're awake."

She'd merely fainted from excessive pain. Of course she would come to. She looked away from him, embarrassed, and unsure of what to say or do.

"Can you please take me back to my room? I do not wish the rest of the staff to know my whereabouts."

"I have no wish to ruin your reputation, Miss Hallaway," he said with affront.

Yes, the circumstances had been dire in this situation. It even made sense for her to be here. As much as she wanted to, she couldn't linger here in his company.

"Did you find any evidence to suspect foul play?"

"Nothing. All the passageways are well sealed. Have been for years. Whoever it was, they could have come though any of the main entrances into the castle. They haven't been closed off to the outside world for years. It'll be easy to cure that bad habit before anything else can happen to the people who live inside these walls."

He stood at the edge of the chaise, his voice soft but brimming with anger. She still hadn't looked up at him. She didn't want to see what his expression held. She knew he worried for her safety. Had gone so far as to care for her himself, instead of calling on the housekeeper to look after her.

"When you attended church, did anyone treat you with scorn?"

She shook her head and dared a glance at him. His arms were loose at his sides, his hands half curled into fists. His jaw clenched, and his immovable mouth was narrowed into a thin line. That he was angry on her behalf shouldn't have sent a jolt of awareness through her body. Especially with the pain still hampering her ankle.

Bits of dust and debris speckled over his dark hair. She wanted to comb the dirt out with her fingers.

"Will you please bring me back to my room?"

Nodding, he said, "Take the ice off and hold it."

She did as he asked and was immediately scooped up into his arms. She hadn't imagined how good being in his embrace had felt earlier. She could, indeed, bask in his arms all day, like a lizard soaking up sun on a rock ledge.

She could have been in his arms sooner had she not been so afraid of her own desires for this brawny man. He lifted her with great ease and with a gentleness that seemed so opposite to his rough exterior. She stared at him. Wanting to catch his gaze, but he was focused on their path straight ahead.

She gave in to the urge she had to run her fingers through the hair at the back of his head.

His arm tightened around her ribs and under her knees. Still, he didn't look at her. They passed through the doors of his room and into the hall.

She brushed the tips of her fingers over the stubble on his face. A tic started at his temple. She touched that, too, wanting to ease any distress he felt from their ordeal this morning.

"Thank you," she whispered.

He looked down at her as he opened her chamber door. Kicking it closed behind him, he strode toward her bed.

"How does your ankle feel?"

As if she could feel her ankle when he held her so tightly against him. Her senses were flooded with a different type of sensation. "Better with the ice on it."

He settled her in the bed, pulled pillows from beside her, and placed them under her leg. Taking the ice, he set it over her ankle with great care.

"I'll have the servants set up a place for you to sit in the morning parlor. I can't imagine you'll take to your bed after a fall."

Elliott got to his feet and caressed the side of her cheek with his hand. His touch nearly undid her. So much so, she clasped it between her palms just as he made to pull away.

This tenderness belied every assumption she'd made of his character.

Had she fallen to her death, she'd have died never knowing what a man truly felt like. Never knowing what it was to be fully a woman. Perhaps she was foolish to keep him at a distance. To avoid him for modesty's sake after everything they had shared. Would it be imprudent to follow through with what she thought was best as opposed to what her heart desired?

Had she not nearly fallen to her death, she might feel differently. But life, at least today, seemed far too short for uncertainties.

"Stay with me awhile longer." She hoped beyond reason that he'd not refuse her now. "The servants won't be up for a bit yet. I don't want to be alone. After what happened . . ."

"You've avoided me, and now you're in want of my company, Miss Hallaway?" There was no censure in his voice, just a note of unsureness and insecurity.

"You called me Abigail earlier."

He nodded once. "I did."

"Won't you do so again?"

She had never been fond of hearing her full name; it reminded her of the times when her sisters had offered some sort of reproach. Coming from Lord Brendall, however, it rang differently. Intimate and for her ears alone.

He clenched his jaw but didn't pull his hand away.

"You cause me a great deal of trouble," he said.

"I'm the youngest of three." She smiled at him, hoping he'd return the gesture. "My main objective as a child was to see how much I could get away with before my father reprimanded me."

He raised one dark brow at her. "We've had very different lives. I cannot confess the same."

Closing her eyes, she took a deep breath. She was damnably tired. So tired it was hard to keep her eyes open, but too frightened to go to sleep just yet. "Please . . . I want you to stay."

"For a short while."

"Thank you," she mumbled, pulling his arm so he had to lean in closer. "Sit with me till then."

With a deep sigh, he walked over to the door and shut it. Clicking over the lock, he said, "I shouldn't want anyone to find us in a compromising position."

"Of course," she responded, a small smile of victory playing on her lips.

What in hell was she about? Yes, she'd been through an ordeal this morning, but her words were sweeter than normal. Her demeanor even more disturbing. For a woman who had avoided him for the better part of a week, why the sudden change?

Was she afraid to be alone? Understandable after everything that had transpired. He didn't have any experience with women like Miss Hallaway. Abby, she'd once said. No, that didn't feel quite right on his tongue or in his head. He much preferred Abigail—a strong name for a strong-willed woman.

Grabbing the pillow from the chair, he tossed it on the bed and climbed in beside her. He leaned against the headboard and focused on his boots. He should remove them, but if he started to remove articles of clothing, he doubted he'd stop till he was quite naked. And then his focus would be getting her quite naked next to him.

She was in pain and he didn't want to cause her any more hurt than she'd already endured.

So he closed his eyes, put his head back, and folded his hands together over his stomach. She rustled around next to him, arranging her skirts and sighing softly as she settled in to rest tightly against his side.

This was not something he'd ever done before. Sit next to a woman in bed, and do nothing of a carnal nature. The very thought had his loins stirring.

He decided right then that doing *this* could kill a man.

He wanted to gather his woman up in his arms, forget that she was his son's governess, and forget that she'd been the one to avoid him after everything they'd shared since her arrival. He'd be able to escape soon. Just as soon as she was asleep. Couldn't be that long. She'd been through an ordeal, to say the least.

"The ice is making me cold," she whispered sleepily, snuggling tighter into him.

He cracked his eyes open to look down at her. Lifting his folded hands away from his stomach, he allowed her to place her head against his chest and her small hand over his abdomen.

He froze. Surely she felt the tension that tightened his body. When she didn't move away, but snuggled in more, he lowered his arms, one lying over her shoulder to keep her from rolling away. With the other, he couldn't help but trace the soft lines of her hand.

Realizing what he was doing, he stopped and put his arm behind his head to lean against it.

She was warm and soft next to him. Her small breasts pressed against his ribs, her hip against his thigh. He hoped to God her eyes were closed, or else she'd see the state she had inadvertently and most likely unintentionally put him in. A state he could do nothing about at the moment.

Although . . . they were alone. The door was locked. And no one would bother them for some time yet.

No, he couldn't demand anything of her. He'd not take her like a damn barbarian. There were more appropriate times to address his want for her, such as after they'd discussed why she'd run off on him the last time they were together.

When she inhaled deeply, her breasts pushed against his side. He swallowed against the tight knot in his throat. How hard would it be to untangle himself from her and escape her chamber? If he didn't . . .

If he didn't get off the bed this very instant, and leave her to her own devices, he'd start touching her.

He moved his hand marginally higher where it rested over her ribs.

He knew immediately that she wore no corset.

No goddamn corset. No wonder he felt the soft give of her breasts against his side: There was nothing between them but a few layers of silk and linen.

The soft plumpness of her breast had him ready to go off in his trousers. Well, damn, this put him in a bad position. He should have told her he couldn't stay. Instead he'd made resisting the need to tumble her damn near impossible.

He'd have to live with the feel of her smaller body crushed alongside his. Her breathing wasn't slow and shallow like someone intent on sleeping. It was deep, but rushed.

She probably heard the rapid beat of his heart where her ear pressed to his chest. If her eyes were open, she'd know exactly what kind of state he was in. How could a man not be in that kind of state when a woman he desired curled up trustingly next to him? She was all soft and so very feminine.

Her fingers did not remain idle. She drew little circles around a button halfway down his shirt. How he wished her hand would move lower.

Shit.

He couldn't remain still for much longer. His hands couldn't keep from exploring her form, either. His left one caressed along her side. He was only human. A man with a larger appetite than normal. But then, what was normal when a woman hadn't graced the castle for nearly seven years? Hadn't been in his bed and stayed the night for even longer than that.

He should tell her to stop her ministrations. To roll away from him so he could get out of the bed without jarring her injury. But there she was. Obviously aware of his state, for she continued to tease him by drawing those little circles over his stomach.

The doctor would be here in another two hours at most. A lot could be done in that time. Although he wondered if she would regret anything they indulged in. Why else would she have avoided him after the time they'd spent together in his study? Simple fact of the matter was, why tamp down her desire this past week if she wanted him as thoroughly as he wanted her?

Without a doubt, they'd be explosive in bed. He knew that.

His conscience chose that moment to pinch him sharply. He started sliding away from her as gently as he could. He couldn't be in her company. It would be impossible to stay sane considering the state he was in.

She wrapped her arm more firmly around his middle, stopping him from leaving the bed.

"Stay," she said again.

"If I stay . . ." He shook his head and thought carefully on his words. She didn't deserve him being snappish. Or angry. It wasn't her fault he was hard as a stone and ready to impale himself between her sweet thighs given the slightest indication that she wanted it.

What should he say? That he'd take advantage of her if she requested his presence for much longer? That he'd try to get her out of her clothes? That he wouldn't be able to keep his damn hands to himself?

"You know where this is leading," was the best response he could come up with.

"Stay," she whispered in that husky voice of hers. "Let me relieve you."

The offer had his prick throbbing and semen pushing out the tip. What was it about this woman? Would he ever know? Would he ever figure her out?

What kind of cad did it make him that he settled back down beside her? That he took her palm and pressed it against his groin and thrust into her palm?

One of these days, he'd get her out of her clothes and all her fine underthings and enjoy the soft give of her body beneath his. Not today, though. Not only because she was injured but because the chances of them righting themselves quickly should someone interrupt would be slight. This would suffice, and he could get his hands on her pretty little cunny while she stroked his cock.

Her hand slid over his cloth-clad erection in even, torturously slow strokes. It wasn't nearly enough. With a flick of his fingers, the fastenings on his trousers parted. Marginally better, even though his smalls still covered him.

Careful about not jarring her injured ankle, Elliott hiked up her skirts and found the slit in her underthings. His fingers met with moisture.

"Shit," he muttered, then groaned as her hand slipped beneath the material, keeping them from skin-to-skin contact.

He couldn't wait to have the little minx. Ride them both to oblivion and back. Tonight. When the castle was settled in to bed, he'd come to her room. Ask her if she truly intended to avoid him. Ask her if she truly didn't want him. If she said no, then they could no longer deny what they both so badly wanted.

Wrapping his free hand around the back of her neck, he pulled her face in closer. He needed to taste her lips. Nibble at their pink plumpness. Now.

She rolled onto her hip, managing to keep her left foot elevated—he checked to be sure he hadn't displaced her leg before he lay siege to her mouth.

She tasted of cinnamon and apples—the tart he'd watched her nibble on earlier. Her lips were warm and supple beneath his. Tracing the seam of her lips with his tongue, he stole into her mouth as her hand ranged over the crown of his penis. Their tongues lazily tangled in a slow loving.

"You make me crazy for your touch."

"I am crazy for yours," she responded.

With the glide of one finger inside her sweet cunny, he stroked the swollen nub at the apex of her thighs with his thumb. Her cream coated all his fingers. He was desperate to taste her again, but thought it better he not get too lost in the moment. He stroked her harder, wanting her to find an end to their mutual insanity.

The faster his hand moved, the faster hers stroked over his prick. Her motions were jerky, unpracticed. Endearing. Her thighs clamped around his hand, squeezing him closer, making it impossible to pull away without a harsh yank. He had no intentions of stopping. Her hand tightened and slowed on his cock as she came gradually to her crisis. He pumped his finger through the slickness of her cunt and kept his mouth busy tasting of her lips and tongue as she rode out her end on his hand, her pelvis moving of its own accord, milking him for every bit of pleasure. As the thrust of her hips slowed, her hand moved again along the heavy length of his cock. He put his hand over hers to increase the tempo.

Feeling his end coming, he grabbed the thin blanket folded on the lower portion of the bed, then pushed her hand away to pump his seed into the wadded-up material.

Head dropping back onto the pillow, he took a deep breath as the final squirt of semen pumped out of him.

Well, damn, if that wasn't the shortest race to the finish line he'd ever had.

Elliott sat up, swinging his feet down to the floor, and fixed his smalls and trousers so he was presentable again. He'd never done that with anyone. Sex and other intimacies, yes, but this . . .

When he stood and faced Abigail, she was pushing down her skirts. He walked over to the other side of the bed, helped her smooth the heavily pleated linen over her legs, and placed the ice-filled cloth back on her ankle, since it had fallen to the floor in their haste.

She did not meet his gaze. Was she embarrassed by her behavior or by committing such an intimate act with him?

He said nothing. Not because it wasn't an appropriate time, but because he didn't know what to say. Words often escaped him. Not so surprising that they did at a time like this. That shouldn't matter; he was more of an observer, never much of a talker. No sense in changing that habit now. Hell, he'd talked to her more than any single person in the span of his life, aside from his son.

Walking over to the window, he propped it open for a moment. The scent of what they'd just done was in the air, and he'd not have anyone judging her for his inability to keep his hands off her. Although she seemed to have as much a problem keeping her hands to herself as he did. Perhaps that reason alone was why she'd avoided him?

Slamming the window tight against the cool air outdoors, he walked over to the mantel and tossed more wood onto the dying fire.

Intelligent woman that she was, she made no comment as he brooded while staring at the flames. What did all this mean for them? Dare he hope that this was an invitation to her bed tonight?

Not willing to put voice to those questions, for fear of her rejecting him again, he walked back to the bed, wadded up the blanket, and stuck it under his arm as he made his way to the door. Turning to her one final time, he caught her confused look at his hasty retreat.

"I'll get rid of this"—he motioned to the material in his arms—"and see if the doctor's arrived."

The doctor wasn't set to arrive for more than hour. He was running from her. Escaping her because he didn't know what to say.

She nodded once and turned her face toward the window. Was she uncomfortable with what they'd just done? Hell if he knew what was playing in her mind right now. Damnable woman. Why did she have to be so difficult to figure out? Why should he care to figure her out at all?

It did him no good standing here. So he left her, intent on washing the blanket in his room and then waiting for the doctor downstairs so he wouldn't have to face her quite yet.

Chapter 13

The king laughed on shutting out the old woman, thinking her a fool, for he already had a son and knew his family would live for generations to come.
—*The Dragon of Brahmors*

Someone had meant to harm her today. She had been lucky to escape from the fall with only a minor injury.

Had the person on the parapet with her intentionally pushed her? Maybe they'd gone for help, or—fearing they'd really done her lasting damage—they'd fled and were still hiding.

She snorted at the realization that she sounded like a witless heroine in a gothic novel.

Shoving more pillows behind her, she leaned back on the cushioned softness. The throbbing in her ankle wasn't nearly as bad now that the ice had brought down the worst of the swelling. Then again, perhaps she couldn't feel the pain because an altogether different kind of throbbing pulsated through her limbs.

What a ninny she was for daring to be so forward with Elliott. Clearly, her mind had gone by the wayside and been trampled on by passersby. She had not one whit of sense left. She'd invited him into her bed, so that she could . . . oh, dear Lord. So that she could do what she did!

She groaned and covered her face. He probably thought her a great hussy. She'd gone and embarrassed herself worse than before. Much worse. What was wrong with her? Every time she was with him, she lost all her good sense. She did things that people simply did not indulge in just for the sake of indulgence.

When a knock came at the door, she didn't even attempt to sit up and greet her guest. She didn't want to put on a smile and pretend that everything was all right with her. It wasn't. She couldn't get Elliott out of her head. Out of her thoughts. Her dreams. He was firmly embedded in everything she did.

Her actions today made it so much worse. How could she be so stupid?

"What have you gone and done to yourself, miss?" Lydia clucked her tongue in disapproval. She had brought fresh linens with her. "Lord Brendall asked me to keep you company till the sawbones arrives."

Was that so he wasn't tempted to find his way back to her chambers? To delight in more wicked things they ought to avoid?

"What happened?" Lydia asked.

"Lord Brendall did not tell you?"

"No. You know how he is now that you've been here the last couple of weeks. That man's not one for talking."

"You're right in that regard." But why did Elliott have to keep her fall a secret? Did he think one of the staff was involved in foul play?

"I was foolish. Out before the sun had fully risen and tripped over some rocks. Lord Brendall saw me fall, so he helped me back to the house. I couldn't stand on my own two feet."

She would have to synchronize her story with Elliott's later. Hopefully he hadn't said anything to the others in the house. Her lies were minimal, so they'd be easy to keep straight.

"You have to be more careful, miss." Lydia shook her head like a mother reprimanding her child, though they were of the same age. "It's an old castle, and you aren't familiar with the way of it yet. Even I find new facets to the grounds I've never noticed before."

"Probably because so much of it lies in disrepair."

"I'm supposing you're right in that regard." Lydia sighed as she stood and flattened a crease from her apron. "Can I get you something to eat? Pa's not back yet with the doctor, and I'm not sure how much longer he'll be gone."

"I had an apple tart earlier. I'm fine for now."

Lydia checked the ice around her ankle; it had melted down significantly. "Is the pain bearable?"

"It's numb right now from the ice. I imagine it'll hurt more as the day wears on."

"Nice of Lord Brendall to fetch it for you. There's not much left from last winter. He's a kindhearted man. Doesn't often show that side of himself."

That remark chafed like a nettle under the skin. Why did everyone dislike his character so much, yet stay on as help? The only person to genuinely care for his lordship seemed to be Thomas. That wasn't to say Lydia disliked Elliott, but it was obvious the other woman remained wary of his lordship, despite having grown up in the castle and having a better understanding of the man than Abby did.

What wasn't she seeing that everyone else was?

If he would but talk to his staff instead of barking out orders to them, and then subsequently ignoring them the rest of the time, maybe they'd warm to him. How was it that she had warmed to him? Surely that had something more to do with her unruly desires.

"I would not have been able to make it back here, if not for him."

"I don't doubt it. You'll have to stop walking the grounds when there's no light to be had. You were out dreadfully early, miss."

"I like the solitude of the morning. I went out to watch the sunrise. It's rather beautiful when it rises over the sea."

Both Lydia's brows arched high on her forehead. "Shame there's no sun to be had today, then."

Abby pursed her lips. She'd been so lost in her thoughts this morning—thinking about Elliott—that she hadn't even noticed the gloomy day and the storm approaching.

"The sky was so pretty and red this morning; I hadn't thought anything of it till the rain let loose in a fury fit for a ride of Valkyries. At least it didn't come down till we were safely back in the house. I'll not be taken unaware again."

"Weather here takes getting used to. A lot of storms roll in from the North Sea unexpectedly. Sometimes they disappear just as fast as they came."

Abby nodded her agreement. She'd noticed the weather could be volatile. The unsettling feeling of that made her crave her familiar home with her sister Emma. She inhaled deeply, closed her eyes, and put her head back on the pillow. She refused to grow maudlin.

"Does it pain you so much?" There was a note of concern in Lydia's voice. "I can fetch more ice."

"Don't waste any more ice on my sprain. I'll be fine as soon as my ankle is bound."

Another knock came at her bedchamber door. This time a young man came in. He was handsome, and so much younger than she expected for a doctor. His hair was a wave of brown, his beard clipped close to his face. His brown eyes were warm and welcoming.

When Lydia stood from the chair she'd pulled close to

the bed, he handed his hat to the maid and kept his focus on his newest patient.

"I heard you had a fall, Miss—"

"Miss Hallaway," she supplied, recognizing him from church.

The doctor approached her. "I'm Dr. Cornwell."

"It would have been a pleasure to have met you under any other circumstance."

He smiled at her. His teeth were full and white beneath his somewhat thin lips. He shrugged out of his navy blue jacket and hung it over the back of the chair Lydia had vacated.

"That'll be all," he told the girl.

Lydia curtsied, her face red at being dismissed so suddenly, and left the room.

Abby noted the presence of Lord Brendall, standing just outside the door. What was he doing here? She had thought he would escape her presence for the rest of the day after what had happened. He seemed just as unsure as she with the positions they often found themselves in.

Dr. Cornwell looked down at her ankle and gently lifted her leg by the calf to better inspect the swollen parts. His touch was cool, but not uncomfortable.

"The ice has helped," he said as he flexed her foot forward slowly.

Abby hissed in a breath and clenched her fists against the pain.

"You'll be off it for at least a week if this movement pains you so much."

He flexed her foot so it was back at its normal position. That seemed to hurt more, and, helpless to hold it back, she made that known by letting out a small pained sound.

Elliott stepped into the room then. A silent brooding presence. But she understood that he worried for her welfare. He didn't like to see her in pain, she decided.

What did he think to do, toss the doctor out on his ear, even though the man had probably been coerced to come up to the castle before the cock could even crow?

Arms crossed over his chest, Elliott wore a scowl that would cause the strongest warrior to take a step back and reassess the situation. Why did he have to stand over her like a Berserker ready for blood retribution? He'd frighten off the doctor if he continued staring after the man in that fashion. Was he so worried about her welfare that it bothered him to see her hurt?

She glared back at him, hoping he'd leave her alone till the doctor could finish up. It was pointless since he ignored her.

Resting her foot back on the perch of pillows, the doctor pressed his fingers into the area around the swollen ankle, then the ankle itself. She hissed in a breath, but didn't cry out again.

"Nothing more than a sprain."

Dr. Cornwell placed his doctor's bag on the chair and opened it. Pulling out a glass bottle filled with liquid and another filled with cream, he held them out to her. She didn't hesitate to take them even though she didn't know what she was supposed to do with either one.

He must have read the confusion in her eyes, since he clarified, "The liquid is laudanum. Should the pain worsen, take no more than a quarter teaspoon in some water. The other is something that will bring the swelling and bruising down. You'll want to apply it directly to the sprain twice daily. I'll check on you again in a week to make sure there are no small fractures."

"What is the cream?" Elliott's voice was edged with curiosity as opposed to distrust.

"A liniment of arnica. Of course, we could bleed her instead to relieve the bad blood." The doctor seemed put out by the suggestion, as though it was the last thing he wanted to do.

Abby had never been bled in all her life. She thought the idea distasteful and said so. "I like this much more. I can't thank you enough for coming up to the castle so early in the morning, Dr. Cornwell."

"It was no bother, Miss Hallaway. I didn't have a chance to introduce myself to you at church last Sunday. Though I'd rather you hale and hearty at church than abed with a bad sprain."

"You are too kind, Dr. Cornwell. I thought you lived in the next township over."

"I do. But I grew up here. So I ride over on Sunday to attend church with my aunt."

He smiled back at her, a dimple flashing in one cheek, then turned back to Elliott. "Will it be possible for her to stay off her feet for at least a few days?"

Elliott merely nodded.

"You're in good hands with Brendall here. I'll see you in a week's time, then, Miss Hallaway."

She should offer the doctor something for his troubles. He was probably bullied out of his bed early this morning.

Abby looked to Elliott. "Lord Brendall, it would please me to speak with Dr. Cornwell alone for a moment."

She thought he'd argue, but after a pointed glare from his lordship to the doctor—who seemed not at all bothered by Elliott's gruff behavior—Elliott turned and left, striding out of the room with his back up like a cat who'd been dunked in water.

"I'm sorry that you were demanded away from your home at so early an hour. I'm grateful that you came."

"I'm glad to be of any service, Miss Hallaway. Brendall and I are old friends; he was no bother."

Unsure how to offer a barter, she boldly said, "I haven't

any coin with me, but I do have some pearl earrings—perhaps for your aunt—that I could give you for your time and your medicines."

Dr. Cornwell raised his hand in objection. "It's not necessary. I'd be well compensated merely by your presence in church again."

Oh, how had she not read his interest before this awkward moment? She couldn't help that a blush stole up her face and neck. Of course no one would think her romantically involved with Elliott. He was such a—a pigheaded oaf of a man. Dr. Cornwell was very handsome. He looked to be around the age of Elliott, maybe a year or two younger.

But he was like every other man she'd met in Town. It seemed she preferred the brooding difficult type as opposed to the kind gentleman standing before her.

"You are too kind, Dr. Cornwell. If I can convince Lord Brendall or even Lydia to church again, we would be happy to share a bench with you."

Martha's daughter, she thought, would make a wonderful wife for Dr. Cornwell. She was well spoken, could read and write, and was dedicated to her duties. Of course, much depended upon the doctor's prospects. Maybe he could not support a wife. Though she had her doubts with his simple but finely cut jacket. Having grown up well provided for, she could see that he had means of his own.

"I will look for you on Sunday, then."

Dr. Cornwell packed up his leather case and, with a tip of his hat before he placed it on his head, he left the room, whistling as he went.

She was left alone for some time. She felt nearly ignored until Elliott came into the room, body strung tight like he wanted to break something. Was he angry that she'd be off her feet? Just because she was supposed to rest her ankle didn't mean she couldn't attend to her duties and instruct his son.

"There was no need for you to offer him payment."

"You were listening?"

"Of course I listened. It's my own damn fault you met with an accident. I look after everyone in this household."

Could he really be upset about something so small? Insignificant, really.

"I didn't mean to offend you, my lord."

"Elliott, please." The anger and tension seemed to drain from his body with his request.

"It wouldn't be proper."

He shoved his hands roughly through his hair, but said not one word in disagreement. It wasn't appropriate to address each other intimately. Not when they couldn't be sure they were alone.

"If you could have the staff help me set up in one of the parlors, I'll meet with your son promptly. He'll not miss his lessons because I've sprained my ankle."

It was such a debutante thing to do—sprain her ankle and require a gentleman to come to her rescue. Though it was arguable that Elliott lived up to what being a gentleman entailed. He was too raw and gruff for so gentle a term.

"You'll rest today," he said. "Tomorrow we'll set you up for lessons downstairs."

"I can't stay in my room all day. I'll die of boredom staring at the walls."

The side of his mouth kicked up in a brief grin. How was it amusing that she'd be whiling away her day abed? She'd not spent a day solely in her bed since she was a child. And even then she couldn't recall a day where she'd done that!

"You can't mean I'm to stay in my room?"

"It would serve you right and teach you to stop wandering the castle at odd hours."

"You've been watching me." He wouldn't know her odd morning hours unless that was the truth.

It was proof enough when he did not answer her question.

"Have you any idea who might have wanted to harm me?" she asked.

"No. And I don't think it wise to advertise that fact quite yet."

"Will we mention this to the rest of the household?"

He shook his head. "No need to worry them. It could have happened by chance, someone camping near the castle or in one of the hidden grottoes startled by your presence. Everyone on staff has worked here for longer than I can remember. I rather doubt it was one of them."

"I have to agree. Makes little sense to want to rid yourself of a governess when you can't keep them here to begin with."

Her comment was a poor attempt at humor. And it made her think . . . what if this *had* happened to the past governesses? Could there be some unsavory character lurking around the castle unknown all these years? Could Elliott be mistaken in that it was someone he knew and trusted who had wanted Abby to meet her maker today?

"I'll call Lydia up to help you dress and do whatever else you women do in the morning." She was caught off guard by the quick change of subject. "Tell her to find me when you're ready to be settled downstairs."

At least he didn't argue with her desire to still be useful despite her injury.

He turned away, intent on leaving her. She should have let him walk away. But she didn't want to see the back of him quite yet. Why did she want his company? He was not an easy companion.

"You are so eager to leave me in the hands of Lydia after your earlier show of *worry*?"

He did not turn to face her as he spoke in a low, somber voice. "I'm trying to do the right thing and walk away." Was he truly afraid she might reject him again? "Earlier . . . I'm sorry."

"I am not the least bit sorry. Please . . . don't walk away."

He turned to her with a quizzical look on his face. "For the devil in me, I can't figure you out, Miss Hallaway."

Nor I you.

Maybe he wasn't the only one fighting his unruly desires.

"Do you want me to leave?" she asked. If they couldn't control their lusts, perhaps she should leave. Though it would kill her a little inside to leave Jacob behind.

"And go where?" There was a thread of worry in his voice. She breathed a sigh of relief that he didn't want her gone from the castle.

"I'm not without connections. I could easily find another position."

He shook his head. "No, I don't want you to leave."

Chapter 14

When winter thawed and spring waned into sum-
mer, a lone guard, near to his death with a knife
wound that had festered at his chest, found his way
back to his king with word of the prince on his dy-
ing breath. —*The Dragon of Brahmors*

After installing Miss Hallaway in the parlor, Elliott went
in search of his son. The boy had disappeared when it had
become apparent that the governess was indisposed in the
first hours of the day. But, vexing and stubborn as ever,
Miss Hallaway had insisted on him retrieving Jacob and
bringing him to her.

Damnable woman. She'd crawled right under his skin.
She made him want something that could never be his.
Namely, her. She was his son's governess. She was under
his employ and protection.

He couldn't offer her marriage, as was the right thing to
do after the intimacies they'd shared. No. Wright men had
no luck where women were concerned.

And he could admit he liked Miss Hallaway far too
much to put her in the same predicament as the women
who'd been mistress of the castle as far back as his great-

grandmother's time. All had died too young. None had been happy. Most had displayed some type of madness before their death.

Yet he couldn't bring their dalliance to an end. Not yet.

Was this the first of many accidents to come? His wife had met with similar events on many occasions, but he'd always thought them of her own making and imagination. None of her accidents had been so dire as being pushed from the parapet wall.

It was frustrating that he hadn't found evidence of an intruder in the castle. Something seemed off about this morning.

But who would wish Miss Hallaway harm? Could it be someone from her past? Could some unsavory character have followed her here? Was that why she'd chosen a place so far from everything and everyone she knew?

Well, damned if he knew what in hell was going on. He'd locked all the passageway doors as he'd walked the grounds and tunnels. They were now barred from everyone without a key, and he was the only one who held those particular keys. Access to those tunnels wouldn't matter to anyone living in the castle, since they rarely made use of the older passageways.

Whoever the intruder was, they had obviously used those old narrow tunnels. There was no other way to get up to the parapet wall undetected. Although the hour had been early, the sun yet to rise . . . who was to say the intruder hadn't come through any of the three gates leading into the castle?

Perhaps it would be safer to send Miss Hallaway to another posting or back to her sisters.

Who would it be safer for, though? Him? Jacob? The rest of the staff, who hadn't an inkling as to what had transpired this morning?

Despite the desire he felt for her, he actually wanted to

spend time with her just for the sake of being in her company. And that put him in a damnable spot.

The stable door was slightly ajar. A sure sign his son was hiding away here.

His son spoke in a low voice. The words not really words, but sounds. What was Jacob doing? Climbing the ladder up to the hayloft, Elliott slowed his steps to listen to his son.

". . . Pah—puh—puh . . . ra—re—ra—rase—ranse . . . purah—prah—prase. Pranse."

There was a question in his son's soft voice. Then a huff of frustration followed by the word *stupid*. Elliott stuck his head up above the landing, his curiosity piqued. His son hadn't noticed his presence as he focused on the book that lay open in his lap.

Elliott felt like he was falling from reality, from everything he thought he knew and understood. His hands gripped the end of the wooden landing until his fingers turned white from the pressure.

His son was reading.

Attempting to learn the words on the page, all on his own. Up to this point, Elliott had never seen his son holding a book. Had never seen Jacob try to read or write anything on paper.

"Prince. Prince!" Jacob shouted, finally making sense of the word that had clearly eluded him for some time.

Jacob looked up—with a smile that showed all the teeth in his mouth—and the excitement drained from his face at being caught. He slammed the book shut and held it behind his back as he got quickly to his feet.

For what reason did Jacob hide the book from him? He'd never given the boy reason to believe reading wasn't a desirable trait. In fact, this was extraordinary. Unexpected and wonderful.

They'd never talked about reading. Elliott had made

sure never to reveal his weakness, his inability to his son. Had he been wrong to do so? Did that make him a bad father? It wasn't as though he could teach Jacob the alphabet or help him to read.

Elliott rested his arms along the landing and stared at Jacob, intrigued.

They were of an image; Jacob hadn't taken after his mother in any way. Well, perhaps there was one way in which he was similar to his mother. The boy had just shown an aptitude for words that Elliott had never possessed.

It upset Elliott that his son felt any need to hide such a development from him and from Miss Hallaway. Why couldn't his son confide this secret in him? Jacob had regaled him with tales of Miss Hallaway's teaching tactics, but had never said a word about his reading. Elliott might never have known if not for accidentally coming upon him.

"Miss Hallaway has done well with your lessons," he said. He had no intention of ignoring the fact that his son was learning in leaps and bounds.

"I didn't mean to take it," Jacob blurted out.

So that was the reason for his odd behavior.

"The book is as much yours as it is mine. My mother wrote it, told me that I could be the dragon." Though he only vaguely remembered the story and he couldn't remember why his mother had told him that. He was sure it had been important all those years ago. "I remember when she sent it to London to be bound. She told me a friend of hers had illustrated all the beautiful pictures for me."

"I can keep it? You won't tell Miss Hallaway I took it?"

"Your secret is safe with me. And speaking of Miss Hallaway, she's still set on lessons today." That seemed to put a small smile back on his son's face. "She's in the morning parlor. Will you come back to the house with me?

Or do you need a moment to collect your things?" Elliott nodded, indicating the book.

Jacob turned away from him, lifted a loose floorboard, and pulled out a ragged gray cloth. Carefully wrapping up the book, he knelt on the floor to hide it in the nook before setting the wooden plank back in place.

"For what reason does it remain hidden?"

"Just till I can learn all the words. It's a surprise for Miss Hallaway."

For Miss Hallaway. Good Lord, his boy adored the woman probably as much as he did.

The first thing Elliott planned to do when he returned to the house was find a nicer cloth to protect the leather-bound book. He'd give it to his son when Miss Hallaway wasn't around.

Stepping down the ladder, he waited for Jacob to follow him, pride filling him like a refreshing breath of air.

Perhaps he wasn't a complete failure where his son was concerned. Not that he'd take any credit for the current strides. No, this was all Miss Hallaway's doing. It made Elliott want to pick her up and swing her around so he could share the joy he felt. To kiss her soundly on the mouth and tell her that he could adore no woman more.

He scratched at his jaw. That wouldn't do. Not at all. He was supposed to talk himself out of liking her so damn much.

Abby gave a cheery smile, not wanting to worry Jacob unnecessarily with her leg perched up on a pillow, wrapped snugly in strips of linen Lydia had torn up for her. Her injury probably looked far worse than it really was.

Elliott followed closely behind, but stopped just inside the door.

"Good morning, young master."

She nodded in the direction of Elliott. Aside from that

small acknowledgment of his presence, it took everything in Abby to not look directly at him. It took every bit of her concentration to focus on Jacob and not hope to catch Elliott's eye. But she desperately wanted to read the thoughts in his gaze. She wondered if he regretted that they'd pleasured each other. Regretted that they couldn't seem to keep their hands to themselves whenever they found themselves ensconced in a room alone.

"What's happened to you, Miss Hallaway?"

Jacob stood frozen in the entry next to his father. Elliott seemed more at ease than she. She hated him a little for that. How unfair that he could compose himself when she felt ragged and confused by all the events of the day.

It probably would have been smarter to rest the remainder of the day, but she could not lie abed doing nothing. There were unexplained happenings in the household and a mystery for her to solve. And solve it she would.

The whole time she'd been trying to make polite conversation with Lydia, she had been wondering about her fall. Did she pose some sort of threat? Had someone noticed her growing attachment to Elliott and despised the fact that she was the hired help? It certainly seemed that no one had noticed them together. They'd been careful. Both had been more intent on ignoring and avoiding each other than anything else over the past week. Or so she had thought.

Elliott bowed and left the room.

Worry was evident in Jacob's expression as he came forward.

"I took a tumble. My own fault for not watching where I walked."

Jacob looked worried enough for her welfare that she didn't want to distress him with so much as a hint of the truth of her morning jaunt.

When he still didn't speak to her, she said, "Our lessons

will be decidedly less exciting now that we'll be confined to the house for the next few days."

"I don't mind." He sat on the cushion at the end of the window seat, staring down at her elevated leg with wide eyes.

He would mind once he realized they'd have to tackle his language studies while stuck indoors. In fact, they'd mostly focus on his reading and writing and less on the subjects he favored.

"I need you to retrieve my journal." Which she used solely for outlining Jacob's lessons. "A few pencils and your writing things."

Jacob's nose scrunched, causing the skin to wrinkle between his eyes, but he stood without so much as a grumble and did her bidding.

Maybe she'd have him remembering the whole alphabet if they worked diligently over the next few days.

Jacob came back into the room. He carried her letter cards, too. When she'd first shown him those cards, he'd told her that he'd never seen a lot of the animals she'd painted, aside from the ones that lived near the castle. Abby could guess picture books held little value to the child since he had never been taught to read the simple words associated with the paintings.

"Thank you." She reached out for the cards and other items she'd requested. "We still haven't found the fable of the dragon prince, have we?"

He shook his head and pulled a chair over to where she was perched in the window seat.

"I will do the math lessons you wrote out later, miss."

She grinned at Jacob. Had she known she'd have his complete cooperation now that she was confined to a bench, she might have been tempted to do herself damage some days ago. It might have saved them both from some aggravation where his language studies were concerned.

Abby shuffled her letter cards to mix the order. The first she pulled was an *e*, and the bird depicted was a confection of tawny brown feathers, long legs, long neck, and big beady amber eyes.

"Emu," Jacob replied easily. There were only a few letters that mixed him up now that he'd been through the cards a handful of times over the past week.

"Very good—now write it down on your board and flip it so I can see it."

He tilted the board toward himself and scratched out the letter with chalk before turning it back to her.

"Excellent. Do you remember the lowercase lettering?"

Without answering, he spun the board around and did as she requested. When he showed her his work, the letter was reversed. She'd not reprimand him for it. What mattered was that he tried, even knowing he was making mistakes.

The good majority of his letters were reversed. She'd noticed that habit of his over the past week. Surely it was common to someone learning language and grasping all its nuances for the first time.

"That'll do," she said. "What other words do you think start with the letter *e*?"

And their lesson went on the remainder of the morning. Elliott visited her when Jacob left to retrieve luncheon for them both.

"I am relieved to see you," she told him. Elliott paused just inside the door, one eyebrow raised in question. "Lydia helped me to my feet earlier."

"The doctor suggested you stay off your feet."

She snorted at that. It was impossible to stay sitting when the maid kept plying her with tea to help with her constitution.

"I will not remain idle for the next few days. I grow ill from being constantly indoors. Could you help me around the grounds for a breath of fresh air after Jacob and I have had something to eat? I really do feel overly confined having to sit here all day. Especially now that the sun has come out."

She thought he'd refuse her. Instead he surprised her by saying, "Once around the bailey, then you are to stay indoors for the remainder of the night."

She smiled her appreciation and was about to ask what she'd do to keep herself occupied come evening when Jacob entered the room with Lydia and two serving trays laden with simple fare.

Lydia curtsied on seeing his lordship. The girl bit her lip and said, "There's not enough for a proper meal for the three of you. Let me retrieve another dish of sweetmeats."

Lord Brendall looked as though he had planned to leave. Instead he nodded toward the maid. "Yes, I'll be taking this meal with my son."

Abby had thought Elliott never dined with his son, especially for the midday meal. Her suspicion was confirmed when Lydia paused, looked back to his lordship with stunned shock coloring her expression before she left the three of them alone in the parlor.

Jacob set down his tray on a round table close to her, close enough that Abby could serve herself. She twisted around on the seat, intent on helping herself to some food.

Lord Brendall picked up one of the dishes and raised a brow in her direction. For some reason, she didn't think he planned on serving himself first. Lydia arrived shortly with more food and another dish.

"Is there anything you object to in the setting?" Elliott motioned toward the platters of sweetmeats, cheeses, and bread.

"No, my lord," Abby responded.

What would Jacob think seeing the lord of the castle

waiting hand and foot on her? "Please . . . let me," she said as he forked a few choice selections of the cheese.

"I insist." He gave her a pointed look, stalling her from getting to her feet. "You'll need to get your strength up if we're to head outdoors."

"True," she agreed, since arguing with the man was like arguing with a stone wall.

Jacob stood away from the table, clearly hungry if the gleam in his round eyes was anything to go by.

Elliott must have noticed. He said, "Serve yourself something, Jacob. I'm taking care of Miss Hallaway."

His tone was gruff, but Jacob was evidently used to it since he didn't flinch at the demand. He didn't step forward to help himself until Elliott came toward her, handing her the plate. She doubted she'd be able to eat the amount of food he had served her.

He picked up the cushion that had toppled to the floor and set it up on the bench again.

Expecting him to stop there, she nearly dropped her platter of food to the floor when he lifted her injured leg and swung her back into a position she'd begun to abhor today.

"Lord Brendall," she admonished, then tempered her voice, realizing Jacob watched them closely as he loaded his plate with sandwiches. "Thank you. I've been forced to endure this seating arrangement for half a day now. I can manage quite well on my own." She loathed the fact that he treated her like the damsel in distress, especially in front of others.

"I'll not take you around the grounds if your ankle swells more because you've not done as the doctor directed."

She'd save her argument that she could take care of herself for when his son wasn't a spectator.

"Very well. I'll do my best to keep rested for the next hour or two." Abby turned to Jacob then and said, "Bring your board over here, so I can show your father what we've worked on these past weeks."

He hesitated only a moment, looking uncomfortable at the prospect of sharing what he'd learned with his father. Reluctantly, he picked up his chalkboard and handed it to her before taking the chair across from her.

They'd been working on the letter *s*. A complicated letter when one was learning language. He still inverted the letter. Handing the board to Elliott, she awaited his response. Hopefully he wouldn't care that the letters were reversed. It was his right, she supposed, to take notice and try to correct the habit in his son. But she hoped he'd take notice of how well his son was doing before lecturing him on how to properly go about writing.

Elliott stared down at the board for a full minute, his brows furrowed. He didn't look as though he were reading the words, just staring at what his son had done. Was he disappointed? Surely not! Jacob had come far and had exceeded her expectations in so short a while.

Jacob remained silent and had in fact stopped eating as he stared inquisitively at his father.

Without saying a word, he handed the small board back to her, stood from the window bench, and walked over to the table to put down his plate. Jacob's only reaction was to shove the remainder of his cold meats in his mouth.

Perhaps she acted too hastily in sharing Jacob's progress. True, it wasn't what other children his age might be capable of. But it was a step in the right direction. And she'd make Elliott take notice of Jacob's improvements. The boy needed the encouragement of his father. Didn't Elliott see that?

* * *

It had been a long day. Inwardly, he had had to battle his want to stay in her company. But spending the day in her company wasn't possible. He had his own tasks to accomplish, his own life to see to. However, in light of everything that had transpired and the subsequent excitement it had put the castle in, he'd declared today a day of rest and minimal work.

Although he hadn't spent the full day in Abigail's company, he'd opted to spend a few hours with her and Jacob after lunch. He'd meant to take her for a short walk around the bailey, then bring her back into the house to rest her ankle. But she'd convinced him to stay outdoors longer.

Jacob had retrieved an old walking stick for his governess and they had followed her lead outside while she hobbled around the grounds. When her strength had started to wane, he'd given her an arm to lean on. It would have been best to go indoors at that point, but the feel of her next to him, all warm and smelling of flowers, had him eager to stay outdoors.

When she'd completely taxed herself of energy and said a few expletives away from the ears of Jacob, he'd wrapped his arm around her waist and only let her do half the work in walking.

He'd said nothing during their time together. Instead, he'd listened as Abigail had shouted out complex mathematical equations and his son had prattled off answers in quick succession. So now he knew what they did while outdoors on their morning, and occasionally afternoon, walks.

It eased his heart to know that she worked diligently with Jacob, whether they were in the library or outside.

And Jacob . . . it was obvious the boy had grown close to her in such a short time. Perhaps he saw a mother-like figure in her. Or a friend. More likely the latter since none of the other governesses had tried so hard as Abigail.

While he currently paced the corridor, he knew she rested in the library with a book in hand; at least that was how he'd seen her an hour ago. Martha and the rest of his staff had retired for the evening. So they were quite alone. It was what he had wanted all day, but now that the time had arrived, he wasn't sure having her all to himself was a good idea. After their early-morning interlude, he'd no idea how their evening would unfold.

He ambled back toward the library. She'd proven well enough this afternoon that she could walk on her own, yet Elliott didn't plan for her to find her way upstairs alone. Not tonight.

On entering the library, he was surprised to find her sitting primly in a chair, her shoeless foot resting on a few cushions that had been placed on the floor.

"I didn't think you'd tarry so long this evening."

He stalled in his steps for only a moment. He hadn't wasted any time in coming for her. But she would not understand his need to protect what was his. He'd not fail another person in his care. Especially not someone he was growing to care for.

For the first time in all his life, Elliott had closed every window and door lock on the main floor of the house. He was always up before the sun rose, so he'd open up the house for the serving staff before they arrived tomorrow. But from this point forward he'd take extra precautions where his governess and his boy were concerned.

He made no response until he approached her and gathered her up in his arms.

She made a sound of protest, saying, "You can't just cart me around as you please, my lord. I do not need your help up to my room."

"I prefer to carry you. Make a choice: my room or yours."

She looked him over a long moment. Did she understand the implication of what was left unsaid? Would she refuse him now? Reject him? His palms felt suddenly damp, but he could do nothing about them right now.

"My room," she finally replied, her hand sliding behind the collar of his shirt, threading through the hair at the back of his head. "Are you always this domineering?"

He chuckled and said, "Yes. A rather unfortunate trait of mine."

He couldn't look at her after responding. If he did that, he'd start kissing her, then they wouldn't make it out of the library for some hours. He had to force himself to go slowly up the stairs, to not take them two at a time as he desperately wanted.

Settling her on her bed, he turned back to the door to lock it behind them. She pushed down the bedding and released the buttons that held a small piece of lace at her wrist.

Unable to take his eyes from her, he watched her loosen the pins in her hair as he placed logs into the fireplace and lit a fire. The room was chilled, but would warm soon enough.

What did she think of him right now? Did she think him a cad, planning on taking advantage of her? Suddenly it dawned on him that nothing could come of tonight. She must be tired after everything that had happened today. He certainly was. They'd sleep, but he'd sleep in her room even though the house was locked up and safe for the remainder of the night. And he'd sleep in her bed because he wanted the feel of her body lying next to him.

If he couldn't spend his days with her, he'd do his damnedest in making sure their evenings were spent together.

"You mean to stay?"

He stood now that the fire was well lit and pulled his shirt from his trousers. "I thought I made that clear in the library."

"What I meant was . . . you intend the spend the whole night sleeping in this bed with me?"

"Yes." He pulled his shirt over his head and hung it on the chair tucked under the escritoire. She chewed on her bottom lip as she stared back at him.

His trousers would have to remain on. Any less clothing between them and he would be tempted to put them in an entirely different position, one with her legs wrapped around his hips.

"Do you think harm will come to me when I'm sleeping or have you something else in mind?"

"Nothing else in mind. You need your rest."

Her look was skeptical.

She didn't believe him. First, he'd locked them in her room so there could be no interruptions. Second, he was very visibly aroused. And she was still fully clothed. What would happen once she undressed for bed? Third, she wanted to reach out and touch the speckling of hair on his beautifully formed chest.

She'd never been overly shy. Even though she'd never undressed for a man before, she didn't feel nervous. Silly to be nervous after the things they had done with each other. Maidenly reservations simply weren't part of her makeup. If there was one thing she had learned from her eldest sister, it was that there was nothing to be ashamed about in nudity. The images her sister painted made the female form appear only beautiful. Of course she wouldn't be completely naked. She'd still have on her unmentionables.

"Are you happy with your son's progress?" She hadn't forgotten his silence this afternoon after seeing the chalkboard.

"More than you can imagine."

"You did not seem pleased when he showed you his board. I understand that his letters are still inverted, but that should correct itself as time goes on. As he practices his writing and reading and gains a better grasp on language in general, it'll start to disappear."

At least that was what she hoped. Jacob had proved to be a bright child, so she trusted what her instincts told her on this matter.

"I was well pleased."

"Then why didn't you appear so to me?" What was odd was that Jacob hadn't seemed bothered by his father's reaction. Maybe she was making too big a deal about this.

"This is a conversation for another day."

She pinched her lips together, disappointed that he wouldn't talk about things of a more personal nature. Things that would surely shine a light upon the deeper feelings this man held for those he cared about.

As she pulled her bodice off, the material got stuck at her elbow. Elliott knelt on the bed and helped her slide the satiny cloth off. He opened the wardrobe to retrieve a hanger.

On opening the door, he stilled. His jaw clenched as he pulled a hanger down, and shoved the material inside.

"I'm sorry I haven't moved your wife's old things from my room. I wasn't sure where to put them."

"No need to apologize. It's Martha who should have had the items removed from here long ago."

"Haven't your other governesses said anything about the dresses?"

"They stayed in another room."

"Oh. Then why didn't you put me in the room they used?"

He shrugged. "This one was made up. Their accommodations were on the main floor, behind the kitchen. You seemed too delicate to put there. All the past governesses were sturdier and hardier in nature. At least they always looked that way to me."

Abby snorted. He obviously didn't know her well enough yet to make such a bold and false statement. She was no weeping, limp willow.

"Don't you find it uncanny to share a bed with me in here? One you shared with your wife?"

"This was her spare room. She never slept here."

"I've been all over this house. This is the second nicest room to yours."

"She slept in my room till Jacob was born."

"And after?"

"There were rooms above the old church."

"The church?" Why in heavens would she be put there? Away from the house, from Elliott, and from her son?

That also meant that the church must have fallen more recently than she'd thought and not during some forgotten battle of centuries past. Should she ask what happened? Eventually she would find out the truth, but not tonight.

Abby slid her skirt from her waist, letting the pleated material fall to the floor. She couldn't be bothered to pick it up since that would mean standing on her foot. She was just too tired to lift another finger. Elliott was right in that they had both had too much excitement today.

She looked at him quizzically as he picked up the flounces of satin and linen and placed it over the chair.

She held out her hand, wanting to feel his warm body tucked alongside hers. She wondered if this was how married couples acted. If they discussed their lives, their day-to-day, before retiring for the evening. She imagined so.

He snuffed the candle; the only thing to see by now was the fire burning warm and bright in the fireplace.

He lifted her from the edge of the bed and placed her in the center as he climbed in next to her. She rolled to her back wanting to see him, talk to him right into the wee hours of the morning if she could.

Elliott propped himself up on his arm next to her and brushed strands of hair away from her face.

"Will you tell me Bethesda's story?"

"She was my mother's nursemaid in the village and Martha's aunt. She lived here until I was around seven, but my father made her leave. My mother walked out into the sea three days after that."

Abby stretched her fingers toward his jawline and traced around the tip in his chin.

Not only had his wife ended her own life, his mother had, too.

"You must remember her fondly. I'm sorry about your mother."

"I am, too. But it's too late to be changed."

"Seems odd that both their lives ended so tragically and in somewhat the same fashion."

Instead of responding, he leaned in close to her and pressed his lips to hers. He parted her mouth enough that he could suck and nibble the lower lip between his, then the upper.

She gave a breathy moan into his mouth, hungry for so much more, but too tired to take what she wanted. He pulled away, turned her to her side, and settled in tight at her back, her rear tucked into his groin, her back along his chest, his arm wrapped around her middle and tucked tightly between the bed and her waist.

The last thing on her mind before sleep took over was: When you fall in love with someone, does your notion of marriage change? Do you ultimately decide that life alone will no longer do? Not that Elliott was offering marriage. It was silly to even think about such things, seeing as she'd always been adamant in not wanting to end up shackled to any man.

She closed her eyes, convinced that all she needed was a good night's sleep. In the morning, she would forget that she had contemplated the ridiculous notion of marriage at all.

Chapter 15

*In lands far away from the Kingdom of Brahmors,
a battle was fought on a blood-spattered field and
the prince fell to his knees, but not from the bite of
a blade.*   —The Dragon of Brahmors

Elliott wasn't sure what had awoken him. He'd been warm
and cozy holding Abigail in his arms, and then he'd heard
something that had made him spring up in bed and look
around the room. Had someone just rattled the doorknob?
Had the noise been the wind shaking the windows?

Nothing seemed out of place. Not that anything should
be since he'd locked the chamber door behind them last
night. There was a clock on her escritoire, but the fire had
died down too much to make out the hour.

Tucking the blankets he'd displaced back around Abigail, he got up to build the fire and listen to the sounds
around him. Unease crept through his body. Something
seemed off. He'd need to check on his son just as soon as
the fire warmed the room again.

Grabbing up his shirt, he tossed it over his head and
found his shoes next. He'd not leave any evidence that he
had been in the governess's room overnight. He'd not leave

any clues that he'd ever been in here aside from when the doctor had visited.

All his things gathered up, he approached the bed one last time. He brushed a few strands of hair away from Abigail's face. He'd confided a lot about himself to her. She'd probably been too tired to rationally digest what he'd said, but he didn't doubt she'd have questions today.

How much should he tell her about his past? He'd not talked about the events that had unfolded during the months leading up to his wife's death. It might have happened seven years ago, but he could recall every detail as if it had happened only yesterday. And it had him thinking, wondering. His wife had been convinced that someone—she often blamed him—wanted to harm her. Had he been blind to some unknown threat or had she really gone mad?

The doctor had confirmed that Madeline's mind was fragile. And Elliott trusted Dr. Cornwell's—Patrick's—opinion. The man had tried to help, had prescribed laudanum after she'd had Jacob, and had even gone so far as to visit every few weeks to see if his wife's condition would improve. It hadn't. And now she lay in a lonely grave soon to be forgotten by the rest of the world.

He knew the local townsfolk thought he had burned down the church with his wife inside. He'd not told anyone about what had transpired that day. He'd never talked about it with Thomas, Martha, or Lydia. It simply wasn't spoken of.

He wondered what else Bethesda had whispered to Abigail in her hatred and rage toward the inhabitants at Brendall Castle, namely him.

He couldn't blame the old woman. She'd been wronged somehow. He was sure his mother had documented it in her journals, only he could read no more than the numbered dates. She'd written multiple times a day in the weeks leading up to her walk into the sea. He could not bring himself to ask Martha to read them. He did not want to shine any ill-begotten lights upon his mother and the memory people had for her.

How much more of that sordid, ugly past would Abigail want him to reveal?

Letting himself out of Abigail's room, he walked down the hall to Jacob's chamber. His boy was sound asleep. Fixing up the fire in his son's room, he went back to his chambers to divest himself of yesterday's clothes and displace the counterpane and sheets to make it look as though he'd slept in his own bed.

Then he walked the corridors of the upper floor. The normal sounds of the old house wouldn't have awakened him from a dead sleep at three in the morning. So something else had to have disturbed him. Taking the stairs to the third floor, he stopped every few paces to listen to the sounds of the night. Nothing unusual to be heard.

The old floorboards creaked in protest under his weight. Elliott hadn't been up to this floor since his son was born, hadn't liked the memories associated with this place and his wife's final months.

The air was stale and dusty. A window probably hadn't been cracked open up here in near to eight years. They'd probably seized shut in this forgotten realm abovestairs. There was no sign of a disturbance in any of the rooms, so he headed down to the main floor. The hour was still too early to unlock the house, so he padded around the house quietly checking each room before moving on to the next.

Nothing seemed out of order. His imagination was getting the better of him in light of yesterday's events.

Making his way to the study, he turned suddenly when he heard a sound that could only be described as someone dragging themselves across the wooden floor. Hand raised to the wall for balance, Elliott tried to determine the direction of the sound, but it stopped just as swiftly as it had come.

Thinking it nothing more than the wind playing tricks on his mind, he entered his study and set himself to lighting a fire to stave off the early-morning chill.

Now that his thoughts weren't focused on finding something untoward and shifty in his home, his mind turned to Abigail.

He'd shocked himself by how much he'd so unwittingly shared. Even though she'd reached out an accepting hand to him last night, that didn't mean she'd remain sympathetic to him today. She knew one of his secrets. Maybe the smallest fact, but it could still have a bearing on what she thought of him come morning when she'd had time to sleep on what he'd revealed.

How would she react if she knew the whole truth surrounding his wife's death? Or the sad truth with regard to his son's lack in aptitude where his studies were concerned?

Abby awoke to a warm room, but a cold bed. She turned on her side and stretched her hand over the spot Elliott had slept in. It shouldn't bother or upset her that he hadn't stayed till morning. The household, and Jacob, could never know of their growing relationship. It would remain a secret for as long as she shared his bed, or he hers as the situation had presented itself last night.

As long as they lived in this house together they'd remain strangers by day, familiar companions by night.

It made her feel like Cinderella, only her allotted time with her prince ceased upon the morning hour, not at the strike of midnight. By day, she was back to the rags of a servant, by night she'd don the opulent silks of a woman fallen and half in love with the man occupying her bed.

Nothing good could come of her time with Elliott. Heartache when it was time for her to leave, but that was her own foolishness for opening up her heart to the man, for allowing herself to feel something that went beyond friendship and closer to love.

Rubbing her eyes, she tossed the thought to the farthest reaches of her mind and yawned her welcome to the day. She couldn't define it as love yet. She hardly knew Elliott. In time, she had no doubt she'd fall in love with him, but now . . . she was merely fascinated by what she didn't understand and craved his company for more carnal reasons. Or at least that was what she would tell herself.

Swinging her legs over the bed, she tested her weight on her injured ankle before she stood. Her ankle felt a great deal better, but she'd not chance putting her full support on it.

Not wanting to lounge about in her chamber too long this morning, she cleaned up quickly at the washstand and dressed.

At some point in the evening, or maybe even early morning, Elliott had brought the walking stick up and set it by the door so she couldn't miss it on her way out of her chamber. The thoughtful gesture made her blood pump faster in her veins as she made her way downstairs.

Elliott stood at the foot of the staircase when she turned on the landing above. She couldn't help the smile that naturally lightened her face on seeing him.

"Good morning," she called to him and grasped the railing before slowly taking her steps.

"And to you." He stepped close to whisper that seductively. His hand came around the small of her back as he lifted her tight against his body and brought her down the last few steps and set her gently on the floor. "It seems a good night's rest has put a healthy glow back in your cheeks."

"I've always had a hearty constitution."

"Glad to know you can't be kept down for long."

There was so much suggestion in his last comment that her heart tripped crazily in her chest. She wanted to close her eyes and lean into him. Tilt her head back and feel the heat of his mouth on hers. Not where anyone could see them, though. Instead of leaning into him, she took a step back and inhaled deeply, trying to gather her thoughts.

"Nothing gets me down for long, my lord." She added the last with a curtsy on seeing Lydia and Martha turning toward them at the far end of the corridor.

Elliott spun around to see what had arrested her gaze and probably to determine the reason she'd suddenly turned formal.

He turned back to her, giving a surprising wink. "Don't strain yourself overmuch today, Miss Hallaway. Jacob needs you well if he's to make further advances in his studies."

With that, he walked toward his study. Lydia gave her a cordial greeting on the way past. Martha said nothing, didn't even so much as glance Abby's way. What had she done to displease the older woman now?

She wouldn't worry on it. Martha would have to learn to like her, because Abby had no plans of seeking employment elsewhere.

Abby found Jacob in the same parlor they'd occupied yesterday. At the door, she said, "You're down before me, young master."

"Father said to help you."

He stood before her, hands clasped in front of him. He was neatly attired in gray short pants and a pressed white shirt; his hair was clean and combed back from his face. Was he making an effort to come to her cleaned up or was the household staff to thank for this sudden change in his appearance? Either way, it pleased her.

"Gather up our materials from yesterday." There were only a few things scattered around the parlor; she left him to collect the items so she wasn't hobbling around on her sore ankle. "I'll not lie here like an invalid for days on end. We'll go back to the library where all my accoutrements are within reach."

He was quick in following her to the other room. She paused on entering, astonished by the progress she'd made with her young pupil. He seemed most apt and willing to learn this morning. More attentive than he'd ever been before.

She gave him an inquiring look. What had changed over the last week? Aside from his grasp on language?

"Have you decided that you like the schoolroom?" she asked.

He scratched at his head and screwed up his face as he thought of an answer. "You're different from the other teachers. They didn't like me. Said I was a heathen child before they could show me any letterings like you did. And they never let me teach them nothing."

"Anything," she corrected, then pressed her lips together in thought.

Did Elliott know of the treatment his son had received prior to her coming here? Not just from Martha, but now she was hearing tales of previous governesses' cruelties. How could anyone treat a child without compassion?

"Perhaps they were the heathens," she teased, getting a smile and laugh out of him. "You should have put frogs in their beds. I did that once, but to my eldest sister. My father laughed and laughed and told her that she should guard her tongue before calling me an unruly child."

"I thought girls didn't like frogs."

"What's not to love about frogs? Perhaps we'll go hunting for them come spring. Don't imagine you can scare me by putting them in my bed. You'll have to be more inventive than that. I should warn you, not even snakes or spiders will scare me."

Jacob's eyes went wide. "I wouldn't, miss. I promise."

She ruffled his hair with a laugh, then hobbled her way over to her chair and sat behind the wide desk. Her ankle ached something fierce. She'd overtaxed herself in their walk yesterday. She'd have to stay indoors today. At least she wasn't confined to a window seat.

"Come, we have much to do this morning."

Jacob pulled his chair around to her side and sat next to her. He placed his mathematics workbook on the desk and opened it to the last lesson she'd given him.

"Did you have any questions or problems with the work I assigned you?"

He shook his head. She looked over the fractions all neatly written out. Not a scratch mark to be found, or an error for that matter, as she checked his fractions added and multiplied and divided correctly.

"You have a great talent for math. When we have you reading better, we'll introduce some word problems to give you more variety."

"Math was the only thing the other governesses taught me. Said I wasn't good for anything else, so they made sure I knew my numbers till I could do them with my eyes closed."

Abby's heart ached for the boy. She stretched her hand out to pat his hands, which were folded over on top of the desk.

"You're an excellent pupil in all subjects, Jacob. Were your governesses often unkind to you?"

He shook his head. "No. I remembered because of what you said about math."

"Do you want to talk about the teachers you've had before me?"

He shook his head again. "None of them stayed long. I can't remember them all."

"I hope I'm not as forgettable, then. I'll do my best to make a positive impression upon your young mind."

"I'll not forget you, Miss Hallaway. Not ever."

She leaned back in her chair and looked her charge over, caught off guard by the sincerity in his voice. She'd never forget him, either. He'd so easily stolen a spot in her heart. She hadn't realized how much she'd loved to be in the company of children.

"I found a children's book a few days ago. If you'll retrieve it from the shelf." She pointed to where she'd set it, facing forward so it could be found again. "It's a simple fable, and I will help you read every single word if we must. I want you to sound out the letters with me so you can learn to recognize them and group them on your own."

When he sat back down next to her, he didn't make so much as a grumble for having to read. Not like their first day together. She was making great improvements with him. She was a little proud of herself for doing so. Never had she thought to be important in someone's life. But that was how she felt when she worked with Jacob.

She'd still make a point of discussing Jacob's past governesses with Elliott. He should know what they'd said about his son. Maybe even talk to Jacob about it, assure him that they were sorely incorrect.

The thought of Elliott had her thinking ahead to her evening. Would he come to her chamber again? She'd never imagined him to be the playful type, but he'd enjoyed teasing her this morning.

Something had changed yesterday between them to bring on that playfulness, or at least last night. After a night in his arms, she could easily forget that what she was doing was wrong. How could anything she shared with Elliott ever be wrong, though?

She'd always insisted on remaining unmarried. Seemed she would get her wish. It shouldn't matter that she was enjoying intimacies with a man in an unsanctified union. She'd not regret it. Not when it felt so right.

She hadn't any room for Elliott in her thoughts right now. Her sole focus should be Jacob. Opening the book on the desk, she pointed to the first word and asked him which letter it was.

Chapter 16

The prince had screamed the sound of death, the noise so splitting that the war ceased and had to end. Where the prince had stood proud and bearing, a dragon festered from the air of despairing.
—*The Dragon of Brahmors*

Elliott watched Miss Hallaway—Abigail—from the library entrance. Her head was bent over a book, her mind solely focused there. He doubted she realized he stood there, which was fine with him; he enjoyed watching her.

He had made a point of coming up to the house to see her and Jacob at least once a day. In the last week, he'd lunched with them thrice and taken supper with his son nightly.

He had stopped outside her bedchamber on a nightly basis, had often come close to tapping his knuckles on the door to see if she'd allow him entrance, but had stopped himself short. He was desperate to have her. Had hardly slept in want of her company, when he remembered the feel of her soft, small body draped over him in sleep. He craved a repeat of that night.

His resolve to leave her be had diminished significantly. At some point this week, he'd talked himself into ignoring decency. She'd shown no outward signs of madness. Though it had taken Madeline some months to become the creature she'd become, he had a feeling Abigail was made of much sterner stuff.

He doubted his ability to walk away from her tonight. After inspecting the whole house, making sure it was locked for the evening and double-checking that they were quite alone, he'd headed in her direction. He couldn't guess what the evening would bring, but he would spend at least part of it with the governess.

They'd built a comfortable friendship of sorts. She told him about his son's accomplishments daily and didn't pester him with any more questions about his past.

He listened to everything she said, his heart full in knowing his son was in good hands with Abigail. She'd not let his boy falter, and if Jacob had any troubles he knew without doubt she'd be there to catch him before he could really stumble.

The top buttons of her dress were loosened, but folded over in a way that he couldn't get a glimpse of her creamy skin beneath. What would it feel like to dip his fingers behind the material, run the back of his knuckles over the top swell of her breasts? Whisk her up into his arms and carry her to her room?

The last time they'd found themselves in each other's arms was three nights ago. The heated kiss had had him hard and aching for release for the remainder of the night. Their embrace had been cut short when they'd heard someone approaching the library and he'd stepped out of view so no one would see him in her company. They'd not been discovered, but it had been a reminder that they should think twice before they acted impulsively.

He didn't want to avoid her any longer. There was no

denying that there was something burning in her gaze, something that told him she wanted more as well. If their want was mutual, then why shy away from it? Why deny it? He was done running from it. He wanted more of her. More time, more gazes, more touches, just more.

Where was his resolve to save her from him now?

As he approached her, he cleared his throat to draw her attention to his presence.

She stood and shut the book she'd been engrossed in. "I hadn't realized it was so late."

She placed the book back on the shelf, sticking out so she'd no doubt find it easily the next time she wanted to read it. He wished he knew what she read. What kinds of stories or poetry she liked.

"I didn't mean to startle you."

She busied herself by righting her desk. Didn't take a genius to figure out that she was nervous. Was it because it was late, and they were all alone? There was no one to interrupt them, no son, no staff. Just them.

"How were lessons today?" he asked, hoping to draw her attention to him and not inanimate objects.

"Your son's skills in math are extraordinary. Did you know?"

He well knew that because it was the only thing he could teach Jacob. He scratched his jaw to hide his amusement at her compliment.

"He's a bright boy."

"I still don't understand why all the past governesses lasted so short a time. Did none show your son compassion?"

He shook his head. He might have had something to do with them leaving; he hadn't liked any of them. They'd been stodgy and uptight, harsh with his son, tight-lipped and temperamental with him. Jacob hadn't liked any one of them . . . until Miss Hallaway.

"The whims of a woman are oft hard to explain."

"Have you just insulted me?" There was no displeasure in her question. She smiled and walked toward the sitting area in the library. "I know you take a glass of whiskey in the evening, but the library is not stocked so I cannot offer you a nightcap."

"We could retire to my study."

Though his purpose in suggesting such had nothing to do with wanting to sip on whiskey—more likely her mouth, her neck, or perhaps he could lick droplets of the fiery liquid from her heated flesh in the throes of passion. His eyes dipped to where the buttons had been loosened on her bodice. The slightest hint of pale skin could be made out beneath.

Should she reject his offer, he'd walk away. He hoped he could temper any disappointment, too.

"And what is in it for me, my lord?"

His eyes met hers again. There was a spark of mischief in hers.

"Does the lady wish a nightcap for herself?"

Her chin jutted up, and one eyebrow rose. "I suppose I would."

Before she could come to him, he was on her, hands tangled at the back of her hair, their mouths crushed together so he could taste what he'd craved most. Her arms wrapped around his neck, her back arched over his other arm. God, a mere look from her and he was hard and raring to go.

Her fingers were tight at his scalp, massaging him there. Holding him in place. He forced himself to slow down, to work the pins loose from her scalp and pull free from her hair. His mouth lightened upon hers, sipping instead of drinking deeply from them.

He said, "I've not been able to get you out of my head for days. Have dreamed of doing this."

She gasped in surprise, fingers sliding away from his scalp to hold on to his shoulders. Did she think he wouldn't have her on his mind constantly?

She nibbled at her lower lip before saying, "Spend the night with me again, Elliott."

How could he deny himself any longer? How could he say no? He knelt to clasp her under the knees and swung her up into his arms.

There'll be no going back after this, he thought. There was no stopping it from happening, either.

Abby hadn't expected him to sweep her up into his arms like some knight errant stealing away a lady. Fingers tracing the hard lines of his face, she felt the firmness in his clenched jaw, the stubble that roughened his face, the dip in his chin that she wanted to lick.

For a week, they'd danced around each other like nothing extraordinary was happening between them. Like they hadn't slept in the same bed overnight and indulged in intimacies that should be shared only between husband and wife. Like they didn't have growing feelings for each other.

She was falling in love with him. There was no denying that fact. Whether he felt the same she couldn't guess. She'd not ask him outright, either.

He'd teased and cajoled her this past week. Had shown a tender side to his character with his sudden presence in his son's daily lessons. He was a good man, despite what he might think of himself and his past.

He was the man she was going to give her heart and her body to. Only she'd not tell him of the former; something held her back from giving that much of herself away. She didn't know what, but until she figured it out she'd say nothing. She'd just enjoy her time with Elliott.

Once in her room, he slowly released his hold on her

legs and let her slide down the front of his body. He searched for the ties holding her skirts in place, and yanked them loose.

Plastered to his front like she was, the stubborn material stayed put. Her hands pressed to his pectorals, the feel of the muscle beneath made her breath rush in and out of her lungs. His back was to the door. He made no move to urge her toward the bed. In fact, he did nothing more than trace his thumb over her cheek and then her lips.

"I've never wanted anything so bad as I have wanted this," he said.

She had no words to respond with. He had as good as admitted the depth of his feelings for her—hadn't he? Did this mean he was falling in love with her, too? She'd never been so afraid in all her life as to admit how she felt. Instead of responding, she stepped away from him and pushed her skirts down, working the ties beneath loose and working her bodice free so she was left standing in nothing but her unmentionables.

He didn't move forward, but savored every reveal; she saw that in the way his eyes grew hooded with sexual intent.

"Are you sure?"

She nodded. She wanted to be wholly his. To be claimed by one man and only one. Him. She needed him, she realized. She didn't want to continue on without knowing this man intimately. There was no backing down, or pulling away. She wanted this as much as she wanted her independence. Once her mind was made up, she went charging forward with the determination of a bull with its sights on red.

She'd let him remove her underclothes when the time came, but first she wanted nothing more than to explore the hard planes of his body under her hands, against her body, around her body.

She pushed his suspenders from his shoulders and hiked

his shirt out of his trousers, brushing her fingers over the firmness of his stomach and torso. He helped her remove the garment, letting it drop to the floor when it was finally over his head.

She studied his chest, the strong lines, felt the muscles of his pectorals, the coarse hair trailing between them and downward. As she brushed her finger over one tight nipple, he let out a harsh groan before muttering, "My turn."

His hands came firm around her. His fingers stretched proprietarily over her lower back, his hand like a hot iron burning through the remaining layers she wore.

She leaned against him, close enough that her breasts were crushed tight to his chest and she could feel the beat of both their hearts. While his fingers worked the laces of her corset loose, she pressed her lips to the dark brown circles of his areola and nipple.

His hands stopped for a moment, his breath hitching when her tongue flicked out to lick at the hardened tip; then he was moving at double the speed to release her from the bindings. The slight burn of the heavy laces being loosened too quickly had her arching her back, thrusting her breasts forward to crest the top edge of the heavy cotton as he worked it free from her body. His urgency made her shiver in anticipation.

He broke away long enough to separate the clasp at the busk of her corset and slide it from between them to toss it to the floor. One less barrier between them.

Gathering up the material of her chemise, Elliott inched it up her body. She raised her hands above her head to aid him in removing it quickly. When the material was high enough to clasp onto with her fingers, she made haste in ridding herself of it. The slip of linen was tossed to the floor with her corset.

Feeling bold and unashamed of what they were about to do, she reached forward and released the ties on his trousers. They fell to below his hips and he pushed them the rest of the way down, stepping out of the material.

The firm ridge of his cock stood thick and needy against the material of his drawers.

"Into the bed with you."

He didn't give her the opportunity to make her way there on her own: He picked her up again and set her down on one side. Then he joined her on the other side so they were face-to-face.

She reached around him to explore the line of his spine and down to the firm roundness of his buttocks.

His hand came down on her rear, squeezed the cheeks as he tilted her pelvis forward, pressing their groins together.

She moaned into his mouth and hitched her thigh over his hip, wanting so desperately to feel his flesh rubbing against hers.

Elliott rolled her onto her back, settling himself above her. His smalls were between them. She couldn't reach far enough below his waist to slide the material down and release the jut of his cock. She wanted all of him around her. Inside her.

Before she could remove the material, he grasped her by the waist and pushed her farther up the bed so he could nibble the top swell of her breast. Then the tip of her breast was being sucked into his mouth, inflaming her desire tenfold.

Abby curled one hand into the soft waves of his hair on a silent gasp. The other she clasped tightly to his side to hold him close as she settled for rubbing herself against the flexed ridges of his stomach. She did so with his encouragement and the guidance of his hand at her hip.

She didn't dissuade him. She couldn't, not only because they'd done stranger things, but because it felt so good.

And right.

"Elliott," she whispered, groaned, moaned—she couldn't tell which. Didn't care how desperate she sounded, either. She was desperate. Needy. Frantic for more, for everything.

All she could feel and comprehend was his mouth and tongue against her skin. His gentle suckling at her breast had her pelvis undulating harder against him, sliding in her own juices against his now slick stomach. Her fingers tightened at his scalp, and she tried to get closer.

Elliott's arms braced on either side of her shoulders as the thrusts of her pelvis grew more frantic. He didn't say anything, only looked at her with those pale blue eyes of his and a small grin turning up one side of his lips as she rode herself to completion.

As he poised himself above her spread thighs, there wasn't anything that could be said. She knew they would finally consummate their union. Not that of husband and wife—which would be a great disappointment to her sisters when they found out just how far she and Elliott had gone—but that of lovers.

She could never be ashamed of what they shared. This was just her and Elliott. The rest of the world didn't matter beyond her room, the castle, the land and sea surrounding them.

There was nothing seedy or wrong in what they were doing. What they shared so intimately with each other. This was just meant to be between them. She'd not detract from something that felt right to her by debasing its meaning.

"Love me," she whispered, not knowing in what context she meant it: love her body, or love her. Both, she supposed.

Bracing himself on one arm for support, he untied his

smalls and kicked them away between the sheets at their feet. The heavy ridge of his cock lay on her lower belly. The intimate feel of him against her wasn't enough. She wanted the rest of her underclothes off so she felt every part of him wrapped around her. Despite the heat of their exerting bodies, she shivered in anticipation beneath him.

"Soon," he promised and lowered his mouth to hers, sucking her tongue against his.

He pressed her thighs farther apart and let the blunt crown of his cock lie intimately between her folds. He did not enter her. She thought maybe he wanted to explore every part of her as she craved to do with him. His fingers lowered between them to rub over her nub.

"You like touching me there." She moaned against his throat, nibbling at his neck as he slicked her own fluids over her privates.

His beard stubble under her mouth prickled all her senses to life. She'd love the feel of his evening shadow against her breasts, her thighs, rubbing over her bare flesh as he loved her.

"I love watching you come."

"Is that the term used?" She let out a soft laugh. "I definitely like to come when you touch me like that."

"Good, because I'm going to do this awhile longer." He scooted down lower on the bed, his face just above her breasts. He muttered, "Small but perfect," before sucking the tip of one breast into his mouth. She arched her back off the bed, wanting him to suck at her harder.

Fluid rushed from her center with the contact of his mouth on her breast. He groaned against her, his hand stilling at her entrance, sliding through the extra fluids, wetting her clitoris more.

She wanted more, less; she couldn't tell which. The feelings and sensations rampaging through her body confused and delighted her. This was so much more than their previous intimacies.

She felt close to her peak. Close to *coming* for him. Her knees spread wider, clasping him around his ribs since he was still taking pleasure in sucking at her breasts. Moving her hands from his scalp to his shoulders as her body came close to release.

Her nipple popped out of his mouth after a deep sucking noise. He said, "I want to put my mouth where my hand is, suck all this sweet juice from your quim."

Her nails dug into his shoulders as her orgasm claimed her, riding her hard, her body throbbing in time with her heartbeat.

His hand eased up. Moving away from that sensitive part of herself.

His expression turned serious. "I don't want to hurt you."

"I trust you," she whispered still feeling her orgasm numbing her limbs. "Completely."

"Seems like too much faith."

"You underestimate yourself, Elliott."

She felt her slickness on his hand as he grasped her waist and moved up her body again, poising himself at her entrance.

He waited a moment, looking down at her, eyes narrowed in question. "Wrap your arms around my shoulders."

His request was firm. Arms tight around his neck and shoulders, she threaded her fingers through his hair once again. It was thick and silky to the touch, different from the feel of hers with its slight wave.

His hand lowered between their bodies so he could grasp the base of his instrument and position himself above her. His other arm remained braced by her head, keeping his weight from crushing her.

Pressing slowly forward, he lodged the tip of his penis within her sheath. The pain was minimal, almost nonexistent aside from a slight discomfort and a feel of stretching.

Lips parted, she kissed his chin, his jaw, and then finally his mouth and dipped her tongue inside to catch his. Both their breaths were coming harshly. Sweat dripped from his temple to hers. She kissed his cheek and tasted the salt of his body. She licked him, wanting to taste everything he was. To take all of him in her at once.

He braced himself on his arms and pulled away from their kiss long enough to say, "I'm sorry," and thrust forward.

Her breath caught in her lungs.

He stayed above her, unmoving. Her body adjusted to him inside her, stretching her. It wasn't precisely painful; the feeling wasn't like anything she knew.

"I'm sorry," he repeated, laying hard kisses against her closed mouth, her cheeks, and her eyelids. The awkward feeling began to ebb the more Elliott kissed her face and ran one hand down the back of her thigh and one buttock in a soothing manner.

"Do you want me to stop?"

There was no censure in his voice.

She shook her head no. Why in all the heavens would she want to stop?

"Don't ever stop," she answered.

He lowered both his hands back down between their bodies and clasped her buttocks in his firm grip. "I won't, then."

He sank into her farther. She wasn't sure how, since she was certain he was already as far as he could go, but the pleasure it brought made her heart flutter and her limbs shake in excitement.

He pulled out halfway and slid slowly back in. A slight pleasure built with each forward thrust of his hips.

Elliott lowered his head closer, his tongue sweeping inside to steal her words before they could properly form on her tongue.

The sting she initially felt ebbed. Had completely diminished as he held himself motionless above her. Her hands loosened from their death-like grip around his neck now that she could feel pleasure languidly radiating from her limbs once again.

Elliott kissed her lips, brushing over them, back and forth, one side to the next.

He pulled out half the distance he'd gained and drove forward with so much force that a sob lodged in her throat. This sob was not derived from pain but quite the opposite.

"Elliott," she moaned.

"Shh . . . I've got you."

He kissed her again. His hands threaded through her hair to keep her head in place even though she strained toward him. Wanting more, or wanting less—she really didn't know—just something to dampen the conflicting feelings tumbling around without a cause or sure outlet inside her.

Her hands moved over him, intent on memorizing the feel of his body on hers. Every contour, every nuance. She caressed the firm swell of his buttocks, the dip at the lower portion of his spine. The muscles straining in his back as he moved in slow, even strokes at a pace meant to titillate and arouse.

This intimacy was something they were meant to share. She'd take and take everything he gave her in their evening cocoon of secret ecstasy. Every second they were together made her want more between them.

A realization dawned on her with that admission: She was irrevocably, wholly his. Just as she'd wanted.

Which meant she'd allowed herself to do the one thing

she'd always promised never to do . . . she'd lost herself to a man. Not because she hadn't wanted it or because they had joined in the most intimate way a man and woman could, and certainly not because he was the only potential suitor in the wilds of Northumbria, but because he'd stolen into her heart bit by bit; wormed his way so deep that he was a permanent fixture there.

She cared for him. No matter that she hadn't fully figured him out, or that he seemed to keep a greater part of himself hidden from those around him—including her. It could not be denied that she might already be in love with him.

"I've lost you," he said, holding still above her, thumbs caressing the side of her face in slow strokes.

She stared back at him. There was something there in his eyes. Was it fear of rejection? From her?

"No. Never that," she replied, and stretched her upper body to wrap her arms around his shoulders again so she was close to his mouth. With no other intention than to taste him, she licked gently at the seam, nibbled at the cleft in his chin like she had wanted to do earlier, and rubbed her cheek against his hair-roughened one.

He rolled over suddenly, changing their positions and putting her astride his thighs.

"What are you about?"

"I want to watch you above me."

She did not shy away.

Tonight they had both shed their shields of self-preservation. Tonight they could love and cherish every moment shared between them.

What would tomorrow bring? Would there be stolen kisses? A desire to feel the heat of their bodies coming together when no one was around to witness them? Would he want more from her than the evening hours offered? Or at dawn would he shrink back into himself and close himself off to her?

These thoughts gave her no peace of mind. She didn't want to think that he didn't desire her as much as she'd come to desire him. She would live in the moment. Share something with him that she'd never shared with another— nor did she want to ever share this intimacy with any other. He, apparently, was the only man she wanted. They were meant for each other in so many aspects. Aspects she'd examine later.

Elliott traced over the line of her spine while she explored the contours of his chest, feeling and molding the strong line of his pectorals, brushing her fingers through the coarse dark hair speckled at the center.

He pulled himself up and put his back to the headboard with her still straddling his muscled thighs. His mouth came to her breast and nibbled at the firm peak.

Hunger radiated from his every pore. His forearms were tense where she clasped them. His hands flexed against her waist and hips, moving her at a slow rocking rhythm. Squeezing and releasing her flesh as he stared at her naked body and traced the lines indenting her skin left behind from the corset.

She thought she'd be too shy to be naked before a man. Maybe her sister's paintings had desensitized her to the female form. She saw nothing wrong in his slow study of her nakedness. Or of the appreciation clear in his gaze as he watched the gentle bounce of her breasts when she moved above him.

She wasn't like the women her sister painted. She was so small in stature that she'd been lucky to develop breasts at all. And not till she'd had her first season in Town. She wasn't embarrassed by that fact; not with the way Elliott stared ravenously upon her, as though she were an oasis on a deep desert trek. He raised one hand and brushed it over the small roundness of her breast, squeezing the firm peak between his two forefingers.

She did not remain idle. She caressed his chest, liking the feel of the firmness of his body and the contrast of coarse hair at the center and soft skin everywhere else she pressed into his flesh.

He was still inside her as they slowly explored each other. She liked the feel of him filling her body. Every now and again she felt a pulse of movement deep inside her. She wasn't sure if that was her body reacting to his now welcome intrusion or the jut of his penis moving within her. All she knew was that it felt good. And it made her want more.

Elliott's movements grew slowly more urgent, until he was thrusting off the bed and into her body. She held his head tight to her breast, wanting him to suck at her harder as she rode his body.

He released her breast and pulled her head down to his as he gave her a few choice thrusts, then completely stilled. She felt the throb of his cock inside her as he found his own release.

They sat holding each other for a long time, Elliott kissing her gently, she doing nothing more than stroking at his hair. What did tonight mean? Did this make her his lover? He hers? Would he want to see her again after she'd so easily given herself to him?

Those were questions for another night. She'd not ruin something beautiful. She was being a ninny again. Of course this meant she was his lover. There were no other women here, none that she knew Elliott to want.

For now . . . this would do. She didn't know how long she could remain merely a lover. Time would tell what was meant for their future.

Elliott left the bed to retrieve a dampened cloth, warmed

it by the fire, and came back to the bed. He cleaned them both with the wet cloth, then tucked himself along her body for sleep.

The only thing she knew with certainly was that she was in a lot of trouble if she couldn't separate her feelings from her desires when it came to Lord Brendall.

Chapter 17

The king asked, "Where has the dragon flown?"
"Here, my liege. He's come home at last, but you
will find him of a different cast."
—The Dragon of Brahmors

Abby walked around Elliott's desk while her fingers traced along the edge of the leather inlay. Various sheaves of paper littered the top. The inkbottle hadn't even been capped. Elliott must have stepped out.

She'd only stolen a few minutes, while Jacob went to eat, to come see Elliott. She'd been thinking about him since she'd awakened this morning. Their *affair*—such a dirty word, but the truth to their circumstances—had continued now for two weeks. How was it that she didn't feel any closer to him even after they'd been intimate with each other?

She slid one of the pages closer to the edge of the desk; it had Martha's familiar handwriting on it. The older woman must act as chatelaine for Brendall Castle.

How odd, she thought, looking closer. The letter was a copy of one sent to her. Did Martha write out two of all her correspondence letters?

With a glance at the door, she confirmed that she was quite alone. She couldn't hear anyone close by, either. Placing her walking stick against the desk—she still used it when her ankle pained her—she moved the quill off the half-filled page Elliott had been working on.

It read oddly. Actually . . . it didn't read at all. She was well versed in both English and French, could recognize a dozen more languages, and this didn't look to be another tongue. She picked up the page and walked over into the stream of light that shone through the window. She recognized some of the letters, but the majority were off. Half appeared inverted and upside down, but written quite neatly—painstakingly precise.

Her fingers curled tight around the bottom corner of the paper, crinkling it up.

How was this possible?

Better yet, why hadn't he said anything?

They'd discussed his son's difficulties on enough occasions that the topic should have come up. Why had he kept this knowledge from her? Did he not trust her enough to tell her?

Her newfound knowledge explained a great many things. No wonder he'd been disinterested in looking over his son's schooling. Did he not trust her?

He didn't trust her!

She was good enough to play his whore, but not good enough to confide his secrets in.

That sent a pang of sorrow right through her heart. She'd been honest—perhaps not completely, but mostly—with him. She had stupidly opened herself up to this hurt. Had she kept her distance, this might not have stung so deeply.

She'd invited the man into her bed, had opened her heart to him and his son, and he didn't think it important to share this one scrap of information with her?

How dare he do this to her. She felt . . . betrayed. And

up to this point, she hadn't realized how much more she had shared of herself than he had. Maybe she was a mere dalliance for him. An amusement while she lived under his roof.

Oh, God, she felt so incredibly stupid. So foolish and on some level humiliated and gullible.

She hadn't noticed his entrance into the study. Elliott approached her despairingly. She held a piece of paper in her hand. The one he'd been working on. He hadn't expected to find her in here. Had he expected her, he would have packed up all his writing appurtenances.

She would know. She did know. It was in the way she studied the page he'd meticulously worked on last night and this morning. The way her brow furrowed and her lips pursed also told him she understood what she was looking at.

He supposed he couldn't keep the truth from her indefinitely. The evidence lay right before her eyes: Martha's neat scroll on the missive, his straggled backward lettering that had never made much sense to him, no matter how long he stared at it. No matter how many times he tried to copy it out. He'd only started practicing his writing again hoping that, like his son, he merely needed to try harder and focus more diligently. It wasn't working, of course. He'd thought that if he tried writing less on a page, like he had to do with his numbers so they didn't get mixed up, maybe the words would start to make sense. Instead, the words moved on the page and never looked the same on a second and third glance.

"What's this about, Elliott?" He saw confusion and hurt in her eyes. Saw it in the way she tilted her head and scrunched her brows.

He stepped back, away from his desk and away from

her. Away from the evidence of his failure. He hadn't wanted her to find out like this. He'd never wanted her to find out.

After the past few days of sleeping in her bed, and enjoying the intimacies they shared, he knew those good times were effectively at an end.

Nothing lasted forever. He more than anyone needed no reminder of that.

He closed his eyes against the knowledge that she now knew his biggest secret. His biggest failure.

He exhaled. "The truth. Nothing more than the bloody truth," he muttered.

She walked over to the desk and pulled another of the pages closer to her, her expression unreadable as she ran her finger across the words on the page. Words that had never made any sense to him and never would.

Why didn't she say something? Tell him he was a letdown like everyone else had. Tell him he was less of a man and a failure in his role as the Earl of Brendall. It was no wonder his son had struggled all these years. How could he not with a father like him?

"Now you know." With that voiced admission he wanted to yell out his frustration. Walk away. Throw something to ease the pain of knowing that their time together was now at an end.

Goddamn it, this was not what he had planned. Tonight he had wanted nothing more than to carry her up to her room and make them both forget everything but what the night had to offer them. She'd not have him now.

He rubbed his eyes and pinched the skin between his brows as he looked back to Abigail. Her back was rigid and straight, her shoulders set firmly back as she stared steadily at him. What was she thinking? What were her thoughts on this whole damn situation? Or for that matter, what did she think of him? Did she hate him? Despise and loathe the fact that she'd lain with a man like him?

Dumb as the day he was born.

Why did she have to find out like this? Why did she have to find out at all? Everything had been perfect. He'd been happier than he'd been in a long time. And now this.

A bitter reminder: nothing good lasted forever. The love for his mother had washed away with her body at sea, the devotion to his sick wife vanishing the day she'd threatened his son's life and then taken her own.

Abigail, at his side, brightening his every day.

The rage he felt was sudden, probably uncalled for, but it couldn't be helped.

A strangled noise of pain escaped him as he stepped forward and swept his hand across the desk, throwing all the papers in a messy array, tossing the inkwell and causing the black liquid to splatter across the pages, marring all his evening's work. Too bad it wouldn't blot out the truth from her eyes.

"I can't read. Is that what you want me to admit? There's your truth. I can't write! I'm the reason Jacob struggles. Say something, woman, and stop looking at me like I'm the biggest fool there ever was."

Her lip trembled. He'd not have her pity him. Cry for him.

"Elliott . . ." Her voice was soft. Too soft. Goddamn. He hadn't wanted her to find out. Not like this. Not ever! "Stop it, Elliott."

She rushed forward, her ankle obviously paining her because she caught the edge of the desk for support. Worry was evident in the way she approached him . . . much as you would an injured dog.

"Leave me be." His request was so hushed he hardly heard the words.

"No. I won't. You can't make me, either. We need to talk about this."

"You're mistaken there."

If she wouldn't leave, he would.

He left her standing in his study, making his way out of the house. He didn't know where he was going. Or what the purpose of leaving was other than the fact that he didn't want to face her after revealing such an ugly truth. He needed to get away. He needed air to clean out his lungs. A long ride to rid him of his thoughts altogether.

He should have denied the evidence of his ineptitude that lay dejectedly about them. Even lying would have been better than seeing the look of sympathy blazing so clear in her eyes. God, he never hated himself so much as he did now.

She followed him to the stable, a silent shadow, but a presence nonetheless that he couldn't outdistance. Wasn't sure he really wanted to leave behind.

When he stopped, she walked right into his back.

"Goddamn you, woman." He spun around, clasped her face between his hands and planted his lips hard against hers. Maybe it was a parting kiss, maybe he did it to scare her off for good.

She didn't fight him, didn't push him away. Instead of being revolted by the truth that made up his character, she clasped onto his arms and held tight, moaning a soft cry into his mouth as she gave him her tongue.

"You're driving me mad," he shouted at her, hating that he was being so cruel to her. Why wasn't she saying anything? Why didn't she yell back at him?

Why did she have to sink into the kiss? Or, for that matter, follow him when he wanted nothing more than to be alone? He broke away from her mouth only long enough to grab her hand and pull her into the stable, away from prying eyes. It was too late for his son to be hiding in here, but those at the keep would have a clear view of him should they be outdoors.

None too gently, because his mood had gotten the better of him, Elliott pushed her up against the wall on the inside of the stable. He stepped forward and assaulted her mouth with his once again. He couldn't taste deeply enough to appease and ease the disjointed anger unfurling inside him. It was rage directed solely at himself.

He ripped himself away from her and paced the floor; once, twice, thrice, jerking his hands roughly through his hair the whole time. Afraid he'd regret any actions he couldn't take back, he grabbed Ivan's saddle and readied his horse.

Abigail didn't move from where he'd placed her. Didn't weep as most women might have from his manhandling of her delicate stature.

"Elliott," she said more firmly as he checked the belt around the barrel of his chestnut.

"Don't," he replied. He didn't want to say any more words he would regret. Didn't want her to say something he would lash out against.

Swinging himself up into the saddle, he took up the reins and turned the horse for the open doors. He gave one more piercing gaze toward Abigail. Her lip trembled. Had he frightened her? Maybe she'd leave tonight, never look back on this pile of rock.

His first assessment of her had been correct. She was a bloody nuisance. A nuisance he had come to enjoy. A woman he had grown to adore in so short a time.

He didn't look back after that. He didn't want to know if she'd followed him out to watch him leave. Didn't want to know if she *didn't*. Goddamn her for making him care. For making him want more than the lot life had dealt him.

He swiped the back of his hand over his dampened

cheek. He looked up to the sky. It wasn't raining. *Great, just bloody great.*

Tightening his thighs, he raced Ivan toward the castle's gates, intent on riding both himself and his horse senseless. He was in a destructive mood, so it was better he left her in the stable to her own devices. He slowed his pace after about a mile, sure he was far enough from his home. Far enough from the truth and from Abigail.

What in hell was he running from? And why?

He'd probably numbered his days with the governess. Bringing Ivan to a canter, he turned the horse back toward the castle, unsure if he wanted to go home or not. Should he have stayed? Was it the right thing to do in leaving her when he wanted nothing more than to lose himself in her?

It would somehow be kinder to send her away. Provided she wasn't already packing her bags.

Pulling Ivan to a stop, he stared up the slope leading into the castle grounds. The giant mound of rock was cursed of any luck. Any love. All the women who came to live here eventually grew to hate it and the men who inhabited the castle.

It was probably because Wright men were an unkind lot. Cads, scoundrels, black-hearted bastards. Madeline had called him those things and more toward the end.

He let out a frustrated sigh and closed his eyes for a moment, blocking the castle from sight.

He had few good memories of his home. His mother kissing him on the cheek, telling him to be a good boy and that she'd forever be proud of him. Reading to him from the storybook she'd written for him. His mother standing in the path of his father's angry tantrums only to be struck in his place. Then finally, the fateful day when his mother had walked out into the sea to never come back.

He wished he understood why she'd left him behind.

His father had beaten him senseless the night his mother had killed herself. Beaten him close to within an inch of his own worthless life. *Worthless life*—those words were pounded into him over the subsequent years and repeated until his father's death. He never remembered his father being kind. Not to him, his mother, the help around the castle. He was a miserable old abusive coot.

There was the memory of his wife coming to the castle for the first time, a shy young woman who knew of his father's cruelties toward the inhabitants, toward his mother. Yet she had still married him. Then he'd put a babe in her belly, and the radiant glow of life slowly leeched from her cheeks as the weeks and months wore on.

The glorious day his son had been born made everything wrong in the world disappear. Until his wife's madness had taken hold of her mind and everything he'd thought to hold dear in the world had been ripped asunder.

His son had nearly died by his wife's hands. Much as he'd nearly died at his father's hands. The castle had come close to burning down in her insanity. Her madness had finally taken her in a blazing inferno of death.

It was hard to say whether she deserved an easy way out of the living world or not. He'd tried to help her, to reason with her, to understand what was wrong with her. All to no avail. She'd not been right after Jacob had been born.

And what of Abigail? Would she grow to hate him as his father had, as his wife had? Why would anyone want to stay with him knowing that the two women he'd loved were dead? Not only dead, but had taken their own lives to be rid of him. And now, he'd proven himself to be dumb. How could she not think less of him knowing that painful truth?

There was no reason for her to stay. He'd been an utter ass to her; a raving madman no better than his father with his moods shifting among lust, want, and fury.

He didn't want her to leave.

He pushed his horse back toward the castle and the woman he wasn't ready to let go of. A woman he deeply cared for. Maybe he could convince her that he was no different from any other man. That he wasn't completely worthless, that he wasn't a raving madman like his father. He'd never lift a finger in anger toward her, never hurt her as his father had hurt his mother.

He had lived here too long alone. If she stayed . . . alone was not what he wanted. But he might need to give her time to come to terms with everything he'd revealed. Time. He was a patient man. Always had been. There was nothing to gain in rushing Abigail's decision to stay. Whether she graced his bed again was another matter entirely.

Abby stood inside the stable door. She couldn't go after him. She knew he wouldn't want her company. He wanted to think about what she had uncovered. Her only purpose in following him out here in the first place was because she hated that he had walked away from her without hearing her out. He'd been hurting when he'd left. Hurting and angry at himself, not with her; she saw that.

His revelation had been shocking. Confusing. It shed light on so many questions she'd had and created more in their place.

Once he was completely gone from her sight, she slowly made her way up to the main house. She should clean up the mess he'd left in the study, hide the evidence of their argument.

Why, though? Why should she play into Elliott's game of unneeded secrecy? Surely the house knew of his lordship's inability to read or write.

He'd chosen to run from her instead of face her as any man in his position should have done.

Making her way back to the house, she closed the study

door behind her and looked around the darkened room. Striding over to the curtain-covered window, she threw the heavy brocade open to let what little light remained in the dreary sky beyond illuminate her surroundings. Perhaps she should feel ill at ease, snooping around his home wanting to know if there were other secrets she'd uncover.

Now that the room had some natural light, she took note of the surroundings. How had she not noticed that there were no books adorning the built-in shelves? Behind the leaded-glass panes, fripperies, clocks, and odd pieces of china filled the shelves instead of dusty old tomes. On the lowest shelf there were tall black leather-bound journals.

She opened the cabinet door and pulled out one of the books, opening it to the middle. Grain counts. Stock shipments. Livestock numbers. Nothing but lists and numbers and simplistic words. Words, she noted, not written in Martha's hand but in Elliott's heavier precise scroll. There were misspellings, and inverted letters even with the most basic of words. Placing the ledger back behind the glass, she walked over to the desk set off to the left of the room.

Kneeling on the carpeted floor, she righted the inkwell. Most of the Indian black had already bled into the pages and Persian rug where it had landed in Elliott's destructive mood. She lifted another page half filled with Elliott's exacting scroll. More grain counts. Is this what he did when he was in here? Copied out inventory lists? Why didn't he just have Martha enter them into the books?

She searched through the papers on the floor to find the original. Unsuccessful, she stood to check the desk. There the list lay in the center of the leather inlay.

She pulled the page closer, inspecting the familiar hand of the woman she'd corresponded with for a month prior to traveling to the castle. Looking through more of the pages on the floor, she tried to understand what Elliott had been doing. Could he be trying to learn the letterings? The words? The language? Was that why he copied out the lists Martha kept?

The heavier pad of slippered feet came down the hall and stopped outside the door. Abby gathered up the papers, sorting them into as neat a pile as she could, and took three steps away from the desk and the evidence that she'd been snooping through.

As though summoned by Abby's thoughts, Martha pushed the door open, first seeing only the stack of papers scattered over the desk in messy piles; then the older woman's eyes alighted on Abby. At least Abby had the sense to compose her features.

"Where's the master?"

"I'm not sure. I came to discuss something with him, but found only an empty room."

Martha's bushy eyebrows drew closer together. "You've no need to be in here, then. And with the door closed."

Abby agreed but she'd not be talked down to like a disobeying dog. Martha had disliked her from the start. It stopped now.

"I thought to pen him a note," she stated, wondering if Martha would give any indication that a note would mean naught to his lordship.

There was nothing but the schooled expression of a woman who had lied so long to herself for her employer that she probably believed her lies to be truths. A kernel of respect sprouted in her heart for Martha, even though Abby wasn't sure what or even how she felt about the recent revelation of Lord Brendall.

Making good on her word, Abby went to the desk, dipped the quill in the inkwell that she'd righted, and scribbled out a note for Lord Brendall. She did it for no other purpose than to appease Martha, who still stood over her like a stern schoolmistress ready to use the rod if Abby so much as blinked wrong.

She wrote that she wanted to speak with his lordship as soon as possible about his son's progress, knowing Martha would read the note once Abby left the room.

Chapter 18

*The king's worst horrors came to life before his
eyes. Unbelieving that the beast was the prince, the
king brandished his sword and stepped into the light
to challenge the monster. With a swipe at the scaled
belly of the dragon, the king dared to destroy the
creature besieging his castle.*

—*The Dragon of Brahmors*

Despite his best intentions to go back up to the castle,
Elliott hadn't. He'd spent the greater part of the early evening outdoors with Ivan, aimlessly wandering the land
surrounding his home. He well knew that made him a
coward. A coward because he couldn't bring himself to
face Abigail even though he'd talked himself into the ne-
cessity of doing so hours ago.

After brushing down Ivan and putting a blanket on
him to guard against the evening frost, he left the stable
and headed for the main house. Once inside, he ensured all
the doors were locked. Nothing untoward had happened
since Abigail's fall, so he wasn't sure why he kept up the
routine.

He returned to his study to clean up the mess he'd left

there. A solitary candle flickered on top of his desk. The papers he'd thrown from his desk were set in a neat pile off to one side, the inkwell capped and sitting atop the papers.

He turned around only to find Abigail sleeping on the sofa. A heavy shawl was wrapped around her, a pillow tucked under her head at the arm.

All the tension that had been racking his body, making it difficult for him to face the rest of the night, drained away on seeing her at ease and asleep in his study. She'd waited for him and he'd been too much of a coward to come back up to the castle and face her after the truths he'd been forced to reveal.

He'd been unkind and cruel to her earlier and regretted it immensely.

He didn't deserve her presence. Didn't deserve for someone like her to wait up for him. It would have served him right had she left him to his own devices. Or even left the castle in pursuit of another less foreboding place, and of a kinder employer. One who wouldn't take advantage of her every chance he could.

But she hadn't left. He didn't have to go on living as he had before. Walking over to her, he brushed the back of his hand over her brow and stared down at her relaxed form.

Her cheeks were rosy, her hair unbound and tucked beneath the shawl. She usually wore her hair braided in a thick rope down the middle of her back at night. He wanted to run his hands through the long loose tresses. He'd desired doing so since first seeing it down the day he'd spied her in her bath and again when he'd seen the fire that lit it under a morning sky. He had been right; it was as fiery as her tenacious nature.

Should he wake her or take them both up to bed? He was tired. He was even a little chilled from staying out so long with Ivan. Would he be welcomed into her bed again? Surely her being here was a good enough indication that she wanted his company. That she wanted more between them. That she wasn't willing to walk away from him no matter how much he might deserve that.

Gathering up his stubborn governess in his arms—stubborn because she'd waited up for him and had probably intended to confront him after everything that had transpired between them—he blew out the candle and carried her up to her room. She snuggled her face into his chest and curled her arms around his neck, murmuring unintelligible words. All he caught was something about men being beasts. It made him smile and had the constriction fisting tight around his heart loosening the smallest bit.

Once in her room, he gently placed her on the bed and turned around to shut and lock her chamber door.

He stripped out of his clothes, including his trousers, since they smelled of horse and rain and sweat. He made quick work of cleaning his body with a washcloth in the basin of tepid water set near the water closet.

He then set himself to removing Abigail's outer clothes. Her skirts were the easiest to pull down from her hips. Her shirtwaist was more difficult to take off since he didn't wish to wake her. She must have been half awake because she aided him in removing the material once he started pulling it down her arms.

Stripped of her day clothes, she curled her arms around a pillow and pulled it close. He wanted her to snuggle into him, not an inanimate object.

Elliott pulled down the bedding and climbed onto the mattress next to her, tucking his body tightly around hers, wrapping his arms around her, afraid to ever let her go. Come morning, she could prove to be livid with him. Might even tell him to leave her be.

Could he prove his worth to her again? Would she be angry with him for sliding into bed next to her?

Abby had been vaguely aware of Elliott carrying her up to her room. She'd waited so long for him that sleep could not be helped. She thought maybe she had slept for a few hours. Her mind slowly came awake. Her body, too, for that matter. Warmth enveloped her.

Elliott had come back to the castle. She assumed, by his presence in her bed, that he wanted to discuss everything that had transpired, as opposed to walking away from it. That, or he wished to continue their affair under everyone's noses and forget everything that had been revealed this afternoon.

She'd not allow for that to happen. She'd not think ill of him, either. Him being here was enough for now. He'd probably been as startled by his forced revelation as she had been to learn the truth.

He had opened himself up to her this afternoon. More than he dared to with others, she imagined. He'd been hurt, been embarrassed, and had expected rejection from her earlier with his admittance.

She'd not walk away from him. There were no secrets too dark for her to dismiss him. With love came acceptance of good and bad, ugly and beautiful.

She nearly snorted . . . yes, this was definitely love. A predicament she'd never expected to find herself in, but one she wouldn't change for the world.

Turning in his arms, she pressed her forehead to his, savoring the feel of his warmth and masculinity surrounding her.

Yes, she loved him. Had for some time now. It was only reaffirmed when he came back to her tonight. She closed her eyes and ran her hands along his hair-roughened face, feeling every contour beneath her fingers.

She pressed her lips to his, wanting to wake him, to admit the truth. No, not yet. It was too soon. They'd just come over their biggest hurdle; she'd not put another obstacle in their path.

She sidled closer to him under their shared blanket, rubbing up against his body, needing to feel his skin next to hers. The burgeoning swell of his cock was firm between them.

Sucking his bottom lip into her mouth, she wrapped her arm around his waist, fingers molding to the bare skin, massaging the muscles there. He came awake slowly. The hand that had been tucked under her breast when she'd woken was now pressing firmly at her lower back, bringing her pelvis tight against his.

"Abigail," he whispered against her lips before sweeping his tongue deep within her mouth.

She accepted him eagerly. His hand slid lower, beneath her drawers, to cup one cheek of her backside to pull her closer. He ground his cock against her center, igniting her passions.

"Don't leave," he panted.

"Never," she responded. "I . . ." What had she been about to say? That she loved him? No, it was too soon. "I won't leave you or Jacob," she finished.

"We'll talk later. Let me love you."

"Yes," she moaned, taking his mouth again in a devouring kiss.

He broke their kiss shortly after to move down her body. Laving his tongue around her nipple, he sucked it into his mouth, pulling deep, making her arch closer to him. He nipped at the underside, squeezing the other firmly with his hand.

"Elliott . . ."

He released her so suddenly she cried out at the loss of his touch.

"Shhh . . ." he soothed. "Flip over on your front."

Her heart ratcheted up in speed, her breath stilling in her lungs in excitement. What did he have in mind?

"Trust me," he said when she stalled too long.

She turned over on hands and knees, bracing herself for whatever he had planned. He squeezed her hip, leaned his much larger frame over her from behind, and gently nipped at her side with his teeth. His fingers found the entrance to her womanhood through the slit in her drawers, slicking her sheath with the juices he'd drawn so easily from her.

Two fingers slid into her, in and out. A rhythmic thrusting that had her pushing her behind out, wanting him to be rougher, faster, harder.

"I want you, Elliott," she groaned into the pillow beneath her head, biting at the edge to keep from screaming out her pleasure.

He moved away from her, to strip himself of his clothes, she assumed, then he was on her, his legs pressed to the back of hers, his instrument sliding deep inside her.

"Oh, God," she moaned.

"Is this what you want? You want me taking you from behind, fucking your sweet cunny with you on your hands and knees?"

"Yes, Elliott, yes!"

He moved inside her. Solid, firm strokes that hit her so deep inside, she thought she'd die from the pleasure. His hand stretched around to grasp her breast and pull teasingly at her distended nipple. The first ripples of her orgasm came quickly. She had to bite the pillow beneath her harder or she would most certainly scream when her release thundered through her body.

"Come for me, Abigail. Come around me. Milk me."

His words were enough to set her aflame. There was no holding back, denying her finale. She came. Just as he demanded. She didn't stop coming for some minutes. Elliott lazily thrust in and out of her, her lubricity quite increased with her orgasm.

"Now for slow again," he said, pulling out of her and turning her to her back.

Elliott skimmed his hands over Abigail's waist, ribs, and breasts, loving the feel of her soft skin under his labor-roughened hands. He couldn't stop touching her, squeezing and stroking her flesh. Feeling every bit of pale skin he exposed to the moonlight.

Her breasts, though small, were perfect for his hands to just cup. The areolas were a flattering pink next to her pale skin, the nipples a deep ruby and glistening wet from the ministrations of his tongue and mouth.

He took his time, in no hurry to reach his finale. With the hand that wasn't exploring her body, he cupped her buttocks and guided her hips in an easy, unrushed rhythm. He'd have to build her desires sure and steady if she was to come again.

If only the joy they found tonight could erase the afternoon's revelation. He wished she'd never learned of his failings. Would she reject him come morning? If not in the morning, would she eventually move on because he was not a man of worth? He didn't want to think about any of these things.

He closed his eyes, effectively shutting out the thoughts bombarding him and focused on Abigail.

He sucked the tip of her breast into his mouth. Her nipple lengthened with his attentions and was like a sweet, hard berry rolling around on his tongue. She slid over his cock faster, making him thrust up into the welcoming haven between her thighs.

He could stay here forever. Forget the world around

them and lock himself in her room for the rest of his days. Or never let her leave the bed, for that matter. Keep her here with him always.

Of course, that would never be possible, but it was a nice fantasy.

Her fingers threaded through his hair and she forced his head away from her breast so she could look him in the eye. She didn't kiss him. Didn't utter a single word. She just stared into his eyes as he did hers. The little flecks of gold danced around the dark of her pupils.

His arms were wrapped tight around her waist, one hand across her lower back and the other between her shoulder blades. He didn't break eye contact with her. Could she see what was inside him? How his heart swelled whenever he thought of her? How he wanted more from her every moment he had her in his arms?

Maybe she was a witch after all. How else had she stolen into his heart and mind so deeply? He knew the dangers of letting anyone get too close. But she'd completely bewitched him. She knew his worst secrets, and here she was opening herself up to him. Giving her most precious gift to him. She was ruined for marriage in lying with him. A shame he could never offer for her hand. He'd not watch her fade as Madeline had.

Hating that his thoughts kept coming back around to this, he focused on the meld of their bodies instead. He picked up the momentum of their thrusting together, grinding and rotating his pelvis against hers. Her legs wrapped around his hips, her ankles locked at his tailbone as her heels dug in, urging him to move faster and harder against her. He took her hands in his and stretched them above her head, his fingers entwined through hers.

He would watch her facial expressions as she came undone this time. She did not remain idle with him atop her. Her pelvis drove up toward his. The hot depth of her cunny seemed to suck hard at his cock. Damn well nearly took everything in him to hold his seed back.

Abigail threw her head back, her neck arched toward him. He nibbled and licked her skin from the dip at the base of her neck all the way up to her chin. He sucked the dainty point of her chin into his mouth and gave it a gentle bite, which made her moan and her hands flex in his.

He pulled his hand away for a moment so he could hitch one of her legs higher. Grasping it behind the knee, he pressed it so it rested against his shoulder. He groaned at the change in position. With her pelvis tilted forward, he felt as though he was inside her as far as he could go. When he slid his hand away, she was forced to hook her knee over his shoulder as he took her hand in his again.

"Look at me," he whispered, pressing his lips against hers. "Look at me while I give you pleasure."

Her eyes drowsily, lustily opened; the green was hard to distinguish around the large black orbs.

The tip of her tongue slowly peeked out from her pink mouth, and she ran it over the top edge of her lip, wetting it as she whetted his appetite to taste her. He slammed into her core and squeezed her hands tightly in his. Her gaze never wavered. Neither did his; it was steady as a pendulum without momentum to keep it from moving away.

His body heaved above hers, rocking their pelvises so tightly together that he felt they were joined as one.

In giving herself to him after everything that had happened today, he realized something: She belonged wholly to him. He'd not let her stray, nor could he ever let her go. She belonged to him just as he belonged solely to her.

He'd fallen hard for his little governess. Faster than a peregrine falcon diving from a cliff . . . only there were no brakes to slow him down, no wings to allow him to soar through the air. He wasn't sure he wanted to stop the life-altering free fall that grasped him by the gut and pulled him in for the thrilling ride. He didn't resist the pull. He embraced it.

Their mouths clashed in a desperate tasting. She nipped at his bottom lip and sucked at his tongue, and their teeth clanked together as they tasted as deeply as they could of each other. Their bodies moved fluidly. Both were desperate for climax but not desperate enough to finish their joining.

Was it possible to fall in love in such a short time? Without knowing all they were? Only that they fit together perfectly, that she was brightness to his darkness, that he was wickedness to her goodness.

He had no idea.

The only thing he knew with any certainty was that it had happened to him. Had happened to him with Abigail. There was no changing what was. He'd not fight against what felt right.

She panted into his mouth, the pounding of their slick bodies forcing a small squeak from her every time he pounded against her tight core.

He fucked her like a man desperate. Like he couldn't get enough of everything she was. And he couldn't. There would never be enough of her; he'd always want, and probably always take when she offered herself so freely. He'd beg and plead on his knees for more if she ever refused him again.

He doubted he'd ever be a complete man if she were absent from his life. Wasn't sure now if he'd ever been complete when she hadn't been here to brighten his home. His life. His son's life.

He wasn't a man falling in love.

He was a man *in* love.

There was no greater gift than this, he decided. Being

tightly wrapped around the woman he loved. Cherished, even.

Her panting turned into high-pitched mewls as his body met hers and rotated over the spread lips of her sex after every propelling thrust forward. Her hands tightened on his, squeezing them so tightly he thought the blood might stop flowing to the tips. He didn't care. He only wanted her to find her climax because he'd soon follow. This felt different from previous times. This felt like more. Like everything.

Her whole body arched off the bed, her fingers grasped his in a death-like grip. Her sweet cunny flexed around his cock, milking it for all he was worth.

He kissed her again as he shot his seed deep into her womb. The only thought going through his mind was that she was his.

In every way, she belonged to him.

They collapsed in each other's arms without any strength to move for a quarter hour.

His cock was still semi-hard in her. The pressure of her cunt like a fist urging him to full mast. The day had been trying. This was enough. They might just have tomorrow. He rolled off her and tucked her tight against his body.

Sleep found her easily. Elliott listened to the soothing deep breaths she took in sleep, trying to imagine what it would be like to not hear that sound. He couldn't picture it. Refused to.

What a state she'd put him in. He'd gone from wanting her from the start, to forcing himself to keep away, to doing everything in his power to secure her as his companion of the night. And now . . . now he was irrevocably in love with her.

Chapter 19

"Father," the dragon cackled. "You have made me this creature and now it is my duty to end your reign."

"Look upon yourself, son, and see the monster you became." —The Dragon of Brahmors

Abby watched Elliott show Jacob how to mix and spread the slop they used to secure the new stone blocks on the wall. It was Saturday, a free day from studies, so she and Jacob had come out to see Elliott and Thomas finishing the last stretch of the wall.

She wondered how she hadn't seen the bond between them before now. Jacob doted upon his father, while Elliott showed so much patience with his son that it made her heart clench maternally. He was a good father. Kindhearted whenever he was with his son—her, too, under the cover of night.

Abby sighed. It made her realize just how much she missed her own father in watching them together. Her father had died four years ago. She'd found him slumped over in the chair behind his great oak desk, hand clenched around a tumbler of whiskey. Father hadn't been all that old—he'd had years ahead of him—but he'd been weak-hearted after Mama had died.

She'd grown up that day. The change had been from a young girl just about to find her way into the world, as her sisters had done before her, to a woman who had better ideas than settling into a life that didn't seem to suit her when she couldn't control the outcome. Life was too short for any uncertainties about one's purpose. Marriage had always been an uncertainty.

She looked up to Elliott. Was he the reason these old memories were resurfacing? She sighed again. There never was much use dwelling on the past. It couldn't change the present, or dictate the future. You could only learn from it. And the day her father had died she had decided to live her life as she saw fit.

"It's rather cool out today. I'm going to head indoors."

"We'll see you for luncheon," Elliott said.

Having at least an hour to herself, Abby made her way back to the house to plan the rest of the week's lessons with Jacob since she had no other pressing matters.

She couldn't believe she'd been here for almost six weeks. She would need to write to her sisters and explain her long absence; otherwise they would be liable to come find her. Not that she'd given them any clear indication to where exactly she was staying, though they did know which town she had taken the train into. It wouldn't be hard for them to find her. It had been terrible of her to not write to her sisters. Especially since she missed them fiercely.

Martha approached her while she unraveled her shawl from her shoulders in the foyer.

"I know we don't have many visitors up here," Martha said. "But you can't use the front door as you please. Walk around the kitchen and enter where the rest of the servants come in."

Abby was shocked by the bitterness in the old woman's voice. She stood there, dumbfounded, the heavy woolen shawl folded over her arm. Should she respond? Was it worth it to defend her actions? She doubted Martha would ever like her, for reasons unknown. Abby probably hadn't helped the situation; she wasn't very good at hiding her feelings toward those she disdained. She was sure she gave that fact away by sneering at Martha every time they happened upon each other.

"For what reason do you dislike me so thoroughly?"

She should have bitten her tongue. Yet . . . she couldn't regret asking the question.

Was it possible that Martha would request her resignation for speaking out of turn? She wouldn't put it past the woman to let her go on so little reason. Martha could tell her she had to leave. But Abby wasn't ready to leave Elliott's side. Not with so much more to explore between them.

She couldn't even ask for Elliott's help in dealing with Martha. Everyone would know why the lord of the manor favored her if she dared to do something so transparent.

"Don't think I'm unaware of what is happening in *my* household."

It was no more Martha's household than hers. Despite the fact that Martha had lived here for a greater number of years, it didn't give the woman any right to treat Abby like an outsider. She'd proven herself with Jacob. Proven that she wanted nothing more than to help Elliott's son as if he were her own child. Had succeeded where all the past governesses had failed.

Of course, it was possible Martha thought her a great whore if she had any inkling as to what happened in the evenings between Abby and Elliott. Could she possibly know? Elliott came to her room once he was sure the house was empty till morning.

"I've done nothing more than I was hired to do."

Not really a lie. She hadn't meant to fall in love. Hadn't meant to find companionship in Elliott's arms. It couldn't be denied that there were strong feelings growing between them. Strong emotions she wanted to explore every facet of.

"Should never have hired you on. You've been more trouble than you're worth. You've got Master Elliott wrapped about your pretty little finger."

"You're wrong." Abby was too stunned by Martha's words to think of a better defense.

Martha smacked the handle end of the broom against the stone floor. The sound was like a hunting rifle going off as it echoed around the foyer's bare marble walls. The out-of-character action made Abby jump back a step. This woman would not rest till Abby left the castle. She saw that now. She hated that that was the case at all.

Abby refused to leave. This was her home. She didn't want to leave Jacob when they'd made leaps and bounds with his language lessons. She didn't want to walk away from Elliott and the love she felt bonding them closer every night they spent in each other's arms. She didn't want to go back to the dull balls and lackluster soirees her sisters hauled her to.

"You mistake my intent," Abby said. "I'm sorry *you* are not pleased with the progress I've made with Jacob."

"I know your type. Should have sent you away when I realized how young you were. Your type aren't welcome in the castle."

Martha pursed her lips and turned the straw broom around to sweep the sand and dirt from the foyer toward the open door much as she might sweep away an unwanted guest.

Abby was not afraid of Martha and showed that by taking a few steps forward, putting the woman within reaching distance. Martha would do no more than scowl and frown at her and deliver a few careful insults. If Martha never grew to like her, so be it. It didn't matter to her.

Abby was here to carve out a path for herself in life. Although . . . that grand plan of independence had changed over the weeks since her arrival. She didn't know precisely what she wanted anymore. She only knew that it wasn't what she had wanted previously.

She was never supposed to want marriage. Or want a man to make up part of her life as though he were her missing half. Life was sometimes cruel and decidedly unfair; it twisted what you didn't want into something tempting. And when you finally gave in to that temptation and realized you'd been wrong all along . . . life shadowed all that seemed bright for the first time.

She would find her way. She didn't have to decide her fate today. More important, she didn't have to leave the castle today.

"I'll be in the library," she told Martha, "should the young master wish to find me before luncheon."

Without giving Martha a chance to respond, she left her in the foyer, furiously sweeping away what was no longer there. The housekeeper mumbled something insulting that Abby couldn't quite make out, didn't want to make out. Abby was a bigger person than Martha; that was all there was to it. She'd be kind and understanding and make the older woman look a fool in front of her master. These things had a way of working themselves out for the better.

Abby circled her fingers in the light dusting of coarse hairs on Elliott's chest, as she often did when they lay in bed at night.

"Elliott?"

"Hmmm," he replied, half asleep with her soothing ministrations.

She was tired, too, but had too much on her mind to find sleep easily tonight. Guilt gnawed at her like a vulture starved and desperate for food. She had to tell him who she really was and why she'd come here. How could she hold back any part of herself from the man she'd fallen in love with? Doing so felt wrong.

"I have something I need to tell you . . ."

She bit at her lip, not sure she wanted to go on, or how to, for that matter. He'd probably fall asleep soon and forget that she'd started a conversation if she remained quiet.

"What is it?" He yawned and barely brought his hand up to cover it in time.

She sighed heavily. No such luck that he would find sleep and forget that she needed to divulge her secrets, which weren't near as life changing as the ones he'd shared with her. That should make it easier to tell him the truth, but it didn't.

Chances were, he'd not care that she was a lady by birth and in standing. Or that she would be a wealthy woman once her inheritance came to her. On the opposite side of the coin, he might care a great deal that she had lied to him. Send her back to her sisters.

This was a burden in desperate need of lifting. It would do her well to tell him the truth.

"You should know something about me. It would never have mattered had we gone on as master and servant."

"You were never a servant in my eyes. Not since the moment we met."

She flattened her palm against his sternum. She needed to stop fidgeting. "And it was with great difficulty that I viewed you as merely my employer. You know I have two sisters."

"I recall you telling me of them."

"What I failed to mention was that they both married rather well. They don't know that I came here to be a governess. I lied to them, you see."

"Then write to tell them the truth."

"I can't."

Abby pushed herself up on her elbow so she could look at Elliott. His eyes were closed, but he opened them when she shifted her position. Stubble darkened his face and shadowed those slashed cheeks and dimpled chin of his.

She wanted him to make love to her body with his mouth so she could feel the prickly scruff of his cheeks sensitizing her skin. She looked away from him and focused on the quilted counterpane that lay bunched up next to them.

"They think I'm here attending a friend's first birth. Had they known I'd taken on a position as governess, they'd have found a way to keep me in London till I was safely wed."

She looked at his face to gauge his expression. He sleepily lifted a brow in question and put one arm behind his head to raise it from the pillows.

"You fear matrimony so much?"

She gave his arm a playful shove.

"No."

Not anymore. But she couldn't voice those words. She knew Elliott had no wish to marry again. He had told her that he was quite happy with how things had turned out and that he never wanted to change their arrangement.

"I might have failed to mention that my sisters are both countesses."

One black brow was still arched in question over his left eye. "And what does that make you, my fair Abigail?"

"I was born into a good family. My father was a viscount."

"Lady Abigail Anne Hallaway, then. Who did your sisters marry? Perhaps I know them by name."

Elliott had admitted an uncanny ability in remembering names and faces; he had to commit a great many things to memory when he couldn't read.

"You may know Emma's husband. He's the Earl of Asbury. I think you are near to the same age."

"I only ever visited London thrice. On one of those occasions, maybe nine or ten years ago, I met Asbury. He was older, so probably not your brother-in-law. His father, perhaps? He helped me with some investments.

"The local villages relied heavily on smuggling in my father's time. When the bans were lifted on the making and distributing of whiskey, the main source of income died here. I remember Asbury because he suggested I invest everything I had into livestock. Cows, sheep, and goats. I thought him a fool. I still took his advice since I had nothing left to lose. He was right."

Elliott proved himself over and over to the people in Northumbria. It upset her to know they disliked him so much. For what reason could they loathe a man who made sure no one under his rule starved? Would she ever know the reason?

"Grace married an Italian count. I left just before her wedding. I fear she'll never forgive me for my hasty departure. In my defense, I'd already accepted the post before news of her marriage."

"I'm sure she will. From what you've carefully said about them before now, they seem as though they love you a great deal."

She nodded. "They do. My sisters wanted nothing more than for me to marry a title. But my heart wasn't in it."

"Your heart wasn't in it?" He was teasing; she knew because the left side of his lip twitched upward, revealing an amused smile despite his even tone of voice. "So you fled as far as the train would take you."

"Yes and no. I did try to appease my sisters. I mingled and danced, dined and flirted all in the hope of finding the perfect suitor for more than three years. There were no potential husbands in my dinner partners."

"I see where your problem lies."

"What do you mean?"

He wouldn't offer marriage, would he? In her revelation, had she hoped him to act a true gentleman and offer for her hand knowing that he'd ruined a lady? She wanted to tell herself that that wasn't what she felt in her heart, but she was done with her lies, even to herself.

He had been clear when he said this was all he could offer her. A life of half sin. Would he change his mind?

And why was she even thinking of marriage? Had she completely forgotten her resolve never to walk down the aisle and say her vows with God as her witness? Hadn't she decided that the best course for any woman was to grasp her future with both hands and make it her own?

"Abigail, darling, there are no perfect men." She ignored the twinge of disappointment that stabbed at her heart and took his tone for what it was, teasing. Mere teasing. "We are all savage beasts no matter how you dress us up or how prettily, or dully, you make us speak when in polite company. We all have the same goal."

"And what is that?"

"Care to guess?" he said, skimming his hand up the inside of her thigh and stopping at the short, crisp hairs at the apex. His blue eyes flickered with naughty intention, and he focused on his hand slowly inching closer.

"And how do you know that's not all a woman desires?"

Turnabout was fair play. Her hand, which rested over his chest, slid down the center of his body over the coarse hairs that trailed low on his belly, pointing the way to her goal. She didn't stop her exploration till she grasped the root of his prick.

"Is it?" His eyes focused back on hers.

He pushed her thighs open so he could glide his fingers between the lips of her sex. Languid, arousing strokes. He definitely wanted to excite her passions again this evening.

Oh, but it took so little to do just that.

"You don't mind that I lied?"

"No. You're still my Abigail."

That had a nice ring to the consonants: *his* Abigail.

She had told all but one of her secrets. Yet the last one wasn't so much a secret as it was a suspicion. Her menses should have come and gone at least once while she'd been at the castle. They hadn't. It was too soon to know anything. Too soon to know if life grew within her.

The rightness of them being together as companions and lovers could never be argued. But in her heart, she had to admit that she craved commitment. Marriage. Would he feel obligated to marry her should she prove to truly be pregnant? She didn't want to force his hand.

The tumultuous thoughts had her stomach flipping in nervous sadness instead of arousal as he inched his fingers closer to her sheath. She banished the worries from her mind. She could think on them tomorrow.

All she wanted was to feel. To forget that her mind warred with her body.

With the back of her hand, she caressed his quickly hardening member.

"Minx," Elliott growled, thrusting two fingers up into her sheath.

Fingers tightening around his rod, she gently pulled the cap back from the head, and reveled when she heard a curse spill from his lips.

Suddenly she was on her hands and knees, rear in the air, his heated palm pressed to her back and forcing her bare chest to the mattress.

"Stay put," he mumbled. He did so enjoy this position.

What did it say about her that she enjoyed his guttural demands? She who never wanted a man to rule her life? Though he hadn't taken command of her life, merely her body.

The backs of his hands stroked over each buttock and the tops of her thighs in tandem.

Should she be embarrassed to be in such a position? Exposed so thoroughly? How could she be? She was with Elliott. He had her explicit trust in all things. He had her heart and soul; if he asked for either, she'd tear them from her body to show her devotion and complete surrender to this man.

"Prettiest sight I've ever seen," he said.

Abby couldn't help that his seductive words had her back bowing and her rear pushing closer to his warm body. She wanted nothing more than for him to blanket her body with his own. She craved the feel of him between her legs.

"Fill me," she asked in a heated whisper.

Her fingers curled into the soft sheets on either side of her head. Her sheath convulsed in anticipation of her request.

"In time."

The palm of his hand came down on her buttock in a playful yet gentle smack.

"Elliott," she groaned, wanting so much more.

Her core tightened and her fluids slicked the skin between her thighs.

"Fill me," she begged. She needed him, was desperate for the feel of him.

He leaned over her, bringing their bodies close together, but not close enough to appease the desire to feel him inside her.

"Do you know, I saw you before you invited me to your bed."

His voice was like hot brandy on her tongue, and it melted her insides all the way down to her belly.

How had he ever seen her? When had he seen her?

"It was your first morning in the castle," he answered her thoughts.

One of his hands slid over her hip and around to her stomach. The tickling touch had her wriggling in his hold. His hand stopped just shy of reaching her breasts. She wanted him to touch her and stop taunting her. She wanted his hand to brand her instead of tease her.

"I came upon you in the kitchen. You were bathing."

His cheek pressed lightly between her shoulder blades, his body finally covered hers as he relayed the first time he'd seen her. The jut of his cock pressed to one cheek of her rear. She felt a bead of his semen wet her skin there.

His free hand smacked down on her buttock again. The sting sent a hot jolt of desire through her whole body and had her biting the sheets to keep from screaming out in pleasure.

Did it make her depraved to enjoy him spanking her rear as if she were a disobedient student? She didn't mind being wicked alongside Elliott. The hardness of his instrument pressed like a rod of steel against her was evidence of his desire for the act he committed. He wanted her to enjoy this erotic game he played at. And she did. Fully. Thoroughly. Completely.

"I wanted to span my hand over this pretty rear of yours when I saw you take off your chemise that morning."

His palm came down on her again. The sensation like

hot wax dribbled on her skin. Thrilling for the momentary rush it filled her with on the initial sting. She wanted it again. And again. And again.

The hand beneath her sternum slid more firmly onto her breast; his body pushed forward, lodging the nut of his cock just inside her. He was intentionally drawing out their time together and the intimacy of their every touch. He enjoyed arousing her every sense, titillating her beyond reason before either of them found their crisis every night.

His hand did not come down on her bottom again. He pushed her legs out farther and, in one long stroke, slid his cock deep inside her.

Abby pushed herself up on her elbows, liking the sensation of him behind her. Loving how much more he filled her body in this position. Loving that he never held back from doing as he wished with her body.

He lifted away from her so he could kneel behind her. His hands rubbed over the globes of her buttocks as he slid in and out of her core at a moderate pace.

He kept her wanting more. And what she wanted more than anything right now was rough and manly and strong. To feel the bulge of his muscles beneath her exploring hands as he filled her body and rode them both to sweet paradise. Tonight she didn't want him holding back. She wanted everything without knowing all that entailed.

"More, Elliott."

"You are anxious tonight." He squeezed her buttocks with both hands. "I'll have to give this part of you more attention in the future if it turns you to melted butter on my tongue."

He leaned over her and licked a hot trail up her spine, sending a shiver of pure delight through her veins. She pushed herself up on her hands. Wanting to feel his chest against her back as they moved together.

Elliott pulled out of her sheath to her utter disappointment and urged her toward the head of the bed, saying, "Grasp the headboard to hold you up."

As soon as her hands wrapped around the intricate molding of the pale wood, he pressed her thighs apart with his knees and slid back inside her. She practically sat on his lap in this position. His hand reached around and squeezed her breast and tweaked her nipple between two of his fingers with every upward thrust to her core.

The feel of their sweaty bodies sliding and grinding together had Abby leaning her head back to Elliott's shoulder and closing her eyes. So many sensations bombarded her that she could do nothing more than hold on to the bed and let Elliott give them both pleasure.

The slide of their bodies together was powerfully arousing. The coarse hairs of his chest at her back a sweet contrast of his hard body against her softer one. Her loose hair stuck to both their bodies and eclipsed them in heated bliss. The smell of their sex and sweat was rapturously delicious with every inhalation and gasp she made. Her fingers curled tighter around the headboard.

"Touch yourself," Elliott commanded.

When she hesitated, not sure what exactly he meant, he uncurled her fingers from the wood and lowered both their hands to the exposed pearl at her center. Her sex was slick with her own fluids. Elliott groaned as their fingers met with the moisture. It was a deep groan, like a contented purr rumbling against her back.

He took the shell of her ear between his teeth, flicked it with his tongue, and demanded more firmly, "Touch yourself."

And she did. Her fingers wrapped around the base of his cock, the feel of him sliding in and out of her more erotic than even the position they were in. She pulled her fingers away from that slick, hot touch to rotate them around the nub of her sex. Elliott's fingers moved with hers, pressed down on hers.

She felt like she was coming undone. Like her whole being was unraveling to the very core of what she was. Her heart sped so fast in her chest that it forced her breathing to come faster, harsher. With every pant she made a little noise in the back of her throat that was high-pitched. Needy.

"Come for me," Elliott said, his hand still atop hers, his other squeezing at her breast. "I want to suck the swollen bud of your sex into my mouth and feel you come around my face."

"Oh, God," she moaned, having no strength for any other words when she was concentrating on all the other feelings ravaging her body into a void of complete surrender.

She felt the tightening of her sheath around his prick. The calmness she inevitably experienced just before her release. His fingers pressed down hard on hers, made them move faster until, finally, she had to pull his hand away and rest her forehead on the cool surface of the wooden headboard.

Her body unraveled, starting in the pit of her pelvis and moving through her limbs in a thrill of excitement so forceful, she could feel nothing but that pleasure for a long moment.

When her body awakened to Elliott's, he still moved inside her. His pace increasing as he shouted out his release and bit at her earlobe. He jerked the final few thrusts inside her before he was completely sated and empty of seed.

Her body felt overworked. Tired. Not even awake enough to speak after such a powerful intimate moment. Her mind had turned inward, anyway.

Guilt in having an affair without the sanctity of the

church filled her with sorrow. Not because it was wrong in God's and everyone else's eyes, but because she could never openly show the love she had for Elliott. Love was sacred. It should be shared. Cherished openly.

Somehow, they ended under the sheets, her body tucked against Elliott's. Neither of them seemed to have the strength to speak. Before she knew it, a need so great for sleep closed in and finally claimed her.

Chapter 20

*"There was ever only one monster in this fair king-
dom, Father. And that was you. I've been gifted a
form that can defeat the evil in this land and here I
am come to claim you."*

—*The Dragon of Brahmors*

Elliott looked at Abigail from across the bedchamber.
She sat on a white silk-covered chair, he on the edge of
her bed.

"I think you need to find another governess. We can't
go on living in secret, Elliott."

"I see no reason why anything needs to change."

"Martha suspects us. Suspects me to be a great harlot
and seducer of all men, I'm sure." She loosened the coil she
kept her hair in during the day, letting ringlets of reddish-
blonde hair fall around her shoulders.

"You're speaking nonsense."

He didn't want to think of the day when she would
have to leave. Jacob would need her guidance until it was
time for him to attend school. That was four years off.
Elliott was so thankful to her for teaching his son to read

that his heart was near to bursting with joy. Reading was something he would never be able to do.

After his initial revelation of that fact, neither of them had talked about it. He wanted to ask her if she could help him with his letters but feared that would get in the way of her teaching his son. He couldn't demand more of her time with their nights and Jacob's lessons during the day.

"I'm simply speaking the truth. I have to be honest with you, Elliott. I can't live in secret for however long you wish it. It's as though what we are doing is shameful. I don't want to feel that way. I don't want this to feel as though we're doing something wrong."

"Then don't think. Just enjoy the time we spend together. Is that so much to ask?"

There was nothing else he could give her. Nothing more permanent than what they already shared. There was marriage, but that was for the fools who thought they were in love and didn't want their lady to escape and reject them later on. That had been him and Madeline. God, he'd been so wrong about her. So very, very wrong.

"Elliott . . . there is going to come a time when I have to leave. It'll be sooner than either of us really wants, I fear."

"More nonsense," he said, pulling his shirt from his trousers.

She stood from her seat and took off her dressing robe. She looked tired tonight. Was it the conversation that tired her or the late nights? Maybe a bit of both. He felt unusually tired, too, but that probably had to do with finishing the repairs on the west wall. It would be done in the next week.

Nothing more than sleep for them both tonight. He shucked his trousers and socks, but left his smalls on and held a hand out to Abigail.

"We'll talk of this another day."

She pursed her lips and nodded. She was reluctant in taking his hand. He hoped that didn't mean she'd start refusing his company in her bed. He craved the feel of her warm body at night. Wanted to watch her sleep and wake with her looking down at him at the first crack of dawn before they had to part for the day.

"I'm not likely to forget that you suggested that."

"I wouldn't expect you to," he replied as she placed her warm palm in his.

Abby stared out at the North Sea. The water was rough, a churning black mass of frothy waves pounding against the rocky shore like angry fists. As far as her eye could see, there was water and sand; farther out she could barely make out the small islands that dotted throughout the water a few miles off from where she stood.

Abby had perched herself on a large rock close to the water's edge. She needed to rest. She'd strained herself in so quickly traversing the sand dunes that surrounded the beach. She'd been desperate to put distance between her and Elliott.

Lifting her heavy shawl from her shoulders, she settled it higher around her neck and ears. It was only early evening but the wind had turned brisk. She could taste the fresh coolness of winter in the air. It would snow soon. Maybe even tonight.

She had come out here to escape all the eyes on her in the house. And to think without anyone to interrupt her thoughts.

Her hand rested on her belly. She had to tell Elliott that a babe grew within her. She had been positive of her state for a few days, but every time she'd tried to tell Elliott, the words got stuck in her throat.

She had so many conflicting feelings about her and Elliott's relationship, about her life at Brendall Castle.

Martha had grown colder toward her—if such a thing were possible. She often treated her poorly by insulting her and talking down to her as though she were no better than vermin. She did this in front of Lydia. Sometimes, even in front of Jacob. Rarely did she do so when Elliott was there to play the witness.

Martha checked to make sure Abby was alone in the library or parlor before taking her leave of the house in the evenings, too. Abby was sure that Martha would have guarded her bedchamber door to make sure she slept alone, had she lived in the main house.

All this made for very uncomfortable living arrangements. Made more uncomfortable by the fact that she wouldn't be able to hide her condition much longer.

She'd felt sick so many mornings. She had even had to run for a chamber pot during the middle of the day to empty the contents of her stomach when something so much as smelled disagreeable—which was almost everything.

She couldn't live like this. In secrecy. In subterfuge. Without the blessing of those around them. Without her sisters to share the joy she felt in her life when she so much as thought about Elliott and about having his child.

She couldn't go on living this way for much longer. How was she going to admit all this to Elliott?

She'd bet her finest ruby necklace that Elliott had never before spent so much time with any of the past governesses. Or any other woman at the castle for that matter. But how obvious was that fact to the rest of the staff? Had she and Elliott not taken enough measures to ensure their affair remained a secret?

Or had Martha recognized Abby's sickness for what it was?

Abby knotted the heavy twill shawl protectively over her stomach and turned back for the castle. She did not want to be trapped on the beach at high tide, which was due any moment with the sun fast setting in the west. Watching the ground for fear of twisting her ankle carelessly since she was overtired, and clumsier than usual these days, Abby took each step gingerly.

A falcon screeched overhead; the sound pierced right to her soul and made her breath catch in her lungs. She swore her heart stopped for a full two beats as the sound sliced through her center.

She glanced up to see the bird circling, then suddenly saw a dark object swinging toward her head. She thought for a moment it was the bird diving in her direction and raised her arms to block the great harpy beast. But the blunt force that knocked her from her feet was not that of a falcon's claws.

She fell like a sack of rocks tossed in the water to drown unwanted kittens. Blotches of black and gray danced across her vision, and her head spun so fast she thought she might be sick.

When she opened her mouth to speak, she screamed instead. Someone grasped her by the chignon she often tied her hair in, and dragged her across the beach. It seemed impossible to get her feet under her and find her balance again. Her head faced the sandy rock-ridden surface beneath. She saw nothing but a dark figure wearing what looked like a ratty old brown habit and—in her peripheral vision—the rush of water washing up on the beach with foamy white fingers.

She attempted to scratch at her captor's strong, unrelenting arms, but her hands only met with thick, rough cloth, not flesh that could be easily maimed with her ungloved fingernails.

She kicked at the ground trying to get her feet under

her and make whomever held her in a death-like grip release her, but her skirts hampered her balance further.

Her captor said not one word as she was dragged closer to the water. She managed one strong kick at her captor's calf, making the dark figure stumble, but it wasn't a hard enough strike to incapacitate her captor or release herself.

Next she knew, ice-cold water slicked through the layers of her skirts and underthings and slithered its death-like touch over her skin. The chill numbed her limbs at an alarmingly quick rate. Her mind trudged slower through a murk of non-understanding. She was cold. So cold that rational thought fled.

How was it possible for her captor to drag her through the water without feeling the cold right down to their marrow?

Abby could do naught but lie in the rough sway of the sea. It would carry her to her death, she thought. The life growing in her would never have a first breath of air. And Elliott didn't know.

Tears warmed her face, but it was not enough warmth to awaken her weak limbs. She hoped death was merciful. Quick. Like the way she was fast losing feeling in her arms, her feet, her lower legs. She hoped the water swallowed her whole and kept her in this state of unfeeling and numbness. She couldn't fight the pain and fog clouding her mind, sucking her into a deep void of nothing. She couldn't fight to live. Not for herself. Not for the babe nestled in her womb.

Such a miserable, lonely way to leave the world. Not at all part of her plan to seize her own fate. Not what she wanted for herself, at all. Drowning in a sea of bitter loneliness was not what she had imagined for her end. Taking the innocent life of her child with her seemed wrong.

Elliott studied the land that surrounded the castle from the window of his bedchamber. He was waiting for her to come back. Night was setting in fast, and Abigail had not come in from her walk. He'd left her to her own devices, understanding her need to collect her thoughts. She said she'd needed time alone. He wondered if she regretted their time together. Did she wish to leave the castle and him behind?

He suspected that to be the case after their previous evening's conversation.

He didn't like the fact that she'd remained out of doors for so long. He'd seen her picking her way down the beach. The gentle push and sound of the waves had been a solace to him many times in his life, so he understood what drew her to the water, but the tide was coming in soon. The water was an unpredictable force of nature once she turned rough-and-tumble, like the fury of a lightning storm striking when least expected.

Surely she understood the dangers in staying down by the water late in the evening.

Not wanting to take any chances where her safety was concerned, especially after the mishap on the parapet wall, he grabbed up his jacket and headed for the door. Martha intercepted him in the main hall.

"My lord." She looked at the coat he held and clucked her tongue like a mother hen. "It's quite chilly outside tonight. Let me find you a warmer, heavier coat before you venture out. There's sure to be snow later this evening."

"I'll be but a short while," he assured her.

Martha had taken up the role as mother to him when his own had passed away. More than twenty years ago now. God, time passed by so quickly. Before he knew it, his son would be a grown man.

Her fingers were still wrapped around his wool coat. Effectively stopping him from going anywhere.

"I can't wait," he said and walked around her, forcing her to release the material from her grasp.

Was Martha intentionally stalling him?

It felt imperative that he locate Abigail. He rubbed at his chest, feeling a bloom of pain and worry settle around his heart.

He found the old wooden door covered in the vines of dried ivy and opened it up to a path leading down to the beach. The door was closed, which seemed odd. If the latch came down, it stopped anyone from returning from whence they came. He was positive he'd seen her come this way.

"Abigail," he called as he pushed through the door and took to a brisk walk over the sand dunes. With practiced ease, he traversed the terrain quickly, making it to the beach in less than five minutes.

No slender figure stood at the edge of the sea, or walked the sandy and pebbled terrain. Had Abigail not had a penchant for colorful dresses and brightly twilled shawls, he would never have seen her in the murk of the water.

He made for the shore at a dead run, throwing his jacket off before he waded into the freezing sea nearly to his waist. His heart lurched at the sight before him. She lay faceup in the water, her heart-shaped face pale and white, lips tinged a deathly shade of blue, and the side of her face and temple marred with a bruise. He might have wondered if her being in the water was an accident if not for the dark swelling at the side of her head.

Her skirts were caught between two rocks and the floating debris of seaweed and a chunk of tree trunk. It was probably the only thing keeping her afloat.

With a supporting arm across her back, he ripped the garments free from where they were wedged, caught her up in his arms, and made his way to the shore.

He placed her gently on the sand—not an ideal place to set her down but he felt he had no choice. He parted her lips to make sure nothing blocked her airway, then lowered his ear to her chest and listened for her breathing. Hearing it faintly, he released a small sigh of relief.

Thank God.

Tucking his discarded jacket around her, he lifted her up in his arms again and made for home. It took him longer to pick his way back over the sand dunes, maybe double the time it had taken to make his way down to the beach. He hoped he wasn't too late to help his Abigail. Their night was far from over. He'd keep vigil for days if he had to, though. He'd not lose her to the sea as he'd lost his mother.

No, Abigail would live because he willed her to do so.

Once she was settled and well again, he'd question each and every person in the castle. Someone must have seen something this time.

Martha. He'd talk to Martha very soon. Something felt off with her lately.

But for now, his first priority lay prone and lifeless in his arms.

He saw no one on his way to his private chambers. He settled her in his bed and worked quickly to strip her of her boots, and then her sodden, ice-cold skirts and bodice. He had to cut the strings of her corset free because the wet laces wouldn't loosen, then he removed her chemise. All of it needed to come off if she were to grow warm again. Tossing his blankets aside, he wrapped her in a sheet, dried her hair with the hand towel from the washstand, and settled her under every blanket and throw at hand.

Building up the fire was his next priority. He didn't stop putting wood inside till he was sweating at his temples and armpits from the heat it let off.

When he approached the bed, her lips were still tinged blue. Sliding his hands beneath the blankets he rubbed at her arm, hoping to bring warmth and a shimmer of blood back to her complexion. It didn't work. She didn't stir or acknowledge that she knew whom she was with, or where she was.

She lay in his bed lifeless.

How long had she been in the water? He knew it was possible to die from the cold like this, and that the only option left to him was to pull off his own clothes and climb in beside her.

It wasn't as though they had not spent many a night naked in each other's arms. Before he stripped, he retrieved a few more blankets from her bedchamber and tossed them on top of his down blanket and counterpane.

He left his smalls on, tossing the rest of his wet clothes in a heap on the floor. Slowly, he climbed in next to Abigail in the wide bed. Her skin was like winter-touched marble. So lifeless and unmoving, it made his breath catch. It was everything she shouldn't be.

Elliott tucked her against his body, wrapping his legs around and through hers, tucking his feet under her icy ones. Her toes were like shards of ice next to his. Hopefully the cold would melt away soon.

He smoothed the flat of his hand along her arm, stroking the life and warmth back into her. His other arm was tucked under her head, the sand in her hair rubbing against his bare skin like sandpaper on wood.

"You cannot die on me, Abigail. Live."

His hand rubbed over her stomach, her thighs; nothing seemed to warm her skin. Nothing seemed to steal the blue from her lips or awaken her from her cold death-like slumber.

"You can't leave me. Not like this."

He raised his hand away from her body long enough to brush the tangled ropes of hair from her face and then rub at her arms once again. He just wanted to bring back everything that was vibrant and fiery about her.

Thinking back to the fire that had claimed his wife, Elliott surprised himself in realizing that the loss of Madeline had been a messy blessing. The thought of losing Abigail played out differently on his emotions. He couldn't help but think a larger part of him would be lost if the cold did not release its grip on her life.

But he couldn't keep her always, could he? She deserved better than him, yet that didn't stop him from finding his way to her bed every night.

For now, he'd hold on to her with everything he was worth, which by his estimation wasn't a whole lot since he wasn't quite a whole man. It would have to be enough for now. Hopefully come morning, she was alive and well and this whole bloody incident could be a thing of the past.

He realized something then: With the ever-constant danger for her, it wasn't safe here. Would he have to ask the woman he loved to leave?

He would find the culprit responsible for her accident. He should have found them before now, but he had become too complacent when no other accidents had happened since her fall from the parapet wall.

Elliott rested his cheek against her ear. The sound of her small breaths was a balm to his soul. It soothed his mind knowing she was still fighting her way up from the sleep that had claimed her.

Chapter 21

*"Dare harm me and our family will no longer thrive
in these lands."*

*"I care not, for I died the day my ladylove ceased
to live."* —The Dragon of Brahmors

Abby was hot. So blistering warm, she felt slippery with
sweat. She rolled her head from the pillow and was brought
up short by the fact that she wasn't so much wet as damp.
Her body felt itchy, as though a thousand feathers tickled
her all at once. Sand, she realized. Sand rolled underneath
her as she uncurled her legs and slid them down a hairy,
masculine set of calves.

Her limbs felt heavy and stiff. As though she hadn't
used them for days, or as though she'd taxed herself after
a full day of riding her horse and hiking through heavy
thicket.

And there was no escaping the fact that she was overly
hot. Which probably had a great deal to do with her much
warmer bed partner. His breathing was deep and even in
sleep, his face a mere inch from her ear. Each exhalation
lifted the hairs lying against the side of her face, causing
them to flutter against her cheek.

She was hot, stiff, and pleasured by the peace she felt in her silent yet drowsily aware moment. She lowered her hands to her belly and sighed out a deep breath. All wasn't lost if she lay in bed next to Elliott.

She wanted to turn around in Elliott's arms, watch him at rest. Indulge in the sight of him in quiet peacefulness. It was her favorite thing to do when he slept in her room at night.

She wanted to remember every part of his face before she told him the news of her pregnancy. It could wait no longer. Her life had nearly been washed to sea.

Uneasy thoughts tumbled around in her mind. She remembered the beach. The feeling of helplessness as someone had clubbed her in the head and dragged her into the ice-cold water. She also recalled the desperation that had clawed at her to free herself from her captor's unrelenting hold.

Her mind had not succumbed so quickly to the deadening sea around her as she had floated in a place between time and matter. Her body neither here nor there. Her mind had been all she'd had left. Troubled thoughts had taunted her and had made guilt almost outweigh the need to survive the ordeal she'd been put through.

She'd lied to so many people, including herself. Had probably hurt everyone in the process, though that would not be apparent until the truth wormed its way out of the rabbit hole.

There were so many ugly truths that could not be ignored for much longer, no matter what she and Elliott had previously revealed. No matter that Elliott had somehow saved her from a fate of nonexistence.

How else would she have ended up in his bed as though her evening were nothing but a bad dream? But the sand rubbing uncomfortably against her skin and the smell of saltwater and seaweed told her it had been no dream.

With a deep inhalation, Abby turned so she faced Elliott. She slid her arms around his broad shoulders to draw circles across his shoulder blades with the tips of her fingers.

His hand had been firmly tucked under her side, his legs wrapped around hers, holding her wedged tightly into his body. It was comforting and arousing all at the same time. They always slept completely entangled with each other. But not quite this entangled.

She slid one hand toward his face to trace the strong, hard line of his jaw. Her fingers prickled over his morning beard, then the indent at his chin.

He did not stir, so she explored further, tracing the thin line of his upper lip, and stretched closer to kiss the lower one. It was the lightest, most fleeting of kisses. She lingered there, relishing the feel of him warm and alive next to her. Which made her also warm and alive, not cold and lonely in the bottom of the sea.

Sliding her hand lower, she traced the firmness of his arms, then lower . . . her touch feather-like because she wasn't sure if she wanted to wake him quite yet. For the first time this morning, she lay awake in his arms, aware of every nuance in the room: the soft tick of a clock, the wind rattling against the house as though a storm raged in a fervor of urgency outside while all remained calm inside.

Only she wasn't calm. She was exhilarated, thankful, confused, needful, tired, and agitated all at the same time. So many emotions fluttered inside her that she didn't know which to focus on. So she focused on the man next to her.

The arousal only grew in intensity with each of her caresses. Sliding her hand between his arm and waist, she explored his pliant yet heavily muscled body. His breathing seemed to come faster, but his eyes remained closed. What would she have to do to bring him to the realm of the living with her right now?

She needn't worry, for his hands moved over her back and pulled her closer so they could wrap around her.

"I'm glad you're awake, Abigail. You frightened me half to death."

"I didn't mean to," she whispered.

What should she say? That it hadn't been her fault? That someone had snuck up on her unexpectedly and she'd been rendered helpless to fight back? She didn't want to say anything at all on the topic. Because that meant thinking about everything that had happened. That meant realizing she couldn't stay here, in this place she called home. That she had to leave Elliott and Jacob behind.

What she couldn't understand was why someone wanted to murder her. The only person who hated her a great deal was Martha. But Martha would not have had the strength to do what was done to her today, would she? Anything was possible, she guessed. But why try to kill her when all she needed to do was tell her she couldn't stay on anymore? Was Martha afraid that Elliott would override her decision?

"You've nothing to apologize for," he said. "Don't even think of apologizing. We'll figure out what happened."

"Will we?"

She wanted to believe him, but this was like the time she'd been pushed from the parapet wall. Nothing had come of his investigation of the house then. Why should that change now? Someone had orchestrated her downfall twice.

She would not give them a third opportunity.

"I will figure this out."

"It has to be someone who lives here."

"Why do you say so?"

"You don't believe me?"

"No, I believe you. It's just a question as to whom." He

rubbed his palm along her back, dusting off the sand that stuck to her. "You should sleep."

"I don't want to. What time do you suppose it is?"

"Around midnight."

She'd give herself one more night in his arms. Just the one was all she needed. She'd have to leave in the coming days. She'd not put the life growing in her womb at risk again.

"Make love to me, Elliott." She looked at his face, into his eyes. She couldn't make out the color in the dark room, but she could see that he stared back at her.

With a slow, lazy smile, he said, "Now that I've got you in this position, I have no desire to let you leave."

He lifted her from the bed, made quick work of losing the sheet they'd lain upon, and shook the sand from the counterpane before putting it back on top of the mattress.

Elliott was gentle, careful even as he helped her back onto the bed. It was as though he was afraid she'd break if he was too demanding on her body. He kissed, licked, and sucked at her breasts, her belly, and even her thighs. His hands did not remain idle in their exploration of her form. Nor did hers, for that matter.

When he finally knelt between her spread thighs, he pushed his way inside her slowly. The slow loving was no less fulfilling than the other times they'd been frantic to have each other. It was like he was remembering her body. Did he plan on sending her away? Even though she knew she needed to leave?

He kept most of his weight off her as they made love. His lips were light on hers as he tasted of her mouth. When his crisis came, his thrusts were harsher. He did not collapse on top of her, but rolled to the side.

"I was too quick," he said.

His hands skimmed down between her thighs, searching

out the bud that would drive her to distraction. She stopped his hand. It was enough just to be together tonight. She was tired and knew she should sleep off the ordeal she'd been through.

"It's fine, Elliott. I just wanted to be with you. To know that you were real and that I was really alive."

He didn't move his hand away, and she wondered if he would insist. Was it silly that she was too tired and too sad to want to find any physical enjoyment beyond what they'd just shared?

"Just hold me, Elliott."

He let out a deep sigh and gathered her close to his body so she could rest her head upon his chest. They said nothing more for some hours, as they both lay awake in each other's arms. Finally, he asked her what had happened, what she had heard, what she had seen as her attacker had dragged her into the water. She told her story. But each rendering gave them no new information as to who had harmed her.

The curtains were drawn from the window. Light tickled at the very edge of the horizon. A subtle reminder and nudge that she could not remain here with Elliott for much longer.

"I should dress. Where are my clothes?"

"I doubt they're dry as yet. I'll retrieve fresh linens for you."

"Don't worry. I'll borrow your dressing robe and return to my room. I should go before the household awakes."

"I'd rather you stay. You need to rest. I nearly lost you yesterday."

She pulled herself higher on his body and pressed her lips to his. She wanted to stay here for the day and do just what they were doing.

"Explain again what happened," he said.

She let out a long breath and recounted her story for

the third time. Was Elliott hoping to catch additional details with each rendition of the events last night? Some obscure detail she'd accidentally left out the first two times? She didn't remember any details aside from the ones she'd already given him.

"I sat down by the water for a quarter hour at most. To rest. I had taxed my energy. I was sure I was alone. I heard nothing but the sea and a few gulls calling overhead."

"Nothing to indicate another on the beach with you. Something doesn't seem right. Anyone approaching would have displaced the rocks and alerted you to their presence."

She knelt atop the bed; her only aim was to dress for the day before the servants could find them together. Or notice that both were absent from their usual morning routine. And she didn't want anyone knowing of her and Elliott's affair.

Elliott pulled her over his body once more, draping her tired, sated body on his muscular form. Without their clothes on it was hard not to notice the state he was in with his cock pressed hard to her belly.

"Tell me truthfully how you feel."

"Shaky," was her honest answer. She was scared for her unborn child, too.

She hadn't found the right moment to reveal the truth of her delicate state, yet.

"I don't think you should be out of bed today. You need to regain your strength. And though your hair covers the gash you took across your skull, I worry that you might have a concussion."

All true. She did need rest. She'd been so tired this past week and had thought their late nights had finally taken their toll on her body. But she had never wanted to put a stop to their evenings. One night away from Elliott was too long as far as she was concerned. She placed her palms lightly on either side of his face.

"I'll manage the day well enough. You know nothing can keep me off my feet."

Tonight she'd tell Elliott her plans to leave and why she had to leave to protect their child.

Come morning, however, she'd look every last servant in the eye to see if their body language so much as hinted that they didn't expect to see her today.

Elliott brushed a few strands of hair from her face and forehead, then grasped her face between his large hands so he could kiss the end of her nose. She closed her eyes and did nothing more than bask in the moment, rubbing the tip of her nose against his once his lips moved away.

"Elliott, I . . ."

I love you she wanted to say. It was hard to concentrate on saying the words when he stared at her with that intensity in his eyes.

When she made no attempt to continue what she'd been about to say, he gave her a lazy self-satisfied smile. Surely he hadn't known what she was about to whisper in an unguarded instant.

"You have given me complete happiness for the first time in my life," he said, instead of waiting for her to fill the silence.

And he her.

Just as she finished the thought a pain deep and intense in her gut had her rolling off his warm body and onto the bed beside him.

She clutched at her lower abdomen, trying unsuccessfully to assuage the pain with her hands.

A low moan tore from her lungs, taken from somewhere so deep inside her she thought maybe it was her very essence, her soul tearing in two. She tried to get her hands and knees under her, but Elliott pulled her back down on her side, his hand pressed like a solid unmovable anchor over hers, locking them in place.

Did he want to take the pain away from her? She didn't want it. She didn't like this one bit. She thought she could pitch all the food she'd stuffed herself full of over the past week.

"Abigail. Oh, Abigail," he said, a hint of sadness in his voice.

The pain was too unbearable to move from the fetal position she'd finally curled into. She wasn't sure what happened or when she became fully aware again, only that time must have passed because Elliott was no longer a shield at her back but stood next to the bed, tears in his eyes.

Tears in his eyes? For what reason? She focused more closely on him, but he wavered from her vision. He had pulled his drawers back on and held linens in his hands.

She felt so cold without him at her side. And strangely empty as she watched him watch her. She was cold, like she was swimming . . . drowning in the frosty, arctic sea all over again.

Her hands were tucked firmly between her clenched thighs. Wet with sweat from her chills, she assumed. She yanked her hands away from the center of her body and wiped the cool rivulets of sweat running down the side of her brow. When she pulled them away from her face, she saw only red staining her skin.

"Abigail." Elliott yanked back all the blankets and gathered her up in his arms, pressing the linen between her thighs. She didn't want to be held, she just wanted the pain to ebb. To stop bleeding.

"Shh . . ." he whispered. "Hold on to me. I'm so sorry. I didn't think."

She swallowed the sobs that were fast building in her throat.

Why was Elliott sorry? He wasn't bleeding. She was.

She tried to push herself up, but the pain in her belly

seemed worse and forced her back down on her side to clutch her hands over the linens Elliott had pressed to her.

Tears of silent misery and agony slipped down her face as she wiped her blood-covered hands over the white sheets around her. She wanted to be rid of the reminder. Wanted this horrible day to disappear into obscurity. To not be reminded of what she stood to lose.

She thought she might hyperventilate. Or worse, scream and have the whole house running to her aid to witness her terror.

There was no air coming from her lungs, though. There was nothing but a deafening silence of numbness. A pain so deep it was debilitating.

Was this punishment for what she'd done? For indulging in her secret desires with Elliott? Had her sins been so great that the devil had cut the cords of life that had sprouted in her womb?

Oh, God, there was no denying the truth of her pregnancy now.

She felt nothing but deadness. A different kind of numbness than she felt when she'd floated in the sea.

She felt nothing but despair as she bled out the beautiful miracle from her unwelcoming body.

She was in Elliott's arms, blankets, sheets and all, unsure how she'd gotten there. Then she was in warm water, his body tucked behind her in the tub as he held his arms tight around her middle and cooed sweet noises of nothing in her ears.

Nothing. It was all nothing. Buzzing silence. Abject loss.

She wished the sea had taken her. Taken her with the babe before it could bleed from her body.

She thought maybe they were in the water for a long time. The water grew cool around them. She felt empty inside. Not just in body but in heart.

The side of Elliot's face rested at the back of her head.

His one arm was snaked tightly around her middle, the other brushing through her hair in slow, methodical calming strokes.

"Elliott." Her voice was barely decipherable; her throat ached to utter his name. Silent agony was all she felt.

"Save your voice. Sleep if you can. I have you."

She closed her eyes not because she wanted to sleep but because they felt so swollen and achy that she needed to rest them.

The water all around them was stained pink. Elliott had braided her hair as she'd half dozed, half slouched against him in the warm water. It hung like a lifeless rope over the edge of the bathtub. Her body now lay limply against his.

Had he not interfered, had he forced himself to remain indifferent to her, she wouldn't be suffering right now. This was his fault.

He drained the tub and filled it once more with warm, almost hot, water. Her blood had stopped flowing. He knew because the water was clear now.

He had suspected that she was carrying his child. Had noticed the increased plumpness and sensitivity to her breasts. The appetite she'd developed late at night that had him raiding his own kitchen for a midnight snack fit for a king. The obvious pallor of her skin and the early hours she went to bed to combat her overtiredness. He'd recognized the signs that she was with child a week or so ago, yet he'd foolishly said nothing.

The miscarriage was probably brought on by her plunge into the cold sea and then their lovemaking afterward. God, he hated himself for that. It tore his heart in two knowing he'd contributed to the destruction of a helpless life. That he'd ripped Abigail's innocence from her and now . . . she suffered.

Standing with her held tight to his body, and with a

hand at the back of her knees, he swooped her up into his arms and dripped all the way to the chaise in his room. It was as though everything she was had drained from her with the blood that had come from her body.

Settling her on the chaise, he stripped the bedding aside and tossed fresh linens down to the center before bringing her back to the bed.

With the extra bath linens he wiped her down till she was completely dry, placed more linens at the center of the bed should she bleed any more, then tossed the blankets atop her. When he was sure she was settled comfortably, he changed out of his damp drawers, tossing the soiled material in with the bedding.

Turning to check the time on the mantel clock, he wondered if he could finish before the servants noticed something was off this morning. It was already six. Martha would be set up in the kitchen for the morning and would have noticed that he wasn't in his study. With a quick decision he donned his day clothes and locked his room behind him.

There was nothing he could do for Abigail right now. He'd join her shortly. Just as soon as he made excuses for them both. With the key he'd taken from Abigail's nightstand, he locked her bedchamber door and headed for the kitchen.

"Master Elliott, what brings you to the kitchen?" Lydia asked. Her mother was absent this morning.

"I was famished," he lied easily. "I saw Miss Hallaway this morning. She's taken a fever so I advised her to rest for the day. Tell your mother."

"I hope she hasn't got that horrible sickness going around the village. There were a dozen people sick from church last Sunday."

Lydia had always been a kind woman. She was eight years his junior, born half a year after Elliott's mother had died. It was a wonder she hadn't married yet. She'd befriended Abigail early on. She was close to the same stature as Abigail, too. Lydia would not have the strength to drag Abigail across the beach and into the water.

Was this how it would be? Would he be suspicious of everyone?

"That could very well be it. I'm feeling off-kilter myself. I am going to rest for the morning in my chamber. Have luncheon left outside my room at noon."

"Yes, my lord." Lydia dipped her head at his request.

He needed to see Martha before he went back to his room. He knew Martha hadn't liked Abigail from the start. Had never cared to figure out why, either. Could Martha—a woman who acted as the matriarch in this household—have done something so vile?

Martha was on the second-floor landing, staring up at the tapestry of his dead wife. "Morning, Master Elliott."

"What brings you to this part of the house so early in the morning?"

"Nothing, my lord, you weren't in your study when I brought a breakfast tray by, so I came to make sure you fared well."

"I have fared better. But I should be well enough soon."

He looked up at the tapestry of his wife. She had been a beautiful woman. Kindhearted and sweet when he'd first brought her here. But it had all changed within the first year of their marriage.

"Always knew there was something off about her," Martha said.

Come to think of it, Madeline had claimed strange things happening in the household against her person. Complained of hearing peculiar noises. Had tried to tell him harm had befallen her more than once. She'd never been hurt, never fallen or been dragged into the sea, but . . .

Elliott looked back to Martha. For what reason? What

motive? It didn't make sense. Martha was a hearty woman; she'd have the strength to drag Abigail into the water. But why? She'd been a part of this family as far back as he could remember.

Thomas could have done it. Only problem with that was Thomas enjoyed Abigail's company. Enjoyed teasing her like a father would a daughter.

He focused on the woman he'd known his whole life.

"You left late from the house last evening."

"Just finished up a few letters for the livestock we sold over the border."

Yet she had carried no parchments on meeting him outside his study. She'd tried to detain him. Tried to stall his leaving.

Martha, then, was his main suspect in Abigail's incidents. Martha would answer to him as soon as he had proof.

"I'll be abed for the remainder of the morning. I have a dreadful pain in my head."

"I'll bring you a drink to ease it."

"No. I'll be fine after a few hours' sleep."

"I haven't seen Miss Hallaway about the household yet. She's usually up for her walk. You haven't seen her, have you?"

There was an expression of genuine care in Martha's question. But was it real? He didn't think so.

"She was ill in the night. She's taken to her bed today. Jacob shouldn't bother either of us. I don't want him sick, too."

"Of course, my lord." Martha descended the stairs.

"I'd like to go over the accounts with you later," he called down to her.

She looked up at him from where she stood on the bottom landing, and replied, "As you wish."

He took the stairs two at a time after that, his only worry Abigail. He wondered if he should call for a doctor.

But then, everyone would know his business. Or maybe not? He'd see her first, then decide. If he had to ride out to get the doctor himself, he would do so.

She didn't know how long she slept, but she woke with a start. Elliott was at her side, gathering her up in his arms.

"Abigail."

"I'm sorry I didn't tell you." The words were so quiet, but to speak them louder and put conviction to them would break her right now. She felt so delicate. Like she'd break if she thought too much on the ordeal.

"I had suspected. It was early on. It's all right."

"It's not fine. Not in the least. I wanted that baby. I wanted it so badly."

Hot fat tears fell from her eyes. There was no stopping this expression of sadness. She'd lost too much today. Although she'd known for certain for only a short a time that she carried Elliott's child, it had been precious to her. A tiny miracle growing inside her. A gift from the heavens despite the sin they lived in.

He brushed her hair back from her face, rocking her gently in his arms in the center of the bed. His thighs flanked hers as he held her tight.

"I know," he whispered against her hair, kissing lightly at her temple. "I'm sorry you've had to experience this at all."

"Don't ever let me go. Oh, God, Elliott. I can't bear this. I can't!"

"Shh . . . I have you."

She fell asleep in his arms, he gently rocking her back and forth, rubbing a soothing hand over her back.

Chapter 22

The king raised his sword, intent on blooding the
great beast, but the dragon was quicker and wasted
no time in ending his plight as he breathed his fire
down unto his cruel father's weak fight.
                                        —The Dragon of Brahmors

Abby stood from the settee and walked dazedly over to
the chair Elliott sat in. They were ensconced in his private chamber, where the servants could not interrupt
them in the early hours of the evening.

She'd lain in bed all morning, still weak and saddened
from her ordeal. Her loss. There had been nothing to do
but think of the situation she was in, and she had come to
some harsh conclusions and realizations today.

Would the small bit of happiness and joy she'd seen
light his eyes these past weeks be completely snuffed when
she told him she couldn't stay? Not unless he offered her
something more than living a lie. Only then would she consider facing whatever danger threatened their happiness.

"I may meet the same fate as your wife."

Abby didn't want to believe it possible. She was stronger

than the woman before her. She knew right down to her bones that she and Elliott could make this work. While she wouldn't allow madness to eat away at her mind, she wasn't sure she could keep looking death in the eye and walk away unscathed indefinitely.

The last accident had been too much for her to bear. She bit her lip hard to squelch the tears that formed in her eyes. She would be strong for this conversation.

"It's possible," he replied.

She wished he had lied. Then she might have convinced herself to stay even though she knew he would not offer marriage.

Elliott tapped the arm of the chair for her to sit on. She couldn't be so close to him. Not when she was going to reject him, run away from him. If she sat next to him, she'd want him to comfort her, to tell her they would get through this. She knew he wouldn't tell her that.

She sat across from him in an identical leather chair instead and curled her feet up under her and crossed her arms over her middle.

"Do you want me to leave?"

"I don't want you to find yourself the victim of another accident. I don't want to find you dead the next time I happen upon you."

She had wanted him to argue that she should stay. It felt as though he was giving up on her.

Yesterday he'd spent the day with her as she'd cried over the loss of the baby. She'd not bled again after he'd bathed her and settled her in bed. Now she felt bereft. Worn out.

She'd thought only a man in love would stand by his woman's side when she experienced something so heart-wrenching. She'd seen tears in his eyes when he'd realized what had happened. It wasn't for her that he had cried . . . it was the tiny life torn from her body that he'd grieved for.

Maybe knowing he'd impregnated her had made him realize that had the child grown in her belly, they'd not be able to hide their affair from the household, or from the village for that matter.

She'd been welcome as a companion, welcomed so easily into his bed as his lover that she hadn't thought to step back and see the worth of her sacrifice in falling so easily in love with him. Yesterday had changed everything.

She gave him a sad smile, her lip quivering where she bit down into the bottom one. "Our match was doomed from the start."

He nodded his agreement and dropped his gaze to the fireplace.

She needed to stay her course. Focus on what her heart was telling her to do—tell him that she would be gone in a couple of days. She only needed time to heal before her journey home.

Numbness, she decided, was too passionless a word to describe how she felt. It was as though she wasn't in her body, but looking down on the scene before her. As though she weren't truly seeing things through her own eyes.

"You are crippled by your worst fears, Elliott. Madeline still has her claws in you."

"Abigail . . ." His tone was even. Careful. "My wife has nothing to do with us."

His wife had everything to do with them, she wanted to scream. Absolutely everything. But the words, the accusation, lodged in her throat.

"I think you want me to stay. But you are afraid to truly let go of your past to embrace a future of a different making. Had this malice toward me never happened, you would open your heart up and let me in. You would give our future a chance."

"What in hell are you talking about?" He rose from the chair.

She stood, too, and raised her hand to his face, cupping the prickly stubble in her soft hand as he came nearer to her. His skin was so dark next to hers. A contrast. An opposite. She'd fallen into a false security these past weeks, thinking him her other half. What a fool she was. A simpering, naive debutante just as she'd always tried not to be.

When they had met in secret over the past weeks, it had felt as if the whole world had ceased to exist around them. It was a nice fantasy, but Abby was no longer willing to settle for merely that. Despite what she had always believed she wanted, she realized how wrong a life of solitude would have been now that she'd invested her heart in the man she loved.

Everything had changed. She felt as though she had changed.

"I can't live the way we are living," she admitted. How strange it felt to voice that opinion. But hearing it made her really believe those words for the truth.

"You've always deserved better than this heap of rock." His hands caressed her arms. It was meant to be soothing, she thought, but didn't feel that way.

"Why do you refuse me a position by your side?"

"I can't offer marriage, Abigail."

She made no response. There was nothing left to be said. She dropped her gaze from his.

"Would marrying me be so awful?" She wasn't sure she wanted him to answer that. But it was better to know than to hope for more.

"You'll grow sick of this place. Marriage would bind you here and you'll eventually want to leave." It was an honest answer. False, but honest. If he couldn't commit to her, then there truly was nothing left for her here.

He shook his head and focused on his hands where they clasped around her arms. He dropped them away and gave her his back. Could he so easily turn away from her? Forget her?

Elliott couldn't look at her, or face the hurt radiating from her like a stove letting off excess heat.

The crackle of the fire in the grate let off little pops as the wood disintegrated in the flame. He heard someone in the hall. He wondered if they listened at the door.

Everything was as it should be, except the part where he was rejecting the woman he loved. Convincing her that there was nothing for her in this cursed place. Agreeing with her leaving, when he knew she wanted him to object.

He felt as though he were discarding her. Betraying her. He was, in a sense. After the mishaps, he couldn't trust that a worse fate wouldn't befall her—a fate like the screaming terror of his wife's voice as fire had engulfed her in an inferno of personal hell.

To keep Abigail safe, he had to let her go.

If she left, she could start afresh. Forget the pain and sadness he'd watched her live through these past two days. Maybe she'd be happier without him. Only time would tell.

He wished he could go with her, but it was better if he stayed away from the vapid gossipmongers that made up the ton. He'd not be subject to their wagging tongues, or play the butt to their jokes should anyone ever learn his secrets. That would only bring down Abigail in their eyes, too.

Besides, he couldn't go when he'd decided the only task for him now was ferreting out the person responsible for hurting Abigail. They'd see no compassion from him. None. He cared not who it was in the household, or how long he'd known them. They'd answer to all the crimes committed, including the death of his unborn babe.

He looked at Abigail again. Her nose was red, her eyes puffy. He hated that he had caused these tears.

"I'll provide for you," he said quietly, feeling the need to fill the silence in the room. She'd want for nothing in her life. She could live independently from her sisters if she so wished it.

"You'll provide for me?" She laughed bitterly. "I've a fortune of my own."

She dashed away a tear that had rolled down her cheek.

"When you realize everything that stands before you is a gift rather than a burden, I fear you'll realize that you have banished another opportunity at love. I was a fool to think I could change you, Elliott, or even hope to persuade you of something far better than the loneliness we both lived with before finding each other. I'm sorry I was wrong."

"You weren't, Abigail. And there is nothing to apologize for. I care a great deal for you."

"I'm not sure who the greater fool is in all this."

"You'll be safer if you leave. You know this. Someone has nefarious intentions toward you. You'll not be safe until I know who it is and put a stop to it."

If he let her walk away as she seemed adamant in doing . . . it would be better for them both. He had to believe that. Didn't believe it, but had to.

"I'll tell the household you are ill. You can remain in your room or mine until you leave."

"What of your son? Do you not care for his well-being?"

"Someone will be able to pick up where you left off."

He knew she'd refuse him entry to her bed, not that he wanted anything more than to watch over her, make sure she slept well. Make sure dreams of losing the babe didn't keep her up at night as they had the past two. He'd find a way to make this up to her.

"I'll leave the day after tomorrow. I only need a cart to the rail. I'll book passage on the first available train home."

"Do you travel to London?"

"Bakewell first. I don't know where my sister is staying right now."

"What about a companion for the trip?"

"There's no need. The trip will be but a few days, no more."

The tears had dried up in her eyes. She held her head high and proud. She was already shutting him out. He felt it like a thick wall of fog growing between them. Separating them.

With four steps, he was in front of her. He'd not let her go without giving her something more.

He took her in his arms and planted his mouth against hers. His hands wrapped in her hair, holding her head close so she couldn't pull away. Not that she attempted to.

She opened her mouth and her arms to him. Their lips melded and nipped a final time.

His hands held either side of her face when he pulled away from the kiss.

For her ears alone, he whispered, "I love you. Remember that I love you."

Tears of silent distress flowed down her cheeks. No sobs racked her body or had her whimpering in his hold. Just silent tears met his declaration. She didn't repeat the sentiment; not that he had expected her to, she was too distraught. Angry with him. Furious with this whole situation.

"You're a scared fool, Elliott. Remember that."

She wiped her sleeve across her face and sniffled, then took a step away from him and walked out of his room. He watched her go. Maybe he *was* a scared fool.

Chapter 23

*The dragon addressed the people: "You once knew
me as the prince of Brahmors. I cannot rule you in
this form but will watch and protect you forevermore. I have no desire to live as a man, for my love
was taken from me with my dying human breath."*
                        —The Dragon of Brahmors

"I see she's packing to leave like the others before her,"
Martha said.

Elliott turned away from the frost and fog mingling
together over the water's surface like long-lost lovers in the
distance. He'd been staring out the window in his study
for at least half an hour, gazing at the chasm of nothing-
ness.

Elliott turned away from the mesmerizing lap of the
water below and looked Martha over with a critical eye.
He recalled this setting and felt a spark of similarity. Same
place, same stance, same question asked by a woman
who'd known him his whole life.

He'd been watching Martha closely these past few days.
Either she knew he was watching her and was careful not

to misstep, or she was innocent of any wrongdoing. He didn't believe the latter.

"She lasted longer than our past governesses," was his response to her flippant remark. "Have you started the process for hiring another?"

"Weeks ago. I have had a few applicants you may like."

Weeks! Not hours, nor a day, but weeks! Abigail hadn't started packing until this morning. Martha had been responsible for hiring Abigail. For what reason would she wish to see the back of her? Why would she want to cause her physical harm?

"I shouldn't want Jacob to go without a teacher now that he's grasped onto his studies with both hands, so to speak. Perhaps it's time he try a tutor again?"

"Aye. A sound plan. I'll have the advertisement changed right away." She turned to leave.

He didn't want her to go yet. Something niggled at the back of his mind like a hammer at his skull.

"Martha?"

She turned back to him.

"How long have you worked here?"

Deep furrows lined her forehead. She seemed puzzled by the question.

"A long time. Long before you were born, Lord Brendall. More than forty years, now."

"You would have been a young woman when you came here." She nodded. "Around thirteen." Another nod. Life had been hard on Martha; she looked a decade older than her true age. "I'm surprised you stayed on. My father was a tyrant."

"My home has always been in the north. I couldn't leave it even with the likes of your father at the helm of the household."

Was there a possibility she'd seen and felt much of the same abuse he had from his father?

She carried on, "Your father was always a hard man."

"An understatement," he interjected.

Cruel, vicious, inhuman were closer to the truth. The old man had been the reason his mother had ended her life. A woman of fortitude and strength browbeaten to a shell of her former self. No one could survive long living under his father's thumb.

Martha interrupted his thoughts. "You didn't want that young one to stay. You won't remember her before long."

"You assume she'll fade as all the others."

"You may not think that now, but time and distance will change your mind."

Was she attempting to make him feel better about letting Abigail go? He shoved his hands in the pockets of his coat and turned back to the window.

There were a lot of reasons to let Abigail leave. First and foremost that of her safety. She'd nearly drowned a few days ago. Drowned! He could have lost her forever. And if she did stay, he could very well impregnate her again. She didn't deserve that. She deserved so much more in life than him. She would only find it if she left.

"I'm glad to know you've sent her away. Spied her in here some weeks ago going through your papers. She could have found any number of things."

Why mention it now? That knowledge served no purpose. But Martha wouldn't know why he'd insisted upon Abigail leaving.

His heart gave a painful jolt recalling the moment in his chamber when he'd torn up the bloody sheets from the miscarriage and tossed them into the fire to hide the evidence of all that had happened. Abigail had slept while he'd wept his regret in silent misery. She'd been far more shocked by the miscarriage than he following her near-deadly trip into the bowels of the sea.

The breath caught in his lungs, and he rubbed at the

pain he felt blooming deep inside his chest. Elliott gave a harsh rub to his eyes.

"I want quiet," Elliott said. Would Martha leave well enough alone where Abigail was concerned now that she'd stated what venom was on her tongue?

"As you wish, my lord."

He walked the house after that. In the library, Abigail's accoutrements were still stacked on the desk in tidy piles. Leather journals where she logged the day's events with his son were set at the edge. Loose sheaves of paper where Jacob had filled out mathematical problems sat atop the journals. The deck of cards depicting each letter of the alphabet lay in the center. He picked them up and turned them over in his hands.

This was where it had started with his son. He doubted he would ever have the aptitude his son displayed. Knew, in fact, that it was an impossibility. He'd tried for so many years to learn what the letters meant.

Fanning out the deck of cards, he looked down at the colorful drawings on the thick parchment. Abigail had taken her time, ensuring the paintings were beautifully, carefully drawn. He'd bet his finest horse that these cards would be around for generations to come.

The animals were well thought out for the letters they represented. Some he didn't even know because he'd never seen them before and couldn't even guess what they were or from whence they hailed. He'd never been one for traveling. Hated it, in fact. Hadn't even liked his trips to London, which had been a necessary evil for his future financial security once his father had died.

He slid one of the cards out from the middle of the spread deck. It was a strange animal with woolly, thick curly hair, like a sheep's. Its doe-like brown innocent eyes stared back. It had long legs and a long neck and the sleek soft face of a lamb. Its ears stood tall and flopped forward where they folded at the middle.

He traced the two straight lines that were the letter it represented; one shot straight up, while the other went out at a right angle. Had he even known what animal it was he still couldn't be sure what the letter was. Perhaps an *i* or an *l* or even a *t*.

Putting the strangely beautiful beast back into the stack, he gathered up the cards into the tidy pile they'd been in before he had displaced them and turned them facedown. He needed no reminders of his failures, though he wondered if Abigail would have been able to teach him as she'd taught Jacob.

Although he'd spent his nights attempting to copy out the letters Martha gave him. Attempted to put the letters, lines, and circles in the same place she did. The sheaves of parchment never looked identical when he held them side by side. The words would always swim before him on the paper.

"Father?"

Elliott had been so focused on the cards and the room around him that he hadn't heard Jacob enter the library. He spun around, about to ask his son if he kept at his reading. Jacob didn't meet his gaze. His fingers fidgeted together and he shifted from leg to leg anxiously, as if he needed to impart something of importance.

"Good afternoon," he said. "What did you wish to tell me?"

His son seemed relieved to be asked. "I came straight here. I was up on the parapet wall. There was someone down below. She didn't see me at first. Martha was talking to her. And then they both looked up. And I ran all the way here."

Elliott placed what he hoped was a soothing, reassuring

hand on his son's shoulder, then steered them out from the library toward his study. He needed to remain calm and not upset his son further. But this was his chance to catch Martha. He'd been waiting for this moment, and here it presented itself so beautifully.

"Slow yourself down, Jacob. Tell me your story slowly so I can make sense of it."

Jacob pinched his lips together and nodded. The best course of action would be for Elliott to ask the questions he needed answered most.

"The woman you saw with Martha, did her clothes look like those of a poor village woman? Worn and ragged?"

"She was like the witch in the dragon fairy tale I took from Miss Abigail."

Bethesda. On speaking terms with her niece, it seemed. What foulness were the two women concocting? Pieces started falling into place in his mind. Bethesda leaving the castle when he was a boy, his mother walking out into the sea, a babe born to Martha not six months later.

The events were related; he just needed to figure out how.

He paused, taken aback by where his thoughts were leading him and coming to a startling conclusion.

Why hadn't he thought of it before? How could he be so blind to the truth? Martha hadn't married Thomas until after Lydia was born. Lydia had been born out of wedlock. Goddamn it. How could he not have figured it out sooner? Simple: There had been no need to.

But how did all this connect to Abigail? Had his wife been a victim of the same mishaps that Abigail had been subjected to? No, he remembered her mood swings, her dementia. Martha couldn't have been part of his wife's demise.

Finally in the sanctuary of his study, Elliott took the key from the lock of the second-to-top drawer of his desk.

"Did you hear any of their conversation?"

"I don't much understand what they were talking about."

"It'll be like a puzzle to solve. Tell me what you heard as best you can."

"I couldn't hear the witch. She spoke so low."

Elliott was surprised and impressed that Jacob had likened Bethesda's character to something so vile—and so accurate. The woman had been a blight on their household. He thought her hatred for them would wane after his father had sent her away.

More than ever, he wished he knew the story and gossip that had surrounded his father and his mother's lady's maid.

Martha was somehow tied into whatever mess his father had created. Just because the main component of the equation had been taken out—Bethesda—hadn't meant the problem had ever been solved.

Was it possible that Thomas and the rest of the household were part of the plot to harm Abigail? His wife? To what end, what ultimate purpose? Revenge against his father?

He focused on his son.

"What of Martha? Her words?"

"She said their plan worked. She told the witch to go through the tunnels. But they are all locked. Except the ones that come up to the house."

His son had obviously been exploring recently to know that. Maybe his son was familiar with and used the old tunnels regularly. It shouldn't surprise Elliott that his boy seemed fearless even in the bowels of the eerie catacombs.

The catacombs.

Anyone who knew the lay of the castle knew of the entrance from the beach into the catacombs. It wasn't part of the tunnels, just an odd connection to the main artery that ran beneath the castle.

"Have you noticed anyone down in the tunnels the last few months?"

"Martha uses them all the time. It's not to go to the keep. I followed her one day . . . she went down to the sea."

That confirmed his suspicion.

Now to catch Martha speaking with the witch that was Bethesda.

He pressed a key into Jacob's palm and clasped tight around Jacob's smaller hands. "I'm giving you this key to let yourself out of this room later." He pointed at the clock on the sideboard. "Not till the little hand is pointed to the six do I want you to leave this room."

Jacob nodded his understanding. Elliott mussed up his hair before striding toward the door. Turning back one last time before he left, he said, "Don't open the door to anyone except Miss Hallaway."

"Yes, Father."

Until he knew who was responsible for the accidents surrounding Abigail, it wasn't safe for even his son to wander the castle. He locked the door behind him and slid the key into the pocket of his jacket.

He wanted to find Abigail, make sure she was tucked away and safe somewhere, but then he might lose the opportunity to confront Martha and Bethesda.

In the kitchen, a servants' entrance opened up to the network of tunnels beneath the main house. It would be the quickest way to intercept the women.

Despite the cold, the tunnels still held a dampness that clung to the stone surface like a second skin. He swore he could taste the salt of the sea in the musty air and feel slickness like seaweed over the walls.

As he approached the ledge that overlooked the village just south of the castle, whispered voices made their way to his ears, echoing off the walls around him. Martha's voice was clearer; Bethesda's was hoarse like a rusty carriage wheel squeaking from disuse.

"He told her to leave," Martha said.

Bethesda said something along the lines of, "You're sure she won't stay?"

Martha *had* been listening at the door when he'd said his good-byes to Abigail. He'd thought someone there all along. His instincts had served him well. Hopefully not too late.

"She hasn't spoken to him since then. It's done. And he's asked for male tutors."

"Good."

"I'll be missed if I'm here much longer. I want to find the boy, make sure he never speaks of seeing us here."

"I still think we should ensure the teacher can't be coming back," Bethesda hissed.

"How do you propose that? She's packing as we speak."

"Don't matter. She can come back. You said she was carrying a child."

"Yes, she has been showing signs of the morning illness."

Elliott's fists clenched so tight, his knuckles cracked with the pressure. How dare they. How dare they think to do something so vile!

"You can't let her have that child. Poison her drink or her food to rid her of the fiend."

"If you think that's best, I'll do so."

"Go, then. There is no time to waste if she's set on leaving today."

As Elliott saw it, he had two options: confront them now, or retrieve the magistrate and charge Martha with plotting against him. The latter would prove more effectual. He suspected Martha wouldn't leave the castle willingly. But he couldn't leave Abigail and his son alone, not with that monster loose in his home.

How could she do this to his family? She'd been there for him growing up when his mother had been absent. Had helped him with all business related to the castle and all correspondence that needed to be drawn up. Had helped him rear his boy when his wife could not be there for him, and later when she'd no longer been around.

That decided it. He'd catch her out. It was the only way. He eased away from the edge. He'd heard enough to damn both women.

"Abigail!" Elliott called out on taking the stairs up to the bedrooms as fast as his legs would carry him.

He'd wanted to go to her on returning to the castle, but he had gone to Jacob instead. His boy was being brave, and Elliott believed he could do what needed to be done.

He'd taken Jacob down to the stable, all without seeing Martha or Bethesda, saddled the boy up on Ivan, and sent him over to the town to collect the magistrate.

Jacob would make him proud. He trusted and knew that right down to the marrow of his bones. The only reason he hadn't gone to Abigail first was because he knew Martha would need time to put something together that would harm his governess.

His son on the other hand needed to be away from the castle and any harm that could befall him if he interfered accidentally with Martha's plan.

She would be caught out.

Abigail opened her chamber door, a scowl wrinkling up her brow. "Must you shout my given name about the house?"

He breathed a sigh of relief on seeing that she was well. Barging into her room, he shut the door behind them.

"What do you think you are doing?"

He ignored her question once his eyes caught sight of a tray with a serving of stew and chunk of bread.

"Have you eaten anything?"

She spun around to see what had arrested his attention. "No, I'm not hungry. I'm eager to quit this place, if you must know."

He grasped her face between his hands, and kissed her soundly on the lips. "Thank God."

"What's this about, Elliott? You can't run through the house intimately calling me by my first name."

"You're safe. That's all that matters."

She stamped her little foot and pulled her face from his grasp. "If you won't tell me what this is about, please leave. I'm nearly finished packing and I won't have you distracting me."

"Abigail. I know who is responsible for your accidents. I've sent my son to collect the magistrate. He should be here in a few hours; he's going to have to collect a third party in Alnwick."

Her eyes were wide. "Who is it?"

There was no sense in keeping the secret from her. Maybe together they could work to expose Martha, get some sort of confession out of her. "Martha."

"That slimy spawn of a devil's fiend."

Abigail stomped her foot again. Her curse got a smile out of him.

"Leave the food. It's been poisoned."

"It can't be, Lydia brought it to me. She wouldn't do such a thing."

"She doesn't know. She's my sister, Abigail. I don't know how I didn't figure that out before, but I realized only today what my father had done."

"Your sister. Why . . . How . . ." She shook her head, confused by the revelation. "What do you need me to do?"

"We need a confession from Martha before the magistrate arrives."

"How?"

This next part hurt him to mention, and would stir sad thoughts in Abigail, too, but it had to be done. "She knew you were in a delicate way. That's why she's poisoned your food. To rid your body of the babe. I don't know what harm it will cause you now that the babe . . ."

Tears welled in her eyes, but they did not fall. Her lower lip trembled. "All this because of an innocent child?" Her voice cracked, then her eyes slowly narrowed and she looked furious.

He could only nod.

"Is Thomas part of this?"

"I don't think so. He married Martha when Lydia was still a small child."

"Get Thomas, Elliott. Make sure he can hear everything. Martha will be in the kitchen, I'm sure. I'll head there now."

She turned to pick up her lunch tray and glared at him when he wouldn't move from the door.

"I understand and feel your anger, but you cannot outright confront her. I can. Move out of my way, Elliott. Make sure you are in the kitchen in no more than ten minutes."

He could see that there was no stopping her. He promised, "I will be there in five. Do not get too close to her, Abigail. I'll not forgive myself if you are hurt again."

"Don't worry about me."

He moved from the door to let her pass. He stopped her with a gentle touch on her elbow.

"I'm sorry," he said.

Sorry for a great many things. The harm that had befallen her, the loss of the baby, their angry exchange of words that had precipitated her leaving. Everything. He was so sorry for everything. And didn't know if things could be fixed between them. Didn't know if they should be fixed between them.

* * *

Abby couldn't believe what Elliott had just told her. She was thankful that her anger overrode her desire to curl up into a ball and cry all over again for the loss of the baby.

How could someone do anything so vile?

She pushed her way through the kitchen door. She'd been right—Martha was putting together a feast for the men for luncheon. Would she stoop so low as to poison them, too? Abby didn't think so.

"Thank you for sending Lydia up with the tray, but I must confess, I've been feeling dreadfully ill for days now."

Martha stared down at the stew.

"It'll warm you for the long, cold trip home. You don't know when another hot meal will present itself in your travels."

"I couldn't eat a bite. It would make me lose the contents already in my stomach."

"Is that so."

"Yes. I've been feeling this way for some weeks. I don't know what the cause could be. No one else is ill, so I doubt it's catching."

A creak sounded at the door. Abby knew it was Elliott, giving her a sign that she should draw whatever confession she needed to out of the old woman. She hated to do this to Thomas. He'd been so kind to her. But he had a right to know his wife was a murderer. She'd taken Abby's baby away from her, and that crime would have her burning in hell for all eternity.

"No, miss. What you got is definitely not catching."

"How do you know?" she asked innocently.

"Your kind of sickness comes from spreading your legs like a whore and letting a man lie with you."

The woman had not shared kind words with her in the past, so the choice of insult didn't shock her. But she gave a surprised gasp at the woman's pronouncement.

"How dare you call me any such thing."

"It's the truth. Now you've gone and put a babe in your belly. You should rid yourself of it. It'll be like its father, and his father before."

"You mean you didn't try to rid me of the child already? Dragging me into the sea and trying to end my life wasn't enough for you?"

"You deserved it, miss. A shame you lived to see another day. I should have held you under the water, and regret not doing so."

"Lord Brendall will know of your crimes."

"No, he'll not." Martha took a step toward her, picking up a rolling pin in the process. "You were too mouthy when you started. Too pretty and too young to be a governess. Knew it the moment I saw you that you'd be trouble to us and nothing more. But you spread your legs quick enough for the master. You're a sluttish whore."

Abby took a step backward. Toward the door. Toward the safety of Elliott's arms. "Do you plan to bludgeon me to death?"

"If I must. The world needs to be rid of you and the bad seed growing in your belly."

Abby would not give the woman the satisfaction of knowing the baby was already lost.

"What did Elliott ever do to you?"

"Brought that last whore into the household. Doted upon her. Put a baby in her when my daughter is the one who should inherit this castle."

"Lydia? What has she to do with the master or me? You'll not convince me she harbors feelings for Elliott and vice versa."

"Stupid girl. They are brother and sister."

Abby took another step back, truly afraid Martha would take a swing at her with the heavy rolling pin.

Her back hit the wall.

"You cannot end my life, Martha. It will not go unnoticed."

There was a madness in Martha's eyes that said otherwise. "Yes, I can. You'll go for another walk into the sea. I'll weigh your lifeless body down this time so you can't rise from the dead. You're no different than Madeline. You'll welcome death when I'm through with you."

The kitchen door slammed open and Thomas came through, his fists clenched at his side. "Martha?"

Martha dropped the rolling pin and smiled for her husband. "Thomas. You frightened me. I was just about to bring you luncheon, so you didn't go hungry on your trip to Alnwick."

"How could you do this to me?" the older man said, his voice full of hurt and betrayal.

Elliott stepped into the room next, his big burly form full of menace and radiating anger like a bee ready to sting.

"You are done, Martha," he hissed through clenched teeth.

Thomas looked his wife over, then turned on his heel and left the room. Abby felt for him. To discover the woman you loved was someone entirely different than you thought would be devastating. Possibly as distressing as the moment she realized she'd lost her baby.

"It would do you well to give up now." Elliott held a piece of rope aloft. "The magistrate arrives soon. You will be taken into custody."

"I did this for you," she pleaded.

"No, you did this for your own ends. I can imagine what my father did to make you turn your hatred on me, but it ends here. Turn about. I don't want to be forced to bind your hands."

"No one will believe you. The townspeople hate you. They'll believe me."

"That's why Thomas was here as witness," he shot back. "I'm sure you fed them poisoned words over the years to make me seem worse than I really am. Turn about, Martha." He held out the rope.

Abby took a step forward, intent on taking the rope from Elliott to bind the woman's hands herself if she must. The old woman was quick, and backhanded her across the face with so much force she fell to the ground. By the time she could focus her eyes again, Elliott held the woman's hands tightly behind her back, the rope already wound around her wrists.

Elliott looked at her. "Are you all right?"

"I'll be fine." Though the loss of her baby stung all the more.

The magistrate took Bethesda into custody before arriving back at the castle. The witch was currently in transport to Newcastle under indictment for the murder of Elliott's wife, which she had admitted quite boldly to playing a part in, and the attempted murder of Abby.

The magistrate had brought a strongman with him in the event that any other members of his staff were involved in Martha's ploys to end the Brendall earldom.

With the sound of the horses, everyone in the household had assembled on the drive before the group reached the inner bailey.

Jacob stayed atop Ivan. Pride swelled in Elliott's chest to see his son thus.

The magistrate held out a parchment and read the words that charged Martha with the crimes of intended murder and attempted murder.

"As confessed by Bethesda of Alnwick, Martha Harrow, you are hereby to be taken into custody for the attempted murder of Lady Abigail Anne Hallaway on the fifth day of November in the year of our Lord eighteen hundred forty-eight. And for the murder of Madeline Harriett Graham-Wright, the sixth Countess of Brendall, on the twenty-fourth day of August, in the year of our Lord eighteen hundred forty-one."

The man who rode with the magistrate dismounted and led a mule forward for Martha.

"I only did what needed to be done!" Martha took a step back from them and toward the house.

The magistrate looked at Martha, his mustache twitching as he sneered down at her in disgust.

"You will be tried by jury at Moot Hall Prison. Until such a time can be arranged, and until the court can hear your plea, you are to remain in custody of the jurisdiction."

Thomas sank into the shadows of the great house. Shock, anger, and confusion mixed in the tight scrunch of his brows. Elliott felt sorry for the man and hoped they didn't grow to dislike each other. He hoped the old man, at least fifteen years Martha's senior, stayed on after his wife was taken away.

She, on the other hand, would live out the rest of her days in prison with her aunt.

A jury would not find them innocent of murder. Not when Bethesda had freely admitted to the heinous crime that had been the end of his wife. All he could think was that it would be over soon. That Martha and Bethesda would never see the light of day again without the bonds of the law trapping them.

He felt at peace with his wife's death for the first time in seven years.

Once the magistrate had left, Elliott sought out Abigail in her bedchamber. Tapping the door lightly, he entered before she could give him permission.

She sniffled into a handkerchief.

"I didn't mean to intrude, but I thought we should discuss the outcome of the day."

She turned to him, eyes swollen and red from crying, and cheeks blotchy and damp from tears. Her hand shook around the rag she held tight.

"Are you going to ask me to stay now that the mystery of the ill deeds has been sorted out?"

"I can't, Abigail."

It was better for her to leave, he told himself. Losing the baby had taught him that he would do nothing but cause Abigail pain. She didn't deserve that. She deserved a better life. With a better man.

Now, with the upcoming trial of Martha and Bethesda, he didn't want her here. She'd be fodder for the gossips. Tongues would wag once the crimes were made public.

"You mean you won't!" She gave him her back, her shoulders shaking as she wept. "We've lost so much, and now you want to turn me out."

"Abigail, you know that's not the truth." God, he was fumbling around this like the bloody fool he was.

"How can it not be? If you loved me as you professed, you'd ask me to stay."

"I can't marry you." *Not right now,* he thought silently.

"Of course. I should have guessed. It's as Martha said. Good enough to spread my legs for you but not worth my salt as wife."

"Don't put words in my mouth! I'm trying to part amicably."

"I understand. You're still a scared fool."

Yes, he was, but he wanted to protect her. And the only way to do that was to let her go. He could not stop the rumors that were sure to spread. If she stayed, he wouldn't be able to think clearly over the duration of the trial. He wouldn't stop loathing himself for causing her so much pain and suffering.

He needed time with his son. Time to figure out what the next step in his household would be. He'd not have her here when there was so much dust to settle. She could carve a decent path in life for herself. She could find happiness. He excelled in ruining beautiful things, like his pixie governess. He'd cause her no more lasting damage.

She cleared her throat and turned back to him. "You don't deserve me, Elliott. I have shared myself with you. My desires, my ambitions, my love, and you throw it away like so much trash."

He walked toward her, at a loss for words, and folded his arms tightly around her. She fought for him to release her, so he held on tighter.

"Never mistake me, my dear. I have never loved another woman as I love you."

Her only response was to sob harder, her whole body shaking with her sorrow. "Then why make me go?"

"It's what we both need. I'm not right for you, Abigail. You could have the world at your fingertips. You should have that and more."

"Did it ever occur to you that that's not what I want? That I only ever wanted you?"

It tore at his heart asking her to leave. Tore his soul right from his chest where it dangled between the earth and a hot place in hell for the damage he'd caused her. For his inability to protect her. For his failure to save her the sorrow she'd experienced this past week.

He always knew she wasn't for him. She was better than him. Which meant he had to make her go. She'd understand in time that what he did now was a blessing for her future, wherever she may end up.

"Go home to your sisters, Abigail. They can comfort you when I cannot."

"Because you will not!" She wrenched herself out of his arms. "I'll go. But don't expect to be forgiven, Elliott. You are a coward."

The barb stung deeply. But he was doing what was right.

She would do well to love another. A man who wouldn't cause the misery he had. She could find a man not broken by his past.

He needed time alone. Knowing his wife hadn't killed herself weighed heavily on his conscience, like the weight of a yoke forged into his shoulders by drudgery.

He had to reconcile himself with his past, find another path in life for Lydia. There was too much to do with Abigail here to witness one failure after another. There was no question of her staying. She had to leave.

Chapter 24

*In killing the disease that had wormed its way into
the land, the dragon had freed the oppression clutch-
ing deep into the sand. The townsfolk cheered upon
the dragon's victory.*

—*The Dragon of Brahmors*

Derbyshire

Abby dropped the bag she carried as she stepped through
the door of her sister's home and ran toward her eldest
sister.

"I've missed you so much, Emma."

She threw her arms around Emma's shoulders and
squeezed her sister close. Afraid if she were to let go that
a barrage of sorrow and tears would be unavoidable once
she faced her sister's loving gaze.

Emma hugged her just as fiercely. Emma's hand
smoothed over her back. A few tears escaped her anyway.

"Oh, Abby. We've all missed you, too. I'm sorry you
missed Grace. She'll be so disappointed not to see you.
Had you written to say you were coming home . . ."

Emma, being the eldest sister, often chastised her two

younger ones. It didn't bother Abby that there was censure in her sister's voice. Emma was probably hurt by the fact that Abby had only written to them once in the two months she'd been absent from their lives.

"I didn't have time. I left so suddenly." And she'd regretted every mile farther from the castle. She should have made Elliott see reason. Made him realize that she would stick by his side even while he went through some of the toughest times in his life.

She stepped away from Emma and chewed on her lower lip. "I have so much to tell you. I'm sorry I lied to you. What a terrible sister I've been."

Emma nodded to her butler to take care of Abby's things and took her arm to lead her into the privacy of the parlor.

"What has you in such a melancholy mood? You've been away from us before."

"When I lived with Papa. I've never been absent from your company for so long. I missed you both fiercely."

"Hush," Emma said, taking Abby in her arms. "You were only gone two months. We've so much to catch up on. Now tell me, when did your friend have her baby?"

Had her sister asked anything else, she could have answered her stoically and calmly as ever. But at the mention of a child—a baby—it was as though a dam broke and let a deluge of tears and sobs flow from her tired and weakened body.

"I'm sorry," she blubbered. "I've done so many things wrong over the months."

The baby, who should not have survived the bleeding, grew strong in her belly and made her cry at the oddest of times. Hopefully her sister would take the tears for guilt.

"Did . . . did the birth not go well?"

"There was no birth. No friend. There was a child, to be certain. I took a job as a governess. I had to leave so suddenly that I thought it better to lie." The words just flowed from her like a geyser shooting strong and straight into the air.

"Whatever have you gotten yourself into?"

"I should have told you before I left, but you were so happy after so many years of being alone that I couldn't reveal the truth. You would have found a way to keep me here, and I needed to do this for myself."

What she couldn't explain to her sister was that she was most definitely in a delicate condition. She'd known about an hour into her trip from Alnwick because she'd had to have a chamber pot at the ready in her private car. She'd thrown up everything she'd eaten over the past three days—or so it felt. The movement of the train swaying side-to-side hadn't helped to ease her nerves or stomach one iota.

The only small relief she'd had was that the sickness had mostly passed when she'd stepped off the train. But for how long would this secret remain untold? How was it even possible for her to be with child?

She wished she could tell Elliott—but how would she get word to him? This was all such a mess.

Her sister was likely to guess in the next month or two as to her condition. For now, she would guard her secret in fear of bewitching her good fortune.

"Don't fret so, Abby. We'll talk about everything over dinner if you like. After you've had the chance to rest up from your trip home. It'll be just the two of us. Richard will understand we have much to discuss."

Abby gave a pitiful laugh followed by a smile. "I'd like that." Then she hugged her sister again, because she needed to.

"Don't think you'll not have to relay your adventures to me. I intend for you to tell me all about your trip up north."

"I wouldn't dream of not sharing the experience with you after I've had a chance to refresh myself. I feel dusty and all-around unpleasant. A nap may be in order."

She'd have to tell her sister why she'd come home. Tell her that she'd fallen in love with her employer. Right now, she wanted to be a tiny bit selfish and just take comfort in her sister. She had a long road ahead of her filled with uncertainty. But she'd never be alone again.

Ablutions were a slow process. Abby could barely hold herself upright, she was so exhausted from the train ride. She had been surprised to find her sister in residence. The mini-season had started just after she'd left for Brendall Castle, and she'd expected her sister to remain in London until winter was full upon them.

She released the frog clasp at her throat and pulled off her short cloak. Folding it, she set it over the arm of the long bench at the end of her bed. She had been given her old room.

Releasing the tiny mother-of-pearl buttons down the front of her charcoal bodice, she took her time to divest herself of her clothes. Untying the outer skirts, she walked over to the window and pulled back the heavy curtains that kept the cool air from invading the house.

The familiar maze of trimmed shrubs lay just beyond the paned glass. Still lushly green. Winter hadn't yet set in here. Looking down on the familiar was comforting.

Her skirts were too thick to fall completely to her feet, so she stepped out of the heavy twill and set it over her cloak. She nearly packed it away in the dressing room herself, then realized a maid would straighten her things around when she went down for supper.

A wide, tall cheval mirror stood on the floor along an empty stretch of wall. She stepped in front of it and loosened the strings of her boneless corset. She let it fall to the soft carpet at her feet. She pulled her chemise over her head and pushed her drawers off her hips. Both items joined the corset. She turned to the side to observe her body for signs of change.

Now that the corset was off, she breathed deeply, feeling like she'd caught her breath for the first time in days. Strange, since her stomach was still flat as ever. She wondered when it would round out with the baby.

A week? A month? Three months? The thoughts filled her with equal measures of dread and joy. Maybe her sisters would send her to the Continent to have the child? Grace would have a house there now that she'd married an Italian count. Maybe she could live there for the rest of her days? Out of reach of the censure London society was sure to yoke around her shoulders.

She faced forward in the mirror. Her breasts were fuller. Heavier.

Maybe she should bind them so her sisters wouldn't notice the difference in her figure. She pressed her hands against them, her intent to flatten them hopeless. They were hard and sore. Perhaps if she bound them in soft linen beneath her corset, no one would be the wiser.

Her gaze dropped in the mirror. Her hips looked wider. Was that something else that changed once a woman was enceinte? Or purely her fanciful imagination?

She sighed, turned her back to the image in the glass, and fished a fresh chemise from the wardrobe.

After she climbed into her bed, already turned down by one of the servants, she stared up at the delicate design in the molding that lined the ceiling.

She'd felt dead to the world around her ever since she'd packed her belongings and left the castle. She barely remembered the ride in the rickety old cart with Thomas. Neither had been of a mind to fill the silence with chatter after the events of the past few days. She'd blindly had her trunks loaded into the train by an attendant, and then she'd been sick the remainder of the trip.

This was the first time she'd had any time to simply think. The first time she realized that she'd walked away from the only man she'd ever loved. A child, too, whom she adored as though he were her own. She liked to think that sentiment was returned by Jacob, but now she'd never know. Would he be disappointed in her for not staying? Or worse, resent her? She hoped not.

She had been too distraught to explain that she was leaving.

She hated all of this.

Hated that she cared so much, and hurt so much. She wanted nothing other than to crawl into the deepest cave like Grendel's mother and never face the world around her again.

She ground the heels of her palms into her eyes, wishing that her life was just as easy to hide from as the pale blue paint she was temporarily blinded to on the ceiling.

Her thoughts turned back to the babe growing in her belly.

If she were roughly four weeks along, she had maybe two to three months to think through what she should do and how she would support herself and the baby until she came into her trust money. She would have an early-summer baby; he or she would be born by June or July.

The knowledge sent a thrill of excitement through her.

She wasn't sure why it felt wrong to tell her sisters the full truth. Maybe it was the fact that Elliott didn't know. Did he have a right to know? He'd sent her away.

Should she send a messenger to him with word of her condition? If there were no further complications with this pregnancy, she would do so out of respect.

She despaired in lying to everyone in the meantime,

but that was one truth that she would reveal only when she was ready. Only when she was sure the baby was safe and growing strong inside her would she reveal the truth.

She slid her hands beneath the blankets and held that thought in her heart as she laid her hands on her still-flat belly.

"I had a little of everything prepared for supper."

More like a grand buffet set out before them. There were no servants to overhear them, either. Emma had been true to her word in that it would be only the two of them.

"You really shouldn't have gone to the trouble, Em."

"It's no bother. Cook prepare steamed pudding and custard just for you."

Abby couldn't help the smile that escaped. It was hard to wallow in self-pity for her circumstances when her sister was offering up her favorite dishes. Unlike some foods, these didn't make her feel ill when she thought about eating them.

Emma handed Abby a plate. "Remind me of why you went to Northumbria."

"The short answer is: I thought maybe I should find my own way in life." Abby turned to look at her sister after putting a sliver of beef on her plate.

Emma frowned down at the bowl of oyster stew in her hands. Abby swallowed and looked away from it. It made her stomach clench and roil. No stew for her.

"And the long answer?" Emma asked.

"I have lived off your kindness too long. It's obvious I'll never marry. I just wanted to strike out on my own and see where it would lead me."

It brought her right back to her sisters. She bit her lip to stop the tremble. She would not cry.

She would not!

"Why ever would you think you're a burden? Papa left you a large dowry, and I have money set aside from my paintings."

"I didn't want charity. And the money Papa left for me doesn't come to me for another two years. I just needed some time on my own."

"You're still young, Abby. It's not too late for you to marry."

"I don't want to marry. I've never wanted to marry. I'm not like you and Grace. I'm content by myself."

Three months ago those words would have been true. Now they soured in her mouth. She'd have been happy to marry Elliott. Never content without him. She doubted she'd ever feel this way for another man.

"How can you say that when you've admitted how much you missed us? You were only gone two months."

Emma set her bowl on the table and sat in her chair. She didn't pick up her spoon till Abby sat next to her. Emma rubbed her hand over Abby's back in reassuring strokes. Abby sniffled, feeling suddenly sentimental.

"You mentioned a child," Emma said.

"I took a position as a governess." She stared her sister in the eye, wondering what her reaction would be.

She merely nodded slowly and said, "Interesting choice. But perhaps suiting since Papa taught you well."

"I enjoyed it. But I didn't like being so far from home." She needed to reveal the reason behind her leaving. "I came home because I took a liking to the master of the house."

Emma's spoon clanked against the bowl, and she turned to Abby with wide, surprised eyes. "Did he know?"

"Yes, and it was a most humiliating experience. He did not return the sentiment." Had he, he would have wanted her to stay. Would have stopped her from leaving. Wouldn't have repeatedly told her to leave. "I'm not ready to share the details. But it precipitated me leaving."

"When you are ready to share the whole story, I want to be the first to hear it."

Abby nodded her agreement.

"I'm sorry and I'm not sorry that it didn't work for the better. Had you stayed in Northumbria, would you have written again?"

"There is a letter in my room I planned to post in town, but didn't have the chance."

"Do you plan on finding another posting as governess?"

"I've had about all the adventure I can handle right now."

And another adventure come summer. Would she rely on her sisters heavily in the first few years? Would they be happy or disappointed with her? Questions she needn't worry about now. Her only focus would be trying to forget Elliott. Forget that she'd found something she had wanted to hold on to with all her might, only to be turned away.

Emma sighed, as if in relief. "I'm glad to hear you'll be staying. I know you've only just arrived, but we leave for Town in a week. You'll want to come. Grace is living in London over the winter. She leaves for Italy come spring."

"I regret missing the wedding more than anything."

Abby looked down at her plate of food. She'd barely touched it. Her appetite just wasn't what it normally was. It was all the melancholy. She must breathe deep and liven up. She must be strong. She picked up her fork again and ate another sliver of meat.

"It was a small ceremony. Grace didn't want an elaborate wedding since this was her second. They honeymooned in Bath for three weeks, then stayed here for a few weeks while they found a town house in London. She'll be so happy to see you! She was so worried when you left. We both were."

"I can't apologize enough for leaving so hastily. I just felt like I needed a change. You were finally happy to have your husband home. I could see that Grace was falling for Mr. Lioni. *Dante.* Seems so strange to call him Dante when I haven't known him all that long."

"They are very much in love."

"And you?"

"And me, too." Emma's smile brightened her whole face. "Our old nemesis, Waverly, is dead."

Abby dropped her fork and grasped her sister's hands in shock. "What do you mean he's dead?"

Waverly had been a bane to them. He had tried to blackmail Emma into becoming his lover by threatening to reveal her talent for painting erotic nudes of women to polite society.

"It was a terrible time. He was trying to get back at Richard for a slight between them years ago. It never had anything to do with us."

"It's shocking."

"Yes, it is. So . . . London?"

"I'd be happy to travel to London with you and Richard. I need something to lift my spirits."

"There are a number of engagements I would like for you to attend with us."

At her skeptical look, Emma clarified, "I promise not to matchmake. Not after you've admitted to falling in love with someone else. Maybe in time we'll find you a husband, but for now . . . we must socialize, with Richard taking his seat in politics. And I'll not leave you at home alone."

"I'd be happy to play the dignitary with you."

"Then it's settled." Emma hugged her. "I'm so happy you're home. I have missed you, too."

Chapter 25

The dragon turned his back on the people who were now his. His wings spread wide and his magic strong, he opened the gates of every door and bid his people to take what they wanted as he descended into the caverns beneath the palace.
—The Dragon of Brahmors

Emma had promised her that tonight was the last ball they were expected to attend. Abby couldn't be happier with the announcement that they'd be going back to the country for the Christmas season.

As the weeks had unfolded, she grew more aware of her body, of the life growing within her. There was no denying the truth. By some miracle, her babe lived. Though her sister Grace had commented on her weight gain—it seemed she was fattening out in the middle and in her breasts—neither of her sisters had asked her the obvious question. Abby suspected they knew but were waiting for her to confirm that fact.

She hadn't been sick since the train ride to London two weeks before. And couldn't be more thankful for that small blessing. She was eating again, and sleeping more than ever. She often fell asleep in the afternoons reading a book, only to be awoken by her sister, followed by a questioning gaze.

Soon. She wasn't ready to reveal that secret yet. She was less than two months along. Another month and she'd be sure the baby was healthy. That was if she could hide her state for that long. Besides, Elliott deserved to know first. But how? The roads were freezing over; travel was dangerous.

She'd had to rely upon the older-style dresses with the high empire waist to hide her slightly distended belly, since wearing a corset pained her too much. Her modiste had at least modernized the style. Had told her it would keep her secrets for a few more months.

Abby had been shocked that the woman had guessed so accurately at her condition. It shouldn't surprise her. This particular modiste had been dressing and fitting her for new styles for three years. The measurements didn't lie, Abby supposed.

Mr. Harnett, a widowed baron, nodded to her from across the room. He'd been to every ball and soiree she and her sisters had attended. Had asked her to dance at every event. She'd given him a few; she didn't want to be rude and refuse him every dance when her card remained empty most nights.

As he headed toward her, she caught movement at the entrance into the ballroom. More servants than usual milled about. A few gentlemen headed toward the entrance to see if they could be of service. Richard left Emma's side to lend his assistance. There was a commotion of some sort—it sounded like voices raised in anger and refusing someone entrance. Everyone turned to see what the ruckus was about, including Mr. Harnett.

Abby edged around the ballroom, hoping to shift herself out of his sight. She didn't want to dance with anyone. She wanted to go home, share the holidays with her sisters and their husbands, and when that was done, she'd send a servant to Brendall Castle with the news to Elliott, because she didn't think she could face him again, and then she'd tell her family about the baby. There would be no more balls for her to attend, no more gentlemen to dance with whom she didn't wish to dance.

Besides, she needed to rest her feet. She couldn't stand for long periods of time anymore. She swore her feet swelled inside her sweaty slippers.

"Abigail," someone shouted.

Elliott?

She paused in her attempted escape and looked around the ballroom, not sure what direction the familiar voice had come from, thinking her fanciful imagination was getting the better of her. She swallowed back a lump of anticipation. Confusion.

What did it mean that Elliott was here? That he was really here?

The room around her went deathly silent and focused on the entrance where the voice had bellowed out. She stepped forward, daring to hope her ears weren't playing tricks on her. Her face was damp when he came into view at the top of the stairs that led to the entrance.

Elliott.

An enclave of gentlemen surrounded him, including her brother-in-law Richard. Elliott shook off someone's hold on his sleeve and took the stairs practically at a run. She wanted to run toward him but was frozen to the spot. Her nerves were running rampant and she thought maybe she'd throw up. And she'd been doing so well in keeping her food down.

Words almost seemed impossible. Were impossible. Her bottom lip was trembling, and she knew she'd sob if she tried to speak.

Seemed Elliott didn't care that she remained silent. He approached her, with everyone in the ballroom watching the most exciting gossip of the season unfold.

She didn't care.

Elliott had realized his folly the day Abigail had left him in the drive without looking back. Had ached for her for weeks on end, hoping his love would dim over the days. It hadn't.

He had missed Abigail every night they were apart. Every day he couldn't catch a glimpse of her walking the grounds.

"Abigail." The words were hoarse.

Elliott looked down at her swimming green eyes. They spilled over as he studied her expression. He wiped the tears from her cheek, uncaring that everyone in the ballroom watched them with rapt curiosity. That they witnessed their reunion moment by moment when this was a private affair between him and Abigail.

Leaning in close, he kissed her tear-streaked face.

"Don't cry." He'd never been able to handle a woman crying.

She opened her mouth to say something, but closed it again. He clasped her hands between his because he couldn't not touch her. They'd been apart for less than three weeks but it felt like an eternity of loneliness.

"Why are you here, Elliott?"

"How could I not come? You mean everything to me. I couldn't stand for you to leave. I was an ass when you left. I wasn't thinking, and for that, I will apologize for a thousand lifetimes."

Those words were torn from the deepest recesses of his heart; he'd been unable to stop them. He hadn't wanted to say so much in front of an audience.

He took one great huff of air and looked at the crowd

around them. He felt decidedly underdressed for this ball. Guests crowded in closer, wanting to hear the exchange between them. Many stood with mouths agape.

He didn't recognize any of the faces around them—not that he would have any reason to know these people. He'd never been part of their world. Part of their system. He'd never wanted to be. But he would do that and more for Abigail.

He couldn't let his nervousness distract him from his purpose. He tore his gaze away from the party and back to Abigail. She seemed too stunned to say anything, or perhaps she hadn't wanted his presence tonight.

During two solid days on a train to Matlock, a carriage ride with his son to the Asbury country home, and then another trip back to the rail so he could make his way to London in the hope of finding her, he hadn't once stopped to think whether she would welcome him back into her life.

Would she forgive him?

They hadn't parted on good terms.

"Martha and her aunt were sent to prison for the murder of my wife and their joint attempt to harm you." He ran the tips of his fingers down the side of her face. "I'd never have forgiven myself if I had lost you. We've already lost too much." He wouldn't damn her and mention the baby.

"There is nothing lost," she whispered. She closed her eyes and rested the side of her face against his. "I missed you so much. I was going to send someone with a message that all is not lost."

How was it possible that life still grew within her? He'd been the one to clean up all the blood. There had been so much blood. One of his hands held the back of her head lightly. He didn't want her to move away from him. Ever.

"I never meant to cause you so much distress. I'll

explain everything when we're alone. My reason for coming is twofold."

Going down on one knee in front of her, he took a fortifying breath and let it out easily. Tongue-twisted, he lightly held her hips and pressed his forehead to her stomach. His baby still grew in her belly.

The thought made him light-headed. Excitement made him want to shout out in joy. Trepidation made him want to sweep Abigail off her feet and take her where there was less noise.

He felt the slight swell beneath and wanted to press kisses there, press his hands over the distension and feel the new life beneath his hands. But doing so would be too much of a declaration and claim over her. He'd not give cause for the gossips to name her a harlot.

"Abigail," he whispered, then took her hands in his. When he looked up to her, tears continued to trail down her cheeks in silent surrender to the moment.

She raised her hands and ran her fingers over the side of his face with a gentleness that stole his breath and ability to speak. He loosened his hold to grasp her wrists. She was so delicate. Fragile.

How could she survive having his child? His wife hadn't fully recovered, and when Madeline's broken body had finally healed from childbearing, her mind had been lost to great sorrow and unaccountable madness. He wondered how susceptible his wife had been to the sickness plaguing her mind, how Martha had harnessed that weakness to make the condition worse.

But his sweet Abigail . . . her eyes still watered, her nose had reddened. She dropped her hands to his shoulders and lowered herself awkwardly to the marble floor with the heavy pleats of her skirt in her way.

There was a collective gasp from the audience around them.

"Don't lower yourself to me."

"We are equal in all things, Elliott. Equal in standing, equal in the power of our minds and the power of our hearts. Equal in everything that can bring one person to see their own greatness through the eyes of the one they love."

He swallowed against the dryness in his throat. Her declaration made him want to crush her to him. To kiss her and claim her as his own woman for the rest of the world to witness.

Not yet.

But the knowledge that she still loved him filled his heart and eased the turmoil that had set in over the weeks they'd been apart.

Releasing her wrists, he cupped her pixie face between his massive hands. "From the very moment you revealed your desire to help Jacob, no matter the challenge that stood in your way and even with the impossibility of the circumstance, I fell in love with you."

Whispers grew in volume around them. He ignored them as he brushed the wetness away from her cheeks again. It was endearing that the tears did not cease to fall.

"I'm a brute in the worst way. I'm unworthy—"

"Never," she declared in a strong voice.

Before he could think better of what he was doing, he threaded his fingers through the fancy updo she'd twisted her hair in and pulled her close to his mouth. Close enough that their lips fleetingly touched.

There were gasps of surprise at this scandalous display. At his daring actions in front of so many witnesses.

"Make me a whole man. Marry me, Abigail Hallaway, for I want nothing more than to call you wife."

"It's not me that makes you a whole man, but you who makes me whole in heart and soul."

He half expected her to refuse him, despite the scandal

she'd stir when she had his babe, unless she planned to leave for the Continent. No, she wasn't running from him. He'd follow her. He wasn't letting her go again.

He waited for the words that would bind them together forever in this life. Her hands trembled against his face for long moments.

"Say something. Tell me yes," he said.

His voice choked up. She couldn't refuse him. He wouldn't accept any answer but an affirmative, resounding yes. Couldn't even bear to think she'd refuse him with a room full of her friends and acquaintances watching on avidly.

"Under one condition will I agree to be your wife."

"Anything. God, Abigail, anything." He kissed her forehead, afraid to see what expression was reflected in her green eyes. "Anything. You need but ask and I'd search for Atlantis herself if you'll come home to me. To Jacob."

"I want nothing more than to be a mother to your son. He's made my heart soar with so many feelings these past months."

She hugged him close then. Her mouth fanning a hot breath into his ear as she whispered, "Procure a special license and take me away from this place. Away from the noise, the stench of the city, this dark world I never wanted to be a part of. Take me back to the sea where the water is a constant soothing din, where the cold air robs me of breath one moment only to embrace me in her strong arms the next. Take me where the birds never stop calling above. Take me where we can be together. Take me home, Elliott."

He'd already planned exactly that. A special license would be procured tonight now that she'd demanded it of him.

He pulled them both to their feet and tucked her arm in his. Abigail's smile was enough to brighten the darkest of nights. He reciprocated the gesture, not feeling at all awkward by something so foreign to him. Nothing could make him a happier man than the moment they shared now.

He let her strength hold him upright and proud as she walked across the ballroom floor with his arm through hers. She approached her brother-in-law. Come to think of it, the younger Asbury looked a lot like the elder he'd known.

"Richard, I require your assistance. It is of utmost importance that we bid our adieus for the evening."

The brother-in-law smiled down at Abigail. It was not a smile of mirth; more likely it sprang from his wicked appreciation that Elliott's little woman was a spitfire to deal with. And when she demanded something, people acted quickly. Another woman came up behind them, her sister perhaps. She was taller and fairer than his Abigail but had the same face shape and mossy green eyes.

Asbury snapped his fingers and held his hand out for his wife to take. Footmen came forward with the women's cloaks and Asbury's coat. Whispers grew into outright tittering as they left the ball.

"I didn't mean to cause a scene," Abigail said once they'd settled themselves in the carriage.

"Think nothing of it," Asbury replied.

The elder sister spoke for the first time. "Abby matters to me more than the people back in that stuffy room." She pointedly looked at Elliott. "We haven't had the pleasure of meeting."

He bowed his head. "Elliott Wright, Earl of Brendall."

"The Archbishop of Canterbury," Asbury said as they alighted on the steps to his town house, "is a family friend. He'll provide a special license so you can marry tomorrow. We'll visit him at first light."

Elliott inclined his head. "I thank you for your assistance in this."

Asbury's only response was, "I'll take you up to your room now."

Jacob came into the foyer then. "Father?" His attention quickly turned to Abigail and, with a bright smile on his face, he ran toward her and hugged her around the waist. "You didn't say good-bye."

Abigail smoothed her hand over his head. "I wanted to. Your father was just going to tell me everything that happened since I left. It's late, though. Shouldn't you be in bed?"

Jacob loosened his hold and looked up at her. "Father said to wait up for him. Said he'd bring you back home with us. We even have a full new staff helping at the castle."

"That is exciting. But it's certainly too late to travel tonight. We're to be married in the morning. How would you feel if we stayed a few days in London before heading home?"

"Do I still have to do my lessons?"

Abigail laughed. "We'll discuss it tomorrow." She nodded toward her sister. "This is Emma, my oldest sister. Do you mind going with her up to your room for the night? She'll show you the way."

"Are you still going to be here in the morning?"

"Yes. I'm not going anywhere. We'll want you at the wedding."

Jacob looked to his father. Elliott nodded and Jacob followed the other woman up the stairs.

"Richard," Abigail said, "I'll show Elliott to his room."

"If you're sure." He seemed hesitant to leave them alone. Was it for propriety's sake?

"I am," she replied.

Asbury left, following after his wife.

When they were alone, Elliott walked toward her and pulled her into his arms. "I shouldn't have let you leave. I thought it would be better for you to start your life again. I didn't realize so many things. I was such a fool. You were right. A scared fool. Scared to take a chance . . ."

"Shh. I just want you to hold me close for a while. I've missed you more than words can ever express."

So he held her. When they broke apart, Abigail stepped up on her toes and kissed him lightly on the mouth.

"Will you sleep in my bed tonight?"

"Every night from this day forward."

She took his hand and led him to her private bed-chamber.

When the door was locked behind him, he tossed down his coat and sat on a bench at the end of her bed to remove his boots.

She came and knelt in front of him to take over the task. "You shouldn't be kneeling on the floor," he said.

"I want to do this for you." She tilted her head up and looked at him. Fresh tears filled her eyes.

"Why are you crying, Abigail?" He pulled her off the floor and sat her in his lap.

"I can't seem to help it anymore. I cry when I'm happy. I cry when I'm sad. I cry all the time and I really hate it."

He placed his hand over her belly. The smallest of bumps had formed there. "I think it's to do with the baby. How is this possible?"

"I don't know. I thank God every day for it, though."

"I will, too." His hand brushed over the mound beneath her dress.

"Maybe it was better for us to part for a short time?"

"It's my fault. I'll not leave you again, Abigail. I refuse to."

Abby released the buttons on Elliott's shirt. She wanted nothing more than to snuggle up to his warm body. She had felt so cold and alone without him by her side at night. She listened as the story unfolded.

"Bethesda had been sent away from the castle when she threatened my father's life. It seemed my father had been forcing himself on Martha for some years. From the time she arrived until she was with child. Bethesda wanted my mother to claim the child as her own. My father wouldn't allow it, of course. So he sent Bethesda away, made Martha stay so no harm would come to the bastard growing in her belly."

"Lydia?"

"Yes. My half sister. The information was always there right in front of me, and I didn't put two and two together. What an idiot I've been."

"Your sister. What's happened to her?"

"Nothing. She is living at Brendall Castle, digesting the information like the rest of us. Thomas is still there. He's sent for his sons from his previous marriage to come on as help. I've hired someone from the local village to look after the house."

"I pity Martha."

"Don't," Elliott said, standing her in front of him so he could remove her clothes. She helped him strip her down to her chemise. She wore no corset. Hadn't been able to when her body ached and felt so tender.

"She was poisoned over the years from my father's violence and abuse. My father had twisted a good woman into a conniving one. She wanted nothing more than to see my father's line die. She preyed upon Madeline's mind. Helped her insecurities fester into madness. It seems Madeline didn't kill herself in that fire."

Abby cupped his face. "Elliott. I'm sorry."

"Don't be. It saddens me to know I was blind to the happenings in my own home, but Madeline was never well. I might not have been able to save her. Now I have you."

"What has happened to Martha and the old woman?"

"They were arrested and sent to Newcastle. Bethesda died a week later. Martha is still there, awaiting her trial. She'll not be freed. She'll be charged with murder at the very least."

She pulled the bedding farther down, scooted into her bed, and waited for Elliott to join her. He slipped out of his trousers. When he turned to her, he was in quite a state of arousal.

"What does this mean for us?"

He climbed into the bed with her.

"We'll be married tomorrow. We can stay here a few days or even spend our Christmas here if that is what you wish."

"I love you, Elliott."

He smiled and wrapped his arms around her.

"And I you." Sliding his hand around to her stomach, he said, "I love this strong little fighter, too. You make me a complete man, Abigail. And there is nothing more a man could desire than holding the woman he loves in his arms, knowing she loves him equally."

Epilogue

Yet there the story does not end, for it has been told that a maiden of beauty and great kindness that could fill the beast's broken heart ventured into the dragon's guarded den . . .
—*The Dragon of Brahmors*

The weather had held up well today, considering they'd had rain for three days straight. The warm break was much needed. They all sat in the garden Elliot'd started building last year. Where the old church used to be.

Most of the fallen rock had been removed; the damaged walls, too. Some remained to offer climbing space for the roses Abigail looked after with great care, and the other walls remaining still had ivy and fern thriving on them.

A dozen graves lay in the small plot off the old vestibule. Some of the slabs had had to be replaced, and the grass was trimmed there now. Any fallen debris from the fire had been removed, and Madeline's grave had a small tree growing behind it. Abigail had insisted on giving both Elliott and his son a nice shady spot for them to sit while they remembered her.

"Elliott," Abigail called, frantic. "Oh, my, look at her. Look at Isabella."

Sitting up where he lounged, Elliott watched his wife with his daughter. They were celebrating her first birthday. Jacob knelt on the grassy lawn a dozen or so steps away, holding his hands out, beckoning his sister to walk to him.

Abigail stood not a foot behind Isabella, arms spread behind her in case she fell.

"That's my girl, Bella," Elliott said. He distracted her halfway from reaching her brother. She stopped in her already unsteady tracks and sat heavily on her rump, throwing her hands up and down in excitement.

"Elliott," Abigail admonished, "you weren't supposed to divert her attention from the goal!"

No reproof laced his wife's sweet voice, though her hands rested on either hip as she laughed at him. She laughed a lot. Brought laughter back into his home. God, he could never remember being surrounded by so much laughter and happiness as he was now.

She was still his Abigail. Working hard with Jacob on his reading and writing. He loved her more for that. Even more that she tried to help him with his letters. He still didn't understand them and was frustrated by that fact. Abigail, though, didn't seem to mind his ineptitude where reading and writing were concerned. She remained ever loving. She had more patience for him than he had for himself.

"Sit and eat with me," he called out.

Abigail plunked Isabella in front of him and knelt next to Jacob over the picnic fare set before them. They both set up the plates of food. Abigail for him, Jacob for his baby sister.

Elliott had been surprised and delighted that Jacob had taken to being a big brother so well. He adored his sister, just as he adored Abigail, no longer his governess but his stepmother and still his ever-patient teacher. He was ten now. Growing fast. And he'd be going off to school in only two years.

On occasion, Elliott had heard him call Abigail "Mum." Yet another thing to put a smile on his face.

"When did you say your sisters would arrive?"

They were going to stay with them for the summer. Lydia would be coming to visit, too. She'd married the doctor in the spring. Their wedding had been small but nice. He'd given his sister a dowry that would last two lifetimes over.

"This week. Emma wrote that she'd been very ill these past months and motion of any sort made it worse. She'll be over her sickness soon, I hope."

"You've been surprisingly well this time around," Elliott said. He'd been waiting days—though it felt like weeks—for her to say something, to tell him and Jacob her news. Their news.

"How did . . ."

He only raised his brow. How could he not tell when the first indication had been the increased swelling of her breasts? He'd noticed that change to her body weeks ago. Had delighted in it. He hoped her bottom would round out like it had the last time. She really did have the prettiest backside.

Abigail brought his plate over and settled beside him, kissing him on the tip of his nose, then his lips. "It's too soon. But now that you mention it . . . we should be having another baby early spring."

The announcement made Elliott feel rather queer. Like he'd just received the best news he could possibly receive. He was teasing and enjoying his wife's company one moment and fighting sudden arousal in the next.

"Jacob, take your sister up to the house for her nap."

Jacob screwed up his face, gave a huff, and carried Isabella up to the house.

When the boy was out of sight, Elliott took the plate from Abigail's hands and set it off to the side. "You should have told me this sooner," he said.

He pressed her down to the blanket and leaned over her. "I think we need to attend to business in our bedchamber immediately."

"Elliott!" She pushed at his shoulder with a laugh. "You've just sent your son off so you could seduce me?"

"Oh, yes. And *seduce* is probably too mild a word." His hand reached under her skirts and slid up her leg till he was at the apex of her thighs.

He parted the material and felt the slickness of her desire there and groaned. His finger parted the lips of her sex, his thumb toying with the bud of her sex. She panted beneath him. Her hand clutched to his arm through all her skirts as she held him tight to her body.

He knew she was going to come when she bit her lip and her thighs tightened around his arm. He kissed her to swallow her cries of passion.

When her pelvis stilled and she let out a sigh, he lifted his mouth from hers.

"Seems I'm not the only one to be aroused by the occasion."

"You are wicked."

"I think that's what you like most about me, darling wife."

He really couldn't help himself. He wanted her with a desperation that quite stole his sanity. He released the ties on his trousers and hitched her skirts up to settle himself between her pretty thighs.

"You can't," she objected. "What if someone should see us?"

"They won't. I need you now."

And now he had her.

Look for the first two novels in this sensational series by

TIFFANY CLARE

THE SURRENDER OF A LADY
ISBN: 978-0-312-37211-8

THE SEDUCTION OF HIS WIFE
ISBN: 978-0-312-38183-7

Available from St. Martin's Paperbacks